James Patterson is one of the best-known and biggest-selling writers of all time. He is the author of some of the most popular series of the past decade: the Women's Murder Club, the Alex Cross novels and Maximum Ride, and he has written many other number one bestsellers including romance novels and stand-alone thrillers. He has won an Edgar Award, the mystery world's highest honour. He lives in Florida with his wife and son.

Praise for James Patterson:

'The man is a master of this genre. We fans will have one wish for him: write even faster'   *USA Today*

'Unputdownable. It will sell millions'   *The Times*

'Packed with white-knuckled twists'   *Daily Mail*

'Breakneck pacing and loop-the-loop plotting'
    Publishers Weekly

'Reads like a dream'   *Kirkus Reviews*

'A fast-paced, electric story that is utterly believable'
    Booklist

'Ticks like a time bomb – full of threat and terror'
    Los Angeles Times

'Absolutely terrific'   *Bookseller*

'Patterson's action-packed story keeps the pages flicking by'
    The Sunday Times

'A fine writer with a good ear for dialogue and pacing. His books are always page-turners'   *Washington Times*

'Patterson is a phenomenon'   *Observer*

'Keeps the adrenaline level high'   *Publishing News*

By James Patterson and available from Headline

When the Wind Blows
Cradle and All
Miracle on the 17th Green *(and Peter de Jonge)*
Suzanne's Diary for Nicholas
The Beach House *(and Peter de Jonge)*
The Jester *(and Andrew Gross)*
The Lake House
Sam's Letters to Jennifer
SantaKid
Honeymoon *(and Howard Roughan)*
Lifeguard *(and Andrew Gross)*
Beach Road *(and Peter de Jonge)*
Step on a Crack *(and Michael Ledwidge)*
The Quickie *(and Michael Ledwidge)*
You've Been Warned *(and Howard Roughan)*

Alex Cross novels
Cat and Mouse
Pop Goes the Weasel
Roses are Red
Violets are Blue
Four Blind Mice
The Big Bad Wolf
London Bridges
Mary, Mary
Cross
Double Cross

The Women's Murder Club series
1st to Die
2nd Chance *(and Andrew Gross)*
3rd Degree *(and Andrew Gross)*
4th of July *(and Maxine Paetro)*
The 5th Horseman *(and Maxine Paetro)*
The 6th Target *(and Maxine Paetro)*

Maximum Ride series
Maximum Ride: The Angel Experiment
Maximum Ride: School's Out Forever
Maximum Ride: Saving the World and Other Extreme Sports

JAMES PATTERSON

POP GOES THE WEASEL

headline

First published in Great Britain in 1999
by HEADLINE BOOK PUBLISHING

This edition published in 2009
by HEADLINE PUBLISHING GROUP

3

Cataloguing in Publication Data is available from the British Library

ISBN 978 0 7553 4933 3

Printed and bound in Great Britain by Clays Ltd, St Ives plc

Headline's policy is to use papers that are natural, renewable
and recyclable products and made from wood grown in
sustainable forests. The logging and manufacturing processes
are expected to conform to the environmental regulations
of the country of origin.

HEADLINE PUBLISHING GROUP
An Hachette UK Company
338 Euston Road
London NW1 3BH

www.headline.co.uk
www.hachette.co.uk

POP GOES THE WEASEL

This is for Suzie and Jack, and the millions of
Alex Cross readers who so frequently ask
– *can't you write faster?*

Pop Goes the Weasel

Chapter 1

Geoffrey Shafer, dashingly outfitted in a single-breasted blue blazer, white shirt, striped tie and narrow gray trousers from H. Huntsman & Son, walked out of his town house at seven thirty in the morning and climbed into a black Jaguar XJ12.

He backed the Jag slowly out of the driveway, then stepped on the accelerator. The sleek sports car rocketed up to fifty before it reached the stop sign at Connecticut Avenue, in the posh Kalorama section of Washington, DC.

When Shafer reached the busy intersection, he didn't stop. He floored the accelerator, picking up more speed.

He was doing sixty-five and ached to crash the Jag into the stately fieldstone wall bordering the avenue. He aimed the Jag closer to the wall. He could see the head-on collision, visualize it, feel it all over.

At the last possible second, he tried to avoid the deadly crash. He spun the wheel hard to the left. The sports car fishtailed all the way across the avenue, tires screeching and burning, the smell of rubber thick in the air.

The Jag skidded to a stop, headed the wrong way on the street, the windshield issuing its glossy black stare at a barrage of early oncoming traffic.

Shafer stepped on the accelerator again, and headed forward *against* the oncoming traffic. Every car and truck began to honk loud, sustained blasts.

Shafer didn't even try to catch his breath or bearings. He sped along the avenue, gaining speed. He zoomed across Rock Creek Bridge, made a left, then another left into Rock Creek Parkway.

A tiny scream of pain escaped from his lips. It was involuntary, coming swiftly and unexpectedly. A moment of fear, weakness.

He floored the pedal again and the engine roared. He was doing seventy, then pressing to eighty. He zigged and zagged around slower-moving sedans, sport-utility vehicles, a soot-covered A&P delivery truck.

Only a few honked now. Other drivers on the parkway were terrified, scared out of their minds.

He exited the Rock Creek Parkway at fifty miles an hour, then he gunned it again.

P Street was even more crowded at that hour than the parkway had been. Washington was just waking up and setting off to work. He could still *see* that inviting stone wall on Connecticut. He shouldn't have stopped. He began searching for another rock-solid object, looking for something to hit very hard.

He was doing eighty miles an hour as he approached Dupont Circle. He shot forward like a ground rocket. Two lines of traffic were backed up at a red light. No way out of this one, he thought. Nowhere to go left or right.

He didn't want to rear-end a dozen cars! That was no way to end this – end his life – by smashing into a commonplace Chevy Caprice, a Honda Accord, a delivery truck.

He swerved violently to the left and veered into the lanes of traffic coming east, coming right at him. He could see the panicked, disbelieving faces behind the dusty, grime-smeared windshields. The horns started to blast, a high-pitched symphony of fear.

He ran the next light and just barely squeezed between an oncoming Jeep and a concrete-mixer truck.

He sped down M Street, then onto Pennsylvania Avenue, and headed toward Washington Circle. The George Washington University Medical Center was up ahead – a perfect ending?

The Metro patrolcar appeared out of nowhere, its siren-bullhorn screaming in protest, its rotating beacon glittering, signaling for him to pull over. Shafer slowed down and pulled to the curb.

The cop hurried to Shafer's car, his hand on his holster. He looked frightened and unsure.

'Get out of the car, sir,' the cop said in a commanding voice. 'Get out of the car right now.'

Shafer suddenly felt calm and relaxed. There was no tension left in his body.

'All right. All right. I'm getting out. No problem.'

'You know how fast you were going?' the cop asked in an agitated voice, his face flushed a bright red. Shafer noticed that his hand was still on his gun.

Shafer pursed his lips, thought about his answer. 'Well – I'd say about thirty, Officer,' he finally said. 'Maybe a little over the speed limit.'

Then he took out an ID card and handed it over. 'But you can't do anything about it. I'm with the British Embassy. I have *diplomatic immunity*.'

Chapter II

That night, as he was driving home from work, Geoffrey Shafer started to feel that he was losing control again. He was beginning to frighten himself. His whole life had begun to revolve around a fantasy game he played called The Four Horsemen. In the game, he was the player called Death. The game was everything to him, the only part of his life with meaning.

He sped across town from the British Embassy, all the way to the Petworth district of Northwest. He knew he shouldn't be there, a white man in a spiffy Jaguar. He couldn't help himself, though, any more than he could that morning.

He stopped the car just before he got to Petworth. Shafer took out his laptop and typed a message to the other players, the Horsemen.

FRIENDS,
DEATH IS ON THE LOOSE IN WASHINGTON.
THE GAME IS ON.

He started the Jag again and rode a few more blocks to Petworth. The usual outrageously provocative hookers were already parading up and down Varnum and Webster Streets. A song called 'Nice and Slow' was playing from a vibrating blue BMW. Ronnie McCall's sweet voice blended into the early evening.

The girls waved to him and showed their large, flat, pert, or flabby breasts. Several wore colorful bustiers with matching hot pants and shiny silver or red platform shoes with pointy heels.

He slowed to a stop beside a small black girl who looked to be around sixteen, and had an unusually pretty face and long slender legs, for such a petite body. She wore too much makeup for his taste. Still, she was hard to resist, so why should he?

'Nice car. Jaguar. I like it a lot,' she cooed, smiled, made a sexy little *o* with her lipsticked mouth. 'You're cute, too, mistah.'

He smiled back at her. 'Jump in, then. Let's go for a test ride. See if it's true love or just infatuation.' He glanced around the street quickly. None of the other girls were working this corner.

'I'm a hundred for full service, sweetie,' she said as she wiggled her tight little butt inside the Jag. Her perfume smelled like eau de bubble gum and she seemed to have bathed in it.

'As I said, get into the car. A hundred dollars is petty cash for me.'

He knew he shouldn't be picking her up in the Jaguar, but he took her for a joy ride anyway. He couldn't help himself now.

He brought the girl to a small wooded park in a part of Washington called Shaw. He parked in a thicket of fir trees that hid the car from sight. He looked at the prostitute and she was even smaller and younger than he had thought.

'How old are you?' he asked.

'How old you want me to be?' she said and smiled. 'Sweetheart, I need the money first. You know how it works.'

'Yes. But do you?' he asked.

He reached into his pocket, and pulled out a switchblade knife. He had it at her throat in an instant.

'Don't hurt me,' she whispered. 'Just be cool.'

'Get out of the car. Slowly. Don't you dare scream. *You* be cool.'

Shafer got out with her, staying close, the knife still pressed to the hollow of her throat.

'This is a fantasy game,' he explained. 'It's all just a game, darling. I play with three other men – in England, Jamaica, and Thailand. Their names are Famine, War, and Conqueror. My name is Death. You're a very lucky girl – I'm the best player of all.'

As if to prove it, he stabbed her for the first time.

Book One

The Jane Doe Murders

Chapter One

Things were going pretty well that day. I was driving a bright-orange school bus through Southeast on a blistering-hot morning in late July and I was whistling a little Al Green as I drove. I was in the process of picking up sixteen boys from their houses and also two foster homes. Door-to-door bus service. Hard to beat.

Just one week earlier I had returned from Boston and the Mr Smith murder case. Mr Smith and a deranged killer named Gary Soneji had both been involved in that one. I needed a rest and I'd taken the morning off to do something I'd been looking forward to for a change.

My partner, John Sampson, and a twelve-year-old named Errol Mignault sat behind me on the bus. John was wearing Wayfarer shades, black jeans, a black T-shirt that read: ALLIANCE OF CONCERNED MEN. SEND DONATIONS TODAY. He is six-nine, a very solid two hundred fifty pounds. We've been friends since we were ten, when I first moved to DC.

He, Errol, and I were talking about the boxer Sugar Ray Robinson, almost shouting over the bus's blustery, occasionally misfiring engine. Sampson had his huge arm lightly draped over Errol's shoulders. Proper physical contact is encouraged when dealing with these boys.

Finally, we picked up the last little guy on our list, an eight-year-old who lived in Benning Terrace, a tough project known to some of us as Simple City.

As we left the project, an ugly smear of graffiti told visitors everything they needed to know about the neighborhood. It read: YOU ARE NOW LEAVING THE WAR ZONE, AND YOU LIVED TO TELL ABOUT IT.

We were taking the boys out to Lorton Prison in Virginia. They would be visiting their fathers for the afternoon. They were all young, between eight and thirteen. The Alliance transports forty to fifty kids each week to see their fathers and mothers in different prisons. The goal is a lofty one: to bring the crime rate in Washington down by a third.

I'd been out to the prison more times than I cared to remember. I knew the warden at Lorton pretty well. A few years back I'd spent a lifetime there, interviewing Gary Soneji.

Warden Marion Campbell had set up a large room on level one, where the boys met with their fathers. It was a powerful scene, even more emotional than I'd expected. The Alliance spends time training the fathers who want to participate in the program. There are four steps: how to show love; accept fault and responsibility; attain parent and child harmonies; new beginnings.

Ironically the boys were all trying to look and act tougher than they actually were. I heard one boy say, 'You weren't in my life before, why should I listen to you now?' But the fathers were trying to show a softer side.

Sampson and I hadn't made the run to Lorton before. It was our first time, but I was already sure I'd do it again. There was so much raw emotion and hope in the room, so much potential for something good and decent. Even if some of it would never be realized, it showed that an effort was being made, and something positive could come from it.

What struck me most was the bond that still existed between some of the fathers and their young sons. I thought about my own boy, Damon, and how lucky we were. The thing about most of the prisoners in Lorton was that they knew what they had done was wrong; they just didn't know how to stop doing it.

For most of the hour and a half, I just walked around and listened. I was occasionally needed as a psychologist, and I did the best I could on short notice. At one little group, I heard a father say, 'Please tell your mother I love her and I miss her like crazy.' Then both the prisoner and his son broke into tears and hugged one another fiercely.

Sampson came up to me after we'd been in the prison for an hour or so. He was grinning broadly. His smile, when it comes, is a killer. 'Man, I love this. Do-gooder shit is the best.'

'Yeah, I'm hooked myself. I'll drive the big orange bus again.'

'Think it'll help? Fathers and sons meeting like this?' he asked me.

I looked around the room. 'I think today, right now, this is a success for these men and their sons. That's good enough.'

Sampson nodded. 'The old one-day-at-a-time approach. Works for me, too. I am *flying*, Alex.'

So was I, so was I. I'm a sucker for this kind of stuff.

As I drove the young boys home that afternoon, I could see by their faces that they'd had positive experiences with their fathers. The boys weren't nearly as noisy and rambunctious on the way back to DC. They weren't trying to be so tough. They were just acting like kids.

Almost every one of the boys thanked Sampson and me as they got off the big orange bus. It wasn't necessary. It sure was a lot better than chasing after homicidal maniacs.

The last boy we dropped off was the eight-year-old from Benning Terrace. He hugged both John and me and then he started to cry. 'I miss my dad,' he said, before running home.

Chapter Two

That night, Sampson and I were on duty in Southeast. We're senior homicide detectives and I'm also liaison between the FBI and the DC police. We got a call at about half past midnight telling us to go to the area of Washington called Shaw. There'd been a bad homicide.

A lone Metro squad car was at the murder scene, and the neighborhood psychos had turned out in pretty fair numbers.

It looked like a bizarre block party in the middle of hell. Fires were blazing nearby, throwing off sparks in two trash barrels, which made no sense, given the sweltering heat of the night.

The victim was a young woman, probably between fourteen and her late teens, according to the radio report.

She wasn't hard to find. Her nude, mutilated body had been discarded in a clump of briar bushes in a small park, less than ten yards off a paved pathway.

As Sampson and I approached the body, a boy shouted at us from the other side of the crime tape. 'Yo, yo, she's just some street whore!'

I stopped and looked at him. He reminded me of the boys we'd just transported to Lorton Prison. 'Dime-a-dozen bitch. Not worth your time, or mine, *dee-fectives*,' he went on with his disturbing rap.

I finally walked up to the young wisecracker. 'How do you know that? You seen her around?'

The boy backed off. But then he grinned, showing off a gold star on one of his front teeth. 'She ain't got no clothes on an' she layin' on her back. Somebody stick her good. Sure sound like a whore to me.'

Sampson eyed the youth, who looked to be around fourteen, but might have been even younger. 'You know who she is?'

'Hell, *no!*' The boy pretended to be insulted. 'Don't know no whores, man.'

The boy finally swaggered off, looking back at us once or twice, shaking his head. Sampson and I walked on and joined two uniformed cops standing by the body. They were obviously waiting for reinforcements. Apparently, we were it.

'You call Emergency Services?' I asked the uniforms.

'Thirty-five minutes ago, and counting,' said the older-looking of the two. He was probably in his late twenties, sporting an attempted mustache and trying to look like he was experienced at scenes like this one.

'That figures.' I shook my head. 'You find any ID anywhere around here?'

'No ID. We looked around in the bushes. Nothing but the body,' said the younger one. 'And the body's seen better days.' He was perspiring badly and looked a little sick.

I put on latex gloves and bent down over the corpse. She did appear to be in her mid to late teens. The girl's throat had been slit from ear to ear. Her face was badly slashed. So were the soles of her feet, which seemed odd. She'd been stabbed a dozen or more times in her chest and stomach. I pushed open her legs.

I saw something, and it made me sick. A metal handle was barely visible between her legs. I was almost sure it was a knife and that it had been driven all the way into her vagina.

Sampson crouched and looked at me. 'What are you thinking, Alex? Another one?'

I shook my head, shrugged my shoulders. 'Maybe, but she's an addict, John. Tracks on her arms and legs. Probably behind her knees, under her arms. Our boy doesn't usually go after addicts. He practices safe sex. The murder's brutal, though. That fits the style. You see the knife?'

Sampson nodded. He didn't miss much. 'Clothes,' he said, 'where the hell did they go? We need to find the clothes.'

'Somebody in the neighborhood probably stripped them off her already,' said the young uniform. There was a lot of disturbance around the body. Several footprints in the dirt. 'That's how it goes around here. Nobody seems to care.'

'We're here,' I said to him. 'We care. We're here for all the Jane Does.'

Chapter Three

Geoffrey Shafer was so happy he almost couldn't hide it from his family. He had to keep from laughing out loud as he kissed his wife, Lucy, on the cheek. He caught a whiff of her Chanel No. 5 perfume, then tasted the brittle dryness of her lips as he kissed her again.

They were standing around like statues in the elegant galley hall of the large Georgian house in Kalorama. The children had been summoned to say goodbye to him.

His wife, the former Lucy Rhys-Cousins, was ash blonde, her sparkling green eyes even brighter than the Bulgari and Spark jewelry that she always wore. Slender, still a beauty of sorts at thirty-seven, Lucy had been at Newnham College, Cambridge, for two years before they were married. She still read useless poetry and literary novels, but spent most of her free time at equally pointless lunches, shopping with her expatriate girl-friends, going to polo matches, or sailing. Occasionally,

Shafer sailed with her. He'd been a very good sailor once upon a time.

Lucy had been considered a prize catch, and he supposed that she still would be, for some men. Well, they could have her skinny, bony body and all the passionless sex they could stomach.

Shafer hoisted up four-year-old twins Tricia and Erica, one in each arm. Two mirror images of their mother. He'd have sold the twins for the price of a postage stamp. He hugged the girls and laughed like the good papa he always pretended to be.

Finally, he formally shook twelve-year-old Robert's hand. The debate being waged in the house was over whether Robert should be sent back to England to boarding school, perhaps to Winchester, where his grandfather had gone. Shafer gave his son a crisp military salute. Once upon a time, Colonel Geoffrey Shafer had been a soldier. Only Robert seemed to remember that part of his life now.

'I'm only going away to London for a few days, and this is *work*, not a holiday. I'm not planning to spend my nights at the Athenaeum or anything like that,' he told his family. He was smiling jovially, the way they expected him to be.

'Try to have some fun while you're away, Dad. Have some laughs. God knows, you deserve it,' Robert said, talking in the lower-octave man-to-man's voice that he seemed to be adopting lately.

'Bye, Daddy! Bye, Daddy,' the twins chorused shrilly,

making Shafer want to throw them against the walls.

'Bye, Erica-san. Bye, Tricia-san.'

'Remember, Orc's Nest,' Robert said with sudden urgency. '*Dragon* and *The Duelist*.' Orc's Nest was a store for role-playing books and gaming equipment. It was in Earlham Street, just off Cambridge Circus in London. *Dragon* and *The Duelist* were currently the two hot-shit British magazines on role-playing games.

Unfortunately for Robert, Shafer wasn't actually going to London. He had a much better plan for the weekend. He was going to play his own fantasy game right here in Washington.

Chapter Four

He sped due east, rather than toward Washington's Dulles airport, feeling as if a tremendously burdensome weight had been lifted. God, he hated his perfect English family, and even more, their claustrophobic life here in America.

Shafer's own family back in England had been 'perfect' as well. He had two older brothers and they were both excellent students, model youths. His father had been a military attaché and the family had traveled around the globe until he was twelve, when they returned to England and settled in Guildford, about half an hour outside London. Once there, Shafer began to expand on the schoolboy mischief he'd practiced since he was eight. The center of Guildford contained several historic buildings and he set out to gleefully deface all of them. He began with the Abbot's Hospital where his grandmother was dying. He painted obscenities on the walls. Then he moved onto Guildford Castle, the Guildhall, the Royal Grammar School, and the Cathedral. He scrawled more obscene words, and also large penises in bright colors. He had no idea why he took such joy in ruining beautiful things, but he did. He loved it – and he especially loved not getting caught.

Shafer was eventually sent to school at Rugby, where the pranks continued. Then he attended St John's College, Cambridge, where he concentrated on philosophy, Japanese, and shagging as many good-looking women as he possibly could. All his friends were mystified when he went into the army at twenty-one. His language skills were excellent and he was posted to Asia, which was where the mischief rose to a new level and he began to play *the game of games.*

He stopped at a 7-Eleven in Washington Heights for coffee – three coffees, actually. Black, with four sugars in each. He drank most of one of the cups on his way to the counter.

The Indian cashier gave him a cheeky, suspicious look, and he laughed in the bearded wanker's face.

'Do you really think I'd steal a bloody seventy-five-cent cup of coffee? You pathetic jerkoff. You pitiful Paki.'

He threw his money on the counter and left before he killed the clerk with his bare hands, which he could do easily enough.

From the 7-Eleven he drove into the Northeast part of Washington, a middle-class section called Eckington. He began to recognize the streets when he was west of

Gallaudet University. Most of the structures were two-storied apartments, with vinyl siding, either red brick, or a hideous Easter-egg blue that always made him wince.

He stopped in front of one of the red-brick garden apartments on Uhland Terrace, near Second Street. This one had an attached garage. A previous tenant had adorned the brick façade with two white concrete cats.

'Hello, pussies,' Shafer said. He felt relieved to be here. He was 'cycling up' – that is, getting high, manic. He loved this feeling, couldn't get enough of it. It was time to play the game.

Chapter Five

A rusted and taped-up purple-and-blue taxi was parked inside the two-car garage. Shafer had been using it for about four months. The taxi gave him anonymity, made him almost invisible anywhere he chose to go in DC. He called it his 'nightmare machine'.

He wedged the Jaguar beside the taxi cab, then he jogged upstairs. Once inside the apartment, he switched on the air-conditioning. He drank another sugar-laced coffee.

Then he took his pills, like a good boy. Thorazine and Librium. Benadryl, Xanax, Vicodin. He'd been using the drugs in various combinations for years. It was mostly a trial and error process, but he'd learned his lessons well. *Feeling better, Geoffrey? Yes, much better, thank you.*

He tried to read today's *Washington Post*, then an old copy of *Private Eye*, and finally a catalog from DeMask, a rubber and leather fetish wholesaler in Amsterdam, the world's largest. He did two hundred pushups, then a few hundred situps, impatiently waiting for darkness to fall over Washington.

At quarter to ten, Shafer began to get ready for a big night on the town. He went into the small, barren bathroom which smelled of cheap cleaner. He stood before the mirror.

He liked what he saw. Very much so. Thick and wavy blond hair that he would never lose. A charismatic, electric smile. Startling blue eyes that had a cinematic quality. Excellent physical shape for a man of forty-four.

He went to work, starting with brown contact lenses. He'd done this so many times, he could almost do it blindfolded. It was a part of his tradecraft. He applied blackface to his face, neck, hands, wrists; thick padding to make his neck seem broader than it was; a dark watch cap to cover every last strand of hair.

He stared hard at himself – and saw a rather convincing-looking black man, especially if the light wasn't too strong. Not bad, not bad at all. It was a good disguise for a night on the town, especially if the town was Washington.

So let the games begin. The Four Horsemen.

At ten twenty-five, he went down to the garage again. He carefully circled around the Jaguar and walked to the purple-and-blue taxi cab. He had already begun to lose himself in delicious fantasy.

Shafer reached into his pants pocket and pulled out three unusual-looking dice. They were twenty-sided, the kind used in most fantasy games, or RPGs. They had numerals on them rather than dots.

He held the dice in his left hand, rolling them over and over.

There were explicit rules to The Four Horsemen; everything was supposed to depend on the dice roll. The idea was to come up with an outrageous fantasy, a mind-blower. The four players around the world were competing. There had never been a game like this – nothing even came close.

Shafer had already prepared an adventure for himself, but there were alternatives for every event. Much depended on the dice.

That was the main point – anything could happen.

He got into the taxi, started it up. Good Lord, was he ready for this!

Chapter Six

He had a gorgeous plan mapped out. He would pick up only those few passengers – 'fares' – who caught his eye, fired up his imagination to the limit. He wasn't in a hurry. He had all night; he had all weekend. He was on a busman's holiday.

His route had been laid out beforehand. First, he drove to the fashionable Adams-Morgan neighborhood. He watched the busy sidewalks, which seemed one long syncopated rhythm of movement. Bar-grazers slouching toward hipness. It seemed that every other restaurant in Adams-Morgan called itself a café. Driving slowly and checking the glittery sights, he passed Café Picasso, Café Lautrec, La Fourchette Café, Bukom Café, Café Dalbol, Montego Café, Sheba Café.

Around eleven thirty, on Columbia Road, he slowed the taxi cab. His heart began to thump. Something very good was shaping up ahead.

A handsome-looking couple was leaving the popular Chief Ike's Mambo Room. A man and a woman, Hispanic, probably in their late twenties. Sensual beyond belief.

He rolled the dice across the front seat: six, five, four – a total of fifteen. A high count.

Danger! That made sense. A couple was always tricky and risky.

Shafer waited for them to cross the pavement, moving away from the restaurant canopy. *They came right toward him.* How accommodating. He touched the handle of the magnum that he kept under the front seat. He was ready for anything.

As they started to climb into the taxi, he changed his mind. He could do that!

Shafer saw that neither of them was as attractive as he'd thought. The man's cheeks and forehead were slightly mottled; the pomade in his black hair was too thick and greasy. The woman was a few pounds heavier than he liked, plumper than she'd looked from a distance in the flattering streetlights.

'Off duty,' he said, and sped away. Both of them gave him the finger.

Shafer laughed out loud. 'You're in luck tonight! Fools! Luckiest night of your lives and you don't even know it.'

The incomparable thrill of the fantasy had completely taken hold of him. He'd had total power over the couple. He had control of life and death.

'Death *be* proud,' he whispered.

He stopped for more coffee at a Starbucks on Rhode Island Avenue. Nothing like it. He purchased three black coffees and heaped six sugars in each.

An hour later, he was in Southeast. He hadn't stopped for another fare. The streets were crowded to the max with pedestrians. There weren't enough taxis, not even gypsies in this part of Washington.

He regretted having let the Hispanic couple get away. He'd begun to romanticize them in his mind, to visualize them as they'd looked in the streetlight. Remembrance of things past, right? He thought of Proust's monumental opening line: 'For a long time I used to go to bed early.' And so had Shafer – until he discovered the game of games.

Then he saw her – a perfect brown goddess standing right there before him, as if someone had just given him a wonderful present. She was walking by herself, about a block from E Street, moving fast, purposefully. He was instantly high again.

He loved the way she moved, the swivel of her long legs, the exactness of her carriage.

As he came up behind her, she began looking around, checking the street. Looking for a taxi? Could it be? Did she want him?

She had on a light cream suit, a purple silk shirt, high heels. She looked too classy and adult to be going to a club. She appeared to be in control of herself.

He quickly rolled the twenty-sided dice again and held his breath. Counted the numerals. His heart leaped. This was what the Horsemen was all about.

She was waving her hand at him, signaling. *'Taxi!'* she called. 'Taxi! Are you free?'

He guided the taxi over to the curb and she took three quick, delicate steps toward him. She was wearing shimmery, silken high heels that were just delightful. She was much prettier up close. She was a nine and a half out of ten.

Then he saw that she was carrying flowers, and wondered why. Something special tonight? Well, that was certainly true. The flowers were for her own funeral.

'Oh, thank you so much for stopping.' She spoke breathlessly as she settled into the taxi. He could tell that she was letting herself relax and feel safe. Her voice was soothing, sweet, down-to-earth, and real.

'At your service.' Shafer turned and smiled at her. 'By the way, I'm Death. You're my fantasy for this weekend.'

Chapter Seven

Monday mornings I usually work the soup kitchen at St Anthony's in Southeast, where I've been a volunteer for the past half-dozen years. I do the seven-to-nine shift, three days a week.

That morning I felt restless and uneasy. I was still getting over the Mr Smith case, which had taken me all over the East Coast and to Europe. Maybe I needed a real vacation, a holiday far away from Washington.

I watched the usual lineup of men, women, and children who have no money for food. It was about five deep and went up Twelfth Street to the second corner. It seemed such a pity, so unfair that so many folks still go hungry in Washington, or are fed only once a day.

I had started helping out at the kitchen years before on account of my wife, Maria. She was doing casework as a social worker at St Anthony's when we first met. Maria was the uncrowned princess of St Anthony's; everybody loved her, and she loved me. She was shot, murdered, in a drive-by incident, not far from the soup kitchen. We'd been married four years and had two small children. The case has never been solved, and that still tortures me. Maybe that's what drives me to solve every case that I can, no matter how bad the odds.

At St Anthony's soup kitchen, I help make sure nobody gets too riled up, or causes undue trouble during meals. I'm six-three, around two hundred and five pounds, and built for peacekeeping, if and when it's necessary. I can usually ward off trouble with a few quiet words and non-threatening gestures. Most of these people are here to eat though, not fight or cause trouble.

I also dish out peanut butter and jelly to anyone who wants seconds, or even thirds of the stuff. Jimmy Moore, the Irish-American who runs the soup kitchen with much love and just the right amount of discipline, has always believed in the healing power of PB and J. Some of the regulars at the kitchen call me 'Peanut Butter Man'. They've been doing it for years.

'You don't look so good today,' said a short, ample woman who's been coming to the kitchen for the past year or two. I know her name is Laura, that she was born in Detroit, and has two grown sons. She used to work as a housekeeper on M Street in Georgetown, but the family felt she'd gotten too old for the job, and let her go with a couple weeks' severance and warm words of appreciation.

'You deserve better. You deserve *me*,' Laura said, and laughed mischievously. 'What do you say?'

'Laura, you're too kind with your compliments,' I said, dishing up her usual dish. 'Anyway, you've met Christine. You know I'm already spoken for.'

Laura giggled, and hugged herself with both arms. She had a fine, healthy laugh, even under the circumstances. 'A young girl has to dream, you know. Nice to see you, as always.'

'Same to you, Laura. As always, nice to see you. Enjoy the meal.'

'Oh, I do. You can *see* I do.'

As I said my cheery hellos and dished out heaped portions of peanut butter, I allowed myself to think about Christine. Laura was probably right, maybe I didn't look so good today; I probably hadn't looked too terrific for a few days.

I still remembered a night about two weeks back. I had just finished the multiple-homicide case in Boston. Christine and I stood on the porch in front of her house out in Mitchellville. I was trying to live my life differently, but it's hard to change. I had a saying I really liked: *Heart leads head.*

I could smell the flowers in the night air, roses and impatiens growing in profusion. I could also smell Gardenia Passion, a favorite perfume that Christine was wearing that night.

She and I had known each other for a year and a half. We'd met during a murder investigation that had ended with the death of her husband. Eventually, we began to go out. I was thinking that it had all been leading to this moment on the porch. At least it had been in my mind.

I had never seen Christine when she didn't look good to me, and make me feel light-headed. She's tall, almost five-ten, and that's nice. She has a smile that could probably light up half the country. That night, she was wearing tight faded jeans and a white T-shirt knotted around her waist. Her feet were bare and her nails were dabbed with red. Her beautiful brown eyes were shining.

I reached out and took her into my arms and suddenly everything seemed right with the world. I forgot all about the terrible case I'd just finished; I forgot about a particularly vicious killer known as Mr Smith.

I cupped her sweet, kind face gently in my hands. I like to think that nothing scares me anymore, and many things don't, but I guess the more good things you have in your life, the easier it is to experience fear. Christine felt so precious to me – so maybe I was scared.

Heart leads head.

It isn't the way most men act, but I was learning.

'I love you more than I've ever loved anything in my life, Christine. You help me see and feel things in new ways. I love your smile, your way with people – especially kids – your kindness. I love to hold you like this. I love you more than I can say if I stood here and talked for the rest of the night. I love you so much. Will you marry me, Christine?'

She didn't answer right away. I felt her pull back, just a little, and my heart caught. I looked into her eyes, and what I saw was pain and uncertainty. It nearly broke my heart.

'Oh, Alex, Alex,' she whispered, and looked as if she might cry. 'I can't give you an answer. You just came back from Boston. You were on another horrible, horrible murder case. I can't take that. Your life was in danger again. That terrible madman was in your house. He threatened your family. You can't deny any of that.'

I couldn't. It had been a terrifying experience, and I had nearly died. 'I won't deny anything you said. But I do love you. I can't deny that either. I'll quit the police force if that's what it takes.'

'No.' A softness came into her eyes. She shook her head back and forth. 'That would be all wrong. For both of us.'

We held each other on the porch and I knew we were in trouble. I didn't know how to resolve it. I had no idea. Maybe if I left the force, became a full-time therapist again, led a more normal life for Christine and the kids. But could I do that? Could I really quit?

'Ask me again,' she whispered. 'Ask me again, sometime.'

Chapter Eight

Christine and I had dated since that night, and it had been the way it always is between us. It just felt right, easy, comfortable, and romantic. Still, I wondered if our problem could be fixed. Could she be happy with a homicide detective? Could I stop being one? I didn't know.

I was brought out of my reverie about Christine by the high-pitched, stuttering wail of a siren out on Twelfth Street, just turning off E. I winced when I saw Sampson's black Nissan pull up in front of St Anthony's.

He turned off the siren on his rooftop, but then beeped the car horn, sat on it. I knew he was here for me, probably to take me somewhere that I didn't want to go. The horn continued to blare.

'It's your friend John Sampson,' Jimmy Moore called out. 'You hear him, Alex?'

'I know who it is,' I called back to Jimmy. 'I'm hoping that he goes away.'

'Sure doesn't sound like it.'

I finally walked outside, crossing through the soup-kitchen line and receiving a few jokey jeers. People I had known for a long time accused me of working half a day, or said that if I didn't like the job, could they have it?

'What's up?' I called to Sampson, before I got all the way out to his black sportscar.

Sampson's side window came sliding down. I leaned inside the car. 'You forget? It's my day off,' I reminded him.

'It's Nina Childs,' Sampson said in a low, soft voice he used only when he was angry or very serious. He tried to deaden his facial muscles, to look tough, not emotional, but it wasn't working real well. 'Nina's dead, Alex.'

I shivered involuntarily. I opened the car door and got in. I didn't even go back to the kitchen to tell Jimmy Moore I was leaving. Sampson jerked the car away from the curbside fast. The siren came on again, but now I almost welcomed the mournful wail. It numbed me.

'What do you know so far?' I asked as we rushed along the intensely bleak streets of Southeast, then crossed the slate-gray Anacostia River.

'She was dumped in a row house, Eighteenth and Garnesville. Jerome Thurman is out there with her. Says she's probably been there since the weekend. Some needlepusher found the body. No clothes or ID, Alex,' Sampson said.

I looked over at him. 'So how did they know it was Nina?'

'Uniform guy on the scene recognized her. Knew her from the hospital. Everybody knew Nina.'

I shut my eyes, but I saw Nina Childs' face and I opened them again. She had been the eleven-to-seven charge nurse in the ER unit at St Anthony's Hospital, where once I ran like a tornado with a dying little boy in my arms. Sampson and I had worked with Nina more times than I could remember. Sampson had also dated Nina for over a year, but then they broke it off. She married a neighborhood man who worked for the city. They had two kids, two little babies, and Nina had seemed so happy the last time I saw her.

I couldn't believe she was lying dead in a tenement on the wrong side of the Anacostia. She had been abandoned, like one of the Jane Does.

Chapter Nine

Nina Childs' body had been found in a battered row house in one of the city's most impoverished, destroyed, and dismaying neighborhoods. There was only one patrol car on the scene, and a single rusted and dented EMS van. Homicides in Southeast don't attract much attention. A dog was barking somewhere and it was the only sound on the desolate street.

Sampson and I had to walk past an open-air drug mart on the corner of Eighteenth Street. Mostly young males, but a few children and two women were gathered there defiantly. The drug marts are everywhere in this part of Southeast. The neighborhood youth activity is the crack trade.

'Daily body pick-up, Officers?' said one of the young men, who was wearing black trousers with black suspenders, no shirt, socks, or shoes. He had a prison-yard physique and tattoos everywhere.

'Come to take out the trash?' An older man cackled from behind an unruly patch of salt-and-pepper beard. 'Take that muhfuckin' barkin'-all-night dog while you here. Make yourselves useful,' he added.

Sampson and I ignored them and continued walking across Eighteenth, then into the boarded-up three-storied row house straight ahead. A black-and-white boxer leaned out of a third-floor window, like a lifetime resident, and wouldn't stop barking. Otherwise the building appeared deserted.

The front door had been jimmied a hundred times, so it just swung open for us. The building smelled of fire, garbage, water damage. There was a gaping hole in the ceiling from a burst steam pipe. It was so wrong for Nina to have ended up in this sad, abominable place.

For over a year I had been unofficially investigating unsolved murders in Southeast, many of them Jane Does. My count was well over a hundred, but no one else in the department was willing to agree to the number, or anything close to it. Several of the murdered women were drug abusers or prostitutes. But not Nina.

We carefully descended a circular stairwell that had a shaky, well-worn wooden railing that neither of us would touch. I could see flashlights shining up ahead and I already had my Maglite turned on.

Nina was deep in the basement of the abandoned building. At least somebody had bothered to tape off the perimeter, frozen the crime scene.

I saw Nina's body – and I had to look away.

It wasn't just that she was dead, it was how she'd been killed. I tried to put my mind and eyes somewhere else until I regained some composure.

Jerome Thurman was there with the EMS team. So was a single patrol officer, probably the one who had identified Nina. No ME was present. It wasn't unusual for a medical examiner not to show up for homicides in Southeast.

There were dead flowers on the floor near the body. I focused on the flowers, still not able to look at Nina again. They didn't fit with the other Jane Does, but the killer didn't have a strict pattern. That was one of the problems I was having. It might mean that his fantasy was still evolving – and that he hadn't finished making up his gruesome story yet.

I noted shreds of foil and cellophane wrappers lying everywhere on the floor. Rats are attracted to shiny things and often bring them back to their nests. Thick cobwebs weaved from one end of the basement to the other.

I had to look at Nina again. I needed to look closely.

'I'm Detective Alex Cross. Let me take a look at her, please,' I finally said to the EMS team, a man and a woman in their twenties. 'I'll just be a couple of minutes, then I'll get out of your way.'

'The other detectives already released the body,' the male EMS worker said. He was rail-thin, with long dirty-blond hair. He didn't bother to look up at me. 'Let us finish our job and get the hell out of this cesspool. Whole area is highly infectious, smells like shit.'

'Just back away,' Sampson barked. 'Get up, before I pull your skinny ass up.'

The EMS techie cursed, but he stood and backed away from Nina's body. I moved in close, tried to concentrate and be professional, tried to remember specific details I had gathered about the previous Jane Does in Southeast. I was looking for some connection. I wondered if a single predator could possibly be killing so many people. If that were true, then this would be one of the most savage killing sprees ever.

I took a deep breath and then I knelt over Nina. The rats had been at her, I could see. The killer had done much worse damage.

It looked to me as if Nina had been beaten to death, with punches, and possibly kicks. She might have been struck a hundred times or more. I had rarely seen anyone given this much punishment. Why did it have to happen? She was only thirty-one years old, mother of two, kind, talented, dedicated to her work at St Anthony's.

There was a sudden noise, like a rifleshot, in the building. It reverberated right through the basement walls. The EMS workers jumped.

The rest of us laughed nervously. I knew exactly what the sound was.

'Just rattraps,' I said to the EMS team. 'Get used to it.'

Chapter Ten

I was at the homicide scene for a little over two hours, much longer than I wanted to be there, and I hated every second. I couldn't fix a set pattern for the Jane Doe killings, and Nina Childs' murder didn't help. Why had he struck her so many times and so savagely? What were the flowers doing there? Could this be the work of the same killer?

The way I usually operate at a crime scene, the homicide investigation takes on an almost aerial view. Everything emanates from the body.

Sampson and I walked the entire crime scene – from the basement to each floor and on up to the roof. Then we walked the neighborhood. Nobody had seen anything unusual, which didn't surprise either of us.

Now came the really bad part. Sampson and I drove from the woeful tenement to Nina's apartment in the Brookland section of Washington, east of Catholic University. I knew I was being sucked in again, but there was nothing I could do about it.

It was a sweltering-hot day and the sun hammered Washington without mercy. We were both silent and withdrawn during the ride. What we had to do was the worst thing about our job, telling a family about the death of a loved one. I didn't know how I could do it this time.

Nina lived in a well-kept brown-brick building on Monroe Street. Miniature yellow roses were blooming out front in bright-green window-boxes. It didn't look as if anything bad should happen to someone who lived here. Everything about the place was so bright and hopeful, just as Nina had been.

I was becoming more and more disturbed and upset about the brutal and obscene murder, and the fact that it probably wouldn't get a decent investigation from the department, at least not officially. Nana Mama would chalk it up to her conspiracy theories about the white overlords and their 'criminal disinterest' in the people of Southeast. She had often told me that she felt morally superior to white people, that she would never, ever treat them the way they treated the black people of Washington.

'Nina's sister, Marie, takes care of the kids,' Sampson said as we rode down Monroe. 'She's a nice girl. Had a drug problem one time, beat it. Nina helped her. The whole family is close-knit. A lot like yours. This is going to be real bad, Alex.'

I turned to him. Not surprisingly, he was taking Nina's death even harder than I was. It's unusual for him to show his emotions though. 'I can do it, John. You stay here in the car. I'll go up and talk to the family.'

Sampson shook his head and sighed loudly. 'Doesn't work that way, sugar.'

He snugged the Nissan up to the curb and we both climbed out. He didn't stop me from coming along to the apartment, so I knew he wanted me there with him. He was right. This was going to be bad.

The Childs' apartment took up the first and second floors. The front door was slightly ornate, aluminum. Nina's husband was already at the door. He had on the proletariat uniform of the DC Housing Authority where he worked: mud-stained work boots, blue trousers, a shirt marked DCHA. One of the babies snuggled in his arms, a beautiful girl who looked at me and smiled and cooed.

'Could we come inside for a moment?' Sampson asked.

'It's Nina,' the husband said, and started to break down right there in the doorway.

'I'm sorry, William.' I spoke softly. 'You're right. She's dead. She's been killed. She was found this morning.'

William Childs started to sob loudly. He was a powerful-looking working man, but that didn't matter. He held his bewildered little girl to his chest and tried to control the crying, but he couldn't.

'Oh God, no. Oh, Nina, Nina baby. How could somebody kill her? How could anybody do that? Oh, Nina, Nina, Nina.'

A young, pretty woman came up behind him. She had to be Nina's sister, Marie. She took the baby from her sister's husband, and the little girl began to scream, as if she knew what had happened. I had seen so many families, so many good people, who had lost loved ones on these merciless streets. I knew it would never completely stop, but I felt it ought to get better, and it never did.

The sister motioned for us to come inside, and I noticed a hall table on which were two pocketbooks, as if Nina were still about. The apartment was comfortable and neat, with light bamboo and white-cushioned furniture. The whirr of a window air-conditioner was constant. A Lladro porcelain figure of a nurse was on an end table.

I was still sorting through details about the homicide scene, trying to connect the murder to the other Jane Does. We learned that Nina had attended a health-care charity dinner on Saturday night. William had been working overtime. The family called the police late Saturday night. Two detectives had shown up, but no one had been able to find Nina until now.

Then I was holding the baby, while Nina's sister took the chill off a bottle of formula. It was such a sad and poignant moment, knowing this poor little girl would never see her mother again, never know how truly special her mother had been. It reminded me of my own kids and their mother, and of Christine, who was afraid I would die during some murder investigation like this one.

The older little girl came up to me while I was holding her baby sister. She was two or three at the most. 'I got a new hairstyle,' she said proudly and did a half-turn to show me.

'You did? It's beautiful. Who did those braids for you?'

'My mommy,' said the girl.

It was an hour later that Sampson and I finally left the house. We drove away in silence and despair, the same way we'd come. After a couple of blocks, Sampson pulled over in front of a ramshackle neighborhood bodega covered with beer and soda posters.

He gave a deep sigh, put his hands to his face, and then John cried. I'd never, ever seen him like this before, not in all the years we'd been friends, not even when we were just boys. I reached out and laid a hand on his shoulder, and he didn't move away. Then he told me something he hadn't shared before.

'I loved her, Alex, but I let her get away. I never told her how I felt. We have to get this sonofabitch.'

Chapter Eleven

I sensed I was at the start of another homicide mess. I didn't want it, but I couldn't stop the horror. I had to try to do something about the Jane Does. I couldn't just stand by and do nothing.

Although I was assigned to the Seventh District as a senior detective, my job as liaison with the FBI gave me some extra status and also freedom to occasionally work without too much supervision or interference. My mind was running free and I'd already made some associations with Nina's murder and at least some of the unsolved killings. First, there had been no identification on the victims at the crime scenes. Second, the bodies had frequently been dumped in buildings where they might not be found quickly. Third, not a single witness had seen anyone who might be a suspect or the killer. The most we ever got was that there had been traffic, or people out on the streets, where one of the bodies had been found. That told me that the killer knew how to blend in, and that he possibly was a black man.

Around six that night, I finally headed home. This was supposed to be a day off. I had things to do there, and I was trying to balance the demands of the job and home life as best I could. I put on a happy face and headed inside the house.

Damon, Jannie, and Nana were singing 'Sit Down You're Rockin' de Boat' in the kitchen. The show tune was music to my ears and other essential parts of my anatomy. The kids looked happy as could be. There is a lot to be said for the innocence of childhood.

I heard Nana say, 'How about "I Can Tell The World"?' Then the three of them launched into one of the most beautiful spirituals I know. Damon's voice seemed particularly strong to me. I hadn't really noticed that before.

'I feel like I just walked into a story by Louisa May Alcott,' I said, laughing for the first time that long day.

'I take that as a *high* compliment,' Nana said. She was somewhere between her late seventies and early eighties now, but not telling, and also not showing her age.

'Who's Louise Maise Alcott?' Jannie said, and made a lemon-sucking face. She is a healthy little skeptic, though almost never a cynic. In that way, she takes after both her father and grandmother.

'Look it up tonight, little one. Fifty cents in your pocket for the correct answer,' I told her.

'You're on.' Jannie grinned. 'You can pay me right now if you like.'

'Me too?' Damon asked.

'Of course. You can look up Jane Austen,' I said to him. 'Now what's with the heavenly harmonizing? I like it very much, by the way. I just want to know what the special occasion is.'

'We're just singing while we prepare dinner,' Nana said, and stuck up her nose and twinkled her eyes. 'You play jazz and the blues on the piano, don't you? We harmonize like angels sometimes. No special reason necessary. Good for the soul, and the soul food, I suppose. Can't hurt.'

'Well, don't stop singing on my account,' I said, but they had already stopped. Too bad. Something was going on, I'd figured out that much. A musical mystery to be solved in my own house.

'We still on for boxing after dinner?' I asked cautiously. I was feeling a little vulnerable because I didn't want them to turn me down for the boxing lesson that has become a ritual.

'Of course,' Damon said, and frowned like I must be out of my mind to even ask such a question.

'Of course. Pshaw. Why wouldn't we be?' Jannie said, and brushed off my silly question with a wave of her hand. 'How's Ms Johnson?' she asked then. 'You two talk today?'

'I still want to know what the singing was all about?' I answered Jannie with a question of my own.

'You have valuable information. Well, so do I. Tit for tat,' she said. 'How do you like that?'

A little later, I decided to call Christine at home. Lately, it had seemed more like the way it had been between us before I got involved with the Mr Smith case. We talked for a while, and then I asked her to go out on Friday.

'Of course. I'd like that, Alex. What should I wear?' she asked.

I hesitated. 'Well, I always like what you choose – but wear something special.'

She didn't ask why.

Chapter Twelve

After one of Nana's roast chicken dinners with baked sweet potatoes and homemade bread, I took the kids downstairs for their weekly boxing lesson. Following the Monday-night fight with the kids, I glanced at my watch and saw that it was already a little past nine.

The doorbell rang a moment later. I set down a terrific book called *The Color of Water* and pushed myself up from my chair in the family room.

'I'll get it. It's probably for me,' I called out.

'Maybe it's Christine. You never know,' Jannie teased, then darted away into the kitchen. Both of the kids adored Christine, in spite of the fact that she was the principal at their school.

I knew exactly who was out on the porch. I had been expecting four homicide detectives from the First District – Jerome Thurman, Rakeem Powell, Shawn Moore and Sampson.

Three of the detectives were standing out on the porch. Rosie the cat and I let them inside. Sampson arrived about five minutes later, and we all gathered in the backyard. What we were doing at the house wasn't illegal, but it wouldn't make us a lot of friends in high places in the police department.

We sat on lawn chairs and I set out beer and low-fat pretzels that two-hundred-seventy-pound Jerome scoffed at. 'Beer and low-fat pretzels. Give me a *break*, Alex. You lost your mind? Hey, you having an affair with my wife? You must have got this bad idea from Claudette.'

'I bought these especially for you, big man. I'm trying to give your heart a break,' I told him, and the others guffawed loudly. We all pick on Jerome.

The five of us had been getting together informally for a couple of weeks. We were beginning to work on The Jane Does, as we called them. Homicide had no official investigation going on; it wasn't trying to link the murders to a serial killer. I'd tried to start one and been turned down by Chief Pittman. He claimed that I hadn't discovered a pattern linking any of the murders, and besides that, he didn't have any extra detectives for duty in Southeast.

'I suppose you've all heard about Nina Childs by now?' Sampson asked the other detectives. All of them had known Nina, and of course Jerome had been at the murder scene with us.

'The good die young.' Rakeem Powell frowned severely

and shook his head. Rakeem is smart and tough and could go all the way in the department. 'Least they do in Southeast.' His eyes went cold and hard.

I told them what I knew, especially that Nina had been found with no ID. I mentioned everything else I had noticed at the tenement crime scene. I also took the occasion to talk some more about the rash of unsolved murders in Southeast. I went over the devastating stats I had compiled, mostly in my free time.

'Statistic like that in Georgetown or the Capitol district, people in this city be enraged. Going ballistic. Be *Washington Post* headlines every day. The president himself be involved. Money no object. National tragedy!' Jerome Thurman railed on and waved his arms around like signal flags.

'Well, we are here to do something about it,' I said in a calmer voice. 'Money *is* no object with us. Neither is time. Let me tell you what I feel about this killer,' I continued. 'I think I know a few things about him.'

'How'd you come up with the profile?' Shawn Moore asked. 'How can you stand thinking about these kinky bastards as much as you do?'

I shrugged. 'It's what I do best. I've analyzed all the Jane Does,' I said. 'It took me weeks working on my own. Just me and the kinky bastard.'

'Plus, he studies rodent droppings,' said Sampson. 'I saw him bagging the little turds. That's his real secret.'

I grinned, and told them what I had so far. 'I think one male is responsible for at least some of the killings.

I don't think he's a brilliant killer, like Gary Soneji or Mr Smith, but he's clever enough not to be caught. He's organized, reasonably careful. I don't think we'll find he has any prior record. He probably has a decent job. Maybe even a family. My FBI friends at Quantico agree with that.

'He's almost definitely caught up in an escalating fantasy cycle. I think he's into his fantasies big time. Maybe he's in the process of becoming someone or something new. He might be forming a new personality for himself. He isn't finished with the killing, not by any means.

'I'll make some educated guesses. He hates his old self, though the people closest to him probably don't realize it. He might be ready to abandon his family, job, any friends he has. At one time he probably had very strong feelings and beliefs about something – law and order, religion, the government – but not anymore. He kills in different ways – there's no set formula. He knows a lot about killing people. He's used different kinds of weapons. He may have traveled overseas. Or maybe he spent time in Asia. I think it's very possible he's a black man. He's killed several times in Southeast – no one's noticed him.'

'Fuck me,' Jerome Thurman said to that. 'Any *good* news, Alex?'

'One thing, and this is a long shot. But it feels right to me. I think he might be suicidal. It fits the profile I'm working on. He's living dangerously, taking a lot of chances. He might just blow himself up.'

'Pop goes the weasel,' Sampson said.

That was how we came to name the killer – the Weasel.

Chapter Thirteen

Geoffrey Shafer looked forward to playing The Four Horsemen every Thursday night, from nine until about one in the morning.

The fantasy game was everything to him. There were three other master players around the world. The players were the Rider on the White Horse, Conqueror; the Rider on the Red Horse, War; the Rider on the Black Horse, Famine; and himself – the Rider on the Pale Horse, Death.

Lucy and the children knew they were forbidden to disturb him for any reason, once he locked himself into the library on the second floor. On one wall was his collection of ceremonial daggers, nearly all of them purchased in Hong Kong and Bangkok. Also on the wall was the oar from the year his college crew were Head of the River. Shafer nearly always won the games he played.

He had been using the Internet to communicate with the other players for years, long before the rest of the world caught on. Conqueror played from the town of Dorking in Surrey, outside London; Famine traveled back and forth between Bangkok, Sydney, Melbourne, and Manila; War usually played out of Jamaica, where he had a large estate by the sea. They had been playing Horsemen for seven years.

Rather than becoming repetitive, the fantasy game had expanded itself. It had grown every year, becoming something new and even more challenging. The object was to create the most delicious and unusual fantasy or adventure. Violence was almost always part of the game, but not necessarily murder. Shafer was the first to claim that his stories weren't fantasies at all, that he lived them in the real world. Now the others would do so as well from time to time. Whether or not they really lived their fantasies, Shafer couldn't tell. The object was to create the evening's most startling fantasy, to get a rise out of the other players.

At nine o'clock his time, Shafer was on his laptop. So were the others. It was rare that one of them missed a session, but if they did, they left lengthy messages and sometimes drawings or even photographs of supposed lovers or victims. Films were occasionally used and the other players had to decide whether or not the scenes were stage-acted or cinema vérité.

Shafer couldn't imagine missing a chapter of the game himself. Death was by far the most interesting character, the most powerful and original. He had missed important social and embassy affairs just to be available for

Thursday nights. He had played when he had pneumonia, and once when he'd had a painful double-hernia operation the day before.

The Four Horsemen was unique in so many ways, but most important, because there was no single gamemaster to outline and control the action of the game. Each of the players had complete autonomy to write and visualize his own story, as long as he played by the roll of the dice, and remained inside the parameters of the character.

In effect, in Horsemen, there were four gamemasters. There was no other fantasy game like it. It was as gruesome and shocking as the participants' imaginations and their skills at presentation.

Conqueror, Famine, and War had all signed on.

Shafer began to type.

DEATH HAS TRIUMPHED AGAIN IN WASHINGTON. LET ME TELL YOU THE DETAILS, THEN I'LL LISTEN TO THE GLORIOUS STORIES, THE IMAGINATIVE POWER OF CONQUEROR, FAMINE, AND WAR. I LIVE FOR THIS, AS I KNOW ALL OF YOU DO AS WELL.

THIS WEEKEND, I DROVE MY FANTASTIC TAXI, 'THE NIGHTMARE MACHINE', ONCE AGAIN . . . LISTEN TO THIS. I CAME UPON SEVERAL CHOICE AND DELECTABLE VICTIMS, BUT I REJECTED THEM AS UNWORTHY. THEN I FOUND MY QUEEN AND SHE REMINDED ME OF OUR DAYS IN BANGKOK AND MANILA.

WHO COULD EVER FORGET THE BLOOD LUST OF THE BOXING ARENA? I HELD A MOCK KICK-BOXING MATCH. GENTLEMEN, I BEAT HER WITH MY HANDS AND FEET. I AM SENDING PICTURES.

Chapter Fourteen

S omething was up, and I didn't think that I'd like it very much. I arrived at the Seventh District Police Station just before seven thirty that morning. I'd been summoned by the powers-that-be to the station, and it was a tough deal. I'd worked until two in the morning trying to get a lead on Nina Childs' murder.

I had a feeling that the day was starting out wrong. I was tense and more uptight than I usually let myself become. I didn't like this early-morning command appearance one bit.

I shook my head, frowned, tried to roll the kinks out of my neck. Finally, I gritted my teeth tightly before opening the mahogany-wood door. Chief of Detectives George Pittman was lying in wait in his office, which consisted of three connecting offices, including a conference room.

The Jefe, as he's called by his many 'admirers', had on a boxy gray business suit, overstarched white shirt, a silver necktie. His gray-and-white-streaked hair was slicked back. He looked like a banker, and in some ways he was. As he never tires of saying, he is working with a fixed budget, and is always mindful of manpower costs, overtime costs, caseload costs. Apparently, he is an efficient manager, which is why the police commissioner overlooks the fact that he's a bully, bigot, racist and careerist.

Up on his wall were three large, important-looking pushpin maps. The first showed two consecutive months of rapes, homicides, and assaults in Washington. The second map did the same for residential and commercial burglaries. The third map showed auto thefts. The maps and the *Post* say that crime is down in DC, but not where I live.

'Do you know why you're here, why I wanted to see you?' Pittman asked point-blank. No socializing or small talk from the Jefe, no niceties. 'Of course you do, Dr Cross. You're a psychologist. You're supposed to know how the human mind works. I keep forgetting that.'

Be cool, be careful, I told myself. I did the thing Chief Pittman least expected – I smiled, and said softly, 'No, I really don't know. I got a call from your assistant. So I'm here.'

Pittman smiled back, as if I'd made a pretty good joke. Then he suddenly raised his voice, and his face and neck turned a bright red; his nostrils flared, exposing the bristly hairs within.

One of his hands was clenched into a tight fist, while the other was stretched open. His fingers were as rigid as the pencils sticking up from the leather cup on his desk.

'You're not fooling anybody, Cross, least of all me. I'm fully fucking aware that you're investigating homicides in Southeast that you aren't assigned to, the so-called Jane Does. You're doing this against my explicit orders. Some of those cases have been closed for over a year. *I won't have it,* I won't tolerate your insubordination, your condescending attitude. I know what you're trying to pull. Embarrass the department, specifically embarrass me, curry fucking favor with the mayor, make yourself some kind of folk hero in Southeast in the process.'

I hated Pittman's tone and what he was saying, but I had learned one trick a long time ago, and it was probably the most important thing to know about politics inside any organization. It's so simple, but it's the key to every petty kingdom, every fiefdom. Knowledge truly is power; it's everything, and if you don't have any, pretend you do.

So I told Chief Pittman nothing. I didn't contradict him; I didn't admit to a thing. I did nothing. Me and Mahatma Gandhi.

I let him think that maybe I was investigating old cases in Southeast – but I didn't admit to it. I also let him think that maybe I had some powerful connections with Mayor Monroe, and God only knows who else in the City on the Hill. I let him think that maybe I was after his job, or that I might have, God forbid, even loftier aspirations.

'I'm working the homicides assigned to me. Check with the captain. I'm doing my best to close as many cases as I can.'

Pittman nodded curtly – *one* nod. His face was still heart-attack red. 'All right, I want you to close *this* case, and I want you to close it fast. A tourist was robbed and gunned down on M Street last night,' he said. 'A well-respected German doctor from Munich. It's front fucking page in today's *Post*. Not to mention the *International Herald Tribune,* and every newspaper in Germany of course. I want you on *that* murder case and I want it solved pronto.'

'This doctor, he's a white man?' I asked, keeping my expression neutral.

'I told you, he's German.'

'I already have a number of open cases in Southeast,' I said to Pittman. 'A nurse was murdered over the weekend.'

He didn't want to hear it. He shook his head – *one* shake. 'And now you have an important case in Georgetown. Solve it, Cross. You're to work on nothing else. That's a direct order . . . from *the Jefe*.'

Chapter Fifteen

As soon as Cross walked out of Chief Pittman's inner office, a senior homicide detective named Patsy Hampton slipped in through a side door that led to the attached conference room. Detective Hampton had been instructed by Pittman to listen in on everything, to evaluate the situation from a street cop's perspective, to advise and counsel.

Hampton didn't like the job, but those were her orders from Pittman. She didn't like Pittman either. He was wound so tight that if you stuck coal up his ass, in a couple of weeks you'd have a diamond. He was mean, petty, and he was vengeful.

'You see what I'm dealing with here? Cross knows how to push all my buttons. In the beginning he would lose his temper. Now he just ignores what I say.'

'I heard everything,' Hampton said. 'He's slick all right.'

She was going to agree with Chief Pittman, no matter what he said.

Patsy Hampton was an attractive woman with sandy-blonde hair cut short, and the most piercing blue eyes this side of Stockholm. She was thirty-one years old, and on a very fast track in the department. At twenty-six, she'd been the youngest homicide detective in Washington. She had much loftier goals in mind.

'You're selling yourself short, though. You got to him. I know you did.' She told Pittman what he wanted to hear. 'He just internalizes it pretty well.'

'You're sure he's meeting with those other detectives?' Pittman asked her.

'They've met three times that I know of, always at Cross's house on Fifth Street. I suspect there have been other times. I heard about it through a friend of Detective Thurman.'

'But they don't meet while any of them are on duty?'

'No, not to my knowledge. They're careful. They meet on their own time.'

Pittman scowled and shook his head. 'That's too god-damn bad. It makes it harder to prove anything really damaging.'

'From what I've heard, they believe the department is holding back resources that could clear a number of unsolved homicides in Southeast and parts of Northeast. Most of the murders involve black and Hispanic women.'

Pittman tensed his jaw and looked away from Hampton. 'The numbers that Cross uses are complete bullshit,' he said angrily. 'They're dogshit. It's all political with him. How much financial resource can we put against the murders of drug addicts and prostitutes in Southeast? It's criminals murdering other criminals. You know how it goes in those black neighborhoods.'

Hampton nodded again, still agreeing when she saw the chance. She was afraid she'd lost him, said the wrong thing by speaking the truth. 'They think that at least some of the victims are innocent women from their neighborhoods. That ER nurse who was killed over the weekend. She was a friend of Cross and Detective John Sampson. Cross thinks a killer could be loose in Southeast, preying on women.'

'A serial killer in the ghetto? Give me a break. We've never had one there. They're rare in any inner city. Why now? Why here? Because Cross wants to find one, that's why.'

'Cross and the others would counter that by saying we've never seriously tried to catch this squirrel.'

Pittman's small eyes suddenly burned into her skull. 'Do you agree with that horseshit, Detective?'

'No, sir. I don't necessarily agree or disagree. I know for a fact that the department doesn't have enough resources anywhere in the city, with the possible exception of Capitol Hill. Now, *that's* political, and it's an outrage.'

Pittman smiled at her answer. The chief knew she was playing him a little, but he liked her anyway. He liked just being in a room with Patsy Hampton. She was such a doll, such a cutie. 'What do you know about Cross, Patsy?'

She sensed that the chief had vented enough. Now he wanted their talk to be more informal. She was certain that he liked her, had a crush on her, but he was too uptight to ever act on his desires, thank God.

'I know Cross has been on the force for just over eight years. He's currently the liaison between the department and the FBI, works with the Violent Criminal Apprehension Program. He's a profiler with a good reputation, from what I hear. Has a Ph.D. in psych from Johns Hopkins. Private practice for three years before he came to us. Widower, two kids, plays the blues on the piano at his house. That enough background? What more do you want to know? I've done my homework. You know me,' Hampton said, and finally smiled.

Pittman was smiling now, too. He had small teeth with spaces between them, and always made her think of Eastern European refugees, or maybe Russian gangsters.

Detective Hampton smiled, though. She knew he liked it when she played along with him – as long as he thought she respected him.

'Any other worthwhile observations at this point?' he asked.

You're such a softy, flabby dick, Patsy Hampton wanted to say, but she just shook her head. 'He has some charm. He's well-connected in political circles. I can see why you're concerned about him.'

'You think Cross is charming?'

'I told you, he's slick. He *is*. People say he looks like the young Muhammad Ali. I think he likes to play the part sometimes. Float like a butterfly, sting like a bee.' She laughed again – and so did he.

'We're going to nail Cross,' Pittman said. 'We'll send him flying back to private practice. Wait and see. You're going to help get it done. You get things done, right, Detective Hampton? You see the bigger picture. That's what I like about you.'

She smiled again. 'That's what I like about me, too.'

Chapter Sixteen

The British Embassy is a plain, federal-style building located at 3100 Massachusetts Avenue. It sits next to the vice-president's house – the Observatory – and also the ambassador's residence, a stately Georgian building with tall, flowing white columns. The Chancery is the actual office building; the embassy is where the ambassador lives.

Geoffrey Shafer sat behind his small mahogany desk at the embassy and stared out onto Massachusetts Avenue. The embassy staff currently counted 415 people, soon to be cut to 414; he was thinking to himself. The staff included defense experts, foreign-policy specialists, trade, public affairs, clerks and secretaries.

Although the US and Britain have an agreement not to spy on each other, Geoffrey Shafer was nonetheless a spy. He was one of eleven men and women from the Security Service, formerly known as MI6, who worked at the embassy in Washington. These eleven ran agents attached to the consulates-general in Atlanta, Boston, Chicago, Houston, Los Angeles, New York, and San Francisco.

He was feeling restless as hell today, getting up from his desk frequently, pacing back and forth across the carpet that covered the creaking parquet floors. He made phone calls he didn't need to make, tried to get some work done, thought about how much he despised his job and the everyday details of life.

He was supposed to be working on a truly silly communiqué about the government's absurd ongoing commitment to human rights. The Foreign Secretary had rather bombastically proclaimed that Britain would support international condemnation of regimes that violated human rights; support international bodies involved in the cause; denounce human rights abuses, *blah, blah, blah, ad nauseam.*

He glanced through a few of the computer games he enjoyed when he was uptight like this – Riven, Mech-Commander, Unreal, TOCA, Ultimate Soccer Manager. None of them appealed to him right now; nothing did.

He was starting to crash, and he knew the feeling. *I'm going down and there is only one certain way to stop it: play The Four Horsemen.*

To make matters worse, it was raining and woefully gray-skied outside. The city of Washington, and also the surrounding countryside, looked forlorn and depressing. Christ, he was in a bad mood, even for him.

He continued to stare east across Massachusetts Avenue, looking into the trees bordering a park dedicated to the pacifist bullshit artist Kahlil Gibran. He tried to day-dream, mostly about fucking various attractive women currently working at the embassy.

He had called his psychiatrist, Boo Cassady, at her home office, but she was about to start a session and couldn't talk for long. They agreed to meet after work. A nasty quickie at her place, before he went home to face Lucy and the sniveling brood.

He didn't dare play Horsemen again tonight. It was too soon since the nurse. But God Almighty – he *wanted* to play. He wished he could take somebody out in some very imaginative way, right there inside the embassy.

He did have one excellent thing to do today – saving it until now, three in the afternoon. He had used the dice already, played a bit of Horsemen, just to help him make a personnel decision.

He had called Sarah Middleton just before lunch and told her they needed to have a chat and could she stop by his office, say at three?

Sarah was obviously tense on the phone and told him she could do it earlier, anytime, at his convenience. 'Not busy then, nothing much to do today?' Shafer asked. Three o'clock would be fine, she answered hastily.

His secretary, the bestial Betty formerly from Belgravia, buzzed him promptly at three. At least he'd finally got through to her about punctuality.

Shafer let her buzz him several times, then picked up the phone abruptly, as if she'd interrupted him at something vital to security.

'What is it, Ms Thomas? I'm extremely busy with this communiqué for the Secretary.'

'I'm sorry to interrupt, Mr Shafer, but Ms Middleton is here. You have a three o'clock appointment with her, I understand.'

'*Hmmm*. Do I? Yes, you're right. Can you ask Sarah to wait? I'll need a few more minutes. I'll buzz when I'm ready to see her.'

Shafer smiled contentedly and picked up a copy of *The Red Coat*, the embassy employee newsletter. He knew Betty hated it when he used Ms Middleton's Christian name. Sarah.

He fantasized about Sarah for the next few moments. He'd wanted to have a go at Mzzz Middleton from their first interview, but he was too careful for that. God, he hated the bitch. This was going to be such fun.

He watched the rain hammer down on the traffic crossing Massachusetts Avenue for another ten minutes. Finally Shafer snatched up the phone. He couldn't wait a minute longer. 'I'll see her now. Send Sarah in.'

He fingered his twenty-sided dice. This could be fun, actually. *Terror at the office.*

Chapter Seventeen

The lovely Sarah Middleton entered his office and managed a cordial look, almost a smile. He felt like a boa constrictor eyeing a mouse.

She had naturally curly red hair, a moderately pretty face, a superior figure. Today she wore a very short suit, red V-necked silk blouse, black stockings. It was obvious to Shafer that she was out to catch a husband in Washington.

Shafer's pulse was beating hard. He was aroused by her, always had been. He thought about taking her, and very much liked that phrase. She didn't look as nervous and unsure of herself as she had recently, so that probably meant she was really scared and trying not to show it. He tried his best to think like Sarah. That made it more fun, though he found it a real challenge to be as squirrely and insecure as she would surely be.

'We certainly needed the rain,' Sarah said, and then

cringed before the sentence was even finished.

'Sarah, please sit down,' he said. He was trying to keep a straight business face. 'Personally, I loathe the rain. It's one of the many reasons I've never been stationed in London.'

He sighed theatrically behind the rigid tent he'd made with his fingers. He wondered if Sarah noticed the length of his fingers and wondered how large he was elsewhere. He would bet anything that she did. It was how people's minds worked, though women like Sarah would never admit it.

She cleared her throat, then put her hands on her knees. The knuckles of her fingers were white. Christ, he was enjoying her obvious discomfort. She looked ready to jump out of her skin. How about out of her tight little skirt and blouse?

He began to stretch the fingers on his right hand, playing his part as dominator to the hilt. 'Sarah, I think I have some bad news, quite unfortunate really, but can't be avoided.'

She sat nervously forward in her chair. She really was nicely built up top. He was getting hard now. 'What is it, Mr Shafer? What do you mean? You *think* you have bad news? You do or you don't?'

'We have to let you go. *I* have to let you go. Budget cuts, I'm afraid,' he said. 'I know you must find this immensely unfair, and unexpected as well. Particularly when you moved halfway across the world from Australia to take this job, and you've been living in Washington for less than six months. Suddenly, the ax falls.'

He could tell she was actually fighting back tears. Her lips were trembling. Obviously she hadn't expected this. She had no idea. She was a reasonably smart and controlled woman, but she couldn't help herself now.

Excellent. He had succeeded in breaking her down. He wished he had a video camera this minute to record the look on her face and play it back countless times in private.

He saw the very instant that she lost it, and treasured it. He watched her eyes moisten, saw the large tears roll over her cheeks, streaking her working-girl makeup.

He felt the power and it was as good as he'd hoped it would be. A small, insignificant game certainly, but a delicious one. He loved being able to instill such shock and pain.

'Poor Sarah. Poor, poor dear,' he murmured.

Then Shafer did the cruelest, most unforgivable thing. Also the most outrageous and dangerous. He got up from his desk and came around to comfort her. He stood behind her, pressing himself against her shoulders. He knew it was the last thing she wanted, to be touched by him, to feel that he was aroused.

She stiffened, and pulled away from him as if he were on fire. 'Bastard,' she said, between clenched teeth, 'you are a consummate prick!'

Sarah left his office, shaking and in tears, running in that stumbling way women often do in heels. Shafer loved it. The sadistic pleasure, not only of hurting someone, but destroying this innocent woman. He memorized the stunning image for all time. He would play it back, over and over.

Yes, he was a prick. Consummate indeed.

Chapter Eighteen

Rosie the cat was perched on the window sill, watching me dress for my date with Christine. I envied the simplicity of her life: *love to eat those mousies, mousies what I love to eat.*

I finally headed downstairs. I was taking the night off from work and I was more nervous, distracted and fidgety than I had been in a long time. Nana and the kids knew something was up, but they didn't know what, and it was driving my three favorite busybodies crazy.

'Daddy, tell me what's going on, *please*?' Jannie clasped her hands in prayer and begged.

'I told you no, and no is no. Not even if you get down on your bony little knees,' I said, and smiled. 'I have a date tonight. It's just a date. That's all you need to know, young lady.'

'Is it with Christine?' Jannie asked. 'At least you can tell me *that* much.'

'*That's* for me to know,' I said as I knotted my tie in the mirror beside the stairs. 'And you *not* to find out, my over-inquisitive girlfriend.'

'You're wearing your fancy blue-striped suit, your fancy dancing shoes, that fancy tie you like. You're *so* fancy.'

'Do I look good?' I turned and asked my personal clothier. 'For my date?'

'You look beautiful, Daddy.' My girl beamed and I knew I could believe her. Her eyes were shiny little mirrors that always told the truth. 'You know you do. You know you're handsome as sin.'

'That's my girl,' I said, and laughed again. *Handsome as sin.* She got that one from Nana no doubt.

Damon mimicked his sister. '*You look beautiful, Daddy.* What a little brownnoser. What do you want from Daddy, Jannie?'

'Do I look good?' I turned to Damon.

He rolled his eyes. 'You look all right. How come you're all duded up? You can tell me. Man to man. What's the big deal?'

'Answer the poor children!' Nana finally said.

I looked her way, and offered up a wide grin. 'Don't use the "poor children" to try to get your gossip quotient for the day. Well, I'm off,' I announced. 'I'll be home before sunrise. Moo-ha-ha-ha.' I did my favorite monster imitation and all three of them rolled their eyes.

It was a minute or so before eight, and as I stepped onto the porch, a black Lincoln town car pulled up in front of the house. It was right on time, and I didn't want to be late.

POP GOES THE WEASEL

'A limousine?' Jannie gasped, and nearly swooned on the front porch. 'You're going out in a *limousine*?'

'Alex Cross!' Nana said. 'What *is* going on?'

I practically danced down the steps. I got into the waiting car, shut the door, told the driver to go. I waved out the back window and stuck out my tongue as the car smoothly pulled away from our house.

Chapter Nineteen

My last image was of the three of them, Jannie, Damon, and Nana, all mugging and sticking out their tongues at me. We do have some fabulously good times together, I was thinking as the car headed over to Prince Georges County, where I had once confronted a homicidal twelve-year-old during the halcyon days of the Jack and Jill killers, and where Christine Johnson lived.

I had my mantra all set for tonight – *heart leads head*. I needed to believe that was so.

'A private car? A limousine?' Christine exclaimed when I picked her up at her house in Mitchellville.

She looked as stunningly beautiful as I've ever seen her, and that's saying a lot. She wore a long sleeveless black shift, black satin pumps with straps, and had a floral brocade jacket over her arm. The heels made her a little over six feet tall. God, how I loved this woman, everything about her.

We walked to the car and got inside.

'You haven't told me where we're going tonight, Alex. Just that it's fancy. Someplace special.'

'Ah, but I've told our driver,' I said. I tapped the partition window and the town car moved off into the summer night. Alex the mysterious.

I held Christine's hands as we drove along on the John Hanson Highway, back toward Washington. Her face tilted toward mine and I kissed her in the cozy darkness. I loved the sweetness of her mouth, her lips, the softness and smoothness of her skin. She was wearing a new perfume that I didn't recognize, and I liked that, too. I kissed the hollow of her throat, then her cheeks, her eyes, her hair. I would have been happy to do just this for the rest of the night.

'It is unbelievably romantic,' she finally said. 'It *is* special. You are something else . . . *sugar.*'

We cuddled and hugged all the way into Washington. We talked, but I don't remember the subject. I could feel her breasts rising and falling against me. I was surprised when we arrived at the intersection of Massachusetts and Wisconsin Avenues. We were getting close to the surprise.

Christine hadn't asked anymore questions. Not until the car eased up in front of Washington National Cathedral, and the driver got out and held the door open for us.

'The National Cathedral?' she said. 'We're going in here?'

I nodded and stared up at the stunning Gothic masterpiece that I'd admired since I was a boy. The

Cathedral crowns over fifty acres of lawns and woods and is Washington's highest point, even higher than the Washington Monument. If I remembered correctly, it was the second largest church in the United States, and possibly the prettiest.

I led the way, and Christine followed me inside. She held my hand lightly. We entered the northwest corner of the nave, which extends nearly a tenth of a mile to a massive altar.

Everything felt special and very beautiful, spiritual, just right. We walked up to a pew under the amazing Space Window at mid-nave. Everywhere I looked there were priceless stained-glass windows, over two hundred in all.

The light inside was exquisite; I felt blessed. There was a kaleidoscope of changing colors on the walls: reds, warm yellows, cool blues.

'Beautiful, isn't it?' I whispered. 'Timeless, sublime, all that good Gothic stuff Henry Adams used to write about.'

'Oh, Alex, I think it's the prettiest spot in Washington. The Space Window, the Children's Chapel. I've always loved it here. I told you that, didn't I?' she asked.

'You might have mentioned it once,' I said. 'Or maybe I just knew it.'

We continued walking until we entered the Children's Chapel. It is small, beautiful, and wonderfully intimate. We stood under a stained-glass window that tells the story of Samuel and David as children.

I turned and looked at Christine and my heart was beating so loud I was sure she could hear it. Her eyes were sparkling like jewels in the flickering candlelight. The black dress shimmered and seemed to flow over her body.

I knelt on one knee and looked up at her.

'I've loved you since the first time I saw you at the Sojourner Truth School,' I whispered, so that only she could hear me. 'Except that when I saw you the first time, I had no way of knowing how incredibly special you are on the inside. How wise, how good. I didn't know that I could feel the way I do – whole and complete – whenever I'm with you. I would do anything for you. Or just to be with you for one more moment.'

I stopped for the briefest pause and took a breath. She held my eyes, didn't pull away.

'I love you so much and I always will. Will you marry me, Christine?'

She continued to look into my eyes, and I saw such warmth and love, but also humility, which is always a part of who Christine is. It was almost as if she couldn't imagine my loving her.

'Yes, I will. Oh, Alex, I shouldn't have waited until tonight. But this is so perfect, so special, I'm almost glad I did. Yes, I will be your wife.'

I took an antique engagement ring out and I gently slid it onto Christine's finger. The ring had been my mother's and I'd kept it since she died when I was nine. The exact history of the ring was unclear, except that it went back at least four generations in the Cross family and was my one and only heirloom.

We kissed in the glorious Children's Chapel of the National Cathedral and it was the best moment of my life, never to be forgotten, never to be diminished in any way.

Yes, I will be your wife.

Chapter Twenty

Ten days had passed without another fantasy murder, but now a powerful mood swing had taken hold of Geoffrey Shafer and he let himself go with the flow.

He was flying high as a kite; hyper, manic, bipolar, whatever the doctors wanted to call his condition. He'd already taken Ativan, Librium, Valium, and Depakote, but the drugs only seemed to fuel his jets.

That night at around six he pulled the black Jaguar out of the lot on the north side of the embassy, passing by the larger-than-life Winston Churchill statue, with its stubby right hand raised in a V for victory, its left hand holding his trademark cigar.

Eric Clapton played guitar loudly on the car's CD. He turned up the volume higher, slapping his hands hard on the steering wheel, feeling the rhythm, the beat, the primal urge.

Shafer turned onto Massachusetts Avenue and then

stopped at a Starbucks. He hurried in and fixed up three coffees his way. Black as his heart, with six sugars. *Mmm, hmmm.* As usual, he had nearly finished the first before he got to the cash register.

Once he was inside the cockpit of his Jag again, he sipped a second cup at a more leisurely pace. He downed some Benadryl and Nascan. Couldn't hurt, might help. He took out the twenty-sided game dice. He had to play tonight.

Anything twelve or higher would dispatch him directly to Boo Cassady's place for a kinky quickie before he went home to the dreaded family. A seven to eleven was total disaster – straight home to Lucy and the kids. Three, four, five, or six meant he could go to the hideaway, for an unscheduled night of high adventure.

'Come three, four, five. Come baby, come! I need this tonight. Need a fix! I need it!'

He shook the dice for what must have been thirty seconds. He made the suspense last, drew it out. Finally, he released the dice onto the gray leather car seat. He watched the roll closely.

Jesus, he'd thrown a four! Defied the odds! His brain was on fire. He could play tonight. The dice had spoken; fate had spoken.

He excitedly punched a number on his cell phone. '*Lucy,*' he said, and he was smiling already.

'Glad I caught you at home, darling ... Yes, you guessed it, first try. We're completely swamped here again. Can you believe it? I certainly can't. They think they own me, and I suppose they're half-right. It's the drug-trafficking rubbish again. I'll be home when I can. Don't wait up, though. Love to the kids. Kisses to everybody. Me too, darling. I love you too. You're the best, the most understanding wife alive.'

Very well played, Shafer thought as he breathed a sigh of relief. Excellent performance, considering the drugs he'd taken. Shafer disconnected from his wife, whose family money, unfortunately, paid for the town house, holidays away, even the Jag, and her fashionable Range Rover, of course.

He punched another number on the cell phone.

'Dr Cassady.' He heard her voice almost immediately. She *knew* it was him. He usually called from the car on his way over to see her. They liked to get each other hot and bothered on the phone. Telephone sex as foreplay.

'They've done it to me again.' Shafer whined miserably into the phone, but he was smiling again, loving his flair for the overdramatic.

A short silence, then, 'You mean they did it to us, don't you? There's *no way* you can get away? It's only a bloody job, and one that you detest, Geoff.'

'You know I would if I possibly could. I do hate it here, loathe every moment. And it's even worse at home, Boo. Jesus, you of all people know that.'

He imagined the tight little frown and Boo pursing her lips. 'You sound high, Geoffrey. Are you, dear? Take your pills today?'

'Don't be horrible. Of course I've taken my medications.

I *am* rushed. I *am* high. On the ceiling, as a matter of fact.
I'm calling between blasted staff meetings. Oh hell, I miss
you, Boo. I want to be inside you, deep inside. I want to do
your pussy, your ass, your throat. I'm thinking about it
right now. Christ, I'm as hard as a rock here in my
government-issue office. Have to beat it down with a stick.
Cane it. That's how we British handle such things.'

She laughed and he almost changed his mind about
standing her up. 'Go back to work. I'll be at home – if you
finish early,' she said. 'I could use a little finishing myself.'

'I love you, Boo. You're so kind to me.'

'I am, and I could probably get into a little caning, too.'

He hung up, and drove to the hideaway in Eckington.
He parked the Jag next to the purple-and-blue taxi in the
garage. He bounded upstairs to change for the game.
God, he loved this, his secret life, his nights away from
everything and everyone he loathed.

He was taking too many chances now, but he didn't
care.

Chapter Twenty-One

Shafer was totally pumped up for a night on the town. The Four Horsemen was on. Anything could happen tonight. Yet he found that he was introspective and pensive. He could flip from manic to depressive in the blink of an eye.

He watched himself as if he were an observer in a dream. He had been a British intelligence agent, but now that the Cold War was ended, there was little use for his talents. It was only the influence of Lucy's father that had kept him in his job. Duncan Cousins had been a general in the army, and now was chairman of a packaged-goods conglomerate specializing in the sale of detergents, soaps, and drugstore perfume. He liked to call Shafer 'the Colonel', rubbing in his 'rise to mediocrity'. The General also loved to talk about the glowing successes of Shafer's two brothers, both of whom had made millions in business.

Shafer shifted his thoughts back to the present. He was

doing that a lot lately, fading in and out like a radio with a bad connection. He took a settling breath, then pulled the taxi out of the garage. Moments later, he turned onto Rhode Island Avenue. It was beginning to rain again, a light mist that made the passing traffic lights blurry and impressionistic.

Shafer drifted over to the curb and stopped for a tall, slender black man. He looked like a drug dealer, something Shafer had no use for. Maybe he would just shoot the bastard then dump the body. That felt good enough for tonight's action. A sleazebag dope dealer whom nobody would miss.

'Airport,' the man announced haughtily as he climbed inside the taxi. The inconsiderate bastard shook off rainwater onto the seat. Then he shut the creaking car door behind him, and was on his cell phone immediately.

Shafer wasn't going to the airport and neither was his first passenger of the night. He listened in on the phone call. The man's voice was affected, surprisingly cultured.

'I think I'll just make the ten o'clock, Leonard. It's Delta *on* the hour, right? I picked up a cab, thank the Lord Jesus. Most of them won't stop anywhere near where my poor mom lives in Northeast. Then along comes this purple-and-blue absolute wreck of a gypsy cab, and merciful God, it stops for me.'

Christ, he'd been identified. Shafer silently cursed his bad luck. That was the way of the game, though, incredible highs and vicious lows. He would have to take this asshole all the way out to National Airport. If he disappeared, it would be connected to a purple-and-blue cab, an 'absolute wreck of a gypsy cab'.

Shafer stepped on the accelerator and sped out toward National. The airport was backed up, even at nine in the evening. He cursed under his breath. The rain was heavy and it was punctuated by rolling thunder and spits of lightning.

He tried to control his building anger, his darkening mood. It took nearly forty minutes to get to the bloody terminal and drop off the passenger. By that time he'd settled back into another fantasy, had another huge mood swing. He was cycling *up* again.

Maybe he should have gone to see Dr Cassady, after all. He needed more pills, especially Lithium. This was like a carnival ride tonight – up and down, up and down. He wanted to push things as far as he could. He also felt crazed. He was definitely losing control.

Anything could happen when he got like this. That was the thing. He pulled into the queue of taxis waiting to get a fare back to DC.

As he moved closer to the front of the line, there was more thunder. Lightning crackled high above the airport. He could see the prospective victims huddled under a dripping canopy. Flights were undoubtedly being postponed and canceled. He savored the cheapseat melodrama, the suspense. The victim *du jour* could be anyone, from a corporate executive to a harried secretary, or maybe even a whole family back from a trip to Disney World.

But not once did he look at the queue of potential victims as he inched closer and closer. He was almost there. Just two more taxis in front of him. He could see the queue out of the corner of his eye. Finally, he had to snatch a quick peek.

It was a tall male.

He peeked again, couldn't help himself.

A white male, a businessman, stepped off the curb and was climbing inside the taxi. He was cursing to himself, pissed off about the rain.

Shafer looked the man over. He was American – late thirties – full of himself. Investment analyst, maybe, or a banker – something like that.

'We can *go* – whenever you're in the mood,' the man snapped at him.

'Sorry, sir,' Shafer said, and smiled obsequiously into the rearview mirror.

He dropped the dice on the front seat: *six*! His heart began to hammer.

Six meant *immediate action*. But he was still inside National Airport. There was a heavy lineup of traffic and cops, bright lights glittering everywhere. It was too dangerous, even for him.

The dice had spoken. He had no choice. The game was *on* right now.

A sea of red rear-lights glowed at him. Cars were everywhere. How could he do this here? Shafer began to perspire heavily.

But he had to do it. That was the point of the game. He

had to do it now. Had to murder this asshole right here at the airport.

He swerved into the nearest parking area. This was not good. He speeded down a narrow lane. Another bolt of lightning flashed overhead; it seemed to underscore the madness and chaos of the moment.

'Where the *hell* are you going?' the businessman shouted at him. He slammed his palm into the back of the seat. 'This isn't the way out, you ass!'

Shafer glared at the business creep in his rearview mirror. He hated him for calling him an ass. The bastard also reminded him of his brothers.

'I'm not going anywhere,' he yelled back. 'But you're going straight to hell!'

The businessman blustered. 'What did you say to me? What did you just say?'

Shafer fired his Smith & Wesson 9mm and hoped no one would hear it above the thunder and honking horns.

He was soaking wet with perspiration, and he was afraid his black face would run and smear. He was expecting to be stopped now. Waiting for policemen to surround the taxi. Bright-red blood was splattered all over the backseat and window. The businessman was slumped in the corner as if he were asleep. Shafer couldn't see where the bloody bullet had exited the taxi.

He made it out of National before he went completely mad. He drove carefully to Benning Heights in Southeast. He couldn't risk being stopped for speeding. But he was out of his head, not sure he was doing the right thing.

He stopped on a side street, checked out the body, stripped it. He decided to dump the corpse out in the open. He was trying his best not to be predictable.

Then he sped away from the crime scene and headed home.

He'd left no identification on the victim. Nothing but the body.

Just a little surprise – a *John* Doe.

Chapter Twenty-Two

I got home from Christine's house at two thirty in the morning, feeling exhilarated, the happiest I'd been in years. I thought about waking Nana and the kids to tell them the news. I wanted to see the surprised looks on their faces. I wished that I had brought Christine home with me, so we could celebrate together.

The phone rang moments after I stepped inside the house. *Oh no,* I thought, *not tonight. Nothing good comes from phone calls at two thirty a.m.*

I picked up in the living room and heard Sampson's voice on the line. 'Sugar?' he whispered.

'Leave me alone,' I said. 'Try again in the morning. I'm closed for the night.'

'No you're not, Alex. Not tonight. Get over to Alabama Avenue, about three blocks east of Dupont Park. A man was found there naked and dead – in the gutter. The guy is white and there's no ID on him.'

First thing in the morning, I would tell Nana and the kids about Christine and me. I had to go. The murder scene was a ten-minute ride across the Anacostia River. Sampson was waiting for me on a street corner. So was the John Doe.

And a lively, mean-spirited crowd. A naked white body dumped in this neighborhood had prompted lots of curiosity, almost like seeing a deer walking down Alabama Avenue.

'Casper the Friendly Ghost been *offed*.' A heckler contributed his twenty-five cents as Sampson and I stooped down under the yellow plastic crime-scene tape. In the background were rows of dilapidated brick buildings that almost seemed to scream out the names of the lost, the forgotten, the never-had-a-chance.

Stagnant water often pools on the street corners here since the storm drains are hardly ever inspected. I knelt over the twisted, naked body that was partly immersed in the cesspool. There would be no tire marks left at the watery scene. I wondered if the killer had thought of that.

I was making mental notes. No need to write them down – I'd remember everything. The man had manicured fingernails and toenails. No calluses showed on either his hands or feet. He had no bruises or distinct disfiguring marks, other than the cruel gunshot wound that had blown away the left side of his face.

The body was deeply suntanned, except where he'd worn swim trunks. A thin, pale ring ran around his left index finger, where he'd probably worn a wedding band, which was missing.

And there was no ID – just like the Jane Does.

Death was clearly the result of the single, devastating gunshot to the head. Alabama Avenue was the primary scene – where the body was found; but I suspected a secondary homicide scene – where the victim was actually murdered.

'What do you think?' Sampson crouched down close beside me. His knees cracked loudly. 'Sonofabitch killer is pissed off about something.'

'Really bizarre that he wound up here in Benning Heights. I don't know if he's connected to the Jane Does. But if he is, the killer wanted us to find this one in a hurry. Bodies around here usually get dumped in Fort Dupont Park. He's getting stranger and stranger. And you're right, he's very angry with the world.'

My mind was rapidly filling with crime-scene notes, plus the usual stream of homicide detective questions. Why leave the body in a street gutter? Why not in an abandoned building? Why in Benning Heights? Was the killer black? That still made the most sense to me, but a very low percentage of pattern killers are black.

The sergeant from the Crime Scene Unit came strolling up to Sampson and me. 'What do you want from us, Detective?'

I looked back at the naked white body. 'Videotape it, photograph it, sketch it,' I told him.

'And take some of the trash in the gutter and side-walk?'

'Take everything. Even if it's soaking wet.'

The sergeant frowned. 'Everything? All this wet trash? Why?'

Alabama Avenue is hilly, and I could see the Capitol Building brightly illuminated in the distance. It looked like a faraway celestial body, maybe heaven. It got me thinking about the *haves* in Washington, and the *have-nots*.

'Just take everything. It's how I work,' I said.

Chapter Twenty-Three

Detective Patsy Hampton arrived at the chilling homicide scene around 2:15. The Jefe's assistant had called her apartment about an unusual murder in Benning Heights that might relate to the Jane Does. This one was different in some ways, but there were too many similarities for her to ignore.

She watched Alex Cross work the crime scene. She was impressed that he'd come out at this early hour. She was curious about him, had been for a long time. Hampton knew Cross by reputation, and had followed a couple of his cases. She had even worked a few weeks on the tragic kidnapping of Maggie Rose Dunne and Michael Goldberg.

So far, she had mixed feelings about Cross. He was personable enough, and more than good-looking. He was a tall, strongly put-together man. She felt that he received undeserved special treatment because he was a forensic psychologist. She'd done her homework on Cross.

Hampton understood that she had been assigned to show Cross up, to win, to knock him down a peg. She knew it would be a tough competition, but she also knew that she was the one to do it; she never failed at anything.

She'd already done her own examination of the crime scene. She had stayed on at the scene only because Cross and Sampson had unexpectedly shown up.

She continued to study Cross – watched him walk the homicide scene several times. He was physically impos- ing, and so was his partner, who had to be at least six-nine. Cross was six-three and weighed maybe two hundred. He appeared younger than his age, which was forty-one. He seemed to be respected by the assisting patrolmen, even by the EMS personnel. He shook a few hands, patted shoulders, occasionally shared a smile with someone working the crime scene.

Hampton figured that was part of his act though. Everybody had one these days, especially in Washington. Cross's was obviously his charisma and charm.

Hell, she had an act herself. Hers was to appear nonthreatening and 'feminine', then perform contrary to the expectations of the males on the force. She usually caught them off-guard. As she'd risen in the department, the men learned that she could be tough. Surprise, surprise. She worked longer hours than anyone else; she was a hell of a lot tougher than the men; and she never socialized with other cops.

But she'd made one big mistake. She broke into a homicide suspect's car without a warrant, and was caught by another detective, a jealous older male. That was how Pittman got his hooks into her, and now he wouldn't let go.

At around a quarter to three, she walked to her forest-green Explorer, noting that it needed a wash. She already had a few ideas about the dead man in the street. There was no doubt in her mind that she would beat Cross.

Book Two

Death Rides a Pale Horse

Chapter Twenty-Four

George Bayer was Famine among The Four Horsemen. He'd been playing the fantasy game for seven years, and he loved it. At least he had until recently, when Geoffrey Shafer started to go out of control.

Famine was physically unimpressive at around five-eight, a hundred ninety pounds. He was paunchy, balding, wore wire-rim glasses, but he also knew that his appearance was deceiving, and he'd made a living off of those who underestimated him. People like Geoffrey Shafer.

He had reread a forty-page dossier on Shafer during his long plane ride from Asia to Washington. The dossier told him everything about Shafer, and also about the character he played, Death. At Dulles Airport Bayer rented a dark-blue Ford sedan, under a false name. He was still detached and introspective during his thirty-minute drive into the city.

But he was also anxious: he was nervous for all of the

Horsemen, especially for himself. He was the one who had to confront Shafer, and he was worried that Shafer might be going mad, that he might blow up in all of their faces.

George Bayer had been an M man, MI6, and he'd known Shafer in the Service. He was in Washington to check out Shafer firsthand. It was suspected by the other players that Geoffrey might have gone over the edge, that he was no longer playing by the rules and was a grave danger to them all. Since Bayer had once been stationed in Washington, and knew the town, he was the one to go there.

Bayer didn't want to be seen at the British Embassy on Massachusetts Avenue, but he had spoken to a few friends who he knew would keep silent about having been contacted. The news about Shafer was as bad as he'd suspected. He was seeing women outside his marriage, and he wasn't being discreet. There was a psychologist, who was a sex therapist, and he had been observed going over to her place several times a week, often during working hours. It was rumored that he was drinking heavily and possibly taking drugs. Bayer suspected the latter. He and Shafer had been friends, and done their share of drugs while posted in the Philippines and Thailand. Of course they were younger and more foolish then; at least that was true of Bayer.

The DC police had recently put in a complaint to the embassy about a reckless-driving incident. Shafer might have been high at the time. His current assignments at the embassy were minimal, and he would have been dismissed, or at least sent back to England, if it wasn't for his wife's father, General Duncan Cousins. What a terrible mess Shafer had made of his life.

But that's not the worst of it, is it, Geoffrey? George Bayer was thinking as he drove into the Northeast section of Washington known as Eckington Place. *There's more, isn't there, dear boy? It's much worse than the embassy thinks. It's probably the biggest scandal in the long history of the Secret Service, and you're right at the heart of it. But of course, so am I.*

Bayer locked the doors of his car as he pulled up to a traffic light. The area looked highly suspicious to him, like so much of Washington these days. What a sad, totally insane country America had become. What a perfect refuge for Shafer.

Famine took in the sights on the mean streets as he continued through the decidedly lower-class neighborhood. There was nothing to compare with this in London. Row upon row of two-storied red-brick garden apartments, many of them in dreadful disrepair. Not so much urban decay as urban apathy.

He saw Shafer's lair up ahead and pulled over to the curb. He knew the exact location of the hideaway from the elaborate fantasy tales Shafer had told the other players. He knew the address. Now he needed to know one more thing: Were the murders that Geoffrey claimed he'd committed fantasies, or were they real? Was he actually a cold-blooded killer operating here in Washington?

Bayer walked to the garage door. It took him only a moment to pick the lock and let himself in.

He had heard so much about the 'nightmare machine', the purple-and-blue taxi that Shafer used for the murders. He was looking at it. The taxi was as real as he was. Now he knew the truth. George Bayer shook his head. Shafer had killed all of those people. This was no longer a game.

Chapter Twenty-Five

B ayer trudged upstairs to the hideaway apartment. His arms and legs felt heavy and he had a slight pain in his chest. His vision was tunneled. He pulled down the dusty blinds and began to look around.

Shafer had boastfully described the garage and taxi several times during the game. He had flaunted the existence of the hideaway and sworn to the other players that it was real and not some fantasy in a role-playing game. Geoffrey had openly dared them to see it for themselves, and that was why Bayer was in Washington.

Well, Geoffrey, the hideaway is real, he agreed. *You are a stone-cold killer. You weren't bluffing, were you?*

At ten o'clock that night Bayer took Shafer's taxi out. The keys were there, almost as a dare. Was it? He figured he had a right to experience exactly what Shafer had. According to Geoffrey, half the fun of the game was foreplay, checking out the possibilities, seeing the whole game board before you made a move.

From ten o'clock until half past eleven Bayer explored the streets of DC, but he didn't pick up a fare. He kept his off-duty sign on. *What a game*, Bayer kept thinking as he drove. *Is this how Geoffrey does it? Is this how he feels when he's prowling the city?*

He was pulled out of his day-dream by an old tramp with a crushed hat, who had wheeled a cart filled with cans and other recyclables right in front of him. He didn't seem to care whether he was run over or not, but Bayer braked hard. That made him think of Shafer. The line between life and death had faded to nothing for him, hadn't it?

Bayer cautiously moved on. He drove past a church. The service was over and a crowd of people were leaving.

He stopped the cab for an attractive black woman in a blue dress and matching high heels. He needed to see what this must be like for Shafer, for Death. He couldn't resist.

'Thank you so much,' the woman said as she slid into the rear of his taxi. She seemed so proper and respectable. He checked her furtively in the mirror. She didn't have much to offer up top. Pretty enough face, though. Long brown legs encased in sheer stockings. He tried to imagine what Shafer might do now, but he couldn't.

Shafer had boasted he was killing people in the poorer sections of Washington, since nobody cared about them anyway. Bayer suspected that he was telling the truth. He knew things about Shafer from when they were in Thailand and the Philippines. He knew Shafer's deepest, darkest secrets.

Bayer drove the attractive and well-spoken black woman to her apartment, and was amused when she gave him a sixty-cent tip for the four-dollar ride. Fifteen percent to the penny. He took the money and thanked her graciously.

'An English cab driver,' she said. 'That's unusual. Have a nice evening.'

He continued to drive until past two in the morning. He drank in the sights; played the dizzying game. And then he had to stop again. Two young girls were hailing for a taxi on the corner. The area was called Shaw, and Howard University was very close according to several signs.

The girls were slender, delectable in stacked heels and shiny clothes that glowed in the dark. One of them wore a microskirt, and he could see the tops of black or navy thigh-highs as he stopped to pick them up. *They must be hookers – Shafer's favorite prey*, Bayer thought to himself.

The second prostitute was even prettier and sexier than the first. She wore white stacked sandals, side-striped white athletic pants, a teeny tank top in blue camouflage.

'Where are we going?' Bayer asked as they scampered over to the taxi.

The girl in the miniskirt did the talking. 'We're going to Princeton Place. That's Petworth, darlin'. Then *you're* going away,' she said. She tossed her head back and issued a taunting laugh. Bayer snickered to himself. He was beginning to get into this now.

The girls climbed in, and Bayer couldn't resist checking them out in the mirror. The foxy one in the microskirt caught him looking. He felt like a schoolboy, found it intoxicating, didn't avert his eyes from hers.

She casually flipped him the finger. He didn't stop looking. Couldn't. *So this was how it felt to Shafer. This was the game of games.*

He couldn't take his eyes off the girls. His heart was pounding. Microskirt wore a tightly fitted ribbed tank top. Her long fingernails were airbrushed in kiwi and mango colors. She had a pager on her belt. Probably a gun in her handbag.

The other girl smiled shyly in his direction. She seemed more innocent. Was she? A necklace that read: BABY GIRL dangled between her young breasts.

If they were going to Petworth, they had to be hooking. They were certainly young and foxy; sixteen, seventeen years old. Bayer could see himself having sex with the girls, and the image was beginning to overpower his imagination. He knew he ought to be careful. This could get completely out of hand. He was playing Shafer's game, wasn't he? And he liked it very much.

'I have a proposition for you,' he said to microskirt.

'All right, darlin',' she said. 'Be one hundred for the half. Plus our ride to Petworth. That's my proposition for you.'

Chapter Twenty-Six

S hafer liked to know when any of the other players traveled, especially if they came to Washington. He had gone through a lot of trouble to hack his way into their computers to keep track of them. Famine had recently bought plane tickets and now he was here in DC. Why?

It wasn't hard to follow George Bayer, once he got to town. Shafer was still reasonably good at it. He'd had plenty of practice at tracking and surveillance, during his years in the Service.

He was disappointed that Famine had decided to 'intersect' with his fantasy. Intersection happened occasionally in the game, but it was rare. Both players were supposed to agree beforehand. Famine was clearly breaking the rules. What did he know, or think he knew?

Then Bayer genuinely surprised him. Not only did he visit Shafer's hideaway but he actually took the taxi for a ride. What the hell was he doing?

At a little past two in the morning, Shafer watched the gypsy cab pick up the two young girls in Shaw. Was Bayer copycatting? Was he setting some kind of trap for Shafer? Or was it something else altogether?

Bayer took the girls to S Street, which wasn't far from the pick-up point. He followed the girls up the darkened stairs of an aging brownstone and then they all disappeared inside.

He had a blue anorak thrown over his right arm and Shafer suspected a pistol was under the coat. Christ! He'd taken two of them. He could have been seen by anyone on the street. The cab could have been spotted.

Shafer parked on the street. He waited and watched. He didn't like being in this part of Shaw, especially without his disguise, and driving the Jaguar. There were some old crumbling brownstones, and a couple of boarded-up, graffiti-covered shacks on the street. No one was outside.

He saw a light blink on the top floor, and figured that was where Bayer had taken the two girls. Probably their flat.

He watched the brownstone from two until close to four. He couldn't take his eyes away. While he waited he imagined dozens of scenarios that might have brought Famine here. He wondered if the others were in Washington, too. Or was Famine acting alone? Was he playing The Four Horsemen right now?

Shafer waited and waited for Bayer to come out of the brownstone. But he didn't come down, and Shafer grew more impatient and worried and angry. He fidgeted. His breathing became labored. He had lurid, paranoid fantasies about what Bayer might have done up there. Had he killed the two girls? Taken their identification? Was this a trap? He thought so. What else could it be?

Still no George Bayer.

Shafer couldn't stand it any longer. He climbed out of the Jaguar. He stood on the street and stared up at the windows of the flat. He wondered if he, too, were being watched. He sensed a trap, wondered if he should flee.

Christ, where the hell was Bayer? What game was Famine playing? Was there a back way out of the building? If so, why had he left the taxi as evidence? Evidence! Damn him!

But then he saw Bayer finally leave the building. He quickly crossed S Street, got into the cab, and drove away.

Shafer decided to go upstairs. He jogged over to the building and found the wooden front door unlocked. He hurried up the steep, winding stairs. He had a flashlight in one hand, turned it on. His semiautomatic was in the other.

Shafer made his way to the fourth floor. He immediately knew which of the two flats was the right one. A poster for Mary J. Blige's *What's the 411* album was on the splintered and scarred door to his right. The girls lived here.

He turned the handle and carefully pushed the door open. He pointed his gun inside, ready.

One of the young girls came out of the bathroom wearing a fluffy black towel on her head, nothing else. She was a hot number with pert little titties. Christ, Famine must have paid for it. What a fool! What a wanker!

'Who the hell are you? What are you doing in here?' the girl shouted angrily.

'I'm Death,' he grinned, and announced, 'I'm here for you and your pretty friend.'

Chapter Twenty-Seven

I had gotten home from the John Doe murder scene at a little past three in the morning. I went to bed, but set my alarm for six thirty. I managed to get myself up before the kids went off to school.

'Somebody was out very, very, very late last night.' Jannie started her teasing before I had made it all the way downstairs and into the kitchen. I continued down and found she and Damon in the breakfast nook with Nana.

'Somebody sure *looks* like they had a late night,' Nana said from her customary cat-bird seat.

'Somebody's cruising for a bruising,' I said to quiet them. 'Now, there's something important I need to tell you before you head out to school.'

'Watch our manners. Always pay attention in class, even if the teacher's boring. Lead with our left if it ever comes to a fight in the school yard,' Jannie offered with a wink.

I rolled my eyes. 'What I was going to say,' I said, 'is that you should be especially nice to Ms Johnson today. You see, last night, Christine said that she'd marry me. I guess that means she's marrying all of us.'

At that point, everything became hugging and loud celebrating in the kitchen. The kids got chocolate milk and bacon grease all over me. I'd never seen Nana happier. And I felt exactly the same. Probably even better than they did.

I eventually made it to work that morning. I had made some progress on the John Doe homicide, and early on Tuesday morning I learned that the man whose body had been dumped on Alabama Avenue was a thirty-four-year-old research analyst named Franklin Odenkirk. He worked at the Library of Congress for the Congressional Research Service.

We didn't release the news to the press, but I did inform Chief Pittman's office as soon as I knew. Pittman would find out anyway.

Once I had a name for the victim, information came quickly and, as it usually is, it was sad. Odenkirk was married and had three small children. He had taken a late flight back from New York that evening, where he'd given a talk at the Rockefeller Institute. The plane landed on time and he deboarded at National around ten. What happened to him after that was a mystery.

For the remainder of Thursday and Friday, I was busy with the murder case. I visited the Library of Congress, and went to the newest structure, the James Madison

Building, on Independence Avenue. I talked to nearly a dozen of Frank Odenkirk's coworkers.

They were courteous and cooperative and I was told repeatedly that Odenkirk, while haughty at times, was generally well-liked. He wasn't known to use drugs or drink to excess; wasn't known to gamble either. He was faithful to his wife. He hadn't been involved in a serious argument at the office for as long as he'd been there.

He was with the Education and Public Welfare Division and spent long days in the spectacular Main Reading Room. There was no apparent motive for his murder, which was what I feared. The killing roughly paralleled the Jane Does so far, but of course the chief of detectives didn't want to hear it. There was no Jane Doe killer, according to him. Why? Because he didn't want to shift dozens of detectives to Southeast and begin an extensive investigation on the basis of my instincts and gut feelings. I had heard Pittman joke that Southeast wasn't part of *his city*.

Before I left the Madison Building I was compelled to stop and see the Main Reading Room once again. It was newly renovated and I hadn't been there since the work had been done.

I sat at a reader's table and stared up at the amazing dome high over my head. Around the room were stained-glass representations of the seals of forty-eight states; also bronze statues of figures, including Michelangelo, Plato, Shakespeare, Edward Gibbon, and Homer. I could imagine poor Frank Odenkirk doing his work here, and it bothered me. Why had he been killed? Had it been the Weasel?

The death was a terrible shock to everyone who had worked with him, and a couple of Odenkirk's coworkers broke down while talking to me about his murder.

I wasn't looking forward to interviewing Mrs Odenkirk, but I drove out 295 and 210 to Forest Heights late on Friday afternoon. Chris Odenkirk was home with her mother, and also her husband's parents, who had flown in from Briarcliff Manor in Westchester County, New York. They told me the same story as the people at the Library of Congress. No one in the family knew of anyone who might want to harm Frank. He was a loving father, a supportive husband, a thoughtful son and son-in-law.

At the Odenkirk home, I learned that the deceased had been wearing a green seersucker suit when he left home, his business meeting in New York had run over, and he was nearly two hours late getting to LaGuardia Airport. He generally took a cab home from the airport in Washington because so many flights arrived late.

Even before I went to the house in Forest Heights I had two detectives sent out to the airport. They showed around pictures of Odenkirk, interviewed airline personnel, shopworkers, porters, taxi dispatchers, and cabdrivers.

Around six I went over to the medical examiner's office to hear the results of the autopsy. All the photos and sketches from the crime scene were laid out. The autopsy had run about two and a half hours. Every cavity of Frank Odenkirk's body had been swabbed and scraped and his brain had been removed.

I talked to the medical examiner while she finished up with Odenkirk at about six thirty. Her name was Angelina Torres, and I'd known her for years. We had both started in our jobs at about the same time. Angelina was a tick under five feet and probably weighed around ninety pounds soaking wet.

'Long day, Alex?' she asked. 'You look used and abused.'

'Long one for you too, Angelina. You look good though. Short, but good.'

She nodded, grinned, then stretched her small, slight arms up over her head. She let out a low groan that approximated the way I felt, too.

'Any surprises for me?' I asked, after allowing her to stretch in peace and moan her little heart out.

I hadn't expected anything, but she had some news. 'One surprise,' Angelina said. 'He was sodomized after he died. Someone had sex with him, Alex. Our killer seems to swing both ways.'

Chapter Twenty-Eight

On the drive home that evening, I needed a break from the murder case. I thought about Christine, and that was much better, easier on the frontal lobe. I even switched off my beeper. I didn't want any distractions for ten or fifteen minutes.

Even though she hadn't talked about it recently, she still felt my job was too dangerous. The trouble was, she was absolutely right. I sometimes worried about leaving Damon and Jannie alone in the world, and now Christine as well. As I drove along the familiar streets of Southeast near Fifth, I considered whether I could actually leave police work. I'd been thinking about going into private practice and working as a psychologist, but I hadn't done anything to make it happen. It probably meant that I didn't really want to do it.

Nana was sitting on the front porch when I arrived home at around seven thirty. She looked peeved, an expression of hers that I know all too well. She can still make me feel like I'm nine or ten years old and she's the one with all the answers.

'Where are the kids?' I called out as soon as I opened the car door and climbed out. A fractured Batman and Robin kite was still up in a tree in the yard and I was annoyed at myself for not getting it down a couple of weeks ago.

'I shackled them to the sink and they're doing the dishes,' Nana said.

'Sorry about missing dinner,' I told her.

'Tell that to your children,' Nana said, frowning up a storm. She's about as subtle as a hurricane. 'You better tell them right now. Your friend Sampson called a little earlier. So did your compatriot Jerome Thurman. There's been more murders, Alex. I used the *plural* noun, just in case you didn't notice. Sampson is waiting for you at the so-called crime scene. Two bodies over in Shaw near Howard University, of all places. Two more young black girls are dead. It won't stop, will it? It never stops in Southeast.'

No, it never does.

Chapter Twenty-Nine

The homicide scene was an old crumbling brownstone in a bad section of S Street in Shaw. A lot of college kids and also young professionals live in the up-and-down, mostly middle-class neighborhood. Lately, prostitution has become a problem there. According to Sampson, the two dead girls were both prostitutes who occasionally worked in the neighborhood but mostly over in Petworth.

A single squad car and an EMS truck were parked at the homicide scene. A uniformed patrolman was posted on the front stoop, and he seemed intent on keeping intruders out. He was young, baby-faced, with smooth butterscotch skin. I didn't know him, so I flashed my detective's shield.

'Detective Cross.' He grunted. I sensed that he'd heard of me.

'What do we have so far?' I asked, before I went inside and trudged up four steep flights. 'What do you hear, Officer?'

'Two girls dead upstairs. Both pros, apparently. One of them lived in the building. Murders were called in anonymously. Maybe a neighbor, maybe the pimp. They're sixteen, seventeen, maybe younger. Too bad. They didn't deserve this.'

I nodded, took a deep breath, and then quickly climbed up steep, winding, creaking stairs to the fourth floor. Prostitutes make for difficult police investigations, and I wondered if the Weasel knew that. On average, a hooker out of Petworth might turn a dozen or more tricks a night, and that's a lot of forensic evidence, just on her body.

The door to apartment 4A was wide open and I could see inside. It was an efficiency – one large room, kitchenette, bath. A fluffy white area rug lay between two daybeds. A lava lamp was undulating green blobs next to several dildos.

Sampson was crouched on the far side of one daybed. He looked like an NBA power forward searching the floor for a missing contact lens.

I walked into a small, untidy room that smelled of incense, peach blossom fragrance, greasy food. A bright red and yellow McDonald's container of fries was open on the couch.

Dirty clothes covered the chairs: bike shorts, short-shorts, Karl Kani urban clothes. At least a dozen bottles of nail polish, remover, files, and cotton balls lay on the floor. There was a heavy, cloying smell of fruity perfume.

I went around the bed to look at the victims. Two very

young women, both naked from the waist down. The Weasel had been here – I could feel it.

The girls were lying one on top of the other, looking like lovers. They looked as if they were having sex on the floor.

One girl wore a blue tank top, the other had on black lingerie. They both had on 'slides', stacked bath sandals that are popular nowadays. Most of the Jane Does had been left naked, but unlike many of the others, we would be able to identify these two fairly easily.

'No actual ID on either girl,' Sampson said, without looking up from his work.

'One of them rents the apartment, though,' I told him.

He nodded. 'Probably pays cash. She's in a cash business.'

Sampson was wearing latex rubber gloves and he was bent down close to the two women.

'The killer wore gloves,' Sampson said, still without looking up at me. 'Don't seem to be fingerprints any-where. That's what the techie says. First look-through. They both were shot, Alex. Single shot to the forehead.'

I was still looking around the room, collecting information, letting the details of the murder scene flow over me. I noticed an array of hair products: Soft Sheen, Care Free Curl, styling gel, several wigs. On top of one of the wigs was a green army garrison cap with stripes. It's commonly called a 'cunt cap' among military personnel because it's effective for picking up women, especially in the South. There was also a pager.

The girls were young and pretty. They had skinny little legs, small, bony feet, silver toe rings that looked like they came from the same shop. Their discarded clothes amounted to insignificant little bundles on the bloodied hardwood floor.

In one corner of the small room, there were vestiges of brief childhoods: a lotto game, a stuffed blue bear that was threadbare and looked about as old as the girls, a Barbie doll, a ouija board.

'Take a good look, Alex. It gets weirder and weirder. Our Weasel is starting to freak out.'

I sighed and bent down to see what Sampson had discovered. The smaller, and perhaps the younger of the two girls was lying on top. The girl underneath was on her back. Her glazed brown eyes stared straight up at a broken light fixture in the ceiling, as if she had seen something terrible up there.

The girl on top had been positioned with her face, actually her mouth, tilted down into the other girl's crotch.

'Killer played real cute games with them after they were dead,' Sampson said. 'Move the one on top a little. Lift her head, Alex. You see it?'

I saw it. A completely new MO for the Jane Does, at least the ones I knew about. The phrase 'stuck on each other' ran through my mind. I wondered if that was the killer's 'message'. The girl on top was connected to the one underneath – by her tongue.

Sampson sighed and said, 'I think her tongue is stapled

inside the other girl. I'm pretty sure that's it, Alex. The Weasel stapled them together.'

I looked at the two girls and shook my head. 'I don't think so. A staple, even a surgical one, would come apart on the tongue's surface . . . Crazy glue would work.'

Chapter Thirty

The killer was working faster so I had to do the same. The two dead girls didn't remain Jane Does for very long. I had their names before the ten o'clock news that night. I continued to ignore the explicit orders of the chief of detectives and to investigate what I felt like.

Early the next morning, Sampson and I met at Stamford, the high school that Tori Glover and Marion Cardinal had attended. The murdered girls were seventeen and fourteen years old.

The memory of the homicide scene had left me with a queasy, sick feeling that wouldn't go away. I kept thinking, *Christine is right. Get out of this, do something else. It's time.*

The principal at Stamford was a small, frail-looking red-haired woman named Robin Schwartz. Her resource officer, Nathan Kemp, had gotten together some students who knew the victims. He had set aside a couple of classrooms for Sampson, Jerome Thurman, and me to use for interviews. Jerome would work in one room, Sampson and me in the other.

Summer school was still in session and Stamford was busy as a mall on a Saturday. We passed the cafeteria on the way there and it was packed at ten thirty. No empty seats anywhere. The room reeked of French fries, the same greasy smell that was in the girl's apartment.

A few kids were making noise, but they were mostly well-behaved. The music of Wu/Tang and Jodeci leaked from earphones. The school seemed to be well-run and orderly. Between classes a few boys and girls embraced tenderly, with loosely locked pinkies and the gentlest brushes of cheeks.

'These were not bad girls,' Nathan Kemp told us as we walked. 'I think you'll hear that from other students. Tori dropped out last semester, but her home life was the main reason. Marion was an honor student at Stamford. I'm telling you, guys, these were not bad girls.'

Sampson, Thurman, and I spent the rest of the morning with the kids. We learned that Tori and Marion were popular all right. They were loyal to their friends, funny, usually fun to be around. Marion was described as 'blazing', which meant she was great. Tori was 'buggin' sometimes', which meant she could be a little crazy. Most of the kids hadn't known that the girls were tricking in Petworth, but Tori Glover was said to always have money.

One particular interview would stick in my mind for a while. Evita Cardinal was a senior at Stamford, and also a cousin of Marion's. She wore white athletic pants and a purple stretchy top. A pair of black-rimmed, yellow-tinted sunglasses were propped on top of her head.

She started to cry her eyes out as soon as she sat down across the desk from me.

'I'm real sorry about Marion,' I said, and I was. 'We just want to catch whoever did this terrible thing. Detective Sampson and I both live nearby in Southeast. My kids go to the Sojourner Truth School.'

The girl looked at me. Her eyes were red-rimmed and wary. 'You won't catch nobody,' she finally said. It was the prevailing attitude in the neighborhood, and it happened to be mostly true. Sampson and I weren't even supposed to be here. I had told my secretary I was out working the murder of Frank Odenkirk. A few other detectives were covering for us.

'How long have Tori and Marion been working in Petworth? Do you know any other girls from school who work over there?'

Evita shook her head. '*Tori* was the one working the street in Petworth. Not Marion. My cousin was a good person. They both were. Marion was my little doggie,' Evita said, and the tears came flowing again.

'Marion *was* there with Tori.' I told her what I knew to be the truth. 'We talked to people who saw her on Princeton Place that night.'

The cousin glared at me. 'You don't know what you're talkin' about, Mister Detective. You're *wrong*. You ain't got the straight.'

'I'm listening to you, Evita. That's why I'm here.'

'Marion wasn't there to sell her body or like that. She was just afraid for Tori. She went to *protect* Tori. She never did nothin' bad for money, and I know that for a fact.'

The girl started to sob again. 'My cousin was a good person, my best girlfriend. She was tryin' to just protect Tori and she got herself killed for it. The police won't do nothin'. You never come back here again after today. Never happen. You don't care about us. We're nothin' to nobody,' Evita Cardinal said, and that seemed to say it all.

Chapter Thirty-One

W*e're nothin' to nobody.* It was a horrifying and absolutely true statement, and it was at the deepest roots of the Jane Doe investigation, the search for the Weasel. It pretty well summed up George Pittman's cynical philosophy about the inner city. It was also the reason I was feeling tired and numb to the bone by six thirty that night. I believed that the Jane Doe murders were escalating.

On the other hand, I hadn't seen nearly enough of my own kids for the last few days, so I decided I'd better head home. On the way, I thought about Christine and calmed down immediately. Since the time I was a young boy, I've been having a recurring day-dream. I'm standing alone on a cold, barren planet. It's scary, but more than anything, it's lonely and unsettling. Then a woman comes up to me. We begin to hold hands, to embrace, and then everything is all right. That woman was Christine, and I had no idea how she had gotten out of my dreams and into the real world.

Nana, Damon, and Jannie were just leaving the house when I pulled up into the driveway. What was this? I wondered.

Wherever they were going, everybody was dolled up and looking especially nice. Nana and Jannie wore their best dresses and Damon had on a blue suit, white shirt and tie. Damon almost never wears what he calls his 'monkey' or 'funeral' suit.

'Where's everybody going?' I said as I climbed out of the old Porsche. 'What's going on? You all aren't moving out on me?'

'It's nothing,' Damon said, strangely evasive, eyes darting all over the front yard.

'Damon's in the Washington Boys' Choir at school!' Jannie proudly blurted out. 'He didn't want you to know until he made it for sure. Well, he made it. Damon's a *chorister* now.'

Her brother swatted her on the arm. Not hard, but enough to show he wasn't pleased with Jannie for telling his secret.

'Hey!' Jannie said, and put up her dukes like the little semipro boxer that she is becoming under my watchful eye.

'Hey, hey!' I said, and moved in like a big-time referee, like that guy Mills Lane, who does the big pro fights. 'No prizefighting outside the ring. You know the rules of the fight game. Now what's this about a choir?'

'Damon tried out for the Boys' Choir and he was selected,' Nana said, and beamed gloriously as she looked over at Damon. 'He did it all by himself.'

'You sing, too?' I said, and beamed at him as well. 'My, my, my.'

'He could be in Boyz II Men, Daddy. Boyz II Boyz, maybe. He's smoo-ooth and silky. His voice is pure.'

'Is that so, Sister Soul?' I said to my baby girl.

'Zatso.' Jannie continued to prattle as she patted Damon on the back. I could tell she was incredibly proud of him. She was his biggest fan, even if he didn't realize it yet. Some day he would.

Damon finally couldn't hold back a big smile, then he shrugged it off. 'No big thing. I sing all right.'

'*Thousands* of other boys tried out,' Jannie said. 'It *is* a big thing, biggest in your small life, brother.'

'Hundreds,' Damon corrected her. 'Only hundreds of kids tried out. I guess I just got lucky.'

'*Hundreds* of *thousands!*' Jannie gushed, and scooted away before he swatted her like the little gnat she can be sometimes. 'And you were *born* lucky.'

'Can I come to the practice?' I asked. 'I'll be good. I'll be quiet. I won't embarrass anybody too much.'

'If you can spare the time.' Nana threw a neat jab. She sure doesn't need any boxing lessons from me. 'Your busy work schedule and all. If you can spare the time, come along with us.'

'Sure, Dad,' said Damon, finally.

So I came along.

Chapter Thirty-Two

I happily walked the six short blocks to the Sojourner Truth School with Nana and the kids. I wasn't dressed up. They were in their finery, but it didn't matter. There was suddenly a bounce in my step. I took Nana's arm, and she smiled as I tucked her hand into the crook of my arm.

'Now that's better. Seems like old times,' I exclaimed.

'You're such a shameless charmer sometimes,' Nana said and laughed out loud. 'Ever since you were a little boy like Damon. You certainly can be one when you want to.'

'You helped make me what I am, old woman,' I confided to her.

'Proud of it, too. And I'm *so* proud of Damon.'

We arrived at the Sojourner Truth School and went directly to the small auditorium in back. I wondered if Christine might be there, but she wasn't anywhere to be seen. Then I wondered if she already knew Damon had made the Boys' Choir, if he had told her first. I kind of liked the thought that he might have told her. I wanted them to be close. I knew that Damon and Jannie needed a mother, not just a father and great-grandmother.

'We're not too good yet,' Damon informed me, before he left to join the other boys. His face clearly showed the fear and anxiety of possibly being embarrassed. 'This is just our second practice. Mr Dayne says we're horrid as a tubful of castor oil. He's tough as nails, Dad. He makes you stand for an hour straight without moving.'

'Mr Dayne's tougher than you, Daddy, tougher than Ms Johnson,' Jannie said, and grinned wickedly. 'Tough as *nails.*'

I had heard that Nathaniel Dayne was a demanding maestro, the Great Dayne, but that his choirs were among the finest in the country and most of the boys seemed to profit immensely from the dedicated training and discipline. He was already organizing the boys up on the stage. He was a very broad man of below-average height. I guessed he carried about two hundred fifty pounds on his five-foot-seven-inch frame. He wore a black suit with a black shirt buttoned at the collar, no tie. He started the boys off with a few playful verses of 'Three Blind Mice' that didn't sound half-bad.

'I'm really happy for Damon. He looks so proud up there,' I whispered to Nana and Jannie. 'He is a handsome devil, too.'

'Mr Dayne is starting a girls' choir in the fall,' Jannie loud-whispered in my ear. 'You watch. I mean, you *listen.* I'll make it.'

'Go for it, girl,' Nana said, and gave Jannie a hug. She is very good at encouraging others.

Dayne suddenly called out loudly, 'Ugh. I hear a *swoop*. I don't want any swoops here, gentlemen. I want clean diction and pure pitch. I want silver and silk. I do not want *swoops*.'

Out of the corner of my eye, I suddenly saw Christine in the hallway. She was watching Dayne and the boys, but then she looked my way. Her face was principal-serious for just a moment. Then she smiled and winked.

I walked over to see her. Be still my heart.

'That's my boy,' I said with mock proudness as I came up to her. She was dressed in a soft gray pantsuit with a coral-pink blouse. God, I loved seeing her now, being with her, hanging out, doing nothing, the works.

Christine smiled. Actually, she laughed a little at me. 'He does everything so damn well.' She didn't hold back, no matter what. 'I was hoping you might be here, Alex,' she whispered. 'I was just this very minute missing you like crazy. You know that feeling?'

'Yes, that feeling and I are well acquainted.'

We held hands as the choir practiced Bach's 'Jesu, Joy of Man's Desiring'. Everything felt so right, and it was hard to get used to.

'Sometimes . . . I still have this dream about George being shot and dying,' she said as we were standing there. Christine's husband had been murdered in her home, and she had seen him die. It was one of the big reasons she was hesitant about being with me: the fear that I might die in the line of duty; also the fear that I could bring terror and violence into the house.

'I remember everything about the afternoon I heard Maria was shot. It eases with time, but it never goes away.'

Christine knew that. She had figured out the answers to most of her questions, but she liked to talk things through. We were both that way.

'And yet I continue to work here in Southeast. I come to the inner city every day. I could choose a nice school in Maryland or Virginia.'

I nodded. 'Yes, Christine, you do choose to work here.'

'And so do you.'

'And so do I.'

She held my hand a little tighter. 'I guess we were made for each other,' she said. 'Why fight it?'

Chapter Thirty-Three

Early the next morning I was back in the write-up room at the Seventh District Station working on the John Doe homicide. I was the first one in there.

Apparently, no one had noticed Frank Odenkirk as he was leaving the airport. His clothing still hadn't been recovered. The ME reported that he had definitely been sodomized after he'd been killed. As I had suspected, there was no semen. The killer had used a condom. Just as with the Jane Does.

The police commissioner was involved in the Odenkirk case, and was putting added pressure on the department. It was making everyone angry and a little crazy. Chief Pittman was riding his detectives hard, and the only case he seemed interested in was the Odenkirk killing, especially since a suspect in the German tourist murder had been arrested.

At around eleven that morning, Rakeem Powell

stopped by my desk. He bent low and whispered, 'Might have something interesting, Alex. Downstairs in the jail, if you've got a minute. Could be a first break on those two murdered girls in Shaw.'

The jail was down a set of steep concrete stairs, just past a tight warren of small interrogation rooms, a holding room and a booking room. All over the ceiling and walls, prisoners had scratched their street names or used black ink from fingerprinting to write the names. This was incredibly dumb of them, since it gave us their street names for our files.

It's purposely kept dark down in the jail. Each cell is six by five feet, with a metal bed and a combination water fountain/toilet. Sneakers had been tossed in the hallways outside several of the cells. It's what experienced prisoners do who don't want to take the laces out of their sneakers. Laces aren't allowed in the jail for safety reasons.

A small-time drug runner and petty thief named Alfred 'Sneak' Streek was seated like the Fresh Prince of DC in one of the holding cells. The street punk looked up at me as I entered his cell. A slicky-sick smirk crossed his face.

Sneak was sporting wraparound sunglasses, dusty dreadlocks, a bright-green and yellow crocheted hat. His white T-shirt had a drawing of Haile Selassie's face and read: HEAD HUNTER. RASTAFARIAN.

'You from the DA's office? I *don't think so*. No dealee, no talkee, my man,' he said to me. 'So get lost.'

Rakeem ignored him as he talked to me. 'Sneak claims to have some useful information about the Glover and

Cardinal homicides. He would like us to extend him some courtesy in return for what he claims to know. He's jammed up on a charge that he may have broken into an apartment in Shaw. He was caught coming out of a bedroom window with a Sony TV in his arms. Imagine that. Not very Sneaky of him.'

'I didn't rob no ticky-tacky apartment. I don't even *watch* TV, my man. And I don't see no assistant district attorney present with the *au-tho-rity* to make a deal.'

'Take off your sunglasses,' I said to him.

He ignored me, so I took them off for him. As one well-known street saying goes, 'His eyes were like tombstones.' I could tell at a glance that Sneak wasn't just running drugs anymore; he was using.

I stood across from Sneak in the jail cell and stared him down. He was probably in his early twenties, angry, cynical, lost in space and time. 'If you didn't rob the apartment, then why would you be interested in seeing a lawyer from the district attorney's office? That doesn't make too much sense to me, Alfred. Now here's what I'll do for you and it's a one-time offer, so listen carefully. If I walk out of here, I *don't* come back.'

Sneak half-listened to what I was saying.

'If you give us information that directly helps solve the murders of those two young girls, *then* we will help you on the robbery charges. I'll go to the mat myself. If you don't give up the information then I'm going to leave you in here with Detective Powell and Detective Thurman. You won't get this generous, one-time offer again. That's another promise, and as these detectives know, I always keep my word.'

Sneak still didn't say anything. A glaze was coming over his eyes. He tried to stare *me* down, but I'm usually better at it than the average TV booster.

I finally shrugged a look at Rakeem Powell and Jerome Thurman. 'Okay, fine. Gentlemen, we need to know what he knows about those murdered girls in Shaw. He gets nothing from us when you're finished with him. It's possible that he's involved with the homicides himself. He could even be our killer, and we need to solve this thing fast. You treat him that way until we know differently.'

I started to get up, when suddenly Sneak spoke.

'Back Door Man. He hang at Downing Park. He, Back Door, maybe see who done those girls. That's how he say it at the park. Say he saw the killer. So how you gonna help me?'

I walked out of the cell. 'I told you the deal, Alfred. We solve the case, your information helps, I'll help you.'

Chapter Thirty-Four

Maybe we were close to something. Two Metro cruisers and two unmarked sedans pulled up to the fenced-in entrance of tiny Downing playground in Shaw. Rakeem Powell and Sampson went with me to visit with Joe 'Back Door' Booker, a well-known neighborhood menace.

I knew Back Door by sight and spotted him right away. He was short, no more than five-seven, goateed, and so good with a basketball that he sometimes played in work boots, just to show off. He had on dusty orange construction boots today. Also a faded black nylon jacket and black nylon pants that accordioned at the ankles.

A full-court basketball game was in progress, a fast, high-level game, somewhere between college and pro in terms of athletic ability. The court couldn't have been more basic – black macadam, faded white lines, metal backboards and rims with chain nets.

Players from two or three other teams sat around waiting their turn to play winners. Nylon shorts and pants and the Nike *swoosh* were everywhere. The court was surrounded by four walls of heavy wire fencing and was known as the 'cage'. Everybody looked up as we arrived, Booker included.

'We got next!' Sampson called out.

The players on and off the court exchanged looks and a couple of them grinned at Sampson's one-liner. They knew who we were. The steady *thump, thump, thump* on the game ball hadn't stopped.

Back Door was on the court. It wasn't unusual for his team to hold winners for an entire afternoon. He had been in and out of reformatories and prisons since he was fourteen, but he could play ball. He was taunting another player who was on the court in gray suit pants, high-tops, a bare chest. 'You suck,' said Back Door. 'Take those church pants off. I play you in baseball, tennis, bowling, *any* game – you suck. Stop suckin'.'

Rakeem Powell blew the silver referee's whistle he always carries. Rakeem works as a soccer ref in his spare time. The whistle is unorthodox, but it gets attention in noisy places. The game stopped.

The three of us walked up to Booker, who was standing near the foul circle at one basket. Sampson and I towered over him. But so did most of the players. It didn't matter, he was still the best ballplayer out there.

He could probably beat Sampson and me if we played him two on one.

'Awhh, leave the brother alone. He didn't do nothin',' one of the other, taller men complained in a deep voice. He had prison-style tattoos all over his back and arms. 'He was here playin' ball, man.'

'Door been here *all day*,' said somebody else. 'Door been here for days. Hasn't lost *a game* in days!'

Several of the young men laughed at the playground humor. Sampson turned to the biggest man on the court. 'Shut the hell up. Stop dribbling that rock, too. Two young sisters been murdered. That's why we're here. This is no game with us.'

The dribbler shut up and picked up the game ball. The yard became strangely quiet. We could hear a jump rope striking the sidewalk in a fast rhythm. Three little girls playing just outside the cage were saying, *'Little Miss Pinky dressed in blue, died last night at half past two.'* It was a jump-rope rhyme, sadly true around here.

I put my arm around Booker's shoulder and walked him away from his friends.

Sampson continued to do the talking. 'Booker, this is going to be so fast and easy you and your friends will be laughing your asses off about it before we're back in our cars.'

'Yeah, uh-huh,' said Joseph Booker, trying to be cool in the extreme heat of Sampson's and my glare.

'I'm serious as a heart attack, little man. You saw

something that can help us with the murder of Tori Glover and Marion Cardinal. Simple as that. You talk and we walk right back out of here.'

Booker glared up at Sampson as if he were staring down the sun. 'I didn't see shit. Like Luki say, I been here for days. I never lose to these sorry chumps.'

I held up my hand, palm out, inches from his squashed moonpie face.

'I'm on a stopwatch here, Booker, so please don't interrupt my flow. I promise you, two minutes and we're out of here. Now here's what's in it for you. One, we go away and you gentlemen finish your game. Two, Detectives Powell and Sampson will owe you one. Three, a hundred dollars now for your time and trouble.

'The clock is ticking,' I said. '*Tick, tick, tick*. Easy money.'

He finally nodded and held out his hand.

'I seen those two girls get picked up. Around two, three in the mornin' on E Street. I *didn't* see no driver, nobody's face or nothin'. Too dark, man. But he was driving a cab. Look like purple-and-blue gypsy. Somethin' like that. Girls get into the back of the cab, drive off.'

'Is that it?' I asked him. 'I don't want to have to come back here later. Break up your game again.'

Booker considered what I'd said, then spoke again. 'Cab driver a white man. Seen his arm stickin' out the side window. Ain't no white boys drivin' the night shift in Shaw, least none I seen.'

I nodded, waited a bit, then I smiled at the other players. 'Gentlemen, as you were. Play ball.'

Thump, thump, thump.

Swish.

Booker could really play ball.

Chapter Thirty-Five

The new pieces of information gave us something to run with. We'd done an incredible amount of thankless street work and something had finally paid off. We had the color of the gypsy cab that had picked up the girls around the time of the murders. The fact that the driver was white was the best lead we had so far.

Sampson and I drove to my house, rather than back to the station. It would be easier to work on the new leads from Fifth Street. It took me about five minutes to come up with more information from a contact at the Taxi Commission. No fleets operating in DC currently had purple-and-blue cabs. That probably meant the car was an illegal gypsy, as Booker had said. I learned that a company called Vanity Cabs had once used purple-and-blue cars, but Vanity had been out of business since '95. The Taxi Commission rep said that half a dozen or so of the old cars might still be on the street. Originally, the fleet had been fifteen cars, which wasn't that many, even if all of them were still around, which was highly doubtful.

Sampson called all the cab companies that regularly did business in Southeast, especially around Shaw. According to their records, there were only three white drivers who had been working that night.

We were working in the kitchen. Sampson was on the phone and I was using the computer. Nana had fixed fresh coffee and also set out fruit and half a pecan pie.

Rakeem Powell called the house at around 4:15. I picked up. 'Alex, Pittman's watchdog is sniffing around here something fierce. Fred Cook wants to know what you and Sampson are working on this afternoon. Jerome told him the Odenkirk murder.'

I nodded and said, 'If the murders in Southeast are connected in any way, that's the truth.'

'One more thing,' Rakeem said, before he let me go. 'I checked with Motor Vehicles. Might be something good for us. A purple gypsy got a summons for running a stop sign around one in the morning over in Eckington, near the university, Second Street. Maybe that's where our boy lives.'

I clapped my hands and congratulated Rakeem. Our long hours working the Jane Doe cases were finally beginning to pay off.

Maybe we were about to catch the Weasel.

Chapter Thirty-Six

He had been much more careful lately. The visit to Washington by George Bayer, Famine, had been a warning, a shot over his head, and Shafer had taken it seriously. The other players could be as dangerous as he was. It was they who had taught him how to kill, not the other way round. Famine, Conqueror, and War were not to be underestimated, especially if he wanted to win the game.

The day after Famine's visit, the others had informed him that Bayer had come to Washington, that he was being watched. He supposed that was his *second* warning. His activity had frightened them and now they were retaliating. It was all part of the game.

After work that night, he headed to the hideaway in Eckington. He spotted what looked like a half-dozen or so policemen canvassing the street.

He immediately suspected the other Horsemen. They

had turned him in, after all. Or were they playing a mind game with him? What were the cops doing here?

He parked the Jaguar several blocks away, then headed toward the hideaway and garage on foot. He had to check this out. He had on a pin-striped suit, city shirt, and tie. He knew he looked respectable enough. He carried a leather briefcase, and definitely looked like a businessman coming home late.

Two African-American policemen were doing door-to-door questioning on Uhland Terrace. This wasn't good – the police were less than five blocks from the hideaway.

Why were they here? His brain was reeling, adrenaline rushing through his nervous system like a flash flood. Maybe this had nothing to do with him, but he couldn't be too careful. He definitely suspected the other players, especially George Bayer. *But why?* Was this the way they planned to end the game, by bringing him down?

When the two policemen up ahead disappeared down a side street off Uhland, Shafer decided to stop at one of the brownstones where they'd been asking questions. It was a small risk, but he needed to know what was happening. A couple of old men were seated on the stoop. An ancient radio played an Orioles baseball game.

'They ask you about some kind of trouble in the neighborhood?' Shafer asked the men in as casual a tone as he could manage. 'They stopped me up the block.'

One of the men just stared at him, terminally pissed off, but the other one nodded and spoke up. 'Sure did, mister. Lookin' for a cab, purple-and-blue gypsy. Connected to some killings, they say. Though I don't recall seeing any purple ones lately. Used to be a cab company called Vanity. You remember, Earl? They had the purple people-eaters.'

'That was some years ago,' the other man said, nodding. 'They went belly up.'

'I guess they were Metro police. Never showed me any ID, though,' Shafer said, and shrugged. He was being careful to speak with an American accent, which he was good at imitating.

'Detectives Cross and Sampson.' The more talkative of the two men volunteered their names. 'Detective Cross showed me his badge. It was the real deal.'

'Oh, I'm sure it was,' Shafer said, and saluted the two old men. 'Good to see the police in the neighborhood, actually.'

'You got that right.'

'Have a nice night.'

'Yeah, you too.'

Shafer circled back to his car, and drove to the embassy. He went straight to his office, where he felt safe and protected. He calmed himself, then turned on his computer and did a thorough search on DC detectives named Cross and Sampson. He found more than he hoped for, especially on Detective Cross.

He thought about how the new developments might

change the game. Then he sent out a message to the Horsemen. He told them about Cross and Sampson – that the detectives had decided to 'play the game'. So, naturally, he had plans for them too.

Chapter Thirty-Seven

Zachary Scott Taylor was a thorough, analytical, and very hard-nosed reporter on the *Washington Post*. I respected the hell out of him. His relentless cynicism and skepticism were a little too much for me to take on a daily basis; otherwise we might have been even closer friends. But we had a good relationship and I trusted him more than I did most journalists.

I met him that night at the Irish Times, on F Street, near Union Station. The restaurant-bar is in an anachronistic stand-alone brick building surrounded by modern office structures. Zachary called it 'a dumpy little toilet of a bar, a perfect place for us to meet'.

In the time-honored tradition of Washington, I have occasionally been one of his trusted sources, and I was about to tell the reporter something important. I hoped he would agree, and that he could convince his editors at the *Post* about the story.

'How're Master Damon and Ms Jannie?' Zachary asked as he sat across from me in a darkened corner under an old photo of a stern-looking man in a black top hat. Zachary is tall, gaunt and thin; he resembles the man in the old photo a little bit. Zachary always talks too fast – with the words running into one another – *How'reMasterDamonandMsJannie?* There was just a hint of Virginia softening his accent.

The waitress eventually came over to our table. He ordered black coffee and I had the same.

'Two coffees?' she asked, to make sure she'd heard us right.

'Two of your very *finest* coffees,' Zachary said.

'This isn't Starbucks, y'know,' she said.

I smiled at the waitress's brio, then at what Zachary had said – his first words to me. I'd probably mentioned my kids' names to him once, but he had an encyclopedic memory for all kinds of disparate information.

'You should go get yourself a couple of kids, Zachary,' I told him, smiling broadly.

He glanced up at an ancient whirring ceiling fan that looked as if it might suddenly spin out of the ceiling. It seemed a nice metaphor for modern life in America, an aging infrastructure threatening to spin out of control.

'Don't have a wife yet, Alex. Still looking for the right woman,' said Zachary.

'Well, okay then, get yourself a wife first, then get a couple of kids. Might take the edge off your neuroses.'

The waitress placed steaming cups of black coffee in

front of us. 'Will that be *all*?' she said. She shook her head, then left us.

'Maybe I don't want the edge taken off my rather stunning neurotic behavior. Maybe I believe that's what makes me such a damn fine reporter, and that without it my work would be pedestrian shit, and then I'd be nothing in the eyes of Don Graham and company.'

I sipped the day-or-two-old coffee. 'Except that if you had a couple of kids, you could never be nothing.'

Zachary squinted one eye shut and smacked the left side of his lips. He was a very animated thinker.

'Except if the kids didn't love, or even like me very much.'

'And you don't consider yourself lovable? But actually you are, Zachary. Trust me. You're just fine. Your kids would adore the hell out of you and you would adore them. You'd have a mutual adoration society.'

He finally laughed and clapped his hands loudly. We usually laugh a good bit when we're together.

'So will you marry me and have my children?' He grinned at me over the top of his steaming cup. 'This is a pick-up joint, after all. Singles from the Bureau of Labor Statistics and the Government Printing Office come here, hoping to bed a staffer from Kennedy's or Glenn's.'

'Actually, it's the best offer I've had all day. Who called this meeting anyway? Why are we here at this dive, drinking really bad coffee?'

Taylor slurped his. 'Coffee's fairly strong, isn't it? That's something to be thankful for. What's up, Alex?'

'You interested in another Pulitzer?' I asked him.

He pretended to think it over, but his eyes lit up. 'Well, I might be. You see, I need to balance the look of my mantelpiece. One of my dates told me that. Never did see the young woman again. She worked for Gingrich, as a matter of fact.'

For the next forty-five minutes or so, I told Zachary exactly what I thought was up. I told him about one hundred and fourteen unsolved murders in Southeast and parts of Northeast DC. I detailed the contrasting investigation of the cases of Frank Odenkirk and the German tourist in Georgetown, and the black teenagers Tori Glover and Marion Cardinal. I filled him in on the chief of detectives, his proclivities and his biases, at least my perception of them. I even admitted that I disliked Pittman intensely, and Zachary knows I'm not that way about too many folks who don't murder for a living.

He shook his head back and forth, back and forth, while I talked, and didn't stop when I was finished. 'Not that I doubt any of what you're saying, but do you have any documentation?' he asked.

'You're such a stickler for details,' I said. 'Reporters are such wusses when you come right down to it.'

I reached down under my seat and lifted up two thick manila folders. His eyes brightened.

'This should help with the story. Copies of sixty-seven of the unsolved homicide reports. Also a copy of the Glover and Cardinal investigation. Note the number of detectives assigned to each. Check the case hours logged.

You'll see a huge discrepancy. That's all I could get my hands on – but the other reports exist.'

'Why would this be happening, this malicious neglect?' he asked me.

I nodded at the wisdom of his question. 'I'll give you the most cynical reason,' I said. 'Some Metro cops like to refer to Southeast as "self-cleaning ovens". That sound like the beginnings of malicious neglect to you? Some victims in Southeast are called NHIs – that's No Humans Involved. The latter is a phrase used by Chief Pittman.'

Zachary quickly leafed through the reports. Then he shook my hand. 'I'm going home to my lonely abode, made bearable only by my single Pulitzer. I have all these fascinating police files on NHIs to read, then hopefully a chilling news exposé to write. We'll see. As always, it's been a party, Alex. My best to Damon, Jannie, Nana Mama. I'd like to meet them one day. Put some faces with the names.'

'Come to the next Washington Boys' Choir performance,' I said. 'All our faces will be there. Damon is a *chorister*.'

Chapter Thirty-Eight

I worked that night until eight thirty, and then I drove to Kinkead's in Foggy Bottom to meet up with Christine. Kinkead's is one of our favorite restaurants and also an excellent place to listen to jazz, and snuggle up to each other.

I sat at the bar and enjoyed the sounds of Hilton Felton and Ephrain Woolfolk until Christine arrived, coming from an event at school. She was right on time, though. She is punctual. Very considerate. Perfect in almost every way, at least in my eyes. *Yes, I will be your wife.*

'You hungry? Want to go to a table?' I asked, after we had hugged as if we'd been separated for many years and thousands of miles.

'Let's just sit here at the bar for a few minutes. You mind?' she asked. Her breath smelled lightly of spearmint. Her face was so soft and smooth that I *had* to lightly cup it in both my hands.

'Nothing I'd rather do in the whole wide world,' I said.

Christine ordered a Harvey's Bristol Cream and I had a mug of beer, and we talked as the music flowed over, around, and right through our bodies. It had been a long day, and I needed this.

'I've been waiting for this all day long. I couldn't wait. Am I being too corny and romantic again?' I said, and grinned.

'Not for me. Never too corny, never too romantic. That won't happen, Alex.' Christine smiled. I loved to see her like this. Her eyes twinkled and danced. I sometimes get lost in her eyes, fall into the deep pools, all that good stuff that people yearn for but few seem to get nowadays, which is sad.

She stared back and my fingers lightly caressed her cheek. Then I held her under her chin. 'Stardust' was playing. It's one of my favorite songs, even under ordinary circumstances. I wondered if Hilton and Ephrain were playing the tune for us, and when I looked at him, Hilton gave me a sly wink.

We moved closer together and danced in place. I could feel her heart beating; feel it right up against my chest. We must have stayed like that for ten or fifteen minutes. No one at the bar seemed to notice; no one bothered us – offered to refill our drinks, or escort us to our table. I guess they understood.

'I really like Kinkead's,' Christine whispered. 'But you know what? I'd rather be home with you tonight. Some place a little more private. I'll make you eggs, whatever you'd like. Is that all right? Do you mind?'

'No, I don't mind at all. That's a perfect idea. Let's go.'

I paid our bar bill, made my regrets about the dinner reservation. Then we went to Christine's.

'We'll start with dessert,' she said and smiled wickedly. I liked that about her too.

Chapter Thirty-Nine

I had been waiting a long time to be in love again, but this was worth it and then some. I grabbed hold of Christine as soon as we were inside her house. My hands began to trace her waist, her hips; they played over her breasts, her shoulders, then touched the delicate bones of her face. We liked to do this slowly, no need to rush. I kissed her lips, then gently scratched her back and shoulders. I pulled her closer, closer.

'You have the gentlest touch,' she whispered against my cheek. 'I could do this all night. Be just like this. You want some wine? Anything? I'll give you anything I have.'

'I love you,' I told her, still lightly scratching her lower back. 'We *will* do this forever. I have no doubt of it.'

'I love you so much,' she whispered, then I heard her breath softly catch. 'So please, try to be careful, Alex. At work.'

'Okay, I will. But not tonight,' I said.

Christine smiled. 'Not tonight. Tonight you can live dangerously. We both will. You *are* handsome, and debonair for a policeman.'

'Or even for an international jewel thief.'

I swept her up and carried her down the hallway to the bedroom. 'Mmm. Strong, too,' she said. She flicked on a hall lamp as we passed. It was just enough light to see where we were going.

'How about a trip somewhere?' I said. 'I need to get away.'

'That sounds good. Yes – before school starts. Anywhere. Take me away from all this.'

Her room smelled of fresh flowers. There were pink and red roses on the nightstand. She has a passion for flowers and gardening.

'You planned this all along, didn't you?' I said. 'You *did*. This is entrapment. You sly girl.'

'I was thinking about it all day,' she confessed and sighed contentedly. 'I thought about being with you all day, in my office, in the hallways, the schoolyard, and then in my car on the way to the restaurant. I've been having erotic day-dreams about you all day.'

'I hope I can live up to them.'

'You will. No doubt about it.'

I took off her black silk blouse in one sweeping motion. I put my mouth to a breast, pulling at it through her demi bra. She was wearing a brushed leather skirt and I didn't take it off, just slowly pushed it up. I knelt and kissed her ankles, the tops of her feet, then slowly came up her long legs. She massaged my neck, my back and shoulders.

'You *are* dangerous tonight,' she said. 'That's a good thing.'

'Sexual healing.'

'Mmm, please. Heal me all over, Doctor.'

She bit down hard into my shoulder, then even harder into the side of my neck. We were both breathing fast. She moved against me then opened her legs for me. I moved inside her. She felt incredibly warm. The bedsprings began to sing and the headboard rocked into the wall.

She pushed her hair to one side, behind an ear. I love the way she does that.

'You feel so good. Oh, Alex, don't stop, don't stop, don't stop,' she whispered.

I did as I was told and I loved every moment, every movement we made together, and I even wondered for a second if we had made a baby.

Chapter Forty

Much later that night we rustled up some eggs with Vidalia onions and cheddar and mozzarella cheeses, opened a nice bottle of Pinot Noir. Then I started a fire, in August, with the air-conditioner turned up high.

We sat in front of the fire, laughed and talked, and planned a quick trip away from Washington. We settled on Bermuda, and Christine asked if we could bring Nana and the kids. I felt as if my life were changing fast, going to a new good place. If only I could get lucky and catch the Weasel somehow. That could be the perfect ending to my career with the Metro police.

I went home to Fifth Street late, got in just before three. I didn't want Damon and Jannie to wake in the morning and not find me there. I was up by eight o'clock the next morning, bounding downstairs to the delectable smells of fresh coffee and Nana's world-famous sticky buns.

The terrible twosome were just about ready to dash off

to the Sojourner Truth School where they were taking advanced classes in the morning. They looked like a pair of shiny angels. I didn't get to feel this good very often, so I was going all the way with it.

'How was your date last night, Daddy?' Jannie said, making her biggest goo-goo eyes at me.

'Who said I had a date?' I made room for her on my knee. She ate a bite of the humongous sweet bun Nana had set on my plate.

'Let's just say a little birdie told me,' she chirped.

'Uh-huh. Little birdie makes good sticky buns,' I said. 'My date was pretty good. How was yours? You had a date, right? Didn't sit home alone, did you?'

'Your date was *pretty* good? You came home with the milkman.' Jannie laughed out loud. Damon was giggling, too. She can get us all going when she wants to; she's been that way since she was a baby.

'Jannie Cross,' Nana said, but she let it go. There was no use trying to make Jannie act like a typical seven-year-old at this point. She was too bright, too outspoken, too full of life and fun. Besides, we have a philosophy as a family: he or she who laughs, lasts.

'How come you two don't live together first?' Jannie asked. 'That's what they all do in the movies and on TV.'

I found myself grinning and starting to frown at the same time. 'Don't get me going on the silly stuff they do on TV and in the movies, little girl. They always get it wrong. Christine and I are going to get married soon, and *then* we'll all live together.'

'You *sure* you asked her?' they all exclaimed.

'I did.'

'And she said yes?'

'Why do you all look so surprised? Of course she said yes. Who could resist being a part of this family?'

'Hooray!' Jannie whooped loudly. I could tell she meant it from the bottom of her little heart.

'Hooray!' echoed Nana. 'Thank God. Oh, thank God.'

'I agree,' Damon piped in. 'It's time that we had a more normal life around here.'

Everybody was congratulating me for several minutes until Jannie finally said, 'I have to go to *school* now, *Pa-pa*. I wouldn't want to disappoint Ms Johnson by being late, now would I? Here's your morning newspaper.'

Jannie handed me the *Washington Post* and my heart jumped a little in my chest. This was a good day indeed. I saw Zachary Taylor's story in the bottom right of the front page. It wasn't the banner headline it deserved to be, but he'd gotten the story on page one.

Potential scandal over unsolved murders in Southeast DC. Possible racial bias seen in police activity.

'Potential scandal indeed,' Nana said, and squeegeed her lower face. 'Genocide always is, isn't it?'

Chapter Forty-One

I entered the station house around nine and Chief Pittman's assistant-lackey came scurrying up to me. Old Fred Cook had been a bad detective once, and now was an equally bad and devious administrator, but Fred was as smooth a buttkisser as could be found in the department or anywhere else in Washington.

'The chief of detectives wants to see you in his office, post-haste. It's important,' Fred told me.'Better move it.'

I nodded at him and tried to keep my good mood intact.'Of course it is, he's the chief of detectives.You have any helpful hints for me, Fred?You happen to know what this is about, what I should expect?'

'It's a big deal,' said Cook, unhelpful and happy about it.'That's about all I can tell you, Alex.'

He walked away, leaving me hanging. I could feel the bile rising in my throat. My good mood had already deserted me.

I walked down the creaking hardwood floors of the hallway to the Jefe's office. I had no idea what to expect; but I sure wasn't prepared for what I found.

I immediately thought about what Damon had said that morning: *It's time that we had a more normal life around here.*

Sampson was seated inside the chief's office. Rakeem Powell and Jerome Thurman were both in there, too.

'Come in, Dr Cross.' Chief Pittman beckoned with an outstretched hand. 'Please come in. We've been waiting for you to arrive.'

'What is this?' I said, pulling up a chair next to Sampson's, whispering in his ear.

'Don't know yet, but it's not too good,' he said. 'The Jefe hasn't said one word to us. Looks like the canary who ate the cat, though.'

Pittman came around in front of his desk and leaned his ample buttocks back against it. He seemed particularly full of himself, and shit, this morning. His mousy gray hair was plastered back and looked like a helmet on his bullet head.

'I can tell you what you want to know, Detective Cross,' he said. 'In fact, I didn't want to tell these other detectives until you got here. As of this morning, Detectives Sampson, Thurman, and Powell have been suspended from active duty. They have been working on cases outside the auspices of this department. Evidence is still being gathered about the full extent of these activities; and also, if any other detectives were involved.'

I started to speak up, but Sampson grabbed my arm – hard. 'Be cool, Alex.'

Pittman looked at the three of them. 'Detectives Sampson, Thurman, Powell, you can go. Your union representative has been informed of the situation. You have questions, or issues with my decision, inform your representative.'

Sampson's mouth was set hard. He didn't say a word to the Jefe, though. He got up and left the office. Thurman and Powell trailed close behind him. Neither of them spoke to Pittman either. The three of them were hard-working, dedicated detectives, and I couldn't stand to watch this happen.

I wondered why the Jefe had spared me so far. I also wondered why Shawn Moore wasn't there. The cynical answer was that Pittman wanted to set us against one another, to make us believe that Shawn had spoken against us.

Pittman reached across his desk and picked up a folded copy of the *Washington Post*. 'You happen to see this article today? Bottom right?'

He pushed the newspaper toward me. I had to catch the paper to keep it from falling to the floor.

'Scandal over unsolved murders in Southeast,' I said. 'Yes, I did. I read it at home.'

'I'll bet you did. Mr Taylor, of the *Post*, quotes unidentified sources in the police department. You have anything to do with the article?' Pittman asked and stared hard at me.

'Why would I talk to the *Washington Post*?' I asked a question in answer to his. 'I told you about the problem in Southeast. I think a repeat killer may be working there. Why go any farther with it than that? Suspending those detectives sure won't help solve the problem. Especially if this sicko is approaching rage, which I believe he is.'

'I don't buy this serial-killer story. I don't see any pattern that's consistent. No one else does but you.' Pittman shook his head and frowned. He was hot, angry, trying to control himself.

He reached out his hand toward me again. His fingers were like uncooked sausages. He lowered his voice almost to a whisper. 'I'd like to fuck you over good, and I will. But for now, it wouldn't be expedient to pull you off the Odenkirk homicide. It wouldn't *look* good, and I suspect it would end up in the *Post*, too. I look forward to your daily reports on the so-called John Doe case. You know, it is time you got some of those unsolved murders off the books. You'll report directly to me on this. I'm going to be all over you, Cross. Any questions?'

I quickly left Chief Pittman's office. Before I hit him.

Chapter Forty-Two

Sampson, Thurman, and Rakeem Powell had already left the building by the time I got out of the Jefe's office. I felt as if I could easily go postal. I nearly walked back inside Pittman's office and wiped up the floor with him.

I went to my desk and thought about what to do next, tried to calm myself down before I did anything rash and stupid. I thought about my responsibilities to the people in Southeast and that helped me. Still, I almost went back after Pittman.

I called Christine and let out some steam. Then, spur of the moment, I asked if she could get away for our long weekend, possibly starting on Thursday night. Christine said that she could go. I went and filled out a vacation form and left it on Fred Cook's desk. It was the last thing he and Pittman would expect from me. But I'd already decided the best thing would be to get away from here, cool down, then decide on a plan to move forward.

As I headed out of the building, another detective stopped me. 'They're over at Hart's bar,' he said. 'Sampson said to tell you they reserved a seat for you.'

Hart's is a very seedy, very popular gin mill on Second Street. It isn't a cops' bar, which is why some of us like it. It was eleven in the morning and the bar room was already crowded, lively, even friendly.

'Here he is!' Jerome Thurman saluted me with a half-full beer mug as I walked inside. Half-a-dozen other detectives and friends were there, too. The word had gotten around fast about the suspensions.

There was a whole lot of laughter and shouting going on. 'It's a bachelor's party!' Sampson said, and grinned. 'Got you, sugar. With a little help from Nana. You should see the look on your face!'

For the next hour and a half, friends kept arriving at Hart's. By noon the bar was full, and then the regular customers started arriving for their lunch-hour nips. The owner, Mike Hart, was in his glory. I hadn't really thought about a bachelor's party, but now that I was in the middle of one, I was glad it happened. A lot of men still guard their emotions and feelings, but not so much at a bachelor's party, at least not at a good one thrown by the people closest to you.

This was a good one. The suspensions that were handed down earlier that morning were mostly forgotten for a few hours. I was congratulated and hugged more times than I could count, and even kissed once or twice.

Everybody was calling me 'sugar', following Sampson's lead. The 'love' word was used, and overused. I was roasted and toasted in sentimental speeches that seemed hilarious at the time. Just about everybody had too much to drink.

By four in the afternoon, Sampson and I were steadying each other, making our way into the blinding daylight on Second Street. Mike Hart himself had called us a cab.

For a brief, clear moment, I was reminded of the purple-and-blue gypsy cab we were looking for – but then the thought evaporated into the nearly white sunlight.

'Sugar,' Sampson whispered against my skull as we were climbing into our cab. 'I love you more than life itself. It's true. I love your kids, love your Nana, love your wife-to-be, the lovely Christine. Take us home,' he said to the driver. 'Alex is getting married.'

'And he's the best man,' I said to the driver, who smiled.

'Yes, I am,' said Sampson, 'the very best.'

Chapter Forty-Three

On Thursday night, Shafer played The Four Horsemen again. He was locked inside his study, but through the early part of the night he could hear the sounds of his family throughout the house. He felt intensely isolated; he was nervous, jittery, and angry for no apparent reason.

While he waited to log on with the other players, he found himself thinking back to the wild car ride through Washington. He relived a particular feeling over and over: the imagined moment of sudden impact with an unmovable object. He saw it as blinding light, and physical objects, and *himself*, shattering like glass and then becoming part of the universe again. Even the pain he would feel would be part of the reassembling of matter into other fascinating forms and shapes.

I am suicidal, he finally thought. *It's just a matter of time. I really am Death.*

When it was exactly nine o'clock, he began to type in a message on his computer. The Horsemen were online, waiting for his response to the visit and warning by George Bayer. He didn't want to disappoint them. What they had done had made him more enthusiastic about playing the game. He wrote:

STRANGELY, DEATH WASN'T SURPRISED WHEN FAMINE APPEARED IN WASHINGTON. OF COURSE HE HAD EVERY RIGHT TO COME. JUST AS DEATH COULD GO TO DORKING, OR SINGAPORE, OR MANILA, OR KINGSTON, AND PERHAPS DEATH WILL PAY ONE OF YOU A VISIT SOON.

THAT'S THE BEAUTY OF THE GAME WE PLAY – ANYTHING CAN HAPPEN.

ULTIMATELY, THE ISSUE IS TRUST, ISN'T IT? DO I TRUST THAT YOU WILL ALLOW ME TO CONTINUE TO PLAY THE FANTASY GAME AS I WISH? AFTER ALL, THAT IS WHAT MAKES THE GAME DISTINCTIVE AND ALLURING, THE FREE-DOM WE EXPERIENCE.

THAT *IS* THE GAME NOW, ISN'T IT? WE HAVE EVOLVED INTO SOMETHING NEW. WE HAVE RAISED THE TABLE STAKES. SO LET'S HAVE SOME REAL EXCITEMENT, FELLOW HORSEMEN. I HAVE A FEW IDEAS TO TRY OUT ON YOU. EVERYTHING IS IN THE SPIRIT OF THE GAME. NO UNNECESSARY RISKS WILL BE TAKEN.

LET'S PLAY THE GAME AS IF OUR LIVES DEPENDED ON IT.

PERHAPS MINE ALREADY DOES?

AS I TOLD YOU – WE HAVE TWO NEW PLAYERS. THEY ARE WASHINGTON DETECTIVES NAMED ALEX CROSS AND JOHN SAMPSON. WORTHY OPPONENTS. I'M WATCHING THEM, BUT I CAN'T HELP WONDERING WHETHER SOON THEY'LL BE WATCHING ME.

LET ME TELL YOU ABOUT A FANTASY SCE-NARIO THAT I'VE CREATED TO WELCOME THEM TO OUR GAME. I'M SENDING PICTURES NOW – DETECTIVES CROSS AND SAMPSON.

Chapter Forty-Four

I t took us a day to get organized for our trip, but everybody seemed to enjoy the spontaneity, and also the special treat that we would all be together on a vacation for the first time. And so, Damon, Jannie, Nana, Christine, and I left DC in the afternoon and arrived in high spirits at Bermuda International Airport late on Thursday evening, the twenty-fifth of August.

I definitely wanted to be out of Washington for a few days. The Mr Smith murder case had been followed too quickly by the Jane Doe investigation. I needed a rest. I had a friend who was part owner of a hotel in Bermuda, and it wasn't a particularly long airplane ride. It was perfect for us.

One scene from the airport will always stick in my mind – Christine singing 'Ja-da, ja-da' with Jannie stuck at her side. I couldn't help thinking that they looked like mother and daughter and that touched me deeply. They were so affectionate and playful, so natural. It was a mind-photo for me to have and to hold. One of those moments that I knew I'd never forget, even as I watched the two of them dancing and singing as if they'd known each other forever.

We were blessed with extraordinarily good weather for our holiday. It was sunny and blue-skied every day, morning until nightfall, when the sky turned a magical combination of reds, oranges, and purples. The days belonged to all of us, but especially the kids. We went swimming and snorkeling at Elbow Beach and Horseshoe Bay, and then raced mopeds along the picturesque Middle and Harbor Roads.

The nights belonged to Christine and me, and we made the most of them. We hit all the best spots: the Terrace Bar at the Palm Reef, the Gazebo Lounge at the Princess, the Clay House Inn, Once Upon a Table in Hamilton, Horizons in Paget. I loved being with her and that thought kept drifting through my mind. I felt that what we shared had been strengthened because I had backed off and given her time and space. And I felt whole again. I kept remembering the very first time I had seen her in the schoolyard at Sojourner Truth. *She's the one, Alex.* That thought still played in my head too.

We sat at the Terrace Bar overlooking the city and harbor of Hamilton. It was dotted with small islands, white sails, ferries back and forth to Warwick and Paget. We held hands and I couldn't stop staring into her eyes, didn't want to.

'Big thoughts?' she finally said.

'I've been thinking a lot about going into private practice again,' I told her. 'I think it might be the best thing to do.'

She stared into my eyes. 'I don't want you to do it for me, Alex. Please don't make me the cause of your leaving your job with the police. I know you love it. Most days you do.'

'The job has been tearing at me lately. Pittman isn't just a difficult boss, I think he's a bad guy. What happened to Sampson and the others is just bullshit. They were working unsolved cases on their own time. I'm tempted to give the story to Zach Taylor at the *Post*. People would riot if they knew the truth. Which is why I *won't* give it to the *Post*.'

She listened and tried to help but she didn't push, and I appreciated that. 'It does sound like a terrible, complicated, nasty mess, Alex. I'd like to punch out Pittman, too. He's choosing politics over protecting people. I'm sure you'll know what to do when the time is right.'

The next morning, I found her walking in the garden, with tropical flowers strewn in her hair. She looked radiant, even more than usual, and I fell in love all over again.

'There's an old saying I've been hearing since I was a little girl,' she told me as I joined her. 'If you have only two pennies, buy a loaf of bread with one, and a lily with the other.'

I kissed her hair, in between the flowers. I kissed her

sweet lips, her cheeks, the hollow in her throat.

The kids and I went back to Horseshoe Bay beach early that afternoon. They couldn't get enough of the deep blue sea, swimming, snorkeling, building sand castles, and of course it was almost time to start school again so everything about our vacation was extra special and intense.

Christine took a moped trip into Hamilton to pick up mementos for a few of the teachers at Sojourner Truth. We all waved until she was out of sight on Middle Road. Then back into the water!

Around five o'clock, Damon, Jannie, and I finally returned to the Belmont Hotel, which sat like a sentinel on lush green hills framed by china-blue skies. All around, everywhere we looked, were pastel-colored cottages with white roofs. Nana was sitting out on the porch, talking to a couple of her new best friends. Paradise regained, I thought, and felt something deep and sacred coming back to life inside me.

As I stared out at the cloudless blue sky, I regretted that Christine wasn't there to share it. I actually missed her in just that short a time. I hugged Jannie and Damon and we were all smiling at the obvious. We loved being here together and we were so damn fortunate to have one another.

'You miss her,' Jannie whispered. It was a statement, not a question. 'That's good, Daddy. That's the way it should be, right.'

When Christine still hadn't returned by six o'clock, I struggled between conflicting thoughts of waiting for her at the hotel or driving into Hamilton myself. Maybe she'd had an accident. *Those damn mopeds*, I thought, having found them fun and perfectly safe just the afternoon before.

I finally spotted a tall, slender woman entering through the front gates of the Belmont, walking against a background of hibiscus and oleander. I sighed in relief, but as I started down the front stairs, I saw that it wasn't Christine.

Christine still hadn't returned, or called the hotel, by six thirty. Or by seven o'clock.

I finally called the police.

Chapter Forty-Five

Inspector Patrick Busby from the Hamilton PD arrived at the Belmont Hotel around seven thirty. He was a small, balding man and from a distance he looked to be in his late fifties or sixties. As he approached the front porch, I could tell he was no more than forty, around the same age as me.

He listened to my story, then said that visitors often lost track of time and themselves in Bermuda. There were also occasional moped accidents on the Middle Road. He promised me that Christine would show up soon with a mild 'road rash', or a 'slightly turned ankle'.

I wouldn't have any of it. She was always punctual, or at the very least, she would have called.

I knew that somehow she'd call if she had a minor accident. So the inspector and I rode together between the hotel and Hamilton, and then we toured the streets of the capital city, particularly Front and Reid Streets. I was silent and solemn-faced as I stared out of the car, hoping to get a glimpse of Christine shopping on some side street, forgetful of the hour. But we didn't see her anywhere, and she still hadn't called the hotel.

When she hadn't turned up by nine, Inspector Busby reluctantly agreed that Christine might be missing. He asked a lot of questions that showed me he was a decent cop. He wanted to know if we'd had any kind of argument or disagreement.

'I'm a homicide detective in Washington, DC,' I finally told him. I'd been holding it back because I didn't want this to get territorial. 'I've been involved with high-profile cases involving mass murders in the past. I've known some very bad men. There might be a connection. I hope not, but that could be.'

'I see,' Busby said. He was such a precise, neat man, with his thin pencil mustache. He looked more like a fussy schoolteacher than a cop, more like a psychologist than I did. 'Are there any other surprises I should know about, Detective Cross?' he asked.

'No, that's it. But you see why I'm worried, and why I called you. I'm working on a series of nasty murders in Washington right now.'

'Yes, I see a reason for your concern now. I will put out a missing persons report forthwith.'

I sighed heavily, then went upstairs and talked to the kids and Nana. I tried my best not to alarm them, but Damon and Jannie started to cry. And then Nana did, too.

We had learned nothing more about Christine or her

whereabouts by midnight. Inspector Busby finally left the hotel at quarter past twelve. He was kind actually, and considerate enough to give me his home number; he asked me to call right away if I heard from Christine. Then he said my family and I would be in his prayers.

At three, I was still up and pacing my hotel room on the third floor, and doing some praying myself. I had just gotten off the phone with Quantico. The FBI was cross-checking all of my homicide cases to see if anyone I'd investigated had connections with Bermuda. They were concentrating on the current series of unsolved murders in Southeast. I'd faxed them my profile on the Weasel.

I didn't have any logical reason to suspect the killer might be here in Bermuda, and yet I feared that he might be. It was just the kind of feeling that the Jefe had been rejecting about the murders in Southeast.

I understood that the Bureau probably wouldn't get back to me until later in the morning. I was tempted to call friends at Interpol, but I held off . . . And then I called Interpol too.

The hotel room was filled with mahogany Queen Anne furniture and wicker, and had dusty-pink carpets. It felt empty, and lonely. I stood like a ghost before tall, water-stained dormer windows and stared out at shifting black shapes against the moonlit sky and remembered how Christine felt in my arms. I felt incredibly helpless and alone without her. I also couldn't believe this had happened.

I hugged myself tightly and became aware of an incredible pain all around my heart. The tightening pain was like a solid column that went from my chest all the way up into my head. I could see her face, her beautiful smile. I remembered dancing with her one night at the Rainbow Room in New York, and dinners at Kinkead's in Washington, and one special night at her place when we'd laughed and thought maybe we'd made a baby. Was Christine out there somewhere on the island? She had to be. I prayed again that she was safe. She had to be safe. I refused to have any other thought for more than a couple of seconds.

The telephone in the room rang, a short burst, at a little past four in the morning.

My heart was stuck in my throat. My skin crawled, felt as if it were shrinking and no longer fit my body. I rushed across the room and grabbed the phone before the second ring. My hand was trembling.

The strange, muffled voice scared me: 'You have e-mail.'

I couldn't think straight. I couldn't think at all.

I'd brought my laptop with me on vacation.

Who knew that I had my computer here? Who knew a small detail like that about me? Who had been watching me? Watching us?

I yanked open the closet door. I grabbed the computer, hooked it up, and logged on. I scrolled down the e-mail to the last message.

It was short and very concise.

SHE'S SAFE FOR NOW. WE HAVE HER.

The curt, cold message was worse than anything I could imagine. Each word was branded into my brain, repeating over and over.

She's safe for now.

We have her.

Book Three

Elegy

Chapter Forty-Six

S ampson arrived at the Belmont Hotel the day after Christine disappeared. I hurried down to the small front lobby to meet him. He threw his large arms around me, clasping me tightly, but gently, as if he were holding a child in his arms.

'You okay? You holding up?' he asked.

'Not even close,' I told him. 'I spent half a day checking the e-mail address I got last night. It came from curtain@mindspring.com. The address was falsified. Nothing is going right.'

'We'll get Christine back. We'll find her.' He muttered what he knew I wanted to hear, but I was sure that he truly believed it in his heart. Sampson is the most positive human being I've ever met. He won't be denied.

'Thanks for coming. It means a lot to all of us. I can't think straight about anything. I'm really rattled, John. I can't even begin to imagine who could have done this.

Maybe the Weasel. I don't know.'

'If you *could* think straight now,' John said, 'I'd be more worried about you than usual. That's why I'm here.'

'I kind of knew you'd come.'

'Of course you did. I'm Sampson. Occam's razor and all that deep philosophical shit at work here.'

There were a half-dozen guests in the hotel lobby and all of them looked our way. The hotel staff knew about Christine's disappearance, and I'm sure that the guests at the Belmont knew as well, as did just about everybody else on the small, chatty island.

'The story's on the front page of the local newspaper,' Sampson said. 'People were reading copies at the airport.'

I told him, 'Bermuda is small, mostly peaceful and orderly. The disappearance of a tourist, or any kind of violent crime, is unusual here. I don't know how the paper got the story so quickly. The leak must have come out of the police station.'

'Local police won't help us. Probably get in the way,' Sampson muttered as we walked over to the hotel registration desk. He signed in, then we trudged upstairs to show Nana and the kids that Uncle John was here.

Chapter Forty-Seven

The following morning, the two of us met for hours with the police in Hamilton. They were professionals, but a kidnapping was a rarity for them. They let us set up in their station house on Front Street. I still couldn't concentrate or focus the way I needed to.

Bermuda is a twenty-one-square-mile island. While the British colony is small, we soon discovered that there are more than twelve hundred roads. Sampson and I split up and covered as much of the island as we possibly could. For the next two days we went from six in the morning until ten or eleven at night, without a break. I didn't want to stop, not even to sleep.

We didn't do any better than the locals, though. No one had seen anything. We'd reached a dead end. Christine had disappeared without a trace.

We were bone tired. After we finished at the station house on the third night, Sampson and I went for a late swim at Elbow Beach, just down the road from the hotel.

I had learned to swim at the municipal pool in DC. Nana had insisted that I learn. She was fifty-four at the time, and stubborn. She made up her mind to learn and took lessons from the Red Cross with us. The majority of people in Southeast didn't know how to swim back then, and she felt it was symbolic of the limiting inner-city experience.

So one summer, we all tackled swimming with Nana at the municipal pool. We went for lessons three mornings a week, and usually practiced an extra hour after that. Nana herself was soon able to swim fifty or more laps. She had stamina, same as now. I rarely get into the water without flashing back to those fine summer days of my youth, when I became a reasonably good swimmer.

Now, Sampson and I floated on the calm surface, out about a hundred yards or so from shore. The sky above was the deepest shade of evening blue, sparkling with countless stars. I could see the curving white line of the beach as it stretched several miles in either direction. Palm and casuarina trees shimmied in the sea breeze.

I felt devastated, totally overwhelmed as I floated on the sea. I kept seeing Christine with my eyes open or closed. I couldn't believe she was gone. I teared up as I thought about what had happened, the unfairness of life sometimes.

'You want to talk about the investigation? My thoughts so far? Little things I learned today? Or give it a rest for the night?' Sampson asked me as we floated peacefully on our backs. 'Talk? Or quiet time?'

'Talk, I guess. I can't think about anything else except Christine. I can't think straight. Say whatever you're thinking. Something bothering you in particular?'

'Little thing, but maybe it's important.'

I didn't say anything. I just let him go on.

'What puzzles me is the first newspaper stories.' Sampson paused and then continued. 'Busby says he didn't talk to anybody the first night. Not a single person, he claims. You didn't either. Story was in the morning edition, though.'

'It's a small island, John. I told you that and you've seen it yourself.'

But Sampson kept at it, and I began to think that maybe there was something in it.

'Listen, Alex, only you, Patrick Busby, and whoever took Christine knew. *He* called it in to the paper. The kidnapper did it himself. I talked to the girl at the paper who got the call. She wouldn't say anything yesterday, but she finally told me late today. She thought it was just a concerned citizen calling. I think somebody's playing with your head, Alex. Somebody's running a nasty game on you.'

We have her.

A game? What kind of nasty game? Who were the players? Was one of them the Weasel? Was it possible that he was still here in Bermuda?

Chapter Forty-Eight

I couldn't sleep back at the hotel. I still couldn't concentrate or focus and it was incredibly frustrating. It was as if I were losing my mind.

A *game*? No, this wasn't a game. This was shock and horror. This was a living nightmare beyond anything I had ever experienced. Who could have done this to Christine? Why? Who was the Weasel?

Every time I closed my eyes, tried to sleep, I could see Christine's face, see her waving goodbye that final time on the Middle Road, see her walking through the hotel gardens with flowers in her hair.

I could hear Christine's voice all through the night – and then it was morning again. My guilt over what had happened to her had doubled, tripled.

Sampson and I continued to canvass Middle Road, Harbour Road, South Road. Every person we spoke to in the police and military believed that Christine didn't simply disappear on the island. Sampson and I heard the same song and dance every day for a week. No one – shopkeepers, taxi or bus drivers – had seen her in Hamilton or St George, so it was possible that she'd never arrived in either town that afternoon.

No one, not one witness remembered seeing her moped on the Middle or Harbour Roads, so maybe she never even got that far.

Most disturbing of all was that there hadn't been any further communication to me about her since the e-mail on the night she'd disappeared. The e-mail address was fake. Whoever had contacted me was a skillful hacker able to conceal their identity. The words I'd seen that night were always on my mind.

She's safe for now.

We have her.

Who was 'we'? And why wasn't there any further contact? What did they want from me? Did they know that they were driving me insane? Was that what they wanted to do? Did the 'Weasel' represent more killers than one? Suddenly that made a lot of sense to me.

Sampson returned to Washington on Sunday, and he took Nana and the kids with him. They didn't want to leave without me, but it was time for them to go. I couldn't make myself leave Bermuda yet. It would have felt as if I were abandoning Christine.

On Sunday night, Patrick Busby showed up at the Belmont Hotel around nine. He asked me to ride with him out past Southampton, about a six-mile drive that he said would take us twenty minutes or more. Bermudians measure distance in a straight line, but all the roads run in wiggles and half-circles, so it always takes longer to travel than you would think.

'What is it, Patrick? What's out in Southampton?' I asked as we rode along Middle Road. My heart was in my throat. He was scaring me with his silence.

'We haven't found Ms Johnson. However, a man may have witnessed the abduction. I want you to hear his story. You decide for yourself. You're the big city detective, not me. You can ask whatever questions you like. Off the record, of course.'

The man's name was Perri Graham, and he was staying in a room at the Port Royal Golf Club. We met him at his tiny apartment in the staff quarters. He was tall and painfully thin, with a longish goatee. He clearly wasn't happy to see Inspector Busby or me on his doorstep.

Busby had already told me that Graham was originally from London, and now worked as a porter and maintenance man at the semiprivate golf club. He had also lived in New York City and Miami, and had a criminal record for selling crack in New York.

'I already told him everything I saw.' Perri Graham spoke defensively as soon as he opened the front door of his room and saw the two of us standing there. 'Go away. Let me be. Why would I hold back anything or—'

I cut him off. 'My name is Alex Cross. I'm a homicide

detective from Washington. The woman you saw was my fiancée, Mr Graham. May we come in and talk? This will only take a few minutes.'

He shook his head back and forth in frustration.

'I'll tell you what I know. *Again,*' he finally said, relenting. 'Yeah, come in. Only because you called me Mr Graham.'

'That's all I want. I'm not here to bother you about anything else.'

Busby and I walked inside the room, which was little more than an alcove. The tile floors and all the furniture were strewn with wrinkled clothes, mostly underwear.

'A woman I know lives in Hamilton,' he said in a weary voice. 'I went to visit her this Tuesday past. We drank too much wine. Stayed the evening, you know how it is. I got up somehow. Had to be at the club by noon, but I knew I'd be late and get docked some of my pay. Don't have a car or nothing, so I hitched a ride from Hamilton, out South Shore Road. Walked along near Paget, I suppose. Damn hot afternoon, I remember. I went down to the water, cool off if I could.

'I came back up over a knobbly hill, and I witnessed an accident on the roadway. It was maybe a quarter of a mile down the big hill there. You know it?'

I nodded and held my breath as I listened to him. I remembered the stifling heat of that afternoon, everything about it. I could still see Christine driving off on a shiny blue moped, waving and smiling. The memory of her smile, which had always brought me such joy, now put a tight knot in my stomach.

'I saw a white van hit a woman riding a blue moped. I can't be sure, but it almost looked like the van hit her on purpose. Driver, he jumped out of the van right away and helped her up. She didn't look like she was hurt badly. Then he helped her inside the van. Put the moped inside, too. Then he drove off. I thought he was taking her to the hospital. Thought nothing else of it.'

'You sure she wasn't badly hurt?' I asked.

'Not sure. But she got right up. She was able to stand all right.'

There was a catch in my voice when I spoke again. 'And you didn't tell anybody about the accident, not even when you saw the news stories?'

The man shook his head. 'Didn't see no stories. Don't bother with the local news much. Just small-time shit and worthless gossip. But then my girl, she keep talking about it. I didn't want to go to the police, but she made me do it, made me talk to this inspector here.'

'You know what kind of van it was?' I asked.

'White van. I think it was maybe a rented one. Clean and new.'

'License plate?'

Graham shook his head. 'Don't have no idea.'

'What did the man in the van look like?' I asked him. 'Any little thing you remember is helpful, Mr Graham. You've already helped a lot.'

He shrugged, but I could tell that he was trying to think back to that afternoon. 'Nothing special about him. Not as tall as you, but tall. Look like anybody else. Just a black man, like any other.'

Chapter Forty-Nine

In a small apartment in a suburb of Washington called Mount Rainier, Detective Patsy Hampton lay in bed, restlessly flipping through the pages of the *Post*. She couldn't sleep, but there was nothing unusual about that. She often had trouble sleeping, ever since she'd been a little girl in Harrisburg, Pennsylvania. Her mother said she must have a guilty conscience about something.

She watched a rerun episode of *ER*, then fetched herself a Stonyfield yogurt with blueberries and logged onto America Online. She had e-mail from her father, now relocated in Delray Beach, Florida; and also from an old college roommate from the University of Richmond, whom she had never been that close to anyway.

The roommate had just heard from a mutual friend that Patsy was a hotshot police detective in Washington, and what an exciting life she must lead. The roommate wrote that she had four children and lived in a suburb of

Charlotte, North Carolina, but that she was bored with everything in her life. Patsy Hampton would have given anything to have just one child.

She wandered back to the kitchen and got a cold bottle of Evian mineral water. She was aware that her life had become ridiculous lately. She spent too much time on her job, but also too much time by herself in the apartment, especially weekends. It wasn't that she couldn't get dates – she was just turned off by men in general lately.

She still fantasized about finding someone compatible, having children. But increasingly, she thought about the depressing and maddening cycle of trying to meet someone interesting. She usually ended up with guys who were hopelessly boring *or* thirty-something jackasses who still acted like teenagers, though without the charm of youth. *Hopeless, hopeless, hopeless*, she thought as she sent off a cheery lie to her dad in Florida.

The phone rang and she glanced at her wristwatch – it was twenty past twelve.

She snatched up the receiver. 'Hampton speaking.'

'It's Chuck, Patsy. Really sorry to call so late. Is it okay? You awake?'

'Sure, no problem, Chucky Cheese. I'm up with the other vampires, yourself included, I guess.'

It was kind of late but she was glad to hear from Chuck Hufstedler, who was a computer geek at the FBI in Washington. The two of them helped each other out sometimes, and she'd recently talked to him about the unsolved murders in Washington, especially the Jane Does. Chuck told her that he was also in contact with Alex Cross, but Cross had trouble of his own right now. His fiancée had been kidnapped, and Patsy Hampton wondered if it had anything to do with the murders in Southeast.

'I'm wide awake, Chuck. What's up? What's on your big mind?'

He started with a disclaimer, which said volumes about Chuck's incredibly low self-esteem. 'Maybe nothing, but maybe something a little interesting on those killings in Southeast, and particularly the two young girls in Shaw. This really comes out of left field, though.'

The FBI computer expert had her attention. 'That's where this killer lives, Chuck, *deep* left field. Tell me what you have. I'm wide awake and listening. Talk to me, Chucky Cheese.'

Chuck hemmed and hawed. He was always like that, which was too bad because he was basically a real nice guy. 'You know anything about RPGs, Patsy?' he asked.

'I know that it stands for role-playing games and, let's see, there's a popular one called Dragon and Dungeons, Dungeons and Dragons – whatever the order.'

'It's Dungeons and Dragons, or Advanced Dungeons and Dragons. Confession time, kiddo. I occasionally play an RPG myself – it's called Millennium's End. I play a couple of hours a day usually. More on weekends.'

'New to me. Go on, Chuck.' God, she thought, cyberspace confessions in the middle of the night.

'Very popular game, even with so-called adults. The characters in Millennium's End work for Black Eagle Security. It's a private organization of troubleshooters who hire themselves out for investigative services around the world. The characters are all good guys, crusaders for good.'

'Uh-huh, Chuck. Say six Hail Marys, now make an Act of Contrition, then get to the damn point. It *is* around twelve thirty, pal.'

'Right, I am heartily sorry, and deeply embarrassed, too. Anyway, there's a chatroom online that I visited. It's called the Gamesters' Chatroom and it's on AOL. As I speak, there's a fascinating discussion going on about a new kind of game. It's more an *anti*-game, though. All the role-playing games I know are about *good* characters trying to conquer chaos and evil. The game under discussion has a couple of evil characters *trying to overcome good*. Specifically, Patsy, one of the characters is attacking and murdering women in the Southeast part of DC. Lots of lurid detail on the murders. These aren't the actual players – but they know about the game. The game itself is probably protected. Thought you should know. It's called The Four Horsemen.'

Patsy Hampton was definitely wide awake now. 'I'm on it. Thanks, Chuck. Let's keep this between the two of us for the moment, okay?'

'Yeah. Okay.'

It took her a couple of minutes to log onto AOL, then get into the Gamesters' Chatroom. She didn't participate, just read what the others had to say. This was interesting. She wondered if she had just stumbled onto her first big break in the Jane Doe case.

The others in the room were named Viper, Landlocked, J-Boy, and Lancelot. They chattered on and on about the hottest fantasy games and cutting-edge magazines, which nearly succeeded in putting her to sleep. The Four Horsemen came up twice, but only in passing as a point of reference. Lancelot was the one who mentioned it. Chuck was right, these probably weren't the actual players, but they knew about the game somehow.

The fantasy nerds were starting to wear really thin with her by quarter past one. Finally, out of frustration, she typed out a message for the little shitheels. She called herself Sappho.

> I CAME IN LATE, BUT HORSEMEN SOUNDS LIKE A NEAT KIND OF REVOLUTIONARY GAME TO ME, LANCELOT. PRETTY AUDACIOUS STUFF, NO?

Lancelot shot back:

> NOT REALLY, *SAPPO*. THERE'S A LOT OF IT GOING AROUND LATELY. ANTI-HEROES, SICKOS. ESPECIALLY IN VAMPIRE GAME CIRCLES.

Hampton typed:

HAVEN'T I READ ABOUT MURDERS LIKE THESE IN THE NEWSPAPERS? BY THE WAY, IT'S SAPPHO, LIKE THE POET.

Lancelot replied:

YEAH, BUT LOTS OF RPGS USE CURRENT EVENTS. NO BIGGIE, REALLY. *SAPPO*.

Hampton grinned. He was an obnoxious little nerd, but she had him – for the moment anyway. And she needed him. How much did he know about The Four Horsemen? Could he be a player? She tried to peek at Lancelot's profile, but he had restricted access to it.

YOU'RE FUNNY. ARE YOU A PLAYER, LAUGHA-LOT, OR JUST AN ART CRITIC?

I DON'T LIKE THE BASIC CONCEPT OF HORSE-MEN. ANYWAY, IT'S A PRIVATE GAME. *STRICTLY* PRIVATE. ENCRYPTED.

YOU KNOW ANY OF THE PLAYERS? I MIGHT LIKE TO TRY IT OUT MYSELF?

There was no response to the question. Patsy thought maybe she'd pushed too hard, too fast. Damn! She should have known better. Damn, damn! Come back, Lancelot. Earth to Lancelot.

I REALLY WOULD LIKE TO PLAY THE FOUR
HORSEMEN. BUT I'M COOL ABOUT IT. NO BIG-
GIE. LANCELOT?

Patsy Hampton waited, and then Lancelot left the
chatroom. Lancelot was gone. And so was her connection to somebody playing a so-called fantasy game
about committing gruesome murders in Washington –
murders that had really happened.

Chapter Fifty

I returned to Washington during the first week of
September and I had never felt stranger in my own
skin. I'd gone to Bermuda with my family and Christine,
and now I was coming home without her. Whoever had
taken Christine had contacted me only once. I missed
her nearly every moment of every day, and I felt so far
away from where she might still be.

It was an unusually cool and windy day when I got back
to the city. It almost seemed as if summer had suddenly
changed to the middle of fall. I felt as if I had been away
much longer than I had. I had been in a fog of unreality in
Bermuda, and I felt nearly the same once I was back in DC
again. I'd never felt this badly before, never so lost, so
unhinged, battered.

I wondered if Christine and I were part of a madman's
elaborate fantasy, what profilers call an escalating fantasy.
If so, who was this madman and where was he now? Was

it the Weasel? Did I know him from some time in my past? The heartless, spineless bastard had communicated *we have her*. And that was it. No further word. Now only silence, which was deafening.

I took a taxi from the airport and I thought of Frank Odenkirk, who had innocently taken a cab one night in August and wound up murdered on Alabama Avenue near Dupont Park. I hadn't thought about the Odenkirk case during the past weeks. I rarely had a thought about the Jane Doe murders while in Bermuda, but I was guiltily reminded of them now. Others had suffered painful losses because of the killer.

I wondered if any progress had been made, and who in the department was running the case, at least the Odenkirk part of it. On the other hand, I didn't feel that I could work on any of the other unsolved murders right now. I felt my place was still in Bermuda, and strange as it sounds, I nearly headed back as soon as I landed.

Then I could see our house up ahead on Fifth Street. Something strange was happening – there was a crowd.

Chapter Fifty-One

Lots of people were standing on the porch and they were also clustered in front of the house when the cab arrived. Cars were parked and double-parked all along the street.

I recognized Aunt Tia. My sister-in-law Cilla and Nana were on the porch with the kids. Sampson was there with a girlfriend named Millie, a lawyer from the Justice Department.

Some of them waved as I pulled up, so I knew everything was all right. This wasn't more trouble. But what was it?

I saw my niece, Naomi, and her husband, Seth Taylor, who had come all the way from Durham, North Carolina. Jerome Thurman, Rakeem Powell, and Shawn Moore were standing on the front lawn.

'Hey, Alex, good to see you.' Jerome's deep voice boomed out at me as I passed near him on my way to the porch. I finally set down my travel bag and started shaking hands, giving out hugs, receiving back pats and kisses from all sides.

'We're all here for you,' Naomi said. She came over to me and hugged me tightly. 'We love you so much. But we'll go away if you don't want us here now.'

'No, no. I'm glad you're here, Scootchie,' I said, and kissed my niece on both cheeks. A while back, she'd been abducted in Durham, North Carolina. I had been there for her and so had Sampson. 'It's good that you and Seth are here. It's good to see everybody. You can't imagine how good it is.'

I hugged relatives and friends, my grandmother, my two beautiful kids, and I realized again how lucky I was to have so many good people in my life. Two teachers from the Sojourner Truth School had also come to the house. They were friends of Christine, and they started to cry when they came up to me. They wanted to know if any progress had been made and if there was anything they could do.

I told them that we had a witness to the abduction, and that we were more hopeful than ever. The teachers were buoyed by the news, which wasn't nearly as good as I made it sound. Nothing more had come of the one eyewitness account of the abduction. No one else had seen the white van that took away Christine.

Jannie finally cornered me in the backyard around nine o'clock. I had just spent half an hour with Damon in the basement, talking man to man, shadowboxing a little bit.

Damon had told me that he was having trouble remembering Christine's face, exactly what she looked like. I told him that it happened with people and that it was all right. We finally shared a long hug.

Jannie had patiently waited to talk with me.

'My turn?' she asked.

'Absolutely, sweetheart.'

Jannie then took my hand and pulled me forward into the house. She quietly led me upstairs, not to her room, but to mine.

'If you get lonely in here tonight, you can come to my room. I *mean* it,' she said as she gently shut the door on the two of us. She is so wise and has such a good perspective on so many things. Both she and Damon are such good kids. Nana says they have 'sound character', and it is building nicely. So far, so good.

'Thank you, sweetie. I will come to your room if it gets bad in here. You're very thoughtful and nice.'

'I am, Daddy. You helped me be this way, and I'm glad of it. Now I have a real serious question for you, Daddy. It's hard, but I have to ask anyway.'

'You go ahead,' I told her, feeling uncomfortable under her serious little gaze. I wasn't completely focused, and I didn't know if I could handle one of Jannie's hard questions. 'I'm listening, sweetheart,' I said. 'Fire away.'

She had let go of my hand, but she took it up again, held my big hand tightly in both her small ones.

'Daddy, is Christine dead?' she asked me. 'You can tell me if she is. Please tell the truth, though. I want to know.'

I almost lost it, sitting on the edge of the bed with Jannie. I'm sure she had no idea how much her question hurt, or how hard it was to answer.

I was hanging over the edge of a dark abyss, just about gone, but I pulled myself together and took a deep breath. Then I tried to answer my little girl's honest question as best I could.

'I don't know yet,' I told her. 'That's the truth. We're still hoping to find her, sweetie. We found one witness so far.'

'But she might be dead, Daddy?'

'Let me tell you the best thing I know about dying,' I said to Jannie. 'The very best thing that I know. Just about the only thing, in fact.'

'You go away, and then you're with Jesus forever,' Jannie said. The way she spoke, though, I wasn't sure if she really believed what she was saying. It sounded like one of Nana's 'gospel truths', or maybe she'd heard it in church.

'Yes, that can be a great comfort to know, baby. But I was thinking of something else. Maybe it's the same thing, but a different way to look at it.'

Her intense little eyes held mine, wouldn't let go. 'You can tell me, Daddy. Please. I want to hear it. I'm very interested in this.'

'It's not a bad thing, but it helps me whenever somebody dies. Think about this. We come into life so easily – from somewhere, from the universe, from God. Why should it be any harder when we leave life? We come – from a good place. We leave – and go to a good place. Does that make any sense to you, Jannie?'

She nodded and continued to stare deeply into my eyes. 'I understand,' she whispered. 'It's like it's in balance.'

She paused a second, thinking it over, then she spoke. 'But Daddy, Christine isn't dead. I just know it. She *isn't* dead. She hasn't gone to that good place yet. So don't you lose hope.'

Chapter Fifty-Two

The character and traits of Death were so much like his own, Shafer was thinking as he sped south along I-95. Death wasn't brilliant, but he was always thorough, and he always won in the end.

As the black Jag raced past the exits for various small towns, Shafer wondered if he wanted to be caught now, if he needed to be unmasked, finally to show his true face to everyone. Boo Cassady believed that he was hiding, even from her, but more importantly, from himself. Maybe she was right. Maybe he did want Lucy and the kids to see who he really was. And the police. But especially the uptight and sanctimonious staff at the embassy.

I am Death – it's who I am. I am a multiple killer – it's who I am. I am not Geoffrey Shafer anymore, maybe I never was. But if I was, it was a long, long time ago.

Shafer had always had a natural mean streak, a vengeful, nasty way. He remembered it from his early years traveling with his family through Europe, then Asia, and finally back to England. His father had been in the military and was always a real tough guy around the house. He struck Shafer and his two brothers often, but not nearly as often as he hit their mother, who died of a fall when Shafer was twelve.

Shafer was large as a boy, and he was one 'tough hombre', a real bully. Other boys feared him, even his brothers, Charles and George, who believed that Geoff was capable of anything. He was.

Nothing in his early days prepared him for being the man who finally emerged once he joined MI6. It was there that he learned he was capable of killing another human being – and Shafer found that he loved it. He had discovered his calling, his true passion in life. He was the ultimate tough guy; Shafer was Death.

He continued traveling south on the interstate highway. Because it was late, traffic was light, mostly high-speeding trucks headed toward Florida, he supposed.

He mentally composed a message to the other fantasy game players.

DEATH GOES TO FREDERICKSBURG, MARYLAND, TONIGHT. A GOOD-LOOKING THIRTY-SEVEN-YEAR-OLD WOMAN LIVES THERE WITH HER MIRROR-IMAGE FIFTEEN-YEAR-OLD DAUGHTER. THE WOMAN IS DIVORCED, A SMALL-TOWN LAWYER, A PROSECUTOR. THE DAUGHTER IS AN HONOR STUDENT AND

A FOOTBALL CHEERLEADER. THE TWO WOMEN WILL BE SLEEPING. DEATH HAS COME TO MARYLAND, BECAUSE WASHINGTON IS TOO DANGEROUS NOW. (YES, I TOOK YOUR WARNING TO HEART.) THE DC POLICE ARE SEARCHING FOR THE JANE DOE MURDERER. A WELL-THOUGHT-OF DETECTIVE NAMED PATSY HAMPTON IS ON THE CASE, AND DETECTIVE CROSS HAS RETURNED FROM BERMUDA. IT WILL BE INTERESTING TO SEE IF HIS CHARACTER HAS CHANGED IN ANY WAY. CHARACTER IS EVERYTHING, DON'T YOU AGREE?

I CAN SEE THE CAHILL HOUSE UP AHEAD. I CAN PICTURE BOTH OF THE LOVELY CAHILL WOMEN. THEY LIVE IN A FOUR-BEDROOM RANCH HOUSE. THE SUBURBAN STREET IS VIRTUALLY SILENT AT 1:00 A.M. NO ONE COULD POSSIBLY CONNECT THESE TWO MURDERS TO THE JANE DOES. I WISH YOU COULD BE HERE WITH ME. I WISH YOU COULD FEEL EXACTLY AS I DO.

Chapter Fifty-Three

S hafer parked his Jag on the shadowy street and felt strangely alone and afraid. He was actually scaring himself. The things he thought and did. No one had a twisted mind like his – no one thought like this. No one ever had such outlandish fantasies and ideas, and then acted them out.

The other players had complicated and very sick fantasy lives of course, but they paled in comparison to his. Famine claimed authorship of a series of psycho-sexual murders in Thailand and the Philippines. War liked to think of himself as the uncrowned head of the group – he claimed to influence the adventures of the others. Conqueror was confined to a wheelchair and made up stories about using his infirmity to lure his prey close enough for the kill.

Shafer doubted that any of them actually had the guts to play the game out in the real world.

But perhaps they would surprise him. Maybe each of the others was living out a homicidal fantasy. Wouldn't that be something?

The Cahill women thought they were so perfectly safe inside the ranch house, less than fifty yards away. He could see a green wooden fence surrounding a stone terrace and lap swimming pool in the back. The house had sliding doors to the pool area. So many possibilities for him to consider.

He might enter the house and murder both of them execution-style. Then he would drive directly back to Washington.

The local police and FBI would be totally baffled. The story might even make network TV. Two women shot and murdered while they slept, a mother and daughter whom everybody in their small town admired. No motive for the horrific crime, no suspects.

He was hard now, and it was difficult to walk. That was comical to Shafer, his absurd hard-on waddle. His mouth formed a smile.

A dog was barking, two or three houses down the street – a small, wimpy dog, from the sound of it. Then a larger dog joined in. They sensed danger, didn't they? They knew he was here.

Shafer knelt beside a maple tree at the edge of the backyard. He stood in shadows while the moon cast a soft white light across the yard.

He slid the twenty-sided dice out of his pocket, then let them fall on the tufts of lawn. *Here we go. Playing by the* rules. *Let's see what the night has to offer.* He counted the numerals on the special dice. They appeared fuzzy in the dark.

Shafer couldn't believe what he saw. He wanted to howl like the crazed and bewildered neighborhood dogs.

The dice count was seven.

Death had to leave! This instant! There could be no murders tonight!

No! He wouldn't do it! To hell with the dice. He wouldn't leave. He couldn't. He was losing all impulse control, wasn't he? Well, so be it. Alea jacta est, he remembered from his schoolboy Latin class. Julius Caesar before he crossed the Rubicon – *the die is cast.*

This was a monumental night. For the first time, he was breaking the rules. He was changing the game forever.

He needed to kill someone and the urge was everything to him.

He hurried to the house before he changed his mind. He was nervous. Adrenaline punched through his system. He used his glass cutter at first, but then just smashed in a small window with a gloved hand.

Once inside he moved quickly down the darkened hallway. He was sweating – so unlike him. He entered Deirdre's bedroom. She was asleep, despite the breaking of the glass. Her bare arms were thrown up over her head, the surrender position.

'Lovely,' he whispered.

She was wearing white bikini panties and a matching

bra. Her long legs were spread delicately, expectantly. In her dreams, she must have known he was coming. Shafer believed that dreams told you the truth, and you had better listen.

He was still hard and was so glad he'd chosen to disobey the rules.

'Who the hell are you?' he heard, suddenly. The voice came from behind.

Shafer whirled around.

It was Lindsay, the daughter. She wore nothing but coral-pink underwear, a brassière and briefs. He calmly raised his gun until it pointed between her eyes.

'Shhh. You don't want to know, Lindsay,' he said, in the calmest voice, not bothering to disguise his English accent. 'But I'll tell you anyway.'

He fired the gun.

Chapter Fifty-Four

For the second time in my life I understood what it felt like to be a victim of a terrible crime rather than the detective investigating it. I was disconnected and out of it. I needed to be doing something positive on a case, or get back to volunteer work at St Anthony's, anything to take my mind off what had happened.

I had to be busy, but I knew I'd lost my ability to concentrate, something that had come so naturally to me. I came across a pair of shocking murders in Maryland that bothered me for some unspecified reason. I didn't follow up on them. I should have.

I wasn't myself; I was lost. I still spent endless hours thinking about Christine, remembering everything about our time together, seeing her face wherever I went.

Sampson tried to push me. He *did* push me. He and I made the rounds of the streets of Southeast. We put the word out that we were looking for a purple-and-blue cab, possibly a gypsy. We canvassed door-to-door in the Shaw neighborhood where Tori Glover and Marion Cardinal had been found. Often we were still going at ten or eleven at night.

I didn't care. I couldn't sleep anyway.

Sampson cared. He was my friend.

'You're supposed to be working the Odenkirk case, right? I'm not supposed to be working at all. The Jefe would be livid. I kind of like that,' Sampson said as we trudged along S Street late one evening. Sampson had lived in this neighborhood for years. He knew all the local hangarounds.

'Jamal, you know anything I should know?' he called out to a goateed youth sitting in shadows on a graystone stoop.

'Don't know nothin'. Just relaxin' my mind. Catchin' a cool night breeze. How 'bout yourself?'

Sampson turned back to me. 'Damn crackrunners working these streets everywhere you look nowadays. Real good place to commit a murder and never get caught. You talk to the police in Bermuda lately?'

I nodded and my eyes stared at a fixed point up ahead. 'Patrick Busby said the story of Christine's disappearance is off the front pages. I don't know if that's good or bad. It's probably bad.'

Sampson agreed. 'Takes the pressure off them. You going back down there?'

'Not right away. But yeah, I have to go back. I have to find out what happened.'

He looked me in the eye. 'Are you here with me right now? Are you *here*, sugar?'

'Yeah, I'm here. Most of the time. I'm functioning okay.' I pointed up at a nearby red-brick building. 'That place would have a view of the front entryway into the girl's building. Any of those windows. Let's get back to work.'

Sampson nodded. 'I'm here as long as you want to be.'

There was something about pounding the streets that appealed to me that night. We talked to everyone in the building that we could find at home, about half the apartments. Nobody had seen a purple-and-blue cab on the street; nobody had seen Tori or Marion either. Or so they said.

'You see any connections anywhere?' I asked as we came down the steep stairs of a fourth-floor walk-up. 'What do you see? What the hell am I missing?'

'Not a thing, Alex. Nothing to miss. Weasel didn't leave a clue. Never does.'

We got back down to the entrance, and met up with an elderly man carrying three clear plastic bags of groceries from the Stop & Shop.

'We're homicide detectives,' I said to him. 'Two young girls were murdered across the street.'

The man nodded. 'Tori and Marion. I know 'em. You want to know 'bout that fella watchin' the buildin'? He was sittin' there most the night. Inside a slick fancy black car,' he said. 'Mercedes, I think. You think maybe he's the killer?'

Chapter Fifty-Five

'I been away awhile, y'see. Visitin' wit' my two old bat sisters in North Carolina for a week of good memories, home-cooked food,' the elderly man said as we climbed to the fourth floor. 'That was why I was missed during the earlier time through here by your detectives.'

This was old-school police work, I was thinking as I climbed stairs – the kind too many detectives try to avoid. The man's name was DeWitt Luke and he was retired from Bell Atlantic, the huge phone company that services most of the Northeast. He was the fifty-third interview I'd had so far in Shaw.

'Saw him sittin' there around two in the mornin'. Didn't think much of it at first. Probably waitin' for somebody. Seemed to be mindin' his own business. He was still there at three, though. Sittin' in his car. Seemed kinda strange to me.' He paused for a long moment as if trying to remember.

'Then what happened?' I prompted the man.

'Fell asleep. But I got up to pee around four thirty. He was *still* in that shiny black car. So I watched him closer this time. He was watchin' the other side of the street. Like some kind of damn spy or somethin'. Couldn't tell what he was lookin' at, but he was studyin' somethin' real hard over there. I thought he might be the police. 'Cept his car was too nice.'

'You got that right,' Sampson said, and barked out a laugh. 'No Mercedes in my garage.'

'I pulled up a card-table chair behind the darkened window in my apartment. Made sure there were no lights on, so he couldn't see me. By now he'd caught my attention some. Remember the old movie *Rear Window*? I tried to figure out why he might be down there sittin', waitin'. Jealous lover, jealous husband, maybe some kinda night stalker. But he wasn't botherin' anybody so far as I could see.'

I spoke again. 'You never got a better look than that? Man sitting in the car?'

'Around the time I got up to pee, he got out of the car. Opened the door, but the inside light didn't come on. That struck me strange, it bein' such a nice car and all. Fueled my mind even more. I squinted my eyes, get a better look.' Another long pause.

'And?'

'He was tall, a blond gentleman. White fella. We don't get too many of them around here at night, or even in the daytime, for that matter.'

Chapter Fifty-Six

Detective Patsy Hampton's investigation of the Jane Doe murders was starting to show forward movement and positive results. She thought she might have something good in the works. She had confidence in her ability to solve the murders. She knew from experience that she was smarter than everybody else.

It helped to have Chief Pittman and all the department's resources on her side. She had spent the past day and a half with Chuck Hufstedler at the FBI building. She knew she was using Chuck a little, but he didn't seem to mind. He was lonely, and she *did* like his company. She and Chuck were still sitting around at three thirty in the afternoon when Lancelot entered the Gamesters' Chatroom again. *Laughalot*, she remembered.

'He couldn't resist, could he?' Hampton said to Hufstedler. 'Gotcha, you fantasy freak.'

Hufstedler looked at her, his thick black eyebrows

arched. 'Three thirty in the afternoon, Patsy. What does that say? Tell you what it says to me. *Maybe* he's playing from work. But I bet our Lancelot is a school kid.'

'Or he's somebody who likes to play with school kids.' She offered a thought that upset her even as she uttered the words.

This time, she didn't try to make contact with Lancelot. She and Chuck just listened in on a stultifying discussion of several role-playing games. In the meantime, he was trying to trace Lancelot.

'He's pretty good at this, a real hacker. He's built a lot of security into his system. Hopefully, we'll get to him anyway.'

'I have confidence in you, Cheeseman.'

Lancelot stayed in the chatroom past four thirty. By then it was all over. Chuck had his name and address: Michael Ormson, Hutchins Place in Foxhall.

At a few minutes before five, two dark-blue vans pulled up in front of the Ormson house on the Georgetown Reservoir. Five agents in blue FBI windbreakers and Detective Patsy Hampton surrounded the large Tudor-style house with an acre or two of front and back lawn and majestic views.

Senior FBI Agent Brigid Dwyer and Hampton proceeded to the front door and found it unlocked. With weapons drawn they quietly entered the house and discovered Lancelot in the den.

He looked to be around thirteen years old. A baby geek. He was sitting at a computer in his shorts and black socks.

'Hey, what the heck is going on? Hey! What are you doing in my house? I didn't do anything wrong. Who are you guys?' Michael Ormson asked in a high-pitched, peeved, but quivering voice.

He was skinny. His face was covered with acne. His back and shoulders had a rash that looked like eczema. Chuck Hufstedler had been right on target. Lancelot was a teenage geek playing with his fancy computer after school. He wasn't the Weasel, though. This boy *couldn't* be the Weasel.

'Are you Michael Ormson?' Patsy Hampton asked the boy. She had lowered her weapon but hadn't holstered it.

The young boy dropped his head and looked ready to weep. 'Oh God, oh God,' he moaned. 'Yes, I'm Michael Ormson. Who are you guys? Are you going to tell my parents?'

Chapter Fifty-Seven

Michael's father and mother were immediately contacted at their jobs at Georgetown University
Hospital and the US Naval Observatory, respectively. The
Ormsons were currently separated, but they both made it
to Foxhall in less than ten minutes, even with rush-hour
traffic starting to build. The other two Ormson children,
Laura and Anne Marie, had come home from high
school.

Patsy Hampton convinced the parents to let her talk to
their son at the house. She told the Ormsons that they
could be present, and could interrupt, and even stop the
interview at any time they wished. Otherwise, she and
Agent Dwyer would have to take Michael to FBI head-
quarters for the interview.

The Ormsons, Mark and Cindy, agreed to let Michael
talk. They were clearly frightened, especially of the FBI
personnel, but they seemed to trust Detective Hampton.

Most people did, she knew. She was pretty, sincere, and had a disarming smile that she used when she needed to.

'I'm interested in the game called The Four Horsemen,' Hampton said to the boy. 'That's the only reason I'm here, Michael. I need your help.'

The teenager dropped his chin to his chest again, and shook his head back and forth. Hampton watched the nervous boy, and decided to take a chance with him. She had a hunch that she wanted to play.

'Michael, whatever you think you've done wrong, it's nothing to us. It's *nothing*. We don't care what you've done on your computer. This isn't about you or your family *or* your hacking. There have been some terrible murders in Washington, and there might be a connection to this game called The Four Horsemen. Please help us, Michael. You're the only one who can. You're the only one.'

Mark Ormson, who was a radiologist at Georgetown University Hospital, leaned forward on the black leather couch in the den. He looked more frightened now than when he'd gotten home. 'I'm beginning to think I better get a lawyer,' he said.

Patsy Hampton shook her head and smiled kindly at both parents. 'This is not about your son, Mr and Mrs Ormson. He's not in any trouble with us, I assure you.'

She turned back to the teenager. '*Michael*, what do you know about The Four Horsemen? We know you're not one of the players. We know it's a very private game.'

The boy finally looked up. She could tell that he liked her, and maybe trusted her some. 'Hardly anything, ma'am. I don't know too much.'

Hampton nodded. 'This is very important to us, Michael. Someone is killing people in the Southeast part of Washington – *for real*, Michael. This is not a fantasy game. I think you can help us. You can save others from getting murdered.'

Michael dropped his head again. He had hardly looked at his mother and father since they arrived. 'I'm good with computers. You probably already figured that out.'

Detective Hampton kept nodding, giving the boy positive reinforcement. 'We know you are, Michael. We had trouble tracing you here. You're *very* good with computers. My friend Chuck Hufstedler at the FBI was really impressed. When all this is over, you can see where he works. You'll like him, and you'll love his equipment.'

Michael finally smiled, showing off large protruding teeth with braces. 'Back at the beginning of summer, probably late in June, this guy came into the Gamesters' Chatroom – where you found me.'

Patsy Hampton tried to hold eye contact with the boy. She needed him badly; she had a feeling that this was a big break, the biggest so far.

Michael continued to speak softly. 'He sort of, like, he took over the conversation. Actually, he was pretty much a control freak about it. He kept putting down Highlander, D&D, Millennium, all the hot games that are out now. Wouldn't let anybody else get a word in. Almost seemed like he was high on something.

'He kept hinting about this completely different game he played called The Four Horsemen. It was like he didn't want to tell us about it, but then he would give out bits and pieces anyway, but not much. He wouldn't shut up.

'He said the characters in D&D, Dune, Condottiere were predictable and boring – which I must admit, they are sometimes. Then he said some of the characters in his game were *chaotic evil* instead of *lawful good*. He said they weren't fake heroes like in most RPGs; his characters were more like people in real life. They were basically selfish, didn't really care about others, didn't follow society's rules. He said Horsemen was the ultimate fantasy game. That was all he would tell us about The Four Horsemen, but it was enough. I mean, you could see it was a game for total psychos.'

'What was his call name?' Agent Dwyer asked Michael.

'Call name, or his real name?' Michael asked, and offered up a sly, superior smile.

Agent Dwyer and Hampton looked at each other. *Call name, or real name?* They turned back to Michael.

'I traced him, just like you tracked me. I got through his encryptions. I know his name, and I know where he lives. Even where he works. It's Shafer – Geoffrey Shafer. He works at the British Embassy on Massachusetts Avenue. He's some kind of information analyst there, according to the embassy's web site. He's forty-four years old.'

Michael Ormson looked sheepishly around the room. He finally made eye contact with his parents, who looked relieved. Then he looked back at Hampton. 'Is any of that stuff helpful to you? Did I help?'

'Yes, you did, Laughalot.'

Chapter Fifty-Eight

G eoffrey Shafer had vowed he would not get high on
pharmaceuticals tonight. He'd also decided he was
going to keep his fantasies under control, under wraps.
He understood precisely what the psycho-babbling profilers on the murder cases would be thinking: his fantasy
life was escalating and he was approaching a rage state.
And the profilers would be exactly right – which was why
he was playing it cool for a while.

He was a skillful cook, skilled at a lot of things, actually.
He sometimes put together elaborate meals for his family,
and even large dinner parties with friends. When he
cooked, he liked to have the family with him in the
kitchen; he loved an audience, even them.

'Tonight, we'll be eating classic Thai,' he announced to
Lucy and the children as they watched him work. He was
feeling a little hyper, and reminded himself not to let
things get out of hand at home. Maybe he ought to take

some Valium before he began to cook. All he'd taken was a little Xanax.

'What sets Thai food apart from other Southeast Asian cuisines are the explicit rules for proportions of ingredients, especially seasonings,' he said as he prepared a centerpiece of carved vegetables.

'Thai is a distinctive cuisine, blending Chinese, Indonesian, Indian, Portuguese, Malaysian. Bet you didn't know that, Tricia and Erica.'

The little girls laughed – confused – so much like their mother.

He put jasmine blossoms in Lucy's hair. Then a blossom each for the twins. He tried the same with Robert but his son pulled away, laughing.

'Nothing too hot tonight, darling,' Lucy said. 'The children.'

'The children, of course, dear. Speaking of hot, the real heat comes from capsaicin, which is stored in the ribs of these chili peppers. Capsaicin is an irritant and burns whatever it touches, even skin, so it's wise to wear gloves. I'm not wearing gloves, of course, because I'm not wise. Also I'm a little crazy.' He laughed. Everyone did. But Lucy looked worried.

Shafer served the dinner himself, without any help, and he announced each dish, both in Thai and English. '*Plaa meuk yaang*, or roast squid. Delicious.' '*Mieng kum*, leaf rolls with "treasurers". Yummy.' '*Plaa yaang kaeng phet*, grilled snapper with red curry sauce. Delectable. A *little* hot, though. Hmmm.'

He watched them tentatively sample each course, and as they tasted the snapper, tears began to run down their faces. Erica began to choke.

'Daddy, it's too hot!' Robert gulped, and complained.

Shafer smiled and nodded blithely. He loved this, the flowing tears, his perfect family in pain. He savored each exquisite moment of their suffering. He'd managed to turn the dinner into a tantalizing game, after all.

At quarter to nine he kissed Lucy and started off on his 'constitutional', as he called his nightly disappearing act. He went out to the Jag and drove a few blocks to Phelps Place, which was a quiet street without many lights.

He took liberal doses of Thorazine *and* Librium, then injected himself with Toradol. He took another Xanax.

Then he went to his doctor's.

Chapter Fifty-Nine

Shafer didn't like the arrogant, asshole doormen at Boo Cassady's building and they didn't like him, he decided.

Who needed their approval anyway? They were shiftless, lazy incompetents, incapable of doing much more than holding open doors and offering up ingratiating smiles to fat-cat tenants.

'I'm here to see Dr Cassady,' Shafer announced to the familiar black wanker with *Mal* jauntily pinned on his lapel. It was probably there so that he wouldn't forget his own name.

'Right,' said Mal.

'Isn't that – right, *sir*?'

'Right, sir. I'll ring up Dr Cassady. Wait right here, sir.'

He could hear Boo through the doorman's staticky phone receiver. She had no doubt left explicit instructions that he be let up immediately. She certainly knew he was coming – they'd talked during the car ride from his house.

'You can go up now, sir,' the doorman finally said.

'I'm fucking her brains out, Mal,' Shafer said. He waltzed to the elevators with a grin. 'You watch that door now. Don't let anyone take it.'

Boo was in the hallway to meet him when the elevator cruised to a stop on ten. She was wearing at least five thousand dollars' worth of clothes from Escada. She had a great body, but she looked like a bullfighter or a marching band leader in the gaudy outfit. No wonder her first two husbands had divorced her. The second husband had been a therapist and treating MD. Still, she was a good, steady mistress who gave much better than she got. More importantly, she was able to get him Thorazine, Librium, Ativan, Xanax. Most of the drugs were samples from drug company representatives. Her husband had left them behind when they'd split. The amount of 'samples' left by the drug reps amazed Shafer, but she assured him it was common. She had other friends who were doctors and she hinted to Shafer that they helped her out for an occasional fuck. She could get all the drugs he needed.

Shafer wanted to take her right there in the hall and knew Boo would like the spontaneity and the passion that was so clearly missing from her life. Not tonight, though. He had more basic needs: the drugs.

'You don't look too happy to see me, Geoff,' she complained. She took his face in her manicured hands. Christ, her long, varnished red nails scared him. 'What happened, darling? Something's happened. Tell Boo what it is.'

Shafer took her in his arms and held her tightly against his chest. She had large soft breasts, great legs, too. He stroked her frosted-blonde hair and nuzzled her with his chin. He loved the power he had over her – his god-damned shrink.

'I don't want to talk about it just yet. I'm here with you. I feel much better already.'

'What happened, darling? What's wrong? You have to share these things with me.'

So he made up a story on the spot, acted it out. Nothing to it. 'Lucy claims she knows about us. God, she was paranoid *before* I started to see you. Lucy always threatens to ruin my life. She says she'll leave me. Sue for what fucking little I have. Her father will have me fired, then blackball me with the government *and* the private sector, which he's perfectly capable of doing. The worst thing is she's poisoning the children, turning them against me. They use the same belittling phrases that she does: "colossal failure", "under-achiever", "get a real job, Daddy". Some days I wonder whether it isn't true.'

Boo kissed him lightly on the forehead. 'No, no, darling. You're well thought of at the embassy. I know you're a loving dad. You just have a bitchy, mean-spirited, spoiled-rotten wife who gets you down on yourself. Don't let her do it.'

He knew what she wanted to hear next, so he told her. 'Well, I won't have a bitchy wife for much longer. I swear to God I won't, Boo. I love you dearly, and I'm going to leave Lucy soon.'

He looked at her heavily made-up face and watched as tears formed and ruined her look. 'I love you, Geoff,' she whispered, and Shafer smiled as if he were pleased to hear it.

God, he was so good at this.

Lies.

Fantasies.

Role-playing games.

He unbuttoned the front of her mauve silk blouse, fondled her, then carried her inside to the sofa.

'This is my idea of therapy,' he whispered hotly in Boo's ear. 'This is all the therapy I need.'

Chapter Sixty

I had been up since before five that morning. Finally, I called Inspector Patrick Busby in Bermuda. I wanted to call every day, sometimes more than once, but I stopped myself.

It would only make things worse, strain my relations with the local police, and signal that I didn't trust them to handle the investigation properly.

'Patrick, it's Alex Cross calling from Washington. Did I catch you at a good time? Can you talk for a moment now?' I asked. I always tried to sound as upbeat as possible.

I wasn't, of course. I had been pacing the house, and already had breakfast with Nana. Then I'd waited impatiently until eight thirty to call Busby at the station house in Hamilton. He was an efficient man, and I knew he was there every morning by eight.

I could picture the thin, wiry policeman as we talked on

the phone. I could see the tidy cubicle office where he worked. And superimposed over everything, I could still see Christine on her moped waving goodbye to me on that perfectly sunny afternoon.

'I have a few things for you from my contact at Interpol,' I said. I told him about an abduction of a woman in Jamaica earlier in the summer, and another in Barbados; both were similar, though not identical, to Christine's disappearance. I didn't think they were connected really, but I wanted to give him something, anything.

Patrick Busby was a thoughtful and patient man; he remained silent until I had finished talking before asking his usual quota of logical questions. I had observed that he was flawed as an interrogator because he was so polite. But at least he hadn't given up.

'I assume that neither abduction was ever solved, Alex. How about the women who were taken? Were they found?'

'No, neither woman was seen again. Not a sign of them. They're still missing.'

He sighed into the phone receiver. 'I hope your news is helpful in some way, Alex. I'll certainly call the other islands and check into it further. Anything else from Interpol or the FBI?'

I wanted to keep him on the line, the lifeline, as I now thought of it. 'A few far-flung possibilities in the Far East, Bangkok, the Philippines, Malaysia. Women abducted and murdered – all Jane Does. To be honest, nothing too promising at this point.'

I imagined him pursing his thin lips and nodding thoughtfully. 'I understand, Alex. Please keep giving me whatever you get from your sources. It's difficult for us to get help outside this small island. My calls for assistance frequently aren't returned. I sincerely wish that I had some good news for you on my end, but I'm afraid I don't.

'Other than Perri Graham, no one saw the man with the van. No one seems to have seen Christine Johnson in Hamilton or St George either. It's truly a baffling mystery. I don't believe that she ever got to Hamilton. It's frustrating for us, too. My prayers are with you and your wonderful family and, of course, John Sampson.'

I thanked Patrick Busby and hung up the phone. Slowly I went upstairs and dressed for work.

I still had nothing really substantial on the murder of Frank Odenkirk, and the Jefe was contacting me daily on e-mail. I certainly knew how the Odenkirk family felt. The media heat about the homicide had died down, though, as it often does. Unfortunately, so had the *Post* stories about the unsolved murders in Southeast.

While I was taking a hot shower, I thought about DeWitt Luke and the mysterious 'watcher' on S Street. What was the man in the Mercedes doing out there so long? Did he have some connection to the murders of Tori Glover and Marion Cardinal? None of this was making complete sense to me. That was the truly maddening thing about the Jane Doe murders and the Weasel. He wasn't like other repeat killers. He wasn't a criminal genius like Gary Soneji, but he was effective. *He got the job done, didn't he?*

I needed to think more about why someone had been lurking outside Tori Glover's apartment. Was he a private detective? A stalker? Or was he actually the murderer? One possibility hit me. Maybe the man in the car was an accomplice of the killer. Two of them working together. I'd seen that before in North Carolina.

I turned up the water, made it hotter. I thought it would help me to concentrate better. Steam out the cobwebs in my brain. Bring me back from the dead.

Nana finally banged on the pipes from downstairs in the kitchen. 'Get down here and go to work, Alex. You're using all my hot water up,' she yelled above the noise of the shower.

'Last time I looked, my name was on the water and gas bills,' I shouted back.

'It's still my hot water. Always was, always will be,' Nana replied.

Chapter Sixty-One

Every day, every night, I was out on the streets of Southeast, working harder than ever, but with nothing much to show for it. I continued to search for the mysterious purple-and-blue cab, and for the late-model black Mercedes DeWitt Luke had seen on S Street.

Sometimes I felt as if I were sleepwalking, but I kept at it, sleepwalking as fast as I could. Everything about the investigation seemed a longshot at best. I received tips and leads every day that had to be followed up; none of them went anywhere, though.

I got home at a little past seven that night but, tired as I was, I still let the kids drag me downstairs for their boxing lesson. Damon was showing me a lot of hand speed, and also some pretty good footwork and power for his age. He always had good spirit, and I was confident that he wouldn't abuse his burgeoning boxing skills at school.

Jannie was more a student of boxing, though she seemed to recognize the value of being able to defend herself. She was quick at mastering techniques, seeing connections, even if her heart wasn't completely into the sport. She preferred to torture her brother and me with her taunts and wit.

'Alex, telephone,' Nana called down from the top of the cellar stairs. I looked at my watch, saw it was twenty to eight.

'Practice your footwork,' I told the kids. Then I trudged up the steep stone stairs. 'Who is it?'

'Wouldn't say who it was,' Nana said as I got up to the kitchen. She was making shrimp and corn fritters and the room was also filled with the glorious smells of honey-baked apples and gingerbread. It was a late dinner for us – Nana had waited until I got home.

I picked up the phone on the kitchen counter. 'Alex Cross.'

'I know who you are, Detective Cross.'

A chill went right through me, and my hands shook.

'There's a pay phone outside the Budget Drugs on Fourth Street. *She's safe for now. We have her.* But hurry. Hurry! Maybe she's on the pay phone right now. I'm serious. *Hurry!'*

Chapter Sixty-Two

I exploded out the back kitchen door without saying a word to Nana or the kids. I didn't have time to explain where I was going, or why. Besides, I didn't really know exactly what was happening. Had I just spoken to the Weasel?

I'm serious. Hurry! Maybe she's on the pay phone right now!

I sprinted across Fifth Street, then down a side alley and over to Fourth. I dashed another four blocks south toward the Anacostia River. People on the streets watched me running. I was like a tornado suddenly roaring through Southeast.

I could see the metal frame of a pay phone from more than a block away as I approached Budget Drugs. A young girl was leaning against the graffiti-covered wall of the drugstore, talking on the phone.

I pulled out my detective's shield as I raced the final block toward her.

The phone gets a lot of use. Some people don't have phones in their homes in the neighborhood.

'Police. I'm a homicide detective. *Get off the phone!*' I told the girl, who looked nineteen or so. She stared at me as if she couldn't care less that a DC policeman was trying to commandeer the phone.

'I'm *using* this phone, mister. Don't care who you are. You can wait your turn like everybody else.' She turned away from me. 'Probably just calling your honey.'

I yanked the receiver away from her, disconnected her call.

'The fuck you think you are!' the girl shouted at me, her face screwed in anger. 'I was talking. The fuck you thinking.'

'I'm thinking you better get out of my face. This is a life-and-death situation. Get away from this phone. *Now! Get out of here!*' I could see she had no intention of leaving. 'There's been a kidnapping!' I was yelling like a madman.

She finally backed away. She was afraid that I was really crazy, and maybe I was.

I stood there with my hand on the phone receiver, trembling, waiting for the call to come in. I was winded. Sweat covered my body.

I stared up and down Fourth Street.

Nothing obvious or suspicious. I didn't see a purple-and-blue cab parked anywhere. No one watching me. Somebody definitely knew who I was. They had contacted me at the Belmont Hotel; they had called me at home.

I could still hear the words echoing loudly inside my head.

She's safe for now.

We have her.

Those were the words sent to me six weeks before in Bermuda. I hadn't heard anything from the sender until now.

My heart was pounding, sounding as if it were amplified in my ears. Adrenaline was rushing like powerful rivers through my blood stream. I couldn't stand this. The caller had stressed that I *hurry*.

A young man approached the pay phone. He stared at my hand on the receiver. 'Wuzup, man? I need to use the phone. The phone? You hear me?'

'Police business.' I gave him a hard stare. 'Take a walk, please. Go!'

'Don't look like no police business to me,' he mumbled.

The man moved away, looking over his shoulder as he retreated down Fourth, frowning, but not stopping to argue with me.

The caller liked to be completely in control, I was thinking as I stood there helpless in front of the busy drugstore. He'd made me wait this long since the Bermuda call, possibly to demonstrate his power. Now he was doing it again. What did he really want, though? Why had he taken Christine? *We* have her, he'd said, and repeated the very same words when he called my house. Was there really a *we*? What kind of group did he represent? What did they want?

I stood at the pay phone for ten minutes, fifteen, twenty. I felt as if I were going mad, but I would stay there all night if I had to. I began to wonder if this was the right phone, but I knew it was. He had been crystal clear, calm, in control.

For the first time in weeks I allowed myself to truly hope that Christine might be alive. I imagined her face, deep brown eyes that showed so much love, and warmth. Maybe, just maybe, I would be allowed to talk to her.

I let my anger build toward the unknown caller. But then I cut it off, shut down my emotions, and waited with a cool head.

People came and went, in and out of the drugstore. A few wanted to use the phone. They took one look at me, then moved on, looked for another phone.

At five minutes to nine, the phone rang. I lifted the receiver instantly.

'This is Alex Cross,' I said.

'Yes, I know who you are. That's already been established. Here's what you should do. *Back all the way off. Just back away. Before you lose everything you care about.* It can happen so easily. In a snap. You're smart enough to understand that, aren't you?'

Then the caller hung up. The line was dead.

I banged the phone with the receiver. I cursed loudly. The manager from the drugstore had come outside and was staring at me.

'I'm going to call the police,' he said. 'That's a public phone.' I didn't bother to tell him I was the police.

Chapter Sixty-Three

Was it the Weasel who had called? Was I dealing with one killer, or more than one?

If only I had some idea who the caller was and who he meant by *we*. The message scared me just as much as the first one had, maybe even more; but it also gave me hope about Christine still being alive.

With hope came a jolting surge of pain. If only they would put Christine on the phone. I needed to hear her voice.

What did they want? *Back all the way off.* Back off from what?

The Odenkirk murder case? The Jane Does? Perhaps even Christine's disappearance? Was Interpol or the FBI getting close to something that had scared them? We weren't close to anything that could solve any of the cases, and I knew timing was critical.

Early Wednesday morning, Sampson and I drove to

Eckington. A woman over there knew where a purple-and-blue cab was garaged. We'd followed up a dozen or so leads like this already, but it didn't matter. Every lead had to be investigated, every single one.

'Cab owner's name is Arthur Marshall,' I told Sampson as we walked from my car toward a red-brick garden apartment that had seen better days. 'Trouble is, Arthur Marshall seems to be a false identity. Landlady has him working at a Target store. According to Target, he doesn't. Never worked at any Target store. Hasn't been seen around for a while, according to the landlady.'

'Maybe we spooked him,' Sampson said.

'I hope not, but you may be right.'

I glanced around at the lower-middle-class neighborhood as we walked. Overhead, the sky was a bright-blue canvas, nearly empty of clouds. The street was packed with one- and two-story homes. Bright orange fliers were sticking out from the mailboxes. Every window was a possible lookout for the Weasel. *Back away*, he had warned. I couldn't. Not after what he'd done. I knew that I was taking a risk though.

He probably spotted us canvassing the streets. If he was responsible for the Jane Doe murders, he had been working undetected for a long while. He was skillful, good at killing, at not getting caught.

The landlady told us what she knew about Arthur Marshall, which wasn't much more than the information she needed to rent him a one-bedroom apartment and the attached garage. She gave us a set of keys for the place and said we could go look for ourselves.

The second house was similar to the landlady's except that it was painted Easter-egg blue. Sampson and I entered the garage first.

The purple-and-blue cab was there.

Arthur Marshall had told the landlady that he owned the cab and operated it as a part-time job. That was a possibility, but it seemed unlikely. The Weasel was close. I could feel it now. Had he known we would find the cab? Probably. Now what? What came next? What was his plan? His fantasy?

'I'm going to have to figure out how to get some techies in here,' I told Sampson. 'There has to be something in the cab, or maybe upstairs in the apartment. Hair, fibers, prints.'

'Hopefully no damn body parts,' Sampson said, and grimaced. It was typical cop humor, and so automatic that I didn't give it a second thought. 'Body parts are always popping up in these cases, Alex. I don't want to see it. I like feet attached to ankles, heads attached to necks, even if all the parts happen to be dead.'

Sampson searched around the front seat of the cab, with latex-gloved hands. 'Papers in here. Candy and gum wrappers, too. Why not call in a favor from Kyle Craig? Get the FBI boys over here.'

'Actually, I talked to Kyle last night,' I said. 'The Bureau's been involved for some time. He'll help out if we say the word.'

Sampson tossed me a pair of gloves and I examined

the cab's backseat. I saw what could be bloodstains in the fabric of the seat cushion. The stains would be easy enough to check out.

John and I finally climbed upstairs into the apartment above the garage. It was dusty, grimy, without much furniture. Eerie and unpleasant on the eyes. It didn't look as if anyone lived there, but if someone did, they were really weird. The landlady had said as much.

The kitchen was mostly empty. An expensive juicer was the only personal indulgence. Not a low-end model – *expensive*. I took out my handkerchief and opened the refrigerator. There was nothing in it but bottled water and some aging fruit. The fruit was rotting and I hated to think of what else we might find here in the apartment.

'Health nut,' Sampson offered.

'Nut anyway,' I said. 'There's a sense of animal fear in here. He gets very tense, excited, when he comes to this place.'

'Yeah,' Sampson said, 'I know the feeling.'

We entered the bedroom, which had a small cot, a couple of stuffed chairs, nothing else. The sense of fear was here, too.

I opened the closet door and what I saw stopped me dead. There was a pair of khaki pants, a blue chambray shirt, a blue blazer – and something else.

'John, come here,' I called. 'John!'

'Oh, shit. Do I have to? Not more bodies.'

'Just come here. It's him. This is the Weasel's place. I'm sure of it. It's worse than a body.'

I opened the closet door wider and let Sampson see what I'd found there.

'Shit,' he groaned. '*Goddamn* it, Alex.'

Someone had put up pictures. Half-a-dozen black-and-white photographs were taped to the wall of the closet. It wasn't a killer's shrine. It was meant to be found.

There were pictures of Nana, Damon, Jannie, me, and Christine. Christine almost seemed to be smiling at the camera, that incredible smile of hers, those big welcoming eyes.

The pictures had been taken in Bermuda. Whoever had rented this apartment had taken them. Finally, I had something to link Christine's abduction to the murders in Washington. I knew who had taken her.

Back off.

Before you lose everything.

I sensed fear again. It was my own.

Chapter Sixty-Four

Patsy Hampton had decided that she wasn't ready to confide in Chief George Pittman just yet. She didn't want the Jefe interfering or crowding her. Also, she flat out didn't trust or like the bastard.

She still hadn't made up her mind what to do about Alex Cross. Cross was a complication. The more she checked him out, the better he looked. He seemed to be a very good, dedicated detective and she felt bad about keeping Chuck Hufstedler's information away from him. Chuck had been Cross's source first, but she'd used the techie's crush on her to gain an advantage. She didn't like herself for doing that.

She drove her Jeep to the British Embassy late that afternoon. She had Geoffrey Shafer under limited surveillance – hers. She could get more teams, but that would mean going to Pittman now, and she didn't want anyone to know what she had. She didn't want to be crowded.

She had done preliminary homework on Shafer. He was in the Security Service, which meant he was British Intelligence, operating outside England. Most likely he was a spy working out of the embassy on Massachusetts Avenue. His reputation was okay, good, actually. His current assignment supposedly had to do with the British Government's human-rights program, which meant the assignment was bullshit. He lived in Kalorama, and that was a high-rent district he shouldn't be able to afford on his salary. So, who the hell was this Shafer chap?

Hampton sat parked in her vehicle outside the embassy on California Street. She smoked a Marlboro Light and started to think things through. She really ought to talk to Cross about where he was with his investigation. Did he know anything that could help? Maybe he was onto Shafer? It was almost criminal for her not to contact Cross and share what she'd gotten from Chucky Cheese.

Pittman's dislike for Cross was well-known; he considered him competition. She didn't know Cross that well, but he got too many headlines. Still, she wished she knew what Cross had in his files, and especially if Geoffrey Shafer might have appeared on Cross's radar.

There was too much fricking noise on the fricking street near the British Embassy. Workers were doing construction on the Turkish Chancery across California Street. Hampton already had a headache – her life was one big headache – and she wished they would stop pounding and hammering and battering and sawing. For some reason or other, there was a crowd of people swarming all over the National Mosque today.

At a few minutes past five Shafer got into his Jaguar in a parking lot outside the glass-walled Rotunda.

She'd seen him twice before and he was in very good shape. Attractive, too, though not a physical type she herself responded to. Shafer sure didn't hang around long after the workday ended. Hampton figured he either had some place to go or he really hated his day job. Possibly both.

She stayed a safe distance behind the black Jag, following it along crowded Massachusetts Avenue. Shafer didn't seem to be heading home, and he wasn't going to Southeast either.

Where are we going tonight? she wondered as she tailed him. *And what does it have to do with The Four Horsemen? What game are you really playing? What are your fantasies?*

Are you a bad man, a murderer, Geoffrey? You don't look like it, Blondie. Such a nice spiffy car for a scumbag killer.

Chapter Sixty-Five

After work, Geoffrey Shafer joined the clogged artery of rush-hour traffic inching along Massachusetts. Turning out of the embassy he had spotted the black Jeep behind him.

The tail was still there as he drove down Massachusetts Avenue.

Who was in the Jeep? One of the other players? DC police? Detective Alex Cross? They had found the garage in Eckington. Now they'd found him. It had to be the bloody police.

He watched the black Jeep as it trailed four cars behind him. There was only one person inside and it looked like a woman. Could it possibly be Lucy? Had she discovered the truth about him? God, had she finally figured out who and what he was?

He picked up his mobile phone and made a call home. Lucy picked up after a couple of rings.

'Darling, I'm coming home, after all. There's a bit of a

lull at the office. We can order in or something – unless you and the children already have plans.'

She blathered on in the usual maddening way. She and the twins had been going to see a movie, *Antz*, but they'd rather stay at home with him. They could order from Pizza Hut. It would be fun for a change.

'Yes, what fun,' Shafer said, and cringed at the thought. Pizza Hut served indigestible cardboard drenched with very bad tomato soup. He hung up, then took a couple of Vicodin and a Xanax. He thought he could feel cracks slowly opening up in his skull.

He made a dangerous U-turn on Massachusetts Avenue and headed toward home. He passed the Jeep going in the opposite direction and was tempted to wave. A woman driver. Now, who was she?

The pizza got to the house at around seven and Shafer opened an expensive bottle of Cabernet Sauvignon. He washed down another Xanax with the wine in the downstairs bathroom. Felt a little confused, fuzzy around the edges. That was all right, he supposed.

Jesus Christ, he couldn't stand being with his family, though; he felt as if he were going to crawl out of his skin. Ever since he'd been a boy in England he'd had a repetitive fantasy that he was actually a reptile and could shed his own skin. He'd had the dream long before he'd read any Kafka; he *still* had the disturbing dream.

He rolled three dice in his hand as he sipped his wine, played the game at the dinner table. If the number seventeen came up, he would murder them all tonight.

He swore he would do it. First the twins, then Robert, and finally Lucy.

She kept prattling on and on about her day. He smiled blithely as she told him about her shopping trip to Bloomingdale's and Bath & Body Works and Bruno Cipriani at the mall. He considered the supreme irony of taking truckloads of antidepressants, and being more depressed. Jesus, he was cycling down again. How low could he go?

'Come, seventeen,' he finally said aloud.

'What, darling?' Lucy suddenly asked. 'Did you just say something?'

'He's already playing tonight's game,' said Robert, and snickered. 'Right, Daddy? It's your fantasy game. Am I right?'

'Right, son,' Shafer replied, thinking, *Christ, I am mad!*

He let the dice gently fall on the dining table, though. He would kill them – if their number came up. The dice rolled over and over, finally banking off the greasy pizza box.

'Daddy and his games,' Lucy said, and laughed. Erica and Tricia laughed. Robert laughed.

Six, five, one, he counted. *Damn, damn.*

'Are the two of us going to play tonight?' Robert asked.

Shafer forced a smile. 'Not tonight, Rob Boy. I'd like to, but I can't. I have to go out again.'

Chapter Sixty-Six

This was getting very interesting. Patsy Hampton watched Shafer leave the large and expensive house in Kalorama around eight thirty. He was off on another of his nightly jaunts. The guy was a regular vampire.

She knew that Cross and his friends called the killer the Weasel, and it certainly fit Shafer. There was something uncomfortable about him, something bent.

She followed the black Jag, but he didn't head toward Southeast, which disappointed her. He drove to a trendy supermarket, Sutton on the Run, which was just off Dupont Circle. Hampton knew the pricey store and called it Why Pay Less.

He parked the sports car illegally, then jogged inside. *Diplomatic immunity.* That pissed her the hell off. What a weasel he was, real Euro-trash.

While he was in the market, Hampton made a command decision. She was pretty sure she was going to talk to Alex Cross. She had thought a lot about it, the pros and cons. Now she figured that she might be endangering lives in Southeast by not sharing at least some of what she knew. If someone died, she wouldn't be able to bear it. Besides, Cross would have gotten the information if she hadn't interceded with Chuck Hufstedler.

Shafer shuffled back out of Sutton on the Run and glanced around crowded Dupont Circle. He had a small bag of overpriced groceries clutched in one arm. Groceries for whom, though? He didn't look in the direction of her Jeep, which was just peeking around the corner.

She followed the black Jag at a safe distance in the light traffic. He got on Connecticut Avenue. She didn't think he'd spotted her, though he was an MI6 man, so she needed to be careful.

Shafer wasn't far from Embassy Row. He wouldn't be going back to work now, would he? Why the groceries if he was headed to the embassy?

The Jaguar eventually turned into the underground garage of a prewar building in Woodley Park. THE FARRAGUT was engraved on a brass sign in front.

Patsy Hampton waited a few minutes, then she pulled into the garage behind the attendant in a small kiosk and identified herself.

'The Jag that came in before me, ever see it here before?' she asked.

The man nodded. He was around her age and she could tell he wanted to impress her if he could. 'Sure. I don't know him to talk to, though. Comes here to visit a lady on ten. Dr Elizabeth Cassady. She's a shrink. I assume he's a patient. He's got a funny look in his eyes,' the attendant said, 'but so do most people.'

'How about me?' Hampton asked.

'Nah. Well, maybe a little,' the attendant said, and grinned.

Shafer stayed upstairs with Dr Cassady for nearly two hours. Then he came down and went straight back to the house in Kalorama.

Patsy Hampton followed him, then watched the house for another half-hour. She thought that Shafer was probably in for the night. She drove to a nearby diner but didn't go inside right away. She picked up her mobile phone before she had too many second thoughts. She knew Cross's street, and got the phone number through information. Was it too late to call? Screw it, she was going through with this.

She was surprised when the phone was picked up on the first ring. She heard a pleasant male voice. Nice. Strong.

'Hello. Alex Cross.'

She almost hung up on him. Interesting that he'd intimidated her for a moment. 'This is Detective Patsy Hampton. I've been doing some work on the Jane Does. I've been following a man who is a suspect. I think we should talk.'

'Where are you, Patsy?' Cross said, without hesitation. 'I'll come to you. Just tell me where.'

'I'm at the City Limits diner on Connecticut Avenue.'

'I'm on my way,' said Cross.

Chapter Sixty-Seven

I wasn't totally surprised that Pittman had assigned someone to the Jane Does. Especially after Zach Taylor's article in the *Washington Post*. I was interested in any leads Detective Hampton might have turned up.

I had seen Patsy Hampton around and she obviously knew who I was. She was supposed to be on a fast track; she was a smart and effective senior homicide detective, though from what I'd heard, she was also a lone wolf. She didn't have any friends in the department, as far as I knew.

She was much prettier than I remembered. She was in very trim, athletic shape, probably early thirties, short blonde hair, piercing blue eyes that cut through the diner haze.

She'd put on bright-red lipstick for our meeting, or maybe she wore it all the time. I wondered what was on her mind and what her motives were. I didn't think I could trust her.

'You or me first?' Detective Hampton asked, after we'd ordered coffee. We were seated at a table in the City Limits diner, near a window looking out on Connecticut Avenue.

'I'm afraid I don't know what this is about,' I told her.

She sipped her coffee and gave me a look over the cup's rim. She was a strong-willed, confident person. Her eyes told me that much.

'You really didn't know someone else was working on the Jane Does?'

I shook my head. 'Pittman said that the cases were closed. I took him at his word. He suspended some good detectives for working the cases after hours.'

'There's a lot of seriously nasty crap going on in the department. So what's new though,' she said as she set down her cup. She gave a deep sigh. 'I thought I could deal with it by myself. Now I'm not so sure.'

'Pittman assigned you to the Jane Does? Personally?'

She nodded, then her blue eyes narrowed. 'He assigned me to the Glover and Cardinal murders, and any others I wanted to look into. Gave me free rein.'

'And you say you have something?'

'Maybe. I've got a possible suspect. He's involved in a role-playing game that features victims being murdered, mostly in Southeast. It's all after-the-fact stuff, so he could have read the news stories and then fantasized about them. He works at the British Embassy.'

This was a new piece of information, and it surprised me. 'How far have you gone with this?'

'Not to Pittman, if that's what you mean. I've done a little discreet checking on the suspect. Trouble is, he seems to be a solid citizen. Very good at his job – supposedly. At least that's the official word from the embassy. Nice family in Kalorama. I've been watching Shafer a little, hoping I'd get lucky. His first name is Geoffrey.'

I knew she was supposed to be a little bit of a loose cannon, and that she didn't suffer fools gladly. 'You're out here alone tonight?' I asked her.

Hampton shrugged. 'That's how I usually operate. Partners slow me down. Chief Pittman knows how I like to work. He gave me the green light. All green, all day long.'

I knew that she was waiting for me to give her something – if I had anything. I decided to play along. 'We found a cab that the killer apparently used in Southeast. He kept it in a garage in Eckington.'

'Anybody see the suspect in the neighborhood?' She asked the right first question.

'The landlady saw him. I'd like to show her pictures of your guy. Or you want to do it yourself?'

Her face was impassive. 'I'll do it. First thing in the morning. Anything revealing in the apartment?'

I decided to be straight with her. She'd initiated the meeting, after all. 'Photographs of me and my family covered a wall in a closet. They were taken of us in Bermuda. While we were on vacation. He was there watching us all the time.'

Hampton nodded gently. 'I heard your fiancée disappeared in Bermuda. Word gets around.'

'There were photographs of Christine too,' I said.

Her blue eyes softened. I got a quick look behind her tough façade. 'I'm really sorry about your loss.'

'I haven't given up yet,' I told her. 'Listen, I don't want any credit for solving these cases, just let me help. He called me at home last night. Somebody did. Told me to back off. I assume that he meant this investigation, but I'm not supposed to be on it. If Pittman hears about us—'

Detective Hampton interrupted me. 'Let me think about everything you've said. You know that Pittman will totally crucify me if he finds out. You have no idea. Trouble is, I don't trust him.' Hampton's gaze was intense and direct. 'Don't mention any of this to your buddies, or Sampson. You never know. Just let me sleep on it. I'll try to do the right thing. I'm not such a hardass really. Just a little weird, you know.'

'Aren't we all,' I said, and smiled. Hampton was a tough detective, but I felt okay about her. I took something out of my pocket. A beeper.

'Keep this. If you get in trouble or get another lead, you can beep me anytime. If you find something out, please let me know. I'll do the same. If Shafer's the one, I want to talk to him before we bring him in. This *is* personal for me. You can't imagine how personal.'

Hampton continued to make eye contact, studying me. She reminded me of someone I'd known a while back, another complicated woman cop named Jezzie Flanagan. 'I'll think about it. I'll let you know.'

'All right. Thanks for calling me in on this.'

She stood. 'You're not in on it yet. Like I said, I'll let you know.' Then she touched my hand. 'I really am sorry about your friend.'

Chapter Sixty-Eight

We both knew I was in, though. We'd made some kind of a deal in the City Limits diner. I just hoped I wasn't being set up by Hampton and Pittman or God knows who else.

During the next two days we talked four times. I still wasn't sure that I could trust her, but I didn't have a choice. I had to keep moving forward. She had already visited the landlady who'd rented out the apartment and garage in Eckington. The landlady hadn't recognized the pictures of Shafer. Possibly he'd worn some kind of disguise when he met with her.

If Patsy Hampton was setting me up, she was one of the best liars I'd met, and I've known some good ones. During one of the calls, she confessed that Chuck Hufstedler had been her source, and that she'd gotten him to keep the information from me. I shrugged it off. I didn't have the time or energy to be angry at either of them.

In the meantime, I spent a lot of time at home. I didn't believe the killer would come after my family, not when he already had Christine, but I couldn't tell that for sure. When I wasn't there, I made sure Sampson or somebody else was checking on the house.

On the third night after I met her, Patsy Hampton and I had a breakthrough of sorts. She actually invited me to join her on the stakeout at Shafer's town house in Kalorama Heights.

He had arrived home from work before six and remained there until past nine. He had a nice-looking ex-pat family, three children, a wife, a nanny. He lived very well. Nothing about his life or surroundings suggested he might be a killer.

'He seems to go out every night around this time,' Hampton told me as we watched him walk to a shiny black Jag parked in a graveled driveway on the side of the house.

'Creature of habit,' I said. A *weasel*.

'Creature anyway,' she said. We both smiled. The ice was breaking up a little between us. She admitted that she had checked me out thoroughly. She'd decided that Chief Pittman was the bad guy in all of this, not me.

The Jaguar pulled out of the drive and we followed Shafer to a night spot in Georgetown. He didn't seem to be aware of us. The problem was that we had to catch him doing something; we had no concrete evidence that he was our killer.

Shafer sat by himself at the bar and we watched him from the street. Did he perch by the window on purpose? I wondered. Did he know we were watching? Was he playing with us?

I had a bad feeling that he was. This was all some kind of bizarre game to him. He left the bar around a quarter to twelve and returned home just past midnight.

'Bastard.' Patsy grimaced, and shook her head. Her blonde hair was soft and had a nice bounce to it. She definitely reminded me of Jezzie Flanagan, a Secret Service agent I'd worked with on the kidnapping of two children in Georgetown.

'He's in for the night?' I asked. 'What was that all about? He leaves the house to watch the Orioles baseball game at a bar in Georgetown?'

'That's how it's been the last few nights. I think he knows we're out here.'

'He's an intelligence officer. He knows surveillance. We also know he likes to play fantasy games. At any rate, he's home for the night, so I'm going home too, Patsy. I don't like leaving my family alone too long.'

'Goodnight, Alex. Thanks for the help. We'll get him. And maybe we'll find your friend soon.'

'I hope so.'

On the drive home, I thought a little about Detective Patsy Hampton. She struck me as a lonely person, and I wondered why. She was thoughtful and interesting once you got past her tough façade. I wondered if anyone could really get through the façade though.

There was a light on in our kitchen when I rolled into the driveway. I strolled around to the back door and saw Damon and Nana, in their bathrobes at the stove. Everything seemed all right.

'Am I breaking up a pajama party?' I asked as I eased in through the back door.

'Damon has an upset stomach. I heard him in the kitchen so I came out to get in his way.'

'I'm all right. I just couldn't sleep. I saw you were still out,' he said. 'It's after midnight.'

He looked worried, and also a little sad. Damon had really liked Christine and he told me a couple of times that he was looking forward to having a mom again. He'd already begun to think of her that way. He and Jannie missed Christine a whole lot. Twice, they'd had important women taken away from them.

'I was working a little late. That's all. It's a very complicated case, Damon, but I think I'm making progress,' I said. I went to the cabinet and took out two tea bags.

'I'll make you tea,' Nana offered.

'I can do it,' I said, but she reached for the bags and I let her take them away from me. It doesn't pay to argue with Nana, especially not in her kitchen.

'You want some tea and milk, big guy?' I asked Damon.

'All right,' he said. He pronounced it *ah-yite*, as they do in the playgrounds, and probably even at the Sojourner Truth School.

'You sound like that poor excuse of an NBA point guard Alan Iverson,' Nana said to him. She didn't much like street slang, never had. She had started off as an English teacher and never lost her love of books and language. She loved Toni Morrison, Alice Walker, Maya Angelou, and also Oprah Winfrey for bringing their books to a wider audience.

'He's the fastest guard in the league, *Grandma Moses*. Shows what you know about basketball,' said Damon. 'You probably think Magic Johnson is still playing in the league. And *Wilt Chamberlain*.'

'I like Marbury with the Timberwolves, and Stoudamire with Portland, formerly with Toronto,' Nana said, and gave a little triumphant smile. '*Ah-yite?*'

Damon laughed. Nana probably knew more about NBA point guards than either of us. She could always get you if she wanted to.

We sat at the kitchen table and drank tea with milk and too much sugar, and we were mostly quiet, but it was kind of nice. I love family, always have. Everything that I am flows from that. Finally, Damon got up from the table. He went to the sink and rinsed out his cup.

'I can probably sleep now,' he reported to us. 'Give it a try anyway.'

He came back to the table and gave Nana and me a kiss before he went back upstairs to bed. 'You miss her, don't you?' he whispered against my cheek.

'Of course I miss Christine,' I said to Damon. 'All the time. Every waking minute.' I didn't make mention of the fact that I was out late because I was observing the sonofabitch who may have abducted her. Nor did I say anything about the other detective on surveillance, Patsy Hampton.

When Damon left, Nana put her hand in mine and we sat like that for a few minutes before I went up to bed.

'I miss her, too,' Nana finally said. 'I'm praying for you both, Alex.'

Chapter Sixty-Nine

The next evening, at around six, I took off early from work and went to Damon's choir practice at the Sojourner Truth School. I'd put together a good-sized file on Geoffrey Shafer, but I didn't have anything that concretely linked him to any of the murders. Neither did Patsy Hampton. Maybe he was just a fantasy-game player. Or maybe the Weasel was just being more careful since his taxi had been found.

It tore me up to go to the Truth School, but I had to go. I realized how hard it must be for Damon and Jannie to go there every day. The school brought back too many memories of Christine. It was as if I was suffocating, all the breath being squeezed out of my lungs. At the same time, I was in a cold sweat that coated the back of my neck and forehead.

A little while after the practice began, Jannie quietly reached over and took my hand. I heard her sigh softly.

We were all doing a lot more touching and emoting since Bermuda, and I don't think we have ever been closer as a family.

She and I held hands through most of the choir practice, which included the Welsh folk song 'All Through the Night'; Bach's 'My heart ever faithful, sing praises'; and a very special arrangement of the spiritual 'O Fix Me'.

I kept imagining that Christine would suddenly appear at the school, and once or twice I actually turned back toward the archway that led to her office. Of course she wasn't there, which filled me with inconsolable sadness and the deepest emptiness. I finally cleared my mind of all thought, just shut down, and let my whole self be the music, the glorious sound of the boys' voices.

After we got home from the choir practice, Patsy Hampton checked in with me from her surveillance post. It was a little past eight. Nana and the kids were putting out cold chicken, slices of pears and apples, Cheddar cheese, a salad of endive and bibb lettuce.

Shafer was still home and, of all things, a children's birthday party was going on there, Patsy reported. 'Lots of smiling kids from the neighborhood, plus a rent-a-clown called Silly Billy. Maybe we're on the wrong track here, Alex.'

'I don't think so. I think our instincts are right about him.'

I told her I would come over at around nine to keep her company; that was the time when Shafer usually left the house.

Just past eight thirty the phone in the kitchen rang again as we were digging into the cold, well-spiced, delicious chicken. Nana frowned as I picked up the phone.

I recognized the voice.

'I told you to back off, didn't I? Now you have to pay some consequences for disobeying. It's your fault! There's a pay phone at the old Monkey House at the National Zoo. The zoo closes at eight, but you can get in through the gardening-staff gate. Maybe Christine Johnson is there at the zoo waiting for you. You better get over there quick and find out. Run, Cross, run. Hurry! *We have her.*'

The caller hung up and I charged upstairs for my Glock. I called Patsy Hampton and told her I'd gotten another call, presumably from the Weasel. I'd be at the National Zoo.

'Shafer's still at his kids' birthday party,' she told me. 'Of course, he could have called from the house. I can see Silly Billy's truck from where I'm parked.'

'Keep in contact with me, Patsy. Phones and beepers. Beeper for *emergencies* only. Be careful with him.'

'Okay. I'm fine here, Alex. Silly Billy doesn't pose too much of a threat. Nothing will happen at his house. Go to the zoo, Alex. *You* be careful.'

Chapter Seventy

I was at the National Zoo by ten to nine. I was thinking that the zoo was actually pretty close to Dr Cassady's apartment at the Farragut. Was it a coincidence that I was so close to Shafer's shrink? I didn't believe in coincidences anymore.

I called Patsy Hampton before I left the car, but she didn't pick up this time. I didn't beep her – this wasn't an emergency, or not so far.

I knew the zoo from lots of visits with Damon and Jannie, but even better from when I was a boy and Nana used to bring me, and sometimes Sampson, who was nearly six foot by the time he was eleven. The main entrance to the zoo was at the corner of Connecticut and Hawthorne Avenues, but the old Monkey House was nearly a mile diagonally across the grounds from there.

No one seemed to be around, but the gardening-staff gate was unlatched – as the caller said it would be. He knew the zoo, too. More games, I kept thinking. He definitely loved to play.

As I hurried into the park, a steep horizon of trees and hills blocked out the lights from the surrounding city. There was only an occasional foot lamp for light, and it was eerie and frightening to be in there alone. Of course, I was sure I wasn't alone.

The Monkey House was farther inside the gates than I had remembered. I finally located it in the dark. It looked like an old Victorian railway station. Across a cobble-stoned circle there was a more modern structure that I knew was the Reptile House.

A sign over the twin doors of the old Monkey House read: WARNING: QUARANTINE – DO NOT ENTER! More eeriness. I tried the tall twin doors, but they were securely locked.

On the wall beside the doors I saw a faded blue-and-white sign – the international pictograph indicating there was a phone inside. *Was that the phone he wanted me to use?*

I shook the doors, which were old and wooden and rattled loudly. Inside, I could hear monkeys starting to scream and act out. First the smaller primates: spider monkeys, chimpanzees, gibbons. Then the deeper grunt of a gorilla.

I caught sight of a dim red glow across the cobble-stoned circle. Another pay phone was over there.

I hurried across the square. Checked my watch. It was two minutes past nine.

He kept me waiting the last time.

I thought about his game-playing. Was this all a role-playing game to him? How did he win? Lose?

I worried that I wasn't at the right phone. I didn't see any others, but there was always the one locked inside the old Monkey House.

Was that the phone he wanted me to use? I felt frantic and hyper. So many dangerous emotions were building up inside me.

I heard a long, sustained '*aaaaahhhh*', like the sound of a football crowd at the opening kickoff. It startled me until I realized it was the apes in the Monkey House.

Was something wrong in there? *An intruder?* Something or someone near the phone?

I waited another five minutes, and then it dragged on to ten minutes. It was driving me crazy. I almost couldn't bear it any longer, and I thought about beeping Patsy.

Then my beeper went off, and I jumped!

It was Patsy. It had to be an emergency.

I stared at the silent pay phone; I waited a half-minute or so. Then I snatched it up.

I called the beeper number and left the number of the pay phone. *I waited some more.*

Patsy didn't call me back.

Neither did the mystery caller.

I was in a sweat.

I had to make a decision now. I was caught in a very bad place. My head was starting to reel.

Suddenly the phone rang. I grabbed at it, almost dropped the receiver. My heart was pounding like a bass drum.

'We have her.'

'Where?' I yelled into the receiver.

'She's at the Farragut, of course.'

The Weasel hung up. He never said she was safe.

Chapter Seventy-One

I couldn't imagine why Christine would be at the Farragut in Washington, but he'd said she was there. Why would he do that if she wasn't? What was he doing to me? To her?

I ran toward where I thought Cathedral Avenue was located. But it was very dark in the zoo, almost pitch-black. My vision was tunneling, maybe because I was close to being in shock. I couldn't think straight.

My mind in a haze, I tripped over a dark slab of rock, went down on one knee. I cut my hands, tore my pants. Then I was up again, running through thick high bushes that grabbed and ripped at my face and arms.

Animals all around the zoo howled, moaned, bellowed insanely. They sensed something was wrong. I could make out the sounds of grizzlies and elephant seals. I realized that I had to be approaching Arctic

Circle, but I couldn't remember where it was in relation to the rest of the zoo or the city streets.

Up ahead was a high Gibraltar-like rock. I clambered up the rock to try and get my bearings.

Down below I saw a cluster of cages, shuttered gift stores and snack bars, two large veldts. I knew where I was now. I hurriedly climbed back down the rock and started to run again. Christine was at the Farragut. Would I finally find her? Could it actually be happening?

I passed African Alley, then the Cheetah Conservation Station. I came to a vast field and what looked like large haystacks scattered everywhere. I realized that they were bison. I was somewhere near the Great Plains Way.

The beeper in my pocket went off again.

Patsy! An emergency! Where was she? Why hadn't she called back at the pay-phone number I'd given her?

I was soaked in sweat and almost hyperventilating. Thank God I could finally see Cathedral Avenue, then Woodley Road up ahead.

I was a long way from where I'd parked my car, but I was close to the Farragut apartment building.

I ran another hundred yards in the dark, then climbed the stone wall separating the zoo from the city streets. There was blood smeared on my hands, and I didn't know where it had come from. The knee I'd scraped? Scratches from swinging branches? I could hear the loud wail of sirens in the near distance. Was it coming from the Farragut?

I headed there in a sprint. It was a little past ten o'clock. Over an hour and a half had already gone by since the call to my house.

The beeper was buzzing inside my shirt pocket.

Chapter Seventy-Two

Something bad had happened at the Farragut. The burping screams of approaching sirens were getting louder as I raced down Woodley. I was reeling, feeling dizzy. I couldn't focus my mind. I realized that, for one of the few times in recent years, I was close to panic.

Neither the police nor the EMS had arrived at the apartment building yet. I was going to be the first on the scene.

Two doormen and several tenants in bathrobes were clustered in front of the underground garage entrance. It couldn't be Christine. It just couldn't be. I raced across a quadrant of lawn toward them. Was the Weasel here at the Farragut?

They saw me coming and looked as frightened as I felt inside. I must have been quite a sight. I remembered that I'd fallen once or twice inside the zoo. I probably looked like a madman, maybe even like a killer. There was blood on my hands and who knew where else.

I reached for my wallet, shook it open to expose my detective's shield.

'Police. What's happened here?' I shouted. 'I'm a police detective. My name is Alex Cross.'

'Somebody has been murdered, Detective.' One of the doormen finally spoke. 'This way. Please.'

I followed the doorman down the steeply sloped concrete driveway leading into the garage.

'It's a woman,' he said. 'I'm pretty sure she's gone. I called nine-one-one.'

'Oh God,' I gasped out loud. My stomach clutched. Patsy Hampton's Jeep was tucked back in a corner space. The door of the Jeep was open and light spilled outside.

I felt terrible fear, pain, and shock as I hurried around the door. Patsy Hampton was sprawled across the front seat. I could tell she was probably dead.

We have her. That was what the message meant. Jesus God, no. They had murdered Patsy Hampton. They had told me to back off. For God's sake, no.

Her bare legs were twisted and pinned under the steering wheel. Her upper body was crumpled over, at almost a right angle. Her head was thrown back and lay partly off the seat, on the passenger's side. Her blonde hair was matted with blood. Her vacant blue eyes stared up at me.

Patsy was wearing a white knit sport shirt. There were deep lacerations around her throat. Bright-red blood was still oozing from the wound. She was naked below the waist. I didn't see any clothes anywhere.

I suspected she'd been strangled with some kind of wire, and that she'd only been dead for a few minutes. A rope or garotte had been used in some of the Jane Doe murders. The Weasel liked to use his hands, to work close to his victims, possibly to watch and feel their pain, maybe even while he was sexually assaulting them.

I saw what looked like paint chips around the deep, ugly neck wounds. Paint chips?

Something else seemed very strange to me. The Jeep's radio had been partly dislodged, but left behind. I didn't understand why the radio had been tampered with, but it didn't seem important right now.

I leaned back out of the Jeep. 'Is anyone else hurt? Have you checked?'

The doorman shook his head. 'No. I don't think so. I'll go look.'

Sirens finally screeched inside the garage. I saw red and blue lights flashing and whirling against the ceiling and walls. Some of the tenants had made it into the garage as well. Why did they have to come and gape at this terrible crime?

A very bad thought flashed in my head. I climbed out of the Jeep, grabbing Patsy's keys out of the ignition. I hurried around to the back. I pushed the release and the rear door came open. My heart was thundering again. I didn't want to look inside, but when I did, there was nothing. *Jesus, Jesus, Jesus. We have her! Was Christine here too? Where?*

I looked around the garage. Up near the entrance I spotted Geoffrey Shafer's sports car, the black Jaguar. He was there at the Farragut. Patsy must have followed him.

I ran across the garage to the Jag. I felt the hood, then the exhaust pipe. Both were still warm. The car hadn't been in the garage very long. The doors were locked. I couldn't break in. I was all too aware of the search and seizure constraints.

I stared inside the Jaguar. In the backseat, I could see dress shirts on wire hangers. The hangers were white and I thought of the chips in Detective Hampton's wounds. Had he strangled her with a hanger? Was Shafer the Weasel? Was he still in the building? What about Christine? Was she here, too?

I said a few words to the patrolmen who'd just arrived, the first on the scene after me. Then I took them with me.

The helpful doorman told me which floor Shafer's therapist's apartment was on. The number was 10D, the penthouse. Like all buildings in DC, the Farragut was restricted to a height no more than the Capitol dome.

I took the elevator with the two uniformed cops, both in their twenties, both scared shitless I'd bet. I was close to rage. I knew I had to be careful; I had to act professionally, to control my emotions somehow. If there was an arrest, there would be questions to answer, such as what I was doing here in the first place. Pittman would be on my case in a second.

I talked to the policemen on the way up, more to calm myself than anything else.

'You okay, Detective?' one of them asked me.

'I'm fine. I'm all right. The killer might still be in the building. The victim was a detective, one of our own. She was on surveillance here. The suspect has a relationship with a woman upstairs.'

The faces of both young cops tightened. It was bad enough to have seen the murdered woman in her car, but to learn that she was a policewoman, a detective on surveillance, made it worse. Now they were about to confront a cop killer.

We hurried out of the elevator to apartment 10D. I led the way and pressed the bell. I saw what appeared to be drops of blood on the hallway carpet near the door. I noticed the blood on my hands, saw the two cops staring at them.

No answer from inside the apartment, so I pounded my fist on the door. Was everyone okay in there? 'Police, open up! DC police!'

I could hear a woman shouting inside. I had my Glock out, the safety off. I was angry enough to kill Shafer. I didn't know if I could hold myself back.

The uniformed patrolmen took their pistols out of their holsters, too. After just a few seconds I was ready to kick down the door, search and seizure constraints or not. I kept seeing Patsy Hampton's face, her dead, vacant eyes, the savage wounds in her crushed throat.

Finally, the door to the apartment slowly opened.

A blonde woman was standing there. Dr Cassady, I assumed. She wore an expensive-looking light-blue suit with lots of gold buttons, but she was barefoot. She looked frightened and angry.

'What do you want?' she demanded. 'What the hell is going on here? Do you know what you've done? You've interrupted a therapy session.'

Chapter Seventy-Three

Geoffrey Shafer stepped into the doorway and stood a few feet behind the irate therapist. He was tall and imposing and very blond. *He was the Weasel, wasn't he?*

'What the hell's the problem here? Who are you, sir, and what do you want?' he asked, in a clipped English accent.

'There's been a murder,' I said. 'I'm Detective Cross.' I showed them my badge. I kept looking past Shafer and Dr Cassady, trying to spot something that would give me probable cause to come inside the apartment. There were lots of plants on the sills, hanging in windows – philodendron, azalea, English ivy. Dhurrie rugs in light pastels, overstuffed furniture.

'No. There's certainly no murderer here,' the therapist said. 'Leave this instant.'

'You should do as the lady says,' Shafer said.

Shafer didn't look like a murderer. He was dressed in a

navy suit, a white shirt, moiré tie, a pocket square. Impeccable taste. Completely unruffled and unafraid.

Then I glanced to look at his shoes. I almost couldn't believe it. The gods had finally smiled at me.

I pulled out my Glock and pointed it at Shafer. At the Weasel. I went up to him and bent on one knee. My whole body was trembling. I examined the right leg of his trousers.

'What the *hell* are you doing?' he asked, pulling away from me. 'This is completely absurd.

'I'm with the British Embassy,' Shafer then stated. 'I'll repeat, I'm with the British Embassy. You have no right to be here.'

'Officers.' I called to the two patrolmen who were still outside the door. I tried to act calm, but I wasn't. 'Come here and look. You see this?'

Both patrolmen moved closer to Shafer. They entered the living room.

'*Stay out of this apartment!*' The therapist raised her voice close to a scream.

'Remove your trousers,' I said to Shafer. 'You're under arrest.'

Shafer lifted his leg and gave a look. He saw a dark stain, Patsy Hampton's blood, smudged on the cuff of his trousers. Fear shot through his eyes and he finally lost his cool.

'You put that blood there! You did it,' he yelled at me. He pulled out an identification badge. 'I am an official at the British Embassy. I don't have to put up with this outrage. I have diplomatic immunity. I will not take off my trousers for you. Call the embassy immediately! *I demand diplomatic immunity.*'

'Get out of here now!' Dr Cassady yelled loudly. Then she pushed one of the patrolmen.

It was just what Shafer needed. He broke free, and ran back through the living room. He rushed into the first room down the hallway, slammed the door, and locked it.

The Weasel was trying to get away. It couldn't happen. I couldn't let it. I got to the door seconds behind him. 'Come out of there, Shafer! You're under arrest for the murder of Detective Patsy Hampton.'

Dr Cassady came screaming down the hall after me.

I heard the toilet flush in the bathroom. No, no, no! I reared back powerfully, and kicked in the door.

Shafer was pulling off his trousers, standing on one leg. I tackled him hard, knocked him over, then held him face down against the tile floor. He screamed curses at me, flailed his arms, bucked his lower body. I pushed his face harder into the floor.

The therapist tried to pull me off Shafer. She was scratching my face, pounding my back with her fists. It took both policemen to restrain her.

'You can't do this to me!' Shafer was yelling at the top of his voice, twisting and turning beneath me, a powerful stallion of a man.

'This is illegal. I have diplomatic immunity!'

I turned to one of the officers.

'Cuff him.'

Chapter Seventy-Four

It was a long and very sad night at the Farragut, and I didn't leave until past three. I had never lost a partner before, although I had once come close with Sampson, in North Carolina. I realized that I'd already come to think of Patsy Hampton as a partner, and a friend. At least we had the Weasel in custody.

I slept in the next morning, allowing myself the small luxury of not setting the alarm. Still, I was wide awake by seven. I'd been dreaming about Patsy Hampton, and also about Christine; different, vivid scenes with each of them, the kind of frenetic dreams where you wake up feeling as tired as when you went to bed. I said a prayer for both of them before I finally rolled out of bed. We had the Weasel. Now I had to get the truth out of him.

I slipped on a somewhat worn white satin robe. Muhammad Ali had worn it in his training camp in Manila before the Joe Frazier fight. Sampson gave it to me for my fortieth birthday. He appreciated that, while most people would use the robe as some kind of sacred exhibit in their house, I routinely wear it to breakfast.

I love the old robe, which is unusual for me since I'm not particularly into mementos and souvenirs. Maybe part of it is that I'm supposed to resemble Ali physically, or so people tell me. I might be a little better looking, but he was definitely the better man.

When I got down to the kitchen, Nana and the kids were sitting at the table watching the small portable TV she keeps there, but doesn't use very often. She prefers to read or chitchat and, of course, cook.

'Ali.' Jannie looked up at me and grinned, but then her eyes went back to the TV. 'You should watch this, Daddy.'

Nana muttered into her cup of tea, 'Your British murderer is all over the news this morning. TV and the newspaper, too. "Diplomatic Immunity May Bar Prosecution of British Embassy Suspect", "Spy Linked to Detective Slay". They already interviewed people in Union Station and on Pennsylvania Avenue. Everybody's mad as a hatter about this diplomatic immunity disgrace, as they call it. It's just terrible.'

'I'm mad. It's not right,' Damon said. 'Not if he did it. Did he, Dad? Did he do it?'

I nodded. 'He did it.' I poured milk into my coffee. I wasn't quite ready to deal with Geoffrey Shafer, or the kids, or especially the terrible, senseless murder the night before. 'Anything else on the news?'

'The Wizards kicked butt,' Damon said with a straight

face. 'Rod Strickland had a double-double.'

'*Shhhh*.' Nana gave us both a mighty look of irritation. 'CNN carried stories *from London*. The media there is already comparing this to that unfortunate nanny case in Massachusetts. They say that Geoffrey Shafer is a decorated war hero and that he claims, with good reasons, he was framed by the police. I assume that means you, Alex.'

'Yes, it does. Let's watch CNN for a few minutes,' I said. Nobody objected, so I switched the channel. A hard knot was forming in my stomach. I didn't like what I was seeing and hearing on TV.

Almost immediately, a reporter came on the screen from London. He introduced himself, and then proceeded to give a pompous thirty-second summary of the previous evening's events.

The reporter looked gravely into the camera. 'And now, in a dramatic development, we have learned that the Washington Police Department is investigating a bizarre twist. According to the American press, the senior detective who arrested Geoffrey Shafer might himself be a suspect in the murder case.'

I shook my head and frowned. 'I'm innocent,' I said, to Nana and the kids. They knew that of course.

'Until proven guilty,' said Jannie, with a little wink.

Chapter Seventy-Five

There was a loud hubbub out in front of the house and Jannie ran to the living-room window to look. She hurried back to the kitchen with wide eyes, loud-whispering, 'It's TV cameras and the newspapers outside. CNN, NBC, lots of them, like that other time with Gary Soneji. Remember?'

'Of course we remember,' said Damon. 'Nobody's retarded in this house except you.'

'Oh good Lord, Alex,' Nana said, 'don't they know decent people are eating breakfast?' She shook her head, rolled her eyes. 'The vultures are here again. Maybe I should throw some meat scraps out the front door.'

'*You* go talk to them, Jannie,' I said, and looked back at the TV. I don't know why I was feeling so cynical, but I was. My remark quieted her down for a half-second, but then she figured it was a joke. She pointed a finger at herself. 'Gotcha!'

I knew they wouldn't go away, so I finally took my mug of coffee and headed toward the front door. I walked out into a beautiful fall morning, temperature probably in the low sixties.

Leaves rustled merrily in the elm and maple trees, dappled sunshine fell on the heads of the TV crew and print journalists gathered at the edges of our front lawn.

The vultures.

'Don't be absurd and ridiculous around here,' I said, and then calmly sipped my coffee as I stared at the noisy press mob. 'Of course I didn't kill Detective Patsy Hampton, or frame anyone for her murder.'

Then I turned on my heels and walked back inside without answering a single question from any of them.

Nana and the kids were right behind the big wooden door, listening. 'That was pretty good,' Nana said, and her eyes sparkled and beamed.

I went upstairs and got dressed for work. 'Go to school. *Now!*' I called back to Jannie and Damon. 'Get straight As. Play nicely with your friends. Pay no attention to the craziness everywhere around you.'

'Yes, Daddy!'

Chapter Seventy-Six

On account of his request for diplomatic immunity, we weren't allowed to question Geoffrey Shafer about Detective Hampton's murder, or anything else. I was incredibly frustrated. We had the Weasel, and we couldn't go near him.

Investigators were lying in wait for me that morning at the station house, and I knew it was going to be a long and excruciating day. I was interviewed by Internal Affairs, then the city's chief counsel, and finally Mike Kersee from the district attorney's office.

Pay no attention to the craziness everywhere around you, I reminded myself over and over, but my own good advice wasn't working too well.

Around three o'clock, the district attorney himself showed up. Ron Coleman is a tall, slender, athletic-looking man; we had worked together many times when he was coming up in the DA's office. I had always found him to be conscientious, well-informed, and directionally committed to rationality and sanity. He'd never seemed very political, so it was a shock to almost everyone when Mayor Monroe appointed him the DA. Monroe loves to shock people though.

Coleman made an announcement. 'Mr Shafer already has an attorney, and he is one of the bright stars of our galaxy. He has retained none other than Jules Halpern. Halpern's probably the one who planted the story that you're a suspect, which you aren't, as far as I know.'

I stared at Coleman. I couldn't believe what I'd just heard. 'As far as you know? What does that mean, Ron?'

The DA shrugged. 'We're probably going to go with Cathy Fitzgibbon on our side. I think she's our best litigator. We'll back her up with Lynda Cole and maybe Daniel Weston, who are also top-notch. That's my take on it as of this morning.'

I knew all three of the prosecutors and they had good reputations, particularly Fitzgibbon. They were on the young side, but tireless, smart, dedicated, a lot like Coleman himself.

'You sound like you're preparing for a war, Ron.'

He nodded. 'As I said, Jules Halpern is Shafer's defense attorney. He rarely loses. In fact, I don't know if he's ever lost a big case like this one. He turns down all the losers, Alex.'

I looked directly into Coleman's dark eyes. 'We have Patsy Hampton's blood on the killer's clothes. We have blood in the bathroom drain, and I'll bet we'll have Shafer's fingerprints somewhere in Hampton's car before the end of the day. We may have the wire hanger he used to strangle her. Ron?'

'Yes, Alex. I know what you're going to say. I know your question. It's the same one that I have.'

'Shafer *has* diplomatic immunity. So why bring in Jules Halpern?'

'That's a very good goddamn question we both came up with. I suspect Halpern's been hired to get us to drop the charges completely.'

'We have substantial evidence. He was *washing Patsy Hampton's blood* off himself in the bathroom. There's residue in the sink.'

Coleman nodded and shrank back into his easy chair. 'I don't understand why Jules Halpern is involved. I'm sure we'll know before too long, though.'

'I'm *afraid* we'll know soon,' I said.

I decided to leave the station by the back way that night, just in case there was press lying in wait out front on Alabama Avenue. As I stepped outside, a small, balding man in a light-green suit popped out from behind the adjacent stone wall.

'That's a good way to get yourself shot,' I told him. I was only half-kidding.

'Occupational hazard,' he lisped. 'Don't shoot the messenger, Detective.'

He smiled thinly as he handed me a white letter-sized envelope. 'Alex Cross, you've hereby been served with a Summons and Complaint. Have a nice night, Detective,' he said in his sibilant whine. Then he walked away as surreptitiously as he'd appeared.

I opened the envelope and quickly scanned the letter. I groaned. Now I knew why Jules Halpern had been retained, and what we were up against.

I had been named in a civil suit for 'false arrest' and 'defamation of the character of Colonel Geoffrey Shafer'. The suit was for fifty million dollars.

Chapter Seventy-Seven

The next morning I was summoned to the District of Columbia Law Department offices downtown. This was not good, I decided. The city's chief counsel, James Dowd, and Mike Kersee from the DA's office were already ensconced in red leather club chairs.

So was Chief of Detectives Pittman, and he was putting on quite a show from his front-row seat. 'You mean to tell me that because Shafer has diplomatic immunity he can avoid criminal prosecution in criminal court? But he can traipse right into our *civil* court and get protection against false arrest and defamation?'

Kersee nodded and made clucking noises with his tongue and teeth. 'Yes, sirree-bob, that's it, exactly. Our ambassadors and their staffs enjoy the same kind of immunity in England and everywhere else around the world. No amount of political pressure will get the Brits to waive immunity. Shafer is a war hero from the Falklands.

Supposedly, he's pretty well-respected inside the Security Service, although lately he seems to have been in some trouble.'

'What kind of trouble?' I asked.

'They won't tell us.'

Pittman was still badgering the lawyers. 'What about that clown from the Baltic Embassy? The one who wiped out the sidewalk café? *He* went to trial.'

Mike Kersee shrugged. 'He was just a low-level staffer from a low-level country that we could threaten. We can't do that with England.'

'Why the hell not?' Pittman frowned and thumped his hand hard against the arm of his chair. 'England isn't worth shit anymore.'

The phone on Dowd's desk rang, and he raised his hand for quiet. 'That's probably Jules Halpern. He said he'd call at ten and he's an efficient bastard. If it is, I'll put him on the speaker box. This should be as interesting as a rectal exam with a cactus.'

Dowd picked up and exchanged pleasantries with the defense attorney for about thirty seconds. Then Halpern cut him off. 'I believe we have matters of substance to discuss. My schedule is rather tight today. I'm sure you're hard pressed as well, Mr Dowd.'

'Yes, let's get down to business,' Dowd said, raising his thick, curly black eyebrows. 'As you know, the police have a qualified privilege to arrest anyone if they have probable cause. You simply don't have a civil case, Counselor—'

Halpern interrupted Dowd before he had finished

speaking. 'Not if that person identifies himself from the outset as having diplomatic immunity, which my client did. Colonel Shafer stood in the doorway of his *therapist's* apartment waving his British Secret Service shield like a stop sign, saying that he had immunity.'

Dowd sighed loudly into the phone. 'There was blood on his trousers, Counselor. He's a murderer, Counselor, *and* a cop killer. I don't think I need to say anymore on the subject. With respect to the alleged defamation, the police also have a qualified privilege to talk to the press when a crime has been committed.'

'And I suppose that the chief of detectives' statement in front of reporters, and several hundred million others around the world, isn't slander *per se*?'

'That's correct, it isn't. There's a qualified privilege with respect to public figures such as your client.'

'My client is not a *public* figure, Mr Dowd. He is a very private individual. He is an intelligence agent. His very livelihood, if not his life, depends on his being able to work undercover.'

The chief counsel was already exasperated, possibly because Halpern's responses were so calm, and yet always delivered rapid-fire. 'All right, Mr Halpern. So why are you calling us?'

Halpern paused long enough to make Dowd curious. Then he began again. 'My client has authorized me to make a very unusual offer. I have strongly advised him against it, but he maintains his right to do so.'

Dowd looked startled. I could tell that he hadn't been

expecting any kind of deal offer. Neither had I. What was this about?

'Go ahead, Mr Halpern,' said Dowd. His eyes were wide and alert as they roamed around the room looking at us. 'I'm listening.'

'I'll bet you are, and all your esteemed colleagues as well.'

I leaned forward to hear every word.

Jules Halpern continued with the real reason for his call. 'My client wants all possibility of a civil case being brought against him waived.'

I rolled my eyes. Halpern wanted to make certain that no one could sue his client in civil court after the criminal court case was concluded. He had no doubt seen how O.J. Simpson had been set free in one court, then bankrupted in the other.

'Impossible!' said Dowd. 'There's no way in hell that will ever happen. No way.'

'Listen to me. There is a way, or I wouldn't have broached the subject. If this is done, and if he and I can be convinced of a speedy route for a criminal trial, my client will *waive diplomatic immunity*. Yes, you heard me correctly. Geoffrey Shafer wants to prove his innocence in a court of law. He insists on it, in fact.'

Dowd was shaking his head in disbelief. So was Mike Kersee. His eyes were glazed with astonishment as he glanced across the room at me.

None of us could believe what we had just heard from the defense attorney.

Geoffrey Shafer wanted to go to trial.

Book Four

Trial and Errors

Chapter Seventy-Eight

Conqueror had watched her work Kensington High Street for nearly six weeks. She became his obsession, his fantasy woman, his 'game piece'. He knew everything there was to know about her. He felt, he knew, that he was starting to act like Shafer. They all were, weren't they?

The girl's name was Noreen Anne and a long time ago, *three years* to be exact, she had traveled to London from Cork, in Ireland, with lovely dreams of being a fashion model on the world stage.

She was seventeen then, nearly five foot ten, slender, blonde, and with a face that all the boys and even older men back home told her was destined for magazine covers, or maybe even the cinema.

So what was she doing here on Kensington High Street at half past one in the morning? She wondered about it as she forced a coquettish smile and occasionally waved a hand at the leering men in slowly passing cars that made the rounds of the High Street, DeVere Gardens, Exhibition Road.

They thought she was pretty all right, just not pretty enough for British or American magazine covers, and not good enough, not classy enough to marry, or be someone's girlfriend.

Well, at least she had a plan, and she thought it was a good one. Noreen Anne had saved nearly two thousand quid since she'd begun to walk the streets. She thought she needed another three thousand or so, and then she would head back to Ireland. She'd start a small beauty shop, because she did know the secrets of beauty, and also a lot about the dreams women have.

So, in the meantime, here I am in front of Kensington Palace Hotel, she thought. *Freezing my fine butt off.*

'Excuse me, miss,' she heard, and turned with a start. She hadn't heard anyone come up on her.

'I couldn't help noticing you standing here. You're an extraordinary beauty. But of course you know that, don't you?'

Noreen Anne felt relief the moment she saw who it was. This one wouldn't hurt her, couldn't if he tried. She could hurt him if it came to that.

He was old, in his late sixties or seventies; he was obscenely fat; and he was seated in a wheelchair.

And so she went off with Conqueror.

It was all part of the game.

Chapter Seventy-Nine

The Americans had promised a speedy route to trial and the fools had actually delivered.

Five months had passed since the murder of Detective Patsy Hampton. Alex Cross had been shuttling back and forth to Bermuda, but still had no idea where Christine had disappeared to. Shafer had been out of jail, but on a very short leash. He hadn't played the game once since Hampton's murder. The game of games had been on hold and it was driving him mad.

Now Shafer sat in his black Jag in the parking lot directly under the courthouse, feeling hopeful. He was eager to stand trial on the count of Aggravated, Premeditated Murder in the First Degree. The rules of play had been established, and he appreciated that.

The suppression hearing from weeks before was still a vivid memory for him. He relished every minute of it – the preliminary hearing was held before jury selection, to determine what evidence would be allowed at the trial. It was held in the spacious chambers of Judge Michael Fescoe. The judge set the rules, so in a way he was the gamemaster. How fabulously droll, how delicious.

Shafer's lawyer, Jules Halpern, argued that Shafer was in a therapy session at Dr Cassady's home office; and he therefore had every right to privacy. 'That privacy was violated. First, Dr Cassady refused to let Detective Cross and the other officers come inside. Second, Colonel Shafer showed his identification to the detective. It proved that he was with the British Embassy and had diplomatic immunity. Cross barged into the therapist's office anyway. Consequently, any evidence obtained, if indeed any evidence was obtained, is the result of unlawful search.'

Judge Fescoe took the rest of the day to consider, then made his decision the next morning. 'As I listened to both sides, it seemed to me that the issues were straightforward and not all that unusual in a murder case. Mr Shafer does, indeed, have diplomatic immunity. However, it is my opinion that Detective Cross acted in a reasonable and lawful manner when he went to Dr Cassady's apartment. He suspected a grave crime had been committed. Dr Cassady opened the door, allowing Detective Cross plain view of Mr Shafer's attire. Colonel Shafer had insisted that his diplomatic immunity denied Detective Cross permission to enter the premises.

'I am therefore going to allow the prosecution to use the clothing Colonel Shafer was wearing the night of the murder, as well as the blood on the carpet outside the apartment door, as evidence.

'The prosecution may also use any evidence found in the parking garage – both in Detective Hampton's car and Colonel Shafer's.' Judge Fescoe continued, and this was the key part of his ruling, 'I will *not allow* evidence found once Detective Cross entered the apartment against the stated wishes of both Colonel Shafer and Dr Cassady. Any and all evidence discovered during the initial or subsequent searches is suppressed and will not be allowed at the trial.'

The prosecution was also told not to make any reference, during the trial, to any other uncharged murders that Shafer was suspected of having committed in Washington. The jury was to understand that Shafer was under investigation only for the murder of Senior Detective Patricia Hampton. Both the prosecution and defense claimed victory at the end of the suppression hearing.

The stone steps outside the courthouse were swarming with a buzzing, unruly crowd on the morning of the first day. Shafer's supporters were wearing UK/OK buttons and waving crisp new Union Jacks. These wondrous fools made him smile as he clasped both hands high over his head in victory. He enjoyed being a hero immensely.

What a glorious time. Even if he was a little high and spacey on a few choice pharmaceuticals.

Both sides were still predicting 'slam dunk' victories. Lawyers were such fabulous bullshitters.

The press was touting the outrageous charade as the 'criminal trial of the decade'. The media hype, expected and ritualistic, thrilled him anyway. He internalized it as tribute and adulation. His due.

He purposely cut quite a dashing figure; he wanted to make an impression – on the world. He wore a soft-shouldered, tailored gray suit, a striped bespoke shirt from Budd, and black Oxfords from Lobb's of St James's. He was photographed a hundred times in the first few moments alone.

He walked inside the courthouse as if in a dream. The most delicious thing of all was that he might lose everything.

Courtroom 4 was on the third floor. It was the largest in the building. Closest to the double set of public doors was a gallery that held around a hundred and forty spectators. Then came the 'bar area', where the attorneys' tables were situated. Then the judge's bench, which took up about a quarter of the room.

The trial began at ten in the morning, and it was all a rattle and hum to him. The lead prosecutor was Assistant US Attorney Catherine Marie Fitzgibbon. He already yearned to murder her, and wondered if he possibly could. He wanted Ms Fitzgibbon's scalp on his belt. She was just thirty-six, Irish-Catholic, single, sexy in her tight-assed way, dedicated to high-minded ideals, like so many others from her island of origin. She favored dark-blue or gray Ann Taylor wardrobes and wore a ubiquitous tiny gold cross on a gold chain. She was known in the DC legal community as the 'Drama Queen'. Her melodramatic telling of the gory details was meant to win the sympathy of the jury. A worthy opponent indeed. A worthy prey as well.

Shafer sat at the defendant's table and tried to concentrate. He listened, watched, felt as he hadn't in a long time. He knew they were all watching him. How could they not?

Shafer sat there observing, but his brain was on fire. His esteemed attorney, Jules Halpern, finally began to speak, and he heard his own name. That piqued his interest all right. He was the star here, wasn't he?

Jules Halpern was little more than five-four, but he cut quite a powerful figure in a court of law. His hair was dyed jet-black and slicked back tightly against his scalp. His suit was from a British tailor, just like Shafer's. Shafer thought, rather uncharitably he supposed, *Dress British, think Yiddish*. Seated beside Halpern was his daughter, Jane, who was the second chair. She was tall and slender, but with the father's black hair and beaked nose.

Jules Halpern certainly had a strong voice for such a slight and small fellow. 'My client, Geoffrey Shafer, is a loving husband. He is a very good father, who happened to be attending a birthday party for two of his children half an hour *before* the murder of Detective Patricia Hampton.

'Colonel Shafer, as you will hear, is a valued and decorated member of the British Intelligence community. He is a former soldier with a fine record.

'Colonel Shafer was clearly set up for this murder charge because the Washington police *needed* this terrible crime to be solved. This I will prove to you, and you will have no doubt of it. Mr Shafer was framed because a particular homicide detective was going through some bad personal times, and lost control of the situation.

'Finally, and this is the most essential thing for you to remember, Colonel Shafer wants to be here. He isn't here because he has to be. He has diplomatic immunity. Geoffrey Shafer is here to clear his good name.'

Shafer nearly stood up in the courtroom and cheered.

Chapter Eighty

I purposely, and probably wisely, skipped the first day, then the second, and the third day of the courtroom circus. I didn't want to face the world press, or the public anymore than I had to. I felt like I was on trial too.

A cold-blooded murderer was on trial, but the investigation continued more feverishly than ever for me. I still had the Jane Does to solve, and the disappearance of Christine, if I could open up any new leads. I wanted to make certain that Shafer would not walk away a free man, and most importantly, I desperately wanted finally to know the truth about Christine's disappearance. I had to know. My greatest frustration was that because of the diplomatic shenanigans, I had never gotten to question Shafer. I would have given anything for a few hours with him.

I turned the southern end of our attic into a war room. There was an excess of unused space up there anyway. I moved an old mahogany dining table out from the shadows. I rewired an ancient window fan and it made the attic space almost bearable most days.

Especially early in the morning and late in the evening, when I did my best work up there – in my hermitage.

I set up my laptop on the table, and I pinned different-colored index cards to the walls, to keep what I considered the most important pieces of the case before me at all times. Inside several bulky and misshapen cardboard boxes I had all the rest of it: every scrap of evidence on Christine's abduction; and everything I could find on the Jane Does.

The murder cases formed a maddening puzzle, created over several years, that was not given to easy solutions. I was trying to play a complex game, against a skillful opponent, but I didn't know the rules of his game, or how it was played. That was Shafer's unfair advantage.

I had found some useful notes in Patsy Hampton's detective logs, and they led me to interview the teenage boy, Michael Ormson, who'd chatted online with Shafer about The Four Horsemen. I continued to work closely with Chuck Hufstedler of the FBI. Chuck felt guilty about giving Patsy Hampton the original lead, especially since I'd come to him first. I used his guilt.

Both the Bureau and Interpol were doing an active search of the game on the Internet. I'd visited countless chatrooms myself, but had encountered no one, other than young Ormson, who was aware of the mysterious game. It was only because Shafer had taken a chance and gone into the chatroom that he'd been discovered. I wondered what other chances he'd taken.

Following Shafer's arrest at the Farragut, we'd had a little time to search his Jaguar, and I also spent nearly an hour at his home – before his lawyers knew I was there. I spoke to his wife, Lucy, and his son, Robert, who confirmed that he played a game called The Four Horsemen. He had been playing for seven or eight years.

Neither the wife nor the son knew any of the other players, or anything about them. They didn't believe that Geoffrey Shafer had done anything wrong.

The son called his father 'the straight arrow of straight arrows'. Lucy Shafer called him 'a good man', and seemed to believe it.

I found role-playing-game magazines as well as dozens of sets of game dice in Shafer's den, but no other physical evidence concerning his game. Shafer was careful. He covered his tracks well. He was in intelligence, after all. I couldn't imagine him throwing dice to select his victims, but maybe that helped to account for the irregular pattern of the Jane Does.

His attorney, Jules Halpern, complained loudly and vigorously about the invasion of Shafer's home, and had I uncovered any useful evidence, it would have been suppressed. Unfortunately, I didn't have enough time, and Shafer was too clever to keep anything incriminating at his home. He'd made one big mistake; he wasn't likely to make another. Was he?

Sometimes, very late at night as I worked in the attic, I

would stop for a while and remember something about Christine. The memories were painful and sad, but also soothing to me. I began to look forward to these times when I could think about her without any interruption. Some nights, I would wander down to the piano in the sun porch and play songs that had been important to us – 'Unforgettable', 'Moonglow', ''Swonderful'. I could still remember how she looked, especially when I visited at her place – faded jeans, bare feet, T-shirt, or maybe a favorite yellow crewneck sweater she liked, a tortoiseshell comb in her long hair that always smelled of shampoo.

I didn't want to feel sorry for myself, but I just couldn't help feeling miserably bad. I was caught in limbo, not knowing one way or the other what had really happened to Christine. I couldn't let her go.

It was paralyzing me, crippling me, making me feel so damn sad and empty. I knew I needed to move on with my life, but I couldn't do it. I needed answers, at least a few of them. *Is Christine part of the game?* I kept wondering. I was obsessed with the game.

Am I part of it?

I believed that I was. And in a way I hoped she was, too. It was my only hope that she might still be alive.

Chapter Eighty-One

And so I found myself a player in a truly bizarre game that was habit-forming for all the wrong reasons. I began to make up my own rules. I brought in new players. I was in the game to win.

Chuck Hufstedler from the FBI offices in DC continued to be helpful. The more I talked to him, the more I realized that he'd had a serious crush on Detective Hampton. His loss, and mine with Christine, had united us.

I climbed up to the attic late on Friday night after watching *The Mask of Zorro* with Damon, Jannie, Nana, and Rosie the cat. I had a few more facts to check before going to bed.

I booted up the computer, logged on and heard the familiar – *you have mail*. Ever since that night in Bermuda, the message gave me a terrible fright, a chill that tightened my body from head to toe.

Sandy Greenberg from Interpol was returning one of my messages. She and I had worked together on the Mr Smith case and had become friends. I'd given her several things to check for me.

CALL ME ANY TIME TONIGHT, ALEX, AND I MEAN ANY TIME. YOUR IRRITATING DOGGED-NESS MAY HAVE PAID OFF. IT'S VITALLY IMPORTANT THAT YOU CALL. *SANDY*.

I called Sandy in Europe and she picked up after the second ring. 'Alex? I think we found one of them. It was your bloody idea that worked. Shafer was playing a game with at least one of his old cronies from MI6. You were spot on.'

'Are you sure it's one of the game-players?' I asked her.

'Pretty sure,' she shot back. 'I'm sitting here now staring at a copy of Dürer's *Four Horsemen,* on my Mac. As you know, the Horsemen are Conqueror, Famine, War and Death. What a creepy bunch. Anyway, I did what you asked. I talked to some contacts from MI6 who found out that Shafer and this one chap regularly keep in touch on the computer. I have all your notes, too, and they're very good. I can't believe how much you figured out from back there in the colonies. You're a very sick puppy too.'

'Thanks,' I said. I let Sandy ramble on for a few minutes. A while back I recognized that she was a lonely person, and, even though she sometimes put up a can-tankerous front, craved company.

'The name he uses in the game is Conqueror. Conqueror lives in Dorking, in England,' Sandy told me. 'His name is Oliver Highsmith, and he's retired from MI6. Alex, he was running several agents in Asia at the same time Shafer was there. Shafer worked under him. It's eight in the morning over here. *Why don't you call the bastard?*' she suggested. 'Send him an e-mail. I have a number for him, Alex.'

I started to wonder about the other players in The Four Horsemen game. Were there four of them – or was that just the name of the game? Who were these players? How was the game actually played? Did all, or indeed any of them, act out their fantasies in real life?

My message to Conqueror was simple and straight-forward, and not too threatening, I hoped. I didn't see how he could resist answering me.

DEAR MR HIGHSMITH,

I AM A HOMICIDE DETECTIVE IN WASHING-TON, DC, LOOKING FOR INFORMATION ABOUT COLONEL GEOFFREY SHAFER PERTAINING TO THE FOUR HORSEMEN. I UNDERSTAND THAT SHAFER WORKED FOR YOU IN ASIA. TIME IS OF THE ESSENCE. I NEED YOUR HELP. PLEASE CONTACT DETECTIVE ALEX CROSS.

Chapter Eighty-Two

I was surprised when a message came right back. Oliver Highsmith, Conqueror, must have been online when my e-mail went through.

DETECTIVE CROSS. I AM WELL AWARE OF YOU, SINCE THE ONGOING MURDER TRIAL IS A RATHER BIG STORY IN ENGLAND, AND IN THE REST OF EUROPE, FOR THAT MATTER. I HAVE KNOWN G.S. FOR A DOZEN YEARS OR MORE. HE DID WORK UNDER ME, BRIEFLY. HE IS MORE AN ACQUAINTANCE THAN A CLOSE FRIEND, SO I HAVE NO EXPERTISE OR BIAS ABOUT HIS GUILT OR INNOCENCE. I HOPE IT'S THE LATTER, OF COURSE.

NOW, AS TO YOUR QUESTION ABOUT THE FOUR HORSEMEN. THE GAME, AND IT *IS* A FAN-TASY GAME, DETECTIVE, IS HIGHLY UNUSUAL

IN THAT ALL OF THE PLAYERS ASSUME THE ROLE OF GAMEMASTER. THAT IS TO SAY, EACH OF US CONTROLS OUR OWN FATE, OUR OWN STORY. G.S.'s STORY IS EVEN MORE DARING AND UNUSUAL. HIS CHARACTER, THE RIDER ON THE PALE HORSE – DEATH – IS DEEPLY FLAWED. ONE MIGHT EVEN SAY EVIL. THE CHARACTER IS SOMEWHAT LIKE THE PERSON ON TRIAL IN WASHINGTON, OR SO IT SEEMS TO ME.

HOWEVER, I MUST MAKE A FEW IMPORTANT POINTS. THE APPEARANCE OF ANY MURDER FANTASIES IN OUR GAME ALWAYS OCCURRED DAYS *AFTER* REPORTS OF MURDERS IN THE NEWSPAPERS. BELIEVE ME, THIS WAS THOR-OUGHLY CHECKED BY US ONCE G.S. WAS ACCUSED. IT WAS EVEN BROUGHT TO THE ATTENTION OF INSPECTOR JONES AT THE SECURITY SERVICE IN LONDON, SO I'M SUR-PRISED YOU WEREN'T INFORMED BEFORE NOW. THE SERVICE HAS BEEN TO SEE ME ABOUT G.S. AND THEY WERE COMPLETELY SATISFIED I ASSUME, SINCE THEY HAVEN'T BEEN BACK.

ALSO, THE OTHER PLAYERS – WHO HAVE BEEN CHECKED OUT BY SECURITY – ARE ALL REPRESENTED BY POSITIVE CHARACTERS IN THE GAME. AND AS I'VE SAID, AS POWERFULLY INVOLVING AS HORSEMEN IS – IT IS ONLY A

GAME. BY THE WAY, DID YOU KNOW THAT BY SOME SCHOLARLY ACCOUNTS THERE IS A FIFTH HORSEMAN? *MIGHT THAT BE YOU, DR CROSS?*

FYI – THE CONTACT AT THE SERVICE IS MR ANDREW JONES. I TRUST HE WILL VOUCH FOR THE VERACITY OF MY STATEMENTS. IF YOU WISH TO CONVERSE FURTHER, DO SO AT YOUR OWN RISK. I AM SIXTY-SEVEN YEARS OF AGE, RETIRED FROM INTELLIGENCE (AS I LIKE TO PUT IT), AND A RATHER FAMOUS WINDBAG. I WISH YOU MUCH LUCK IN YOUR SEARCH FOR TRUTH AND JUSTICE. I MISS THE CHASE MYSELF.

CONQUEROR

I read the message, then reread it. *Much luck in your search?* Was that as loaded a line as it sounded?

And was I a player – *the Fifth Horseman?*

Chapter Eighty-Three

I went to court every day of the following week, and like so many other people, I got hooked on the trial. Jules Halpern was the most impressive orator I had ever watched in a courtroom; but Catherine Fitzgibbon was effective as well. It would depend on who the jury believed more. It was all theater, a game. I remembered that as a kid I used to regularly watch a courtroom drama with Nana called *The Defenders*. Every show began with a deep-voiced narration saying something to the effect that 'the American Justice System is far from perfect – but it is still the very best justice system in the world'.

That might be true, but as I sat in the courtroom in Washington, I couldn't help thinking that the murder trial, the judge, the jury, the lawyers, and all the rules were just another elaborate game; and that Geoffrey Shafer was already planning his next foray, savoring every move that the prosecution made against him.

He was still in control of the game board. He was the gamemaster. He knew it, and so did I.

I watched Jules Halpern conduct smooth examinations that were designed to give the impression that his monstrous, psychopathic client was as innocent as a newborn baby. Actually, it was easy to drift off during the lengthy cross-examinations. I never really missed anything, though, since all the important points were repeated over and over *ad nauseam*.

'Alex Cross . . .'

I heard my name mentioned and refocused my attention on Jules Halpern. He produced a blown-up photograph that had appeared in the *Post* on the day after the murder. The photo had been taken by another tenant at the Farragut and sold to the newspaper.

Halpern leaned in close to the witness on the stand, a man named Carmine Lopes, a night doorman at the apartment building where Patsy Hampton was murdered.

'Mr Lopes, I show you Defendant's Exhibit "J", a photograph of my client and Detective Alex Cross. It was taken in the tenth-floor hallway soon after the discovery of Detective Hampton's body.'

The blow-up was large enough for me to see most of the detail from where I was sitting in the fourth row. The photo had always been a shocker to me.

Shafer looked as if he had just stepped out of the pages of *GQ*. In comparison my clothes were tattered and dirty. I had just come off my crazy marathon run from the zoo; I had been down in the garage where I found poor Patsy.

My fists were clenched tightly and I seemed to be roaring out anger at Shafer. Pictures *do* lie. We know that. The photograph was highly inflammatory, and I felt it could cause prejudice in the minds of the jurors.

'Is this a fair representation of how the two men looked at ten thirty that evening?' Halpern asked the doorman.

'Yes, sir. It's very fair. That's how I remember it.'

Jules Halpern nodded as if he were receiving vital information for the first time. 'Would you now describe, *in your own words*, what Detective Cross looked like at that time?' he asked.

The doorman hesitated and seemed slightly confused by the question. I wasn't. I knew where Halpern was going now.

'Was he dirty?' Halpern jumped in and asked the simplest possible question.

'Er, dirty . . . sure. He was a mess.'

'And was he sweaty?' the defense lawyer asked.

'Sweaty . . . yeah. We all were. From being down in the garage, I guess. It was a real hot night.'

'Nose running?'

'Yes, sir.'

'Were Detective Cross's clothes ripped, Mr Lopes?'

'Yes, they were. Ripped and dirty.'

Jules Halpern looked at the jury first, then at his witness. 'Were Detective Cross's clothes bloodstained?'

'Yes . . . they sure were. That's what I noticed first, the blood.'

'Was the blood anywhere else, Mr Lopes?'

'On his hands. You couldn't miss it. I sure didn't.'

'And Mr Shafer, how did Mr Shafer look?'

'He was clean, not mussed at all. He seemed pretty calm and collected.'

'Did you see any blood on Mr Shafer?'

'No, sir. No blood.'

Halpern nodded, then he faced the jury. 'Mr Lopes, which of the two men looked more like someone who might have just committed a murder?'

'Detective Cross,' the doorman said, without hesitation.

'Objection!' the district attorney screamed, but not before the damage had been done.

Chapter Eighty-Four

T hat afternoon, the defense was scheduled to call Chief of Detectives George Pittman. The assistant district attorney, Catherine Fitzgibbon, knew that Pittman was on the docket and she asked me to meet with her for lunch. 'If you have an appetite before Pittman goes on,' she added.

Catherine was smart, and she was thorough. She had put away nearly as many bad guys as Jules Halpern had set free. We got together over sandwiches at a crowded deli near the courthouse. Neither of us was thrilled about Pittman's upcoming appearance. My reputation as a detective was being ruined by the defense, and it was a hard thing to watch and do nothing.

She bit down into a hefty Reuben sandwich that squirted mustard onto her forefinger and thumb. Catherine smiled. 'Sloppy, but worth it. You and Pittman are really at odds, right? More like you hate each other's guts?'

'It's serious dislike, and it's mutual,' I told her. 'He's tried to do me in a couple of times. He thinks I'm a threat to his career.'

Catherine was attacking her sandwich. '*Hmmm*, there's a thought. Would you be a better chief of detectives?'

'Wouldn't run, wouldn't serve if elected. I wouldn't be good cooped up in an office playing political ping-pong.'

Catherine laughed. She's one of those people who can find humor almost anywhere. 'This is just fricking great, Alex. The defense is calling the chief of detectives as one of *their* goddamn witnesses. They've listed him as hostile, but I don't think he is.'

Catherine and I finished off the rest of her sandwich. 'Well, let's find out what Mr Halpern has up his sleeve today.'

At the start of the afternoon session, Jules Halpern did a careful and thorough setup of Pittman's credentials, which sounded reasonably impressive in the abstract. Undergrad at George Washington, then law school at American; twenty-four years on the police force, with medals for bravery and citations from three different mayors.

'Chief Pittman, how would you describe Detective Cross's record in the department?' asked Halpern.

I cringed in my seat. Felt my brow wrinkle, my eyes narrow. Here we go, I thought.

'Detective Cross has been involved in some high-profile cases that the department has solved,' he said, and left it at that. Not exactly praise, but at least he hadn't gone on the attack.

Halpern nodded sagely. 'What, if anything, has changed his performance recently?'

Pittman looked my way, then answered. 'A woman he was seeing disappeared while they were on a trip together in Bermuda. Since that time, he's been distracted and distant, quick to anger, not himself.'

Suddenly I wanted to speak up in the courtroom. Pittman didn't know the first thing about Christine and me.

'Chief Pittman, was Detective Cross ever a suspect in the disappearance of his girlfriend, Ms Christine Johnson?'

Pittman nodded. 'That's standard police procedure. I'm sure he was questioned.'

'But his behavior on the job has changed since her disappearance?'

'Yes. His concentration isn't the same. He's missed days of work. It's all a matter of record.'

'Has Detective Cross been asked to seek professional help?'

'Yes.'

'Did you ask him to seek help yourself?'

'I did. He and I have worked together for a number of years. He was under stress.'

'He's under a *lot* of stress? Is that fair to say?'

'Yes. He hasn't closed a single case recently.'

Halpern nodded. 'A couple of weeks before the Hampton homicide, you suspended some detectives he was friendly with.'

Pittman's look was somber. 'Unfortunately, I did.'

'Why did you suspend the detectives?'

'The detectives were investigating cases outside the auspices of the department.'

'Is it fair to say they were making up their own rules, acting like vigilantes?'

Catherine Fitzgibbon rose to her feet and objected, but Judge Fescoe allowed the question.

Pittman answered. 'I don't know about that. Vigilantes is a strong word. But they were working without proper supervision. The case is still under investigation.'

'Was Detective Cross part of the group that was making up its own rules to solve homicides?'

'I'm not certain. But he was spoken to about the matter. I didn't believe he could handle a suspension at that time. I warned him and let it slide. I shouldn't have,' said Pittman.

'No further questions.'

None needed, I thought.

Chapter Eighty-Five

That night after he left the courthouse, Shafer was flying high. He thought that he was winning the game. He was manic as hell, and it felt both good and bad. He was parked in the dark garage under Boo Cassady's building. Most manics aren't really aware that they're exhibiting signs of a manic episode, but Shafer knew. His 'spirals' didn't come out of nowhere, they built and built.

The irony, and the danger, of being back in her building wasn't lost on him. Scene of the crime and all that rot. He wanted to go to Southeast tonight, but that was too risky. He couldn't hunt – not now. He had something else in mind: the next few moves in his game.

It was unusual, though not unheard of, for the defendant in a first-degree homicide trial to be out roaming the streets, but that had been one of the prerequisites of dropping his immunity. What choice did the prosecution have? None at all. If they didn't agree, he had a free pass to keep him out of jail.

Shafer followed a tenant he'd seen several times into the lift from the garage and took it to Boo's apartment. He rang the doorbell. Waited. Heard her padding across the parquet floor. Yes, Act One of tonight's performance was about to begin.

He knew she was watching him through the door's peephole, just as he had watched Alex Cross there on the night Patsy Hampton got her just deserts. He had seen Boo a few times after his release, but then he cut her off.

When he stopped seeing her, she lost it. Boo called him at work, then at home – and constantly on his car phone until he changed the bloody number. At her worst, she reminded him of the nutcase Glenn Close had played in the movie *Fatal Attraction*.

He wondered if he could still push her buttons. She was a fairly bright woman – and that was a large part of her problem. She thought far too much, double and triple think. Most men, especially dull-witted Americans, didn't like that, which made her even crazier.

He put his face against the door, felt its cool wood on his cheek. He started his act.

'I've been petrified to see you, Boo. You don't know what it's been like. One slipup, anything they can use against me, and I'm finished. And what makes it worse is that I'm innocent. You know that. I talked to you the whole time from my house to yours that night. You know I didn't kill that detective. Elizabeth? Boo? Please say something. At least swear at me. Let the anger out . . . Doctor?'

There was no answer. Actually, he rather liked that. It made him respect her more than he had. What the hell, she was more screwed up than he was.

'You know exactly what I'm going through. You're the only one who understands my episodes. I need you, Boo. You know I'm manic-depressive, bipolar, whatever the hell you shrinks want to call my condition. Boo?'

Then Shafer actually started to cry, which nearly made him laugh. He uttered loud, wrenching sobs. He crouched on his haunches and held his head. He knew he was a far better actor than so many of the high-priced fakers he saw in movies.

The door to the apartment slowly opened. 'Boo hoo,' she whispered. 'Is poor Geoff in pain? What a shame.'

What a bitch, he thought, but he had to see her. She was testifying soon. He needed her tonight, and he needed her help in the courtroom.

'Hello, Boo,' he whispered.

Chapter Eighty-Six

Act Two of the evening's performance.

She stared at him with huge dark-brown eyes that looked like amber beads, the kind she bought at her swanky shops. She'd lost weight, but that made her sexier to him, more desperate. She wore navy walking shorts and an elegant pink silk T-shirt – but she also wore her pain.

'You hurt me like no one ever has before,' she whispered.

He held himself under control, play-acting, a truly award-winning performance. 'I'm fighting for my life. I swear, all I think about is killing myself. Haven't you heard anything I've said? Besides, do you want your picture all over the tabloids again? Don't you see? That's why I've been staying away from you.'

She laughed, bitterly, haughtily. 'It's going to happen anyway, when I testify. The photographers will be everywhere I go.'

Shafer shut his eyes. 'Well, that will be your chance to hurt me back, darling.'

She shook her head and frowned. 'You know I wouldn't do that. Oh, Geoff, why didn't you at least call? You're such a bastard.'

Shafer hung his head, the repentant bad boy. 'You know how close I was to the edge before all this happened. Now it's worse. Do you expect me to act like a responsible adult?'

She gave a wry smile. He saw a book on the hallway table behind her, *Man and His Symbols*. Carl Jung. How fitting. 'No, I suppose not, Geoff. What do you want? Drugs?'

'I need you. I want to hold you, Boo. That's all.'

That night, she gave him what he wanted. They made love like animals on the gray velvet loveseat she used for her clients, then on the JFK-style rocking chair, where she always sat for her sessions. He took her body, and her soul.

Then she gave him drugs – antidepressants, painkillers, most of her samples. Boo was still able to get the samples from her ex, a psychiatrist. Shafer didn't know what *their* relationship was, and frankly, he didn't care. He took some Librium and shot up Vicodin at her place.

Then he took Boo again, both of them naked and sweating and frenzied on the kitchen counter. *The butcher's block*, he thought.

He left her place around eleven. He realized he was feeling worse than before he'd gone there. But he knew what he was going to do. He'd known before he went to Boo's. It would explode their little minds. Everyone's. The press. The jury.

Now for Act Three.

Chapter Eighty-Seven

At a little past midnight, I got an emergency call that blew off the top of my head. Within minutes I had the old Porsche up close to ninety on Rock Creek Parkway, the siren screaming at the night, or maybe at Geoffrey Shafer.

I arrived in Kalorama at 12:25. EMS ambulances, squad cars, TV news trucks were parked all over the street.

Several neighbors of the Shafers were up and had come outside their large, expensive houses to observe the nightmare scene. They couldn't believe this was happening in their upscale enclave.

The chatter and buzz of several police radios filled the night air. A news helicopter was already hovering overhead. A truck marked CNN arrived and parked right behind me.

I met a detective named Malcolm Ainsley standing on the front lawn. We knew each other from other homicide scenes, even a few parties. Suddenly the front door of the Shafer house opened.

Two EMTs were carrying a stretcher outside. Dozens of cameras were flashing.

'It's Shafer,' Ainsley told me. 'Sonofabitch tried to kill himself, Alex. Slit his wrist and took a lot of drugs. There were open prescription packets everywhere. Must've had second thoughts, though. Called for help.'

I had enough information about Shafer from the discovery interviews preceding the trial and my own working profile on him to begin to make some very educated guesses about what might have happened. My first thought was that he suffered from some kind of bipolar disorder featuring both manic and depressive episodes. A second possibility was cyclohymia, in which case there can be numerous hypomanic episodes and also depressive symptoms. Associated symptoms could include inflated self-esteem, decreased need for sleep, excessive involvement in 'pleasurable' activities, increase in goal-directed activity – such as winning his game.

I moved forward as if I were floating in a very bad dream, the worst I could imagine. I recognized one of the EMS techies, Nina Disesa. I'd worked with her a few times before in Georgetown.

'We got to the bastard just in time,' Nina said and narrowed her dark eyes. 'Too bad, huh?'

'Serious attempt?' I asked her.

Nina shrugged. 'Hard to tell for sure. He hacked up his wrist pretty good. Just the left one, though. Then the drugs, *lots* of drugs, doctor's samples.'

I shook my head in utter disbelief. 'But he definitely called out for help?'

'According to the wife and son, they heard him call out from his den: "Daddy needs help. Daddy is dying. Daddy is sick." '

'Well, he got that part right. Daddy is incredibly sick. Daddy is a monumental sicko.'

I continued trudging forward toward the red-and-white ambulance. News cameras were still flashing all over the street. My mind was unhinged, reeling. *Everything is a game to him. The victims in Southeast, Patsy Hampton, Christine. Now this. He's even playing with his own life.*

'His pulse is still strong,' I heard as I got close to the ambulance. I could see one of the EMT workers checking the EKG inside the van. I could even hear beeps from the machine.

Then I saw Shafer's face. His hair was drenched in perspiration, and his face as pale as a sheet of white paper. He stared into my eyes, trying to focus. Then he recognized me.

'You did this to me,' he said, mustering strength, suddenly trying to sit up on the stretcher. 'You ruined my life for your career. You did this! You're responsible! Oh God, oh God. My poor family! Why is this happening to us?'

The TV cameras were rolling film, and they got his entire Academy Award-quality performance. Just as Geoffrey Shafer knew they would.

Chapter Eighty-Eight

The trial had to be recessed due to Shafer's suicide attempt. The courtroom shenanigans probably wouldn't resume until the following week.

Meanwhile, the media had another feeding frenzy, including banner headlines in the *Washington Post*, *New York Times*, *USA Today*. At least it gave me time to work on a few more angles. Shafer was good; God, he was good at this.

I had been talking with Sandy Greenberg nearly every night. She was helping me collect information on the other game players. She had even gone and talked with Conqueror. She said she doubted that Oliver Highsmith was a killer. He was late sixties, seriously overweight, and wheelchair-bound.

Sandy called the house at seven that night. She's a good friend. Obviously, she was burning the midnight oil for me. I took the call in the sanctuary of my attic office.

'Andrew Jones of the Security Service will see you,' she announced in her usual perky and aggressive manner. 'Isn't that great news? I'll tell you – *it is*. Actually, he's eager to meet with you, Alex. He didn't say it to me directly, but I don't think he's too keen on Colonel Shafer. Wouldn't say why. Even more fortuitous, he's in Washington. He's a top man. He matters in the intelligence arena. He's very good, Alex, a straight shooter.'

I thanked Sandy and then immediately called Jones at his hotel. He answered the call in his room. 'Yes. Hello. Andrew Jones speaking. Who is this, please?'

'It's Detective Alex Cross of the Washington police. I just got off the line with Sandy Greenberg. How are you?'

'Good, very good. Well, hell, not really. I've had better weeks, months. Actually I stayed here in my room hoping that you'd call. Would you like to meet, Alex? Is there somewhere we wouldn't stand out too much?'

I suggested a bar on M Street in half an hour, and I arrived there a minute or two early. I recognized Jones from his description on the phone: 'Broad, beefy, red-faced. Just your average ex-rugby type. Though I never bloody played, don't even watch the drivel. Oh yes, flaming red hair and matching mustache. That should help, shouldn't it?'

It did. We sat at a dark booth in back and got to know one another. For the next forty-five minutes, Jones filled me in on several important things, not the least of which was politics and decorum within the English intelligence and police communities; Lucy Shafer's father's good name and standing in the army, the concern for his reputation; and the desire of the government to avoid an even dicier scandal than the current mess.

'Alex, if it were true that one of our agents had committed cold-blooded murders while posted abroad, and that Intelligence knew nothing about it, the scandal would be a true horror and major embarrassment. But if MI6 *knew anything* about what Colonel Shafer is suspected of doing! Well, it's absolutely unthinkable.'

'Did they?' I asked him. 'Is this situation unthinkable?'

'I won't answer that, Alex, you know I can't; but I am prepared to help you if I possibly can.'

'Why?' I asked, then. 'Why now? We needed your help on this before the trial began.'

'Fair question, good question. We're prepared to help because you now have information that could cause us a hell of a lot of trouble. You're privy to the *unthinkable*.'

I said nothing. I thought I knew what he was alluding to, though.

'You've discovered a fantasy game called The Four Horsemen. There are four players, including Shafer. We know you've already contacted Oliver Highsmith. What you probably don't know yet, but will find out eventually, is that all the players are former or current agents. That is to say, Geoffrey Shafer might just be the beginning of our problems.'

'All four of them are murderers?' I asked.

Andrew Jones didn't answer; he didn't have to.

Chapter Eighty-Nine

'We think that the game originated in Bangkok, where three of the four players were posted in ninety-one. The fourth, Highsmith, was a mentor of George Bayer, who is Famine in The Four Horsemen. Highsmith has always worked out of London.'

'Tell me about Highsmith,' I said.

'As I said, he's always been in the main office, London. He was a high-level analyst, then he actually ran several agents. He's a very bright chap, well thought of.'

'He claimed that The Four Horsemen was just a harmless fantasy game.'

'It could be for him, Alex. He might be telling the truth. He's been in a wheelchair since eighty-five. Road accident. His wife had just left him and he cracked. He's an enormous fellow, about three hundred pounds. I doubt that he's going about murdering young women in the seedier areas of London. That's what you believe Shafer was doing here in Washington? The Jane Doe murders?'

Jones was right and I didn't deny it. 'We know he was involved in several murders, and I think we were close to catching him. He was picking up victims in a gypsy taxicab. We found the cab. Yes, we knew about him, Andrew.'

Jones tented his thick fingers, pursed his lips. 'You think Shafer knew how close you and Detective Hampton were getting?'

'He might have, but there was a lot of pressure on him. He made some mistakes that led us to an apartment he rented.'

Jones nodded. He seemed to know a great deal about Shafer, which told me he'd been watching him, too. Had he been watching me as well?

'How do you think the other game-players might react to Shafer's being so out of control?' I asked.

'I'm fairly sure they felt threatened. Who wouldn't? He was a risk to all of them. He still is.'

Jones continued. 'So, we have Shafer, who's probably been committing murders here in Washington, acting out his fantasies in real life. And Highsmith, who probably couldn't have, but could be a sort of controller. Then there's a man called James Whitehead, in Jamaica, but there have been no murders of the Jane Doe variety on the island, or any nearby island. We've checked thoroughly. And there's George Bayer in the Far East.'

'What about Bayer? I assume you've investigated him, too?'

'Of course. There's nothing specific on his record, but there was an incident, a possible connection to follow up on. Last year, in Bangkok, two girls who worked in a strip bar in Pot Pol disappeared. They just vanished into the noisy, *teeming* streets. The girls were sixteen and eighteen respectively, bar dancers and prostitutes. Alex, they were found nailed together in the missionary position, wearing only garters and stockings. Even in jolly old Bangkok that caused quite a stir. Sounds distressingly similar to the two girls who were killed in Shaw.'

I nodded. 'So we have at least two unsolved Jane Does in Bangkok. Has anyone actually questioned Bayer?'

'At this point, no, but he's being watched. Remember the politics, the fear of a scandal that I mentioned earlier? There's an ongoing investigation of Bayer and the others, but to some extent our hands are tied.'

'My hands aren't tied,' I said. 'That's what you wanted me to say, isn't it? What you expected? It's why you met with me tonight?'

Jones turned very serious. 'It's how the world works, I'm afraid. Let's do this together from here on. If you do ... I promise to do what I can to find out what happened to Christine Johnson.'

Chapter Ninety

The trial resumed sooner than expected, the following Wednesday in fact. There was speculation in the press about how serious Shafer's self-inflicted wounds had been. None of the public's perverse interest in the case seemed to have been lost.

It seemed impossible to predict the outcome, a fact of life I tried not to let get me down too much. Both Shafer and I were present in the packed courtroom that first morning. Shafer looked pale, weak, an object of sympathy perhaps. I certainly couldn't take my eyes off him.

Things got stranger and stranger. At least they did for me. Sergeant Walter Jamieson was called that morning. Jamieson had been at the Police Academy when I attended. He had taught me my craft, and he was still there, teaching others. I couldn't imagine why he was in court as a witness in Patsy Hampton's murder case.

Jules Halpern approached the witness with a heavy-looking hardback book open in his hands.

'I read to you from the textbook *Preserving the Crime Scene: A Detective's Primer*, which you wrote twenty years ago and which you still use in your classes: "It is *imperative* that the detective not disturb the crime scene until backup can be brought in to corroborate charges effected by the detective to unearth evidence, lest those charges be misconstrued to be those of the perpetration. Gloves *must* be worn at all times at a crime scene." Did you write that, Sergeant Jamieson?'

'Yes, I did. Most certainly. Twenty years ago, as you said.'

'Still stand by it?' Halpern asked.

'Yes, of course. A lot of things have changed, but not that.'

'And you heard earlier testimony that Detective Cross wore gloves both inside Detective Hampton's car and at the Cassady apartment.'

'Yes, I heard the testimony. I also read the grand jury transcripts.'

Halpern turned on the overhead projector in the courtroom. 'I direct your attention to prints number 176 and 211 provided by the DA's office. You see the ones denominated?'

'Number 176 and 211. I see them.'

'Now, the prints are denominated "Detective Hampton Belt Buckle: ID: Alex Cross/Right Thumb." And "Left Side Dashboard: ID: Alex Cross/Left Forefinger." What does that mean? Can you explain the markings to us?'

'It means that Alex Cross's prints were found on Detective Hampton's belt as well as on the dashboard of her car.'

Jules Halpern paused for a full ten seconds before he went on. 'And may we not therefore conclude, Sergeant Jamieson, that Detective Cross himself could be our murderer.'

'Objection!' Catherine Fitzgibbon stood up and shouted.

'Withdrawn,' said the defense attorney. 'I'm finished here.'

Chapter Ninety-One

Lawyers for both the prosecution and defense continued to regularly appear on Larry King and other TV shows and boast that their cases were 'slam dunks'. If you listened to the lawyers, neither side could lose.

In the courtroom, Jules Halpern had the fierce look and body language of someone brimming with confidence and determination. He was riding the case hard. He looked like a jockey whipping his thoroughbred to victory.

The bailiff stood and announced, 'The defense calls Mr William Payaz.'

I didn't recognize the name. Now what? Now *who*?

There was no immediate response in the courtroom.

No one came forward.

Heads craned around the room. Still no one responded. Who was the mystery witness?

The bailiff repeated a little louder, 'Mr Payaz, Mr William Payaz.'

The double doors in the back of the room suddenly opened, and a circus-style clown walked in. The gallery began to whisper loudly and a few people laughed. What a world we lived in; what a circus indeed.

The clown took the stand and both the prosecution and defense were immediately called forward for a side-bar by Judge Fescoe. A heated discussion ensued that none of the rest of us could hear. The clown issue was apparently resolved in favor of the defense. After being sworn in, the clown was asked his name for the record.

His white-gloved right hand raised, he said, 'Billy.'

The bailiff asked, 'Last name, please?'

The clown said, 'First name, Silly. Last name, Billy, Silly Billy. I had it legally changed,' he confided to the judge.

Jules Halpern took over, and he treated the clown with respect and seriousness. First, he asked him to state his credentials, which the clown did politely. Then Halpern asked, 'And what brings you here today?'

'I did a party for Mr Shafer out in Kalorama on the fateful and terrible night of the murder. It was his twins' fifth birthday. I did a party when they were four as well. I brought a video along. Want to see?' he said, speaking as if he were addressing a crowd of three-year-olds.

'Of course,' said Jules Halpern.

'Objection!' Catherine Fitzgibbon called out loudly.

The video was admitted over the prosecution's objections and yet another lengthy sidebar. The newspapers had claimed that Judge Fescoe was intimidated by Jules Halpern, which seemed the case.

The tape began with an arresting closeup of a painting of a clown's face. As the camera pulled back, everyone in the courtroom could see it was the sign on Silly Billy's van, which was parked in front of a handsome red-brick town house with a glass conservatory linked to the main building. The Shafer house.

The next scene showed Silly Billy ringing the front bell and apparently surprising the Shafer children at the door.

Once again the prosecution objected to the videotape. There was another sidebar. The lawyers returned to their seats and the tape resumed.

The other children at the birthday party ran to the door. The clown handed out toys from a sack over his shoulder – teddy bears, dolls, shiny red firetrucks.

Silly Billy then performed magic tricks and gags on the sunporch, which looked out onto the backyard. The yard was very pretty, with potted orange trees, white climbing roses, jasmine vine, lush green grass.

'Wait! I hear something outside!' He had turned and spoken to camera. Now he ran and disappeared from sight.

The kids all followed. The tension of surprise and imminent fun was in the children's eyes.

A pale white pony appeared, cantering slowly around the corner of the house. Silly Billy was riding on the horse.

But when the clown dismounted, the kids discovered that the clown was actually Geoffrey Shafer! The kids went wild, but especially the Shafer twins. They ran and hugged their daddy, who seemed the perfect father.

There were heartwarming, candid shots of the children eating frosted cake and playing party games. There were more shots of Shafer laughing and playing with several of the children. I suspected that Jules Halpern himself supervised the final editing of the tape. It was very convincing.

The adult guests, all dressed up and looking sophisticated, were a glowing testimonial that Geoffrey Shafer and his wife were outstanding parents. No longer in his clown costume but in a smart navy suit, Shafer modestly deflected the tributes. He had changed into the same clothes he had worn when he was apprehended at the Farragut.

The tape ended with the smiling and quite beautiful twins telling the camera that they loved their mommy and daddy for making their 'dream come true'. The lights came up. The judge granted a brief recess.

I felt incredibly angry that the video had been shown. It made Shafer seem such a wonderful father – and *victim*.

The jury was all smiles, and so was Jules Halpern. He had argued masterfully that the tape was crucial to establish Geoffrey Shafer's state of mind shortly before Patsy Hampton's murder. Halpern was so skillful an orator he'd actually made the outrageous request sound logical. At any rate, it was moot now.

Shafer himself was smiling broadly, as were his wife

and son. It suddenly occurred to me that Shafer had been riding a pale horse at the party for his children. He was Death from The Four Horsemen.

It was all theater and games to him, his entire life.

Chapter Ninety-Two

Sometimes I wanted to shut my eyes tight and not have to watch another moment of the trial. I wanted things to be the way they were before the Weasel.

Catherine Fitzgibbon was doing a very good job with each witness, but the judge seemed to be favoring the defense whenever possible. It had begun at the crucial suppression-of-evidence hearing and it continued now.

Lucy Shafer took the witness stand early that afternoon. The warm, homespun videotaped images of the Shafer family were still fresh in the minds of the jury.

I had been trying to understand Lucy Shafer's odd and perplexing relationship with her husband since the first time I had met her, the night of Patsy Hampton's murder. What kind of woman could live with an unrepentant monster like Shafer and not know it? Could this woman be that much in denial? Or was there something else that motivated her, somehow held her captive to Shafer? I had seen all kinds of marital relationships in my therapy practice, but nothing like this.

Jane Halpern conducted the questioning and she looked every bit as confident and winning as her father. She was tall and slender, with wiry black hair tied in a bow with a dark crimson ribbon. She was twenty-eight, just four years out of Yale Law School, but seemed older and wiser.

'Mrs Shafer, how long have you and your husband known each other?'

Lucy Shafer spoke in a gentle but clear voice. 'I've known Geoffrey for most of my adult life, actually. My father was his commanding officer in the army. I believe I was just fourteen when I first met Geoff. He was nine years older. We married when I was nineteen, after my second year at Cambridge. Once when I was studying for exams, he showed up in full military dress: polished saber, medals, shiny black leather riding boots – right in the middle of the library. I was studying in a sweatshirt or some such awful getup, and I don't think I'd washed my hair for days. Geoff told me it didn't matter. He didn't care a bit about appearances. He said he loved me and always would. I must tell you, he's kept that promise.'

'Very nice,' Jane Halpern said, seemingly utterly charmed, as if she'd never heard the story before. 'And has he remained romantic?'

'Oh, yes, even more so. Scarcely a week goes by that

Geoff doesn't bring me flowers, or perhaps a beautiful Hermès scarf, which I collect. And then there are our "ouch" excursions.'

Jane Halpern wrinkled her nose and her dark-brown eyes twinkled. 'What are "ouch" excursions?' she asked, with the exuberant curiosity of a morning TV show host.

'Geoff will take me to New York, or maybe Paris, or back to London, and I get to shop for clothes until he says "ouch". He's very generous, though.'

'A good husband, then?'

'The best you could imagine. Very hardworking, but not so much that he forgets about his family. The children adore him.'

'Yes, we could tell that from this morning's film, Mrs Shafer. Was the party an unusual occasion?'

'No. Geoffrey's always throwing parties. He's very joyful, full of life, full of fun and surprises. He's a sensitive, very creative man.'

I looked from Lucy Shafer to the jury box. She had them in a spell, and they couldn't take their eyes off her. She was also credible. Even I had the sense that she genuinely loved her husband, and more important, that she believed he loved her.

Jane Halpern milked the testimony for all it was worth. I couldn't blame her. Lucy Shafer was attractive and seemed nice, kind, and very much in love with her husband and children, but she didn't appear to be a fool. Just someone who had found exactly who she wanted and valued him deeply. That someone was Geoffrey Shafer.

It was the indelible image the jury took away with them at the end of the day.

And it was an amazing lie – spun by a master.

Chapter Ninety-Three

I talked things over with Andrew Jones when I got home
after court that afternoon. I'd tried to contact Oliver
Highsmith again, but so far hadn't gotten any response.
Also, there was nothing new to link Shafer to the Jane
Doe murders in Washington. Shafer didn't seem to have
murdered anyone, at least locally, in the past several
months.

After a dinner of chicken pot pie, salad, rhubarb pie,
Nana gave the kids the night off from their chore of doing
the dishes. She asked me to stay and help, to be her
'partner in grime', as we used to call it.

'Just like the good old days, same as it ever was,' I said
as I splashed soap and water onto silver and dishes in the
porcelain sink that's as old as the house.

Nana dried the kitchenware as quickly as I got it to her.
Her fingers were still as nimble as her mind. 'I like to
think we're older *and* wiser,' she chirped.

'I don't know. I'm still the one getting dishwater hands.'

'I haven't told you something, and I should have,' Nana said, suddenly going serious on me.

'Okay,' I said, and stopped splashing water and soap bubbles around in the sink. 'Shoot.'

'What I wanted to say – is that I'm proud of the way you've been able to handle the terrible things that have happened. Your strength and your patience have given me inspiration. And I'm not easily inspired, especially by the likes of you. I know it has had the same effect on Damon and Jannie. They don't miss a thing.'

I leaned over the sink, suddenly feeling in a confessional mood. 'It's the worst stretch of my life, the hardest thing I've ever had to do. It's even worse than when Maria died, Nana, if that's possible. At least back then I knew for sure she was dead. I could let myself grieve. I could finally let her go and breathe again.'

Nana came around the sink and took me in her arms, which always surprised me with their strength.

She looked me squarely in the eyes, just like she always has since I was around nine years old. She said, 'Let yourself grieve for her, Alex. Let her go.'

Chapter Ninety-Four

Geoffrey Shafer had an attractive, loving wife, and that incongruous and monstrously unfair fact bothered me a lot. I couldn't understand it as a psychologist or as a detective.

The clever testimony of Lucy Shafer continued early the following morning, and lasted just over an hour. Jane Halpern wanted the jury to hear more about Lucy's wonderful husband.

Finally, it was Catherine Fitzgibbon's turn. In her own way, she was as tough, and maybe as formidable, as Jules Halpern.

'Mrs Shafer, we've all been listening to you intently, and it all sounds very charming and idyllic, but I'm troubled and confused by something. Here's what troubles me. Your husband tried to commit suicide eight days ago. Your husband tried to kill himself. So maybe he isn't quite what he seems to be. Maybe he isn't so well-balanced and sane. Maybe you're mistaken about who he really is.'

Lucy Shafer stared directly into the prosecuting attorney's eyes. 'In the past few months, my husband has seen his life, his career, and his good name falsely put in jeopardy. He couldn't believe that these horrible charges had been made against him. This whole Kafkaesque ordeal drove him, quite literally, to despair. You have no idea what it means to lose your good name.'

Catherine Fitzgibbon smiled, and quipped, 'Sure I do. Of course I do. Haven't you read the *National Enquirer* lately?' That got a laugh from the courtroom audience, even the jury members. I could tell that they liked Catherine. So did I.

She continued, 'Isn't it true that your husband has been treated for "despair" for many years? He's seeing a psychologist, Mrs Shafer. He suffers from manic-depression, or bipolar disorder, correct?'

Lucy shook her head. 'He's had a mid-life crisis. That's all it is. It's nothing unusual for men of his age.'

'I see. And were you able to help him with his crisis?'

'Of course I was. Although not with respect to his work. So much of what he does is classified and top secret. You must understand that.'

'I must,' the prosecutor said, then quickly went on, 'So your husband has a great many secrets he keeps from you?'

Lucy frowned, and her eyes shot darts at the wily prosecutor. 'In his *work*, yes.'

'You knew that he was seeing Dr Cassady? Boo Cassady?'

'Yes, of course I did. We often talked about it.'

'How often did he see her? Do you know? Did he tell you that? Or was it *top secret*?'

Jane Halpern shouted, 'Objection!'

'Sustained. Ms Fitzgibbon,' warned Judge Fescoe, with an arched brow.

'Sorry, your honor. Sorry, Lucy. All right, then. How often did your husband see Boo Cassady?'

'He saw her as much as necessary, I suppose. I believe her name is *Elizabeth*.'

'Once a week? Twice? Every day?' Fitzgibbon pressed on, without missing a beat.

'I think once a week. Usually it was once a week.'

'But the doormen at the Farragut testified they saw your husband much more than that. Three and four times a week on average.'

Lucy Shafer shook her head wearily and glared at Fitzgibbon. 'I trust Geoffrey completely. I don't keep him on a lead. I certainly wouldn't *count* his therapy sessions.'

'Did you mind that Dr Cassady, *Elizabeth*, is such an attractive woman?'

'No, don't be absurd.'

Fitzgibbon looked genuinely surprised. 'Why is that absurd? I don't think it is. I think I'd mind if my husband was seeing an attractive woman at her home office two, three, four times a week.'

Fitzgibbon moved swiftly. 'Didn't it bother you that Boo

Cassady was a surrogate *sex* therapist for your husband?'

Lucy Shafer hesitated, seemed surprised, and glanced quickly at her husband. *She hadn't known.* It was impossible not to feel sorry for her.

Jane Halpern quickly rose from her seat. 'Objection! Your honor, there is no foundation that my client was seeing a sex surrogate.'

Lucy Shafer visibly pulled herself together on the witness stand. She was clearly stronger than she looked. Was she a game-player, too? Could she be one of the Horsemen? Or did she and her husband play a completely different kind of game?

She spoke. 'I'd like to answer the question. Madam Prosecutor. My husband, Geoffrey, has been such a good husband, such a good father, that even if he felt it necessary to see a sex therapist, and did *not* want to tell me about it because of the hurt or shame he felt, I would understand.'

'And if he committed *cold-blooded murder* – and did not want to tell you?' the prosecutor asked, then turned to the jury.

Chapter Ninety-Five

E lizabeth 'Boo' Cassady was in her late thirties, slender and very attractive, with lustrous brown hair that she had worn long since she was a young girl. She was a regular shopper at Neiman Marcus, Saks, Nordstrom, Bloomingdale's, and various chic specialty shops around Washington. It showed.

She had gotten the nickname 'Boo' as an infant because she always laughed and laughed whenever she heard the sound of somebody playing 'peek-a-boo' with her. She soon learned to make it herself, muttering *'boo, boo, boo, boo'*. In school, right through college, she kept the name, friends said, because she could be a little scary at times.

For her important day in court she'd chosen a single-breasted pantsuit, beautifully cut, very soft and flowy. Her outfit was an eye-pleasing mix of coffee and cashmere cream. She looked like a professional person, and a successful one.

Jules Halpern asked her to state her name and occupation for the record. He was amiable but businesslike, a little cooler than he had been with other witnesses.

'Dr Elizabeth Cassady. I'm a psychotherapist,' she replied evenly.

'Dr Cassady, how do you know Colonel Shafer?'

'He's a patient of mine and has been for over a year. He sees me at my office at 1208 Woodley Avenue once or twice a week. We increased the sessions recently since Mr Shafer's attempted suicide.'

Halpern nodded. 'What time are the sessions?'

'Usually early evenings. They can vary according to Mr Shafer's work schedule.'

'Dr Cassady, I direct your attention to the evening of the murder of Detective Hampton. Did Geoffrey Shafer have a therapy session with you that night?'

'Yes, he did. At nine p.m., nine until ten. I think he may have arrived a little earlier that night. But the session was scheduled for nine.'

'Could he have arrived as early as eight thirty?'

'No. That isn't possible. We were talking to each other on cell phones from the time he left his house in Kalorama until he arrived at my building. He was feeling a great deal of guilt about his latest dark mood coming too close to his daughters' birthday party.'

'I see. Was there any break in your conversation with Colonel Shafer?'

'Yes. But it was a very short one.'

Halpern kept the pace brisk. 'How much time passed

between the time the two of you stopped talking on the cell phone and his arrival at your office?'

'Two or three minutes, five at the most. While he parked and came upstairs. No more than that.'

'When he arrived at your office, did Geoffrey Shafer seem unsettled in any way?'

'No, not at all. He appeared relatively cheerful, actually. He had just hosted a successful birthday party for the twins. He felt it had gone very well and he dotes on his children.'

'Was he out of breath, tense, or perspiring?' Halpern asked.

'No. As I said, he was calm and looked quite fine. I remember it very clearly. And after the intrusion by the police, I made careful *notes* to keep everything accurate and fresh,' she said, then glanced at the prosecutor's table.

'So, you made notes for the sake of accuracy?'

'Yes, I did.'

'Dr Cassady, did you notice any blood anywhere on Colonel Shafer's clothing?'

'No, I did not.'

'I see. You saw no blood on Shafer. And when Detective Cross arrived, did you see any blood on him?'

'Yes, I saw dark stains or streaks of blood on his shirt and suit coat. Also on his hands.'

Jules Halpern paused to let everything sink in with the jury. Then he asked a final question. 'Did Colonel Shafer look as if he had just murdered someone?'

'No, certainly not.'

'I have nothing further,' said the defense attorney.

Daniel Weston did the cross-exam for the prosecution. He was twenty-nine years old, bright, quick-witted, a rising star, and known to be a ruthless hatchetman in the prosecutor's office.

Dan Weston was also good-looking, blond, and rugged. He got physically close to Boo Cassady. They made a fetching couple, which was the visual idea he wanted to communicate.

'Ms Cassady, you weren't Mr Shafer's *psychiatrist*, were you?'

She frowned slightly, but then managed a weak smile. 'No, a psychiatrist has to be a medical doctor. You know that, I'm sure.'

'And you are not a medical doctor?'

She shook her head. 'I am not. I have a doctorate in sociology. You know that, too.'

'Are you a *psychologist*?' Weston asked.

'A psychologist usually has a graduate degree in psychology, sometimes a Ph.D.'

'Do you have a graduate degree in psychology?'

'No. I'm a psychotherapist.'

'I see. Where was your training to be a psychotherapist?'

'American University. I graduated with a Ph.D. in social work.'

Daniel Weston kept coming at Cassady. There was hardly a beat between question and answer. 'This "psychotherapy office" of yours at the Farragut. What sort of furnishings does it have?'

'A couch, desk, lamp. It's basically very spare. Lots of plants, though. My patients find the atmosphere functional but also relaxing.'

'No box of tissues by the couch? I thought that was a must,' Weston said with a thin smile.

The witness was clearly annoyed now, and maybe even shaken. 'I take my work very seriously, Mr Weston. So do my patients.'

'Was Geoffrey Shafer referred to you by someone?'

'Actually, we met in the National Gallery . . . at the Picasso Erotic Drawing Exhibit. That's been covered in depth by the press.'

Weston nodded, and a thin smile crossed his lips. 'Ah, I see. Are your sessions with Geoffrey Shafer erotic? Do you ever discuss sex?'

Jules Halpern rose quickly; a regular Jules-in-the-box. 'Objection! Doctor/patient privilege. It's confidential.'

The young prosecutor shrugged, flipped back his blond curls with his hand. 'I'll withdraw the question. No problem. Are you a sexual surrogate?'

'No, I am not. As I stated earlier, I am a psychotherapist.'

'On the evening of the murder of Detective Hampton, did you and Geoffrey Shafer discuss—'

Jules Halpern quickly rose again. 'Objection. If the prosecution is inquiring into the patient's privileged disclosures—'

Weston raised both arms in frustration. He smiled at the jury, hoping they felt the same way. 'All right, all right. Let me see. I'll take this out of the so-called doctor/patient realm and ask you, quite simply, if you, Ms Cassady, a woman, have had sexual relations with Geoffrey Shafer, a man?'

Elizabeth 'Boo' Cassady hung her head and stared down at her lap.

Daniel Weston smiled, even as Jules Halpern objected to the question and was upheld by Judge Fescoe. Weston felt that he had made his point.

Chapter Ninety-Six

'**C**all Detective Alex Cross.'

I took a deep breath, composed my mind, body, soul, then walked up the wide center aisle of the court-room to testify. Everyone in the room was watching me, but the only person I really saw was Geoffrey Shafer. The Weasel. He was still playing the part of the wronged innocent man and I wanted to bring him down. I wanted to cross-examine him myself, to ask the real questions that needed to be asked, to tell the jury about all the suppressed evidence, to bring justice crashing down on him with all its force.

It was a hard thing to have worked honestly for so many years – and now be accused of being a rogue cop, someone who had tampered with evidence, and maybe worse. It was ironic, but now maybe I had the opportunity to set the record straight; to clear my name.

Jules Halpern smiled cordially at me as I sat down in

the witness stand. He established eye contact, quickly looked over at the jury, then back at me. His dark eyes radiated intelligence and it seemed an incredible waste that he was working for Shafer.

'I want to start by saying that it is an honor to meet you, Detective Cross. For years I, like most of the jurors I'm sure, have read in the Washington papers about the murder cases you have helped solve. We admire your past record.'

I nodded and even managed a grudging smile of my own. 'Thank you. I hope you'll admire my present and future record as well,' I said.

'Let's hope so, Detective,' Halpern said. He moved on. We parried for half an hour or so, before he asked, 'You suffered a terrible personal tragedy a short time before the arrest of Colonel Shafer. Could you tell us about it?'

I fought the urge to reach out and grab the polite-sounding, insidious little man by the neck. I leaned closer to the mike, struggled for control.

'Someone dear to me was kidnapped while we were in Bermuda on vacation. She's still missing. I haven't given up hope that she'll be found. I pray every day that she's still alive.'

Halpern clucked sympathetically. He was good, much like his client. 'I really am sorry. Did the department give you adequate time off?'

'They were understanding and helpful,' I said, feeling my jaw stiffen with resentment. I hated that Halpern was using what happened to Christine to unsettle me.

'Detective, were you officially back on active duty at the time of Detective Hampton's murder?'

'Yes, I went back on full-time duty about a week before the murder.'

'Was it requested that you stay off active duty for a while longer?'

'It was left up to me. The chief of detectives did question my ability to resume my duties. But he made it my choice.'

Halpern nodded thoughtfully. 'He felt your head might be elsewhere? Who could blame you if it was?'

'I was upset, I still am, but I've been able to work. It's been good for me. The right thing to do.'

There were several questions about my state of mind, then Halpern asked, 'When you found out that Detective Hampton had been murdered, how upset were you?'

'I did my job. It was a bad homicide scene.' *Your client is a butcher. Do you really want to get him off? Do you realize what you're doing?*

'Your fingerprints were on Detective Hampton's belt and on the dashboard of her car. Her blood was on your clothes.'

I paused for several seconds before I spoke again. Then I tried to explain. 'There was a huge jagged tear in Detective Hampton's jugular vein. Blood was everywhere in the car, and even on the cement floor of the garage. I tried to help Detective Hampton – until I was certain she was dead. That's why there were fingerprints in the car and Detective Hampton's blood on my clothes.'

'You tracked blood upstairs?'

'No, I did not. I checked my shoes carefully before I left the garage. I checked *twice*. I checked because I *didn't* want to track any blood up into the building.'

'But you were upset, you admit that much. A police officer had been murdered. You forgot to put on gloves when you first searched the scene. There was blood on your clothes. How can you possibly be so sure?'

I stared directly into his eyes and tried to be as calm as he was. 'I know exactly what happened that night. I know who killed Patsy Hampton in cold blood.'

He raised his voice suddenly. 'No, you do not, sir. That's the point. *You do not*. In frisking Colonel Geoffrey Shafer, isn't it fair to say that you were in physical contact with him?'

'Yes.'

'And isn't it possible that blood from your clothes got onto his? Isn't it even likely?'

I wouldn't give him an inch. I couldn't. 'No, it isn't possible. There was blood on Geoffrey Shafer's trousers *before* I arrived.'

Halpern moved away from me. He wanted me to sweat. He walked over to the jury box, occasionally looking back at me. He asked several more questions about the crime scene, and then—

'But Dr Cassady didn't see any blood. The two other officers didn't see any blood – *not until after you came into contact with Colonel Shafer*. Colonel Shafer was on the phone until three to five minutes before he met his therapist. He came straight there from his children's birthday party. *You have no evidence, Detective Cross!* Except what you brought into Dr Cassady's apartment yourself. You have absolutely no evidence, Detective! You arrested the wrong man! You framed an innocent man!'

Jules Halpern threw up his hands in disgust. 'I have no further questions.'

Chapter Ninety-Seven

I took a back way out of the courthouse. I usually did, but on this day it was essential. I had to avoid the crowds and the press, and I needed to have a private moment to recover from my time on the witness stand.

I'd just had my ass pretty well kicked by an expert asskicker. Tomorrow, Cathy Fitzgibbon would try to undo some of the damage in cross-exam.

I was in no hurry as I walked down a back stairway that was used by maintenance and cleaning people in the building, and was also a fire escape.

It was becoming clear to me that there was a chance that Geoffrey Shafer would be acquitted. His lawyers were the best. We'd lost important evidence at the suppression hearing.

And, I *had* made a mistake at the homicide scene in my rush to help Patsy Hampton without putting on gloves.

It was an honest mistake, but it probably created doubt

in the minds of the jurors. I'd had more blood on me than Shafer. That was true. Shafer might actually get away with murder, and I couldn't stand the thought. I felt like yelling as I descended the twisting flight of stairs.

And that's what I did, finally. I yelled at the top of my voice and it felt so damn good to get it out. Relief flowed through my body, however temporary it might be.

At the bottom of the concrete stairs was the basement of the courthouse. I headed down a long darkened hallway toward the rear lot where the Porsche was parked. I was still lost in my thoughts, but calmer after hollering my fool head off in the stairwell.

There was a sharp bend in the hallway near the exit to the parking lot. I came around the turn and saw him. I couldn't believe it. The Weasel was right there.

He was first to speak. 'What a surprise, Dr Cross. Sneaking away from the madding, or is it maddening crowd? Tail between your legs today? Don't fret, you did all right upstairs. Was that you yelling in the halls? Primal screams are the best, aren't they?'

'What the hell do you want, Shafer?' I asked him. 'We're not supposed to meet or talk like this.'

He shrugged his broad shoulders, wiped his blond hair away from his eyes. 'You think I care about rules? I don't give a shit about rules. *What do I want?* My good name restored. I want my family not to have to go through any more of this. I want it all.'

'Then you shouldn't have killed all those people. Especially Patsy Hampton.'

Shafer finally smiled. 'You're very sure of yourself, aren't you? You don't back down. I admire that, to a degree. I played the game of being a hero once myself. In the army. It's interesting for a while.'

'But it's much more interesting to be a raving lunatic murderer,' I said.

'See? You just don't back down from your pig-headed opinions. I love it. You're wonderful.'

'It's not opinion, Shafer. You know it, and so do I.'

'Then prove it, Cross. Win your pitiful sodding case, will you? Beat me fair and square in a court of law. I even gave you home advantage.'

I started to walk toward him; I couldn't help myself. He stood his ground.

'This is all an insane game to you. I've met assholes like you before, Shafer. I've beaten better. I'll beat you.'

He laughed in my face. 'I sincerely doubt it.'

I walked right past him in the narrow tunnel.

He pushed me – hard, from behind. He was a big man, but even stronger than he looked.

I stumbled, almost went over onto the stone floor. I wasn't expecting the outburst of anger from him. He held it in so well in court, but it was close to the surface. The madness that *was* Geoffrey Shafer. The violence.

'Then go ahead, beat me. See if you can,' he yelled at the top of his voice. 'Beat me right here, right now. I don't think you can, Cross. I know you can't.'

Shafer took a quick step toward me. He was agile and athletic, not just strong. We were almost the same size, six foot two or three, two hundred pounds. I remembered that he'd been an army officer, then MI6. He still looked in excellent shape.

Shafer pushed me again with both hands. He made a loud grunting noise. 'If you've beaten better, then I should be a pushover. Isn't that so? I'm just a *pushover*.'

I almost threw a punch; I wanted to. I ached to take him down, to wipe the smug, superior look off his face.

Instead, I grabbed him hard. I slammed Shafer up against the stone tunnel wall and held him there.

'Not now. Not here,' I said, in a hoarse, raw whisper. 'I'm not going to hit you, Shafer. What? Have you run to the newspapers and TV. But I am going to bring you down. Soon.'

He came out with a crazy laugh. 'You are fucking hilarious, do you know that? You're a *scream*. I love it.'

I walked away from Shafer in the dark tunnel. It was the hardest thing I've ever had to do. I wanted to beat the answers out of him, get a confession. I wanted to know about Christine. I had so many questions, but I knew he wouldn't answer them. He was here to bait me, to *play*.

'You're losing . . . everything,' he said to my back.

I think I could have killed Geoffrey Shafer on the spot.

I almost turned, but I didn't. I opened the creaking door and went outside instead. Sunlight streamed into my eyes, half-blinding me for a dizzying moment. Shading my face with an arm, I climbed stone stairs to the parking area, where I got another unwanted surprise.

A dozen grim-faced members of the press, including some important reporters, were gathered in the back parking lot. Someone had alerted them; someone had tipped them off that I was coming out this way.

I looked back at the gray metal door, but Geoffrey Shafer didn't come out behind me. He had retreated and disappeared back into the basement.

'Detective Cross.' I heard a reporter call my name. 'You're losing this case. You know that, don't you?'

Yes, I knew. I was losing everything. I just didn't know what I could do to stop it.

Chapter Ninety-Eight

The following day was taken up with my cross-examination by Catherine Fitzgibbon. Catherine did a good job of redressing some of the harm done by Jules Halpern, but not all of it. Halpern consistently broke up her rhythm with his objections. Like so many recent high-profile trials, this one was maddening. It should have been easy to convict and put away Geoffrey Shafer, but that wasn't the case.

Two days later, we got our best chance to win, and Shafer himself gave it to us, almost as if he was daring us. Now we realized that he was even crazier than we'd thought. The game was his life; nothing else seemed to matter.

Shafer agreed to take the stand. I think that I was the only one in the courtroom who wasn't completely surprised that he was testifying, that he was playing the game right in front of us.

Catherine Fitzgibbon was almost certain that Jules Halpern had lectured, pleaded and advised him against it; but there Shafer was anyway, striding toward the witness stand, looking as if he had been called up there to be ceremoniously knighted by the Queen.

He couldn't resist the stage, could he? He looked every bit as confident and in control as he had the night I arrested him for Patsy Hampton's murder. He was dressed in a navy-blue double-breasted suit, white shirt, and gold tie. Not a single blond hair was out of place, nor was there any hint of the anger boiling just under the surface of his meticulously groomed exterior.

Jules Halpern addressed him in conversational tones, but I was certain that he was uneasy about this unnecessary gamble.

'Colonel Shafer, first I want to thank you for coming to the witness stand. This is completely voluntary on your part. From the beginning, you've stated that you wanted to come here to clear your name.'

Shafer smiled politely, and then cut off his lawyer with a raised hand. The lawyers on both sides of the bar exchanged looks. What was happening? What was he going to do?

I leaned way forward in my seat. It struck me that Jules Halpern might actually *know* that his client was guilty. If he did, he wouldn't have been able to cross-examine him. Legally, he couldn't ask questions that disguised the real facts as he knew them.

This was the only way that Shafer could have his

moment in the sun: a soliloquy. Once called to the stand, Shafer could give a speech. It was unusual, but absolutely legal – and, if Halpern knew his client was guilty, it was the only way that Shafer could take the stand and not be incriminated by his own attorney.

Shafer had the floor. 'If you will please excuse me, Mr Halpern, I believe I can talk to these good people myself. I really can manage. You see, I don't need a lot of expert help telling the simple truth.'

Jules Halpern stepped back, nodded sagely, and tried to keep his poise. What else could he do under the circumstances? If he hadn't known his client was an egomaniac or insane, he surely knew it now.

Shafer looked toward the jury. 'It has been stated here in court that I am with British Intelligence, that I was MI6, a spy. I'm afraid that I am actually a rather unglamorous agent, Double-O-Nothing if you will.'

The light, well-aimed jab at himself drew laughter in the courtroom.

'I am a simple bureaucrat, like so many others who toil away their days and nights in Washington. I follow well-established procedures at the embassy. I get approvals for virtually everything I do. My home life is simple and orderly as well. My wife and I have been married nearly sixteen years. We love each other dearly. We're devoted to our three children.

'So I want to apologize to my wife and children. I am so frightfully sorry for this hellish ordeal they've had to go through. To my son, Rob, and the twins, Tricia and Erica,

I'm so sorry. If I had any idea what a circus this would become, I would have insisted on diplomatic immunity, rather than clear my name, our name, *their* name.

'While I'm making heartfelt apologies, I'll make one to all of you for being a bit of a bore right now. It's just that – when you're accused of murder, something so heinous, so unthinkable, you want desperately to get it off your chest. You want to tell the truth more than anything else in the world. So that's what I'm doing today.

'You've heard the evidence – and there simply isn't any. You've heard character witnesses. And now you've heard from me. I did not kill Detective Patsy Hampton. I think you all know that, but I wanted to say it to you myself. Thank you for listening,' he said, and bowed slightly in his seat.

Shafer was brief, but he was poised and articulate, and, unfortunately, very believable. He always held eye contact with the jury members. His words weren't nearly as important as the way he delivered them.

Catherine Fitzgibbon came forward to do the cross-examination, and she was careful with Shafer at first. She knew that he had the jury on his side for the moment.

She waited until near the end of her cross-exam to go after Shafer where he might be most vulnerable.

'That was very nice, Mr Shafer. Now as you sit before this jury you claim that your relationship with Dr Cassady was strictly professional, that you did not have a sexual relationship with her? Remember you are under oath.'

'Yes, absolutely. She was, and hopefully will continue to be, my therapist.'

'Notwithstanding the fact that she admits to having a sexual relationship with you?'

Shafer held his hand toward Jules Halpern, signaling for him not to object. 'I believe that the court record will show that she did not admit to such.'

Fitzgibbon frowned. 'I don't follow? Why do *you* think she didn't answer counsel?'

Shafer shot back. 'That's obvious. Because she didn't care to *dignify* such a question.'

'And when she hung her head, sir, and looked down at her lap? She was nodding assent?'

Shafer now looked at the jury, and shook his head in amazement. 'You misread her completely. You missed the point again, Counselor. Allow me to illustrate, if I may. As Charles the First said before being beheaded, "Give me my cloak lest they think I tremble from fear." Dr Elizabeth Cassady was deeply embarrassed by your associate's crude suggestion, so was my family, and so am I.'

Geoffrey Shafer looked at the prosecutor with steely eyes. He then acknowledged the jury again. 'And so am I.'

Chapter Ninety-Nine

The trial was almost over, and now came the really hard part: waiting for a verdict. That Tuesday, the jurors retired to the jury room to commence their deliberations in the murder trial of Geoffrey Shafer. For the first time, I allowed myself to actually think the unthinkable: that Shafer might be set free.

Sampson and I sat in the rear row of the courtroom and watched the twelve members depart: eight men and four women. John had come to court several times, calling it the 'best and sleaziest show this side of the Oval Office', but I knew he was there to give me support.

'The sonofabitch is guilty, he's mad as little Davey Berkowitz,' Sampson said as he watched Shafer. 'But he has a lot of good actors on his side: doting wife, doting mistress, well-paid lawyers, Silly Billy. He could get away with it.'

'It happens,' I agreed. 'Juries are hard to read. And getting harder.'

I watched as Shafer courteously shook hands with the members of his defense team. Both Jules and Jane Halpern had forced smiles on their faces. *They knew, didn't they? Their client was the Weasel, a mass murderer.*

'Geoffrey Shafer has the ability to make people believe in him when he needs to. He's the best actor I've seen.'

I said goodbye to John, then I snuck out the back way again. This time neither Shafer nor the press was lying in wait downstairs or in the rear parking lot.

In the lot, I heard a woman's voice and I stopped moving. *I thought it was Christine.* A dozen or so people were walking to their cars, seemingly unaware of me. I felt fevered and hot as I checked them all. None of them was her. Where had the voice come from?

I took a ride in the old Porsche and listened to George Benson on the CD player. I remembered the police report about Shafer's thrill-seeking ride ending near Dupont Circle. It seemed a strangely appealing prospect. I took my own advice not to try and guess how the jury would decide the case. It could go either way.

I finally let myself think about Christine, and I choked up. It was too much. Tears began to stream down my cheeks. I had to pull over.

I took a deep breath, then another. The pain in my chest was still as fresh as it had been the day she had disappeared in Bermuda. She had tried to stay away from me, but I wouldn't let her. I was responsible for what had happened to her.

I drove around Washington, riding in gently aimless circles. I finally reached home more than two and a half hours after I left the courthouse.

Nana came running out of the house. She must have seen me pull into the driveway. She'd obviously been waiting for me.

I leaned out of the driver's side window. The DJ was still talking congenially on Public Radio.

'What is it, old woman? What's the matter now?' I asked Nana.

'Ms Fitzgibbon called you, Alex. The jury is coming back. They have a verdict.'

Chapter One Hundred

I was apprehensive as I could be. But I was also curious beyond anything I could remember.

I backed out of the driveway and sped downtown. I got back to the courthouse in less than fifteen minutes, and the crowd on E Street was larger and more unruly than I had seen it at the height of the trial. At least a half-dozen Union Jacks waved in the wind; contrasting that were American flags, including some painted across bare chests and faces.

I had to push and literally inch my way through the crush of people up close to the courthouse steps. I ignored every question from the press. I tried to avoid anyone with a camera in hand, or the hungry look of a reporter.

I entered the packed courtroom just before the jury filed back inside. *You almost missed it,* I said to myself.

Judge Fescoe spoke to the crowd as soon as everyone

was seated. 'There will be no demonstrations when this verdict is read. If any demonstrations occur, marshals will clear this room immediately,' he instructed in a soft but clear voice.

I stood a few rows behind the prosecution team and tried to find a regular breathing pattern. It was inconceivable that Geoffrey Shafer could be set free; there was no doubt in my mind that he'd murdered several times, not just Patsy Hampton, but at least some of the Jane Does. He was a wanton pattern killer, one of the worst, and had been getting away with it for years. I realized now that Shafer might be the most outrageous and daring of the killers I'd faced. He played his game with the pedal pressed to the floor. He absolutely refused to lose.

'Mr Foreperson, do you have a verdict for us?' Judge Fescoe asked in somber tones.

Raymond Horton, the foreperson, spoke to Judge Fescoe. 'Your honor, we have a verdict.'

I glanced at Shafer and he appeared confident. As he had been for every day of the trial, he was dressed in a tailored suit, white shirt and tie. He had no conscience whatsoever; he had no fear of anything that might happen. Maybe that was a partial explanation for why he'd run free for so long.

Judge Fescoe appeared unusually stern. 'Very well. Will the defendant please rise and face the jury,' he said.

Geoffrey Shafer stood at the defense table and his longish hair gleamed under the bright overhead lighting. He towered over Jules Halpern and his daughter, Jane.

Shafer held his hands behind him, as if he were cuffed. I wondered if he might have a pair of twenty-sided dice clasped in them, the kind I had seen in his study.

Judge Fescoe addressed Mr Horton again. 'As to count one of the indictment, Aggravated, Premeditated Murder in the First Degree, how do you find?'

Mr Horton answered, 'Not guilty, your honor.'

I felt as if my head had suddenly spun off. The audience packed into the small room went completely wild. The press rushed to the bar. The judge had promised to clear the room, but he was already retreating to his chambers.

I saw Shafer walk toward the press, but then he quickly passed them by. What was he doing now? He noticed a man in the crowd, and nodded stiffly in his direction. Who was that?

Then Shafer continued toward where I was, in the fourth row. I wanted to vault over the chairs after him. I wanted him so bad, and I knew I had just lost my chance to do it the right way.

'Detective Cross,' he said in his usual supercilious manner. 'Detective Cross, there's something I want to say. I've been holding it in for months.'

The press closed in; the scene becoming smothering and claustrophobic. Cameras flashed on all sides. Now that the trial was ended, there was nothing to prevent picture-taking inside the courtroom. Shafer was aware of the rare photo-opportunity. Of course he was. He spoke again, so that everyone gathered around us could hear.

Suddenly it was quiet where we stood, a pocket of silence, foreboding expectation.

'You killed her,' he said, and stared deeply into my eyes, almost to the back of my skull. *'You killed her.'*

I went numb. My legs were suddenly weak. I knew he didn't mean Patsy Hampton.

He meant Christine.

She was dead.

Geoffrey Shafer had killed her. He had taken everything from me, just as he warned me he would.

He had won.

Chapter One Hundred
and One

S hafer was a free man, and he was enjoying the bloody
hell out of it. He had gambled, and he had won big
time. *Big time!* He had never felt anything quite like this
exhilarating moment following his verdict. He'd wagered
his life.

He accompanied Lucy and the children to a
by-invitation-only press conference held in the pompous,
high-ceilinged Grand Jury room. He posed for countless
photos with his family. They hugged him again and again,
and Lucy couldn't stop crying like the brain-dead, hopelessly spoiled and crazy child that she was. If some people
thought *he* was a drug abuser, they'd be shocked by
Lucy's intake. Christ, that was how he'd first learned
about the amazing world of pharmaceuticals.

He finally punched his fist into the air and held it there
as a mocking sign of victory. Cameras flashed everywhere. They couldn't get enough of him. There were

nearly a hundred reporters wedged into the room. The women reporters loved him most of all. He was a legitimate media star now, wasn't he? He was a hero again.

A few gate-crashing agents of fame and fortune pressed their cards at him, promising obscene amounts of money for his story. He didn't need any of their tawdry business cards. Months before, he had picked out a powerful New York and Hollywood agent.

Christ, he was free as a bird! He was absolutely flying now. After the press conference, claiming concern for their safety, he sent his family ahead without him.

He stayed behind in the court law library and firmed up book deal details with Jules Halpern and the Bertelsmann Group, now the most powerful book publishing conglomerate around the world. He had promised them his story – but of course they weren't going to get anything close to the truth. Wasn't that the way with the so-called 'tell-all, bare-all' nonfiction published these days? Bertelsmann knew this, and still they'd paid him a fortune.

After the meeting, he took the slow-riding lift down to the court's indoor car park. He was still feeling incredibly high, which could be dangerous. A set of twenty-sided dice was burning a hole in the pocket of his suit trousers.

He desperately wanted to play the game. Now! The Four Horsemen. Better yet, Solipsis. *His* version of the game. He wouldn't give in to that urge, not yet. It was too dangerous, even for him.

Since the beginning of the trial, he had been parking the Jaguar in the same spot. He *did* have his patterns after all. He never bothered to put coins in the meter, not once. Every day there was a pile of five-dollar tickets under the windshield wiper.

Today was no exception.

He grabbed the absurd parking tickets off the windshield and crumpled them into a ball in his fist. Then he dropped the wad of paper onto the oil-stained concrete floor.

'I have diplomatic immunity,' he smiled as he climbed into his Jag.

Book Five

Endgame

Chapter One Hundred and Two

S hafer couldn't believe it. He had made a very serious and perhaps irreversible mistake. The result wasn't what he had expected, and now his whole world seemed to be falling apart. At times he thought that it couldn't have been worse if he had gone to prison for the cold-blooded murder of Patsy Hampton.

Shafer knew that he wasn't just being paranoid or mad. Several of the pathetic wankers inside the embassy were watching him every bloody time he stepped from his office. They seemed to resent him and openly despise him, especially the women. Who had turned them against him? Somebody surely was responsible.

He was the white, English O.J. Simpson. A weird off-color joke to them. Guilty though proven innocent.

So Shafer mostly stayed inside his office with the door closed, sometimes locked. He performed his few remaining duties with a growing sense of irritation and frustration, and a sense of the absurd. It was driving him mad to be trapped like this, to be a pathetic spectacle for the embassy staff.

He idly played with his computer and waited for the game of The Four Horsemen to resume, but the other players had cut him off. They insisted that it was too dangerous to play, even to communicate, and *not one of them* understood that that was exactly why this was the perfect time to play.

Shafer stared out onto Massachusetts Avenue for interminably long stretches during the day. He listened to call-in talk shows on the radio. He was getting angrier and angrier. He needed to play.

Someone was knocking on the door of his office. He turned his head sharply, and felt a spike of pain in the back of his neck. The phone had begun to ring. He picked up and heard the voice of the temp he'd been given. Ms Wynne Hamerman was on the intercom.

'Mr Andrew Jones is here to see you,' she said.

Andrew Jones? Shafer was shocked. Jones was a director from the Security Service in London. Shafer hadn't known he was in Washington. What the hell was this visit about? Andrew Jones was a high-level, very tough bastard who wouldn't just drop by for tea and biscuits. *Mustn't keep him waiting too long.*

Jones was standing there, and he looked impatient, almost angry. What was this about? His steely-blue eyes were cold and hard; his face as rigid as that of an English soldier in Belfast. In contrast, his brilliant red hair and mustache made him look benign, almost jolly. He was called 'Andrew the Red' back in London.

'Let's go inside your office, shall we? Shut the door behind you,' Jones said, in a low but commanding tone.

Shafer was just getting over his initial surprise, but he was also starting to become angry. Who was this pompous asshole to come barging into his office like this? By what right was he here? How dare he? The toad! The glorified lackey from London.

'You can sit down, Shafer,' Jones said. Another imperious command. 'I'll be brief and to the point.'

'Of course,' Shafer answered. He remained standing. 'Please do be brief. I'm sure we're both busy.'

Jones lit up a cigarette, took a long drag, then let the smoke out slowly.

'That's illegal here in Washington,' Shafer goaded him.

'You'll receive orders to return to England in thirty days' time,' said Jones, who continued to puff furiously on the cigarette. 'You're an embarrassment here in Washington, as you will be in London. Of course, over there the tabloids have recreated you as a martyr of the brutal and inefficient American police and judicial system. They like to think of this as *DC Confidential*, more evidence of wholesale corruption and naiveté in the States. Which we both know, in this case, is complete crap.'

Shafer smiled contemptuously. 'How dare you come in here and talk to me like this, Jones. I was framed for a heinous crime I didn't commit. I was acquitted by an American jury. Have you forgotten that?'

Jones frowned, and continued to stare him down. 'Only because crucial evidence wasn't allowed in the trial. The blood on your trousers? That poor woman's blood in the bathroom drain at your mistress's?' He blew smoke out of the side of his mouth. 'We know everything, you pathetic fool. We know you're a stone-cold killing freak. So you'll *go* back to London – until we catch you at something. Which we will, Shafer. We'll make something up if we have to.

'I feel sick being in the same room with you. Legally, you've escaped punishment this time, but we're watching you very closely now. We will get you, somewhere, some day soon.'

Shafer looked amused. He couldn't hold back a smile. He knew he shouldn't, but he couldn't resist the play. 'You can try, you insufferable, sanctimonious shit. You can certainly try. But join the queue. And now, if you please, I have work to do.'

Andrew Jones shook his head. 'Well actually, you don't have any work to do, Shafer. But I am happy to leave. The stench in here is absolutely overpowering. When was the last time you had a bath?' He laughed contemptuously. 'Christ, you've completely lost it.'

Chapter One Hundred
and Three

That afternoon I met with Jones and three of his agents at the Willard Hotel, near the White House. I had called the meeting. Sampson was there, too. He'd been reinstated in the department, but that didn't stop him from doing what had originally gotten him into trouble.

'I believe he's crazy,' Jones said of Shafer. 'He smells like a lavatory at boot camp. He's definitely going down for the count. What're your thoughts on his mental state?'

I knew Geoffrey Shafer inside and out by now. I'd read about his family: his brothers, a long-suffering mother, the domineering father. Their travels from military base to base until he was twelve. 'Here's what I think. It started with a serious bipolar disorder, what used to be called manic-depression. He had it when he was a kid. Now he's strung out on pharmaceutical drugs: Xanax, Benadryl, Haldol, Ativan, Valium, Librium, several others. It's quite a cocktail. Available from local doctors for the right price. I'm surprised he can function at all. But he survives. He doesn't go down. He always wins.'

'I told Geoff he has to leave Washington. How do you think he'll take it?' Jones asked. 'I swear his office smelled as if a dead body had been festering there for a couple of days.'

'Actually his disorder can involve an accompanying odor, but it's usually steely – like metal, very pungent, sticks to your nostrils. He probably isn't bathing. But his instincts for playing the game, for winning and surviving, are amazing,' I said. 'He won't stop.'

'What's happening with the other players?' Sampson inquired. 'The so-called Horsemen?'

'They claim that the game is over, and that it was only a fantasy game for them. Oliver Highsmith stays in touch, to keep tabs on us, I'm sure. He's actually a scary bastard in his own right. Says he's saddened by the murder of Detective Hampton. He's still not a hundred percent sure that Shafer is the killer. Urges me to keep my mind open on that one.'

'Is your mind open on it?' I asked, looking around the room at the others.

Jones didn't hesitate. 'I have no doubt that Geoffrey Shafer is a multiple murderer. We've seen enough, and heard enough from you. He is quite possibly a homicidal maniac beyond anything we've ever seen. And I also have no doubt that eventually he's going down.'

I nodded my head. 'I agree,' I said, 'about everything you just said. But especially the homicidal maniac part.'

Chapter One Hundred
and Four

S hafer was talking to himself again that night. He couldn't help it, and the more he tried to stop, the worse it became; the more he fretted, the more he talked to himself.

They can all bugger off. Jones, Cross, Lucy and the kids, Boo Cassady, the other spineless players. Screw them all. There was a reason behind The Four Horsemen, he knew. *It wasn't just a game. There was more to it than simple horseplay.*

The house at Kalorama was empty, much too quiet at night. It was huge and ridiculous, as only an American house can be. The 'original' architectural detail, the double living room, six fireplaces, long-ago-dead flowers, unread books in gold and brown leather binding, Lucy's Marmite. It was driving him up the twelve-foot-high walls.

He spent the next hour or so trying to convince himself that he wasn't crazy; specifically that he wasn't an addict. Recently, he'd added another doctor in Maryland to his sources for the drugs. Unfortunately, the illegal prescriptions cost him a fortune. He couldn't keep it up forever. The Lithium and Haldol were to control his mood swings – which were very real. Thorazine was for acute anxiety, which was fucking bloody real as well. Narcan had also been prescribed for his mood swings. The multiple injections of Loradol were for something else, some pain from he couldn't remember when. He knew there were good reasons for the Xanax, Compazine, Benadryl.

Lucy had already fled home to London, and she'd taken the traitorous children with her. They'd left exactly one week after the trial ended. Her father was the real cause. He'd come to Washington, spoken to Lucy for less than an hour, and she'd packed up and left, like the Goody Two-Shoes she'd always been. Before she departed, Lucy had the nerve to tell Shafer she'd stood by him for the sake of the children and her father, but now her duty was over. She didn't believe he was a murderer, as her father did; but he was an adulterer, and that she couldn't take for one moment longer.

God, how he despised his little wifey. Before Lucy left, *he* made it clear to *her* that the real reason she'd performed her 'duty' was so he wouldn't reveal her unsavory drug habits to the press, which he *would* have, and might do anyway.

At eleven o'clock he had to go out for a drive, his nightly constitutional. He was feeling unbearably jittery and claustrophobic. He wondered if he could control himself for another night, another minute. His skin was crawling, and he had dozens of irritating little tics. He couldn't stop tapping his goddamn foot!

The dice were burning a bloody hole in his trouser pocket. His mind was racing in a dozen haphazard directions, all of them very bad. He wanted to, needed to, kill somebody. It had been this way with him for a long time, and that had been his dirty little secret. The other Horsemen knew the story; they even knew how it had begun. Shafer had been a decent soldier, but ultimately too ambitious to remain in the army. He had transferred into MI6 with the help of Lucy's father. He thought there was more room for advancement in MI6.

His first posting had been Bangkok, which was where he met James Whitehead, George Bayer, and eventually Oliver Highsmith. Whitehead and Bayer spent several weeks working on him, recruiting Shafer for a specialized job: he would be an assassin, their own personal hit man for the worst sort of wet work. Over the next two years he did three sanctions in Asia, and found that he truly loved the feeling of power that killing gave him. Oliver Highsmith, who ran both Bayer and Whitehead from London, once told him to depersonalize the act, to think of it as a game, and that was what he did. He had never stopped being an assassin.

Shafer turned on the CD in the Jag. *Loud*, to drown out the multiple voices raging in his head. The old-age-home rockers Jimmy Page and Robert Plant began a duet inside the cockpit of his car.

He backed out of the drive and headed down Tracy Place. He gunned the car and had it up close to sixty in the block between his house and Twenty-Fourth Street. Time for another suicidal drive? he wondered.

Red lights flashed on the side of Twenty-Fourth Street. Shafer cursed as a DC police patrol car eased down the street toward him. *God damn it!*

He pulled the Jag over to the curb and waited. His brain was screaming. 'Assholes. Bloody impertinent assholes! And you're an asshole, too!' he told himself in a loud whisper. 'Show some self-control, Geoff. Get yourself under control. Shape up. Right now!'

The Metro patrol car pulled up behind him, almost door to door. He could see two cops lurking inside.

One of them got out slowly and walked over to the Jag's driver-side window. The cop swaggered like a hot-shit all-American cinema hero. Shafer wanted to blow him away. Knew he could do it. He had a hot semi-automatic under the seat. He touched the grip, and God, it felt good.

'License and registration, sir,' the cop said, looking unbearably smug. A distorted voice inside Shafer's head screeched, *Shoot him now. It will blow everybody's mind if you kill another policeman.*

He handed over the requested identification, though, and managed a wanker's sheepish grin. 'We're out of Pampers at home. Trip to the 7-Eleven was in order. I know I was going too fast, and I'm sorry, Officer. Blame it on baby brain. You have any kids?'

The patrolman didn't say a word; not an ounce of civility in the bastard. He wrote out a speeding ticket. Took his sweet time about it.

'There you go, Mr Shafer.' The patrol officer handed him the speeding ticket. 'Oh, and by the way, we're watching you, shithead. We're all over you, man. You didn't get away with murdering Patsy Hampton. You just think you did.'

A set of car lights blinked on and off, on and off, on the side street where the patrol car had been sitting a few moments earlier.

Shafer stared, squinted back into the darkness. He recognized the car, a black Porsche.

Cross was there, watching. Alex Cross wouldn't go away.

Chapter One Hundred and Five

A ndrew Jones sat in the quiet, semi-darkened front seat of the Porsche with me. We'd been working closely together for almost two weeks. Jones and the Security Service were intent on stopping Shafer before he committed another murder. They were also tracking War, Famine, and Conqueror.

We watched silently as Geoffrey Shafer slowly turned the Jaguar around and drove back toward his house.

'He saw us. He knows my car,' I said. 'Good.'

I couldn't see his face in the darkness, but I could almost feel the heat rising from the top of his head. I knew he was crazed. The phrase 'homicidal maniac' kept drifting through my mind. Jones and I were looking at one, and he was still running free. He'd already gotten away with murder, several of them.

'Alex, aren't you concerned about possibly putting him into a rage state?' Jones asked, as the Jaguar eased to a stop in front of the Georgian-style house. There were no lights on in the driveway area, so we couldn't see Geoffrey Shafer for the next few seconds. We couldn't tell if he'd gone inside.

'He's already in a rage state. He's lost his job, his wife, his children, the game he lives for. Worst of all, his freedom to come and go has been curtailed. Shafer doesn't like limitations put on him, hates to be boxed in. He can't stand to lose.'

'So you think he'll do something rash.'

'Not rash, he's too clever. But he'll make a move. It's how the game is played.'

'And then we'll mess with his head yet again?'

'Yes, we will. Absolutely.'

Late that night, as I was driving home, I decided to stop at St Anthony's. The church is unusual in this day and age; it's open at night. Monsignor John Kelliher believes that's the way it should be, and he's willing to live with the vandalism and petty theft. Mostly, though, the people in the neighborhood watch over St Anthony's.

A couple of worshipers were inside the candlelit church around midnight, when I arrived. There usually are a few 'parishioners' inside. Homeless people aren't allowed to sleep there, but they wander in and out all through the night.

I sat watching the familiar red-and-gold votive lamps flicker and blink. I sucked in the thick smell of incense from Benediction. I stared up at the large gold-plated crucifix and the beautiful stained-glass windows that

I've loved since I was a boy.

I lit a candle for Christine, and I hoped that somehow, some way, she might still be alive. It didn't seem likely. My memory of her was fading a little bit, and I hated that. A column of pain went from my stomach to my chest, making it hard for me to breathe. It had been this way since the night she disappeared, almost a year ago.

And then, for the first time, I admitted to myself that she was gone. I would never see her again. The thought caught like a shard of glass in my throat. Tears welled in my eyes. 'I love you,' I whispered to no one. 'I love you so much and I miss you terribly.'

I said a few more prayers, then I finally rose from the long wooden pew and silently made my way toward the doors of the vestibule. I didn't see the woman crouching in a side row. She startled me with a sudden movement.

I recognized her from the soup kitchen. Her name was Magnolia. That was all I knew about her, just an odd first name, maybe a made-up one. She called out to me in a loud voice. 'Hey, Peanut Butter Man, now you know what it's like.'

Chapter One Hundred and Six

Jones and Sandy Greenberg, from Interpol, had helped get the other three Horsemen under surveillance. The net being cast was large, as the catch could be, if we succeeded.

The huge potential scandal in England was being carefully watched and monitored by the Security Service. If four English agents were murderers involved in a bizarre game, the fallout would be widespread and devastating for the intelligence community.

Shafer dutifully went to the embassy to work on Wednesday and Thursday. He arrived just before nine and left promptly at five. Once inside, he stayed out of sight in his small office, not even venturing out for lunch. He spent hours on America Online, which we monitored.

Both days, he wore the same gray slacks and a double-breasted blue blazer. His clothes were uncharacteristically wrinkled and unkempt. His thick blond hair was combed back, looked dirty and greasy, and it resisted the high winds flowing through Washington. He looked pale, seemed nervous and fidgety.

Was he going to crash?

After dinner on Friday night, Nana and I sat out in back of the house on Fifth Street. We were talking, and spending more time together than we had in years. I knew she was concerned about me, and I let her help as much as she wanted. For both our sakes.

Jannie and Damon were washing the dishes inside and they managed not to squabble too much. Damon washed while Jannie dried. Damon's tape deck played the beautiful score from the movie *Beloved*.

'Most families have a disher and dryer these days,' Nana said, after she'd taken a sip of her tea. 'Slavery has ended in America, Alex. Did you happen to hear about that?'

'We have a dishwasher and dryer, too. Sounds like they're in good working order. Low maintenance, low cost. Hard to beat.'

Nana clucked. 'See how long it lasts.'

'If you want a dishwasher we can buy it, or are you just practicing the fine art of being argumentative before you launch into something more deserving of your talents? As I remember, you are a fan of Demosthenes and Cicero.'

She nudged me with her elbow. 'Wiseapple,' she said. 'Think you're so smart.'

I shook my head. 'Not really, Nana. That's never been one of my big problems.'

'No, I suppose not. You're right, you don't have a big head about yourself.' Nana stared into my eyes. I could almost feel her peering into my soul. She has an ability to look very deeply into things that really matter. 'You ever going to stop blaming yourself?' she finally asked. 'You look just terrible.'

'Thank you. Are you ever going to stop nagging me?' I asked, and finally smiled at her. Nana could always bring me out of the doldrums, in her own special way.

She nodded her small head. 'Of course I will. I'll stop one day. Nobody lives forever, grannyson.'

I laughed. 'You probably will, though. Live longer than me or the kids.'

Nana showed lots of teeth – her own, too. 'I *do* feel pretty good, considering everything,' she said. 'You're still chasing him, aren't you? That's what you're doing nights. You and John Sampson, that Englishman, Andrew Jones.'

I sighed. 'Yeah, I am. And we're going to get him. There may be four men involved in a series of murders. Here, in Asia, Jamaica, London.'

She beckoned to me with a bent, crabbed forefinger. 'Come closer now.'

I grinned at her. She's such a soft touch really, such a sweetie, but such a hardass, too. 'You want me to sit down on your lap, old woman? You sure about that?'

'Good Lord, no. Don't sit on me, Alex. Just bend over and show some respect for my age and wisdom. Give me a big hug, while you're at it.'

I did as I was told, and I noticed there wasn't any fuss

or clatter coming from the kitchen anymore.

I glanced at the screen door, and saw my two little busybodies were watching, their faces pressed against the mesh wire. I waved them away from the door, and their faces disappeared.

'I want you to be so very, very careful,' Nana whispered as I held her gently. 'But I want you to get him somehow, some way. That man is the worst of all of them. Geoffrey Shafer is the worst, Alex, the most evil.'

Chapter One Hundred and Seven

The game had never really ended – but it had changed tremendously since the trial in Washington.

It was five thirty in the evening in London and Conqueror was waiting at his computer. He was both anxious and feverishly excited about what was happening: The Four Horsemen was starting up again.

It was twelve thirty a.m. in Manila in the Philippines. Famine was ready for a message, and a new beginning to the game he loved.

And War awaited news of The Four Horsemen at his large house on the island of Jamaica. He too was obsessed with how it would end, and whether he would be the winner.

It was twelve thirty in Washington. Geoffrey Shafer was driving fast to the White Flint Mall, from the embassy. He had a lot to accomplish that afternoon. He was revved and manic.

He sped up Massachusetts Avenue, past the British Embassy and the vice-president's house. He wondered if he was being followed and assumed it was possible. Alex Cross and the other police were out there, just waiting to get him. He hadn't spotted them yet, which only meant that they were getting serious now.

He made a quick right, hit a traffic circle, and shot onto Nebraska Avenue headed toward American University. He snaked around back roads near the university, then got on Wisconsin, and sped toward the mall.

He entered Bloomingdale's, found the department store sparsely crowded, a little depressing actually. Good, he despised the American shopping scene anyway. It reminded him of Lucy and her brood. He walked at a leisurely pace through the men's clothing section. He picked up a few overpriced Ralph Lauren Polo sport shirts, and then two pairs of dark trousers.

He draped a black Giorgio Armani suit over his arm and took the bundle into the changing rooms. At a security desk inside he handed the clothes to an attendant on duty, to curtail shoplifters, no doubt.

'Changed my mind,' he said.

'That's not a problem, sir.'

Shafer then jogged down a narrow corridor that led to a rear exit. He sprinted toward the glass doors, then burst into a parking lot in back. He saw signs for Bruno Cipriani and Lord & Taylor, and knew he was heading in the right direction.

A Ford Taurus was parked there near the F pole. Shafer

jumped inside, started it up, and drove up the Rockville Pike to Montrose Crossing, a little over a mile away.

He didn't think anyone was following now. He passed Montrose, and headed north to the Federal Plaza shopping center. Once he was there, he entered Cyber Exchange, which sold new and used software and lots of computers.

His eyes darted left and right, until he saw exactly what he needed.

'I'd like to try out the new iMac,' he told the salesperson who approached him.

'Be my guest. You need any assistance, holler,' the salesperson said. 'It's easy.'

'Yes, I think I'm fine. I'll call if I get stuck. I'm pretty sure I'm going to buy the iMac, though.'

'Excellent choice.'

'Yes. Excellent, excellent.'

The lazy clerk left him alone and Shafer immediately booted on. The display model was connected online. He felt a rush of manic excitement, but also a tinge of sadness as he typed in his message to the other players. He'd thought this through and knew what had to be said, what had to be done.

GREETINGS AND SALUTATIONS. THIS GLORI-OUS AND UNPRECEDENTED ADVENTURE OF EIGHT YEARS, THE FOUR HORSEMEN, IS NEARLY AT AN END NOW. YOU HAVE STATED YOUR CASE VERY LOGICALLY, AND I ACCEPT

THE REGRETTABLE CONCLUSION YOU'VE REACHED. THE GAME HAS BECOME TOO DANGEROUS. SO I PROPOSE THAT WE CREATE AN UNFORGETTABLE ENDING. I BELIEVE THAT A FACE-TO-FACE MEETING IS A FITTING END. IT'S THE ONLY CONCLUSION THAT I CAN ACCEPT.

THIS WAS INEVITABLE, I SUPPOSE, AND WE HAVE DISCUSSED IT MANY TIMES BEFORE. YOU KNOW WHERE THE GAME ENDS. I PROPOSE THAT WE START PLAY ON THURSDAY. TRUST ME, I WILL BE THERE FOR THE GRAND FINALE. IF NECESSARY, I CAN BEGIN THE GAME WITHOUT YOU. DON'T MAKE ME DO THAT...
DEATH.

Chapter One Hundred and Eight

At nine o'clock on Monday morning, Shafer joined the monotonous, stomach-turning line of workaday morons stuck in traffic headed in the direction of Embassy Row. He had the intoxicating thought that he would never be going to work again after today. Everything in his life was about to change. He couldn't go back.

His heart was pounding as he stopped and waited at the green light on Massachusetts Avenue near the embassy. Car horns beeped behind him, and he was reminded of his suicide run a year ago. Those were the days, damn it. Then he blasted through on the red. He ran. He had rehearsed his escape. This was for keeps.

He saw two blocks of clear roadway ahead and he floored the gas. The Jaguar leaped forward, raw phallic power, as it were. The sports car rocketed toward the puzzle of side streets around American University.

Ten minutes later he was turning into the White Flint

Mall at fifty, gunning the Jag up to fifty-five, sixty, sixty-five as he sped across the mostly empty lot. He was sure no one had followed him.

He drove toward a large Borders Books & Music store, turned right, then zoomed up a narrow side lane between the buildings.

There were five exits out of the mall that he knew of. He accelerated again, tires squealing.

The surrounding neighborhood was a warren of narrow streets. Still no one was behind him, not a single car.

He knew of a little-used one-way entrance onto the Rockville Pike. He got on the road, heading out against the barrage of traffic streaming to work in the city. He hadn't spotted any cars speeding behind him inside the mall, or on the side streets, or on the Pike.

They probably had only one, or at most two cars on him in the morning. That made the most sense to Shafer. Neither the Washington Metro police nor the Security Service would approve a large surveillance detail to follow him. He didn't think so anyway.

He'd probably lost them. He whooped loudly and started blaring the Jag's horn at all the pathetic suckers and fools stuck in the oncoming lanes, headed toward work. He'd been waiting nearly eight years for this.

It was finally here.

Endgame.

Chapter One Hundred
and Nine

'**W**e've still got him?' I asked Jones, nervously looking around at the half-dozen agents working in the crisis room inside the British Embassy. The room was filled with state-of-the-art electrical equipment including half-a-dozen video monitors.

'Still got him. He won't get away that easily, Alex. Besides, we think we know where he and the others are going now.'

We had a tiny, sophisticated homing device on the Jaguar, but there was a reasonable chance Shafer would discover it. So far, he hadn't. And now he was running in the Jag, running with the bait, at least that was what we thought was happening.

The Horsemen were all on the move. Oliver Highsmith had been followed from his home in Surrey to Gatwick Airport, outside London. Agents at the airport made sure that Conqueror got on the British Airways flight to New

York, then called Washington to report he was en route.

A couple of hours later, an agent called from the Philippines. George Bayer was at Ninoy Aquino Airport in Manila. Famine had purchased a ticket to Jamaica, with a stopover in New York.

We already knew that James Whitehead had retired to Jamaica, and he was on the island at this time. War was waiting for the others to arrive.

'I'm trying to get a fixed pattern for The Four Horsemen game, but there are several points of view at work. That's what they like about the game, what makes it so addictive,' I said to Jones as we waited for more information to come in.

'We know that at least three of them have been playing the game since they were stationed in Thailand in ninety-one. Around that time, bar girls and prostitutes began to disappear in Bangkok. The local police didn't spend much time on the investigation. Girls in Pot Pol had disappeared before. The police have somewhat the same attitude here in Washington with respect to the Jane Doe killings. These girls didn't mean much. They were written off. Murders and disappearances in Southeast certainly aren't investigated like the ones in Georgetown or on Capitol Hill. It's one of Washington's dirty little secrets.'

Jones lit a new cigarette with the butt of his last one. He puffed, then said, 'It might just be Shafer who's involved in the actual murders, Alex. That, or the others are much more careful than he is.'

I shrugged my shoulders. I didn't think so, but I didn't have enough concrete evidence to argue my case effectively with Jones, who was no slouch as a detective.

'The end of The Four Horsemen is coming, right? Can they really end their little fantasy game?' Sampson asked.

'It sure looks like they're getting together,' I said. 'Four former British agents, four grown men who love to play diabolical games. In my opinion, four murderers.'

'Possibly.' Andrew Jones finally admitted that the unthinkable could be true. 'Alex, I'm afraid that you could be right.'

Chapter One Hundred and Ten

J amaica must have been chosen because it was relatively private, and because James Whitehead owned a large beach house there. But perhaps there were other angles attached to the game of The Four Horsemen. I hoped that we would know soon enough.

Oliver Highsmith and George Bayer arrived on the island within minutes of each other. They met at baggage inside Donald Sangster Airport, then drove for about an hour to the posh Jamaica Inn in Ocho Rios.

We were on the move, too. Sampson and I had gotten there on an early-morning flight from DC. The weather was glorious. Blue skies, warm breezes. We heard strains of English and Jamaican Creole at the airport, reggae and ska. The rustle of banana trees, as the sea breeze rushed through them, was like a soft chorus.

The hotel in Ocho Rios was very private and old-fashioned, just forty-five rooms overlooking the sea. We arrived there simultaneously with four English teams. There were also two teams of detectives from Kingston.

The English High Commission office in Kingston had been alerted about our presence and our purpose here. Full cooperation had been promised. Everyone was committed to bringing down all four game-players, whatever the consequences, and I was very impressed with the English group, and also the local detectives.

We waited for Geoffrey Shafer. Sampson and I were strategically positioned to watch the narrow, shaded road that led to the hotel. We were on a lush hillside between the hotel and the sparkling blue Caribbean sea. Andrew Jones and another agent were in a second car hidden near the hotel's rear entrance. Six of his agents were posing as porters and maintenance workers at the hotel. Jamaican detectives were also on the grounds.

We'd had no news about Shafer. He had finally lost us. But we believed he would join the rest of the Horsemen. Jones complained that there weren't enough of us to stop Shafer if he was coming after the others. I agreed. If Shafer was playing kamikaze, there would be no adequate defense.

So we waited and waited. Continual updates came in over the car's short-wave radio. The messages didn't stop all afternoon. They were a kind of electronic heartbeat for our surveillance detail.

Oliver Highsmith is still in his room. Doesn't want to be disturbed apparently . . .

Bayer is in his room as well. Subject was spotted on the

terrace about ten minutes ago, checking out the beach with binoculars . . .

Bayer has left his room. He's taking a dip in the deep blue sea. Subject is in a red-striped swimming costume. Difficult to miss. Makes the job easier. Not on the eyes, though . . .

A black Mercedes arriving at the front gate. Driver's tall and blond. Could be Geoffrey Shafer. You see him, Alex?

I reported in immediately. 'The blond man isn't Shafer. Repeat, it isn't Shafer. Too young, probably American. Young wife and two children tagging along. False alarm. It isn't Shafer.'

The radio reports continued.

Highsmith has just ordered up from room service. Two English breakfasts in the middle of the day. One of our people will bring it up to him . . .

Bayer is back from his swim. He's well-tanned. Little guy, but muscular. Tried to hit on some ladies. Struck out.

Finally, at around six o'clock, I made another report. 'James Whitehead just drove up in a green Range Rover! He's coming inside the hotel. War is here.'

Only one more game-player to go.

We waited. Death had yet to arrive.

Chapter One Hundred and Eleven

Shafer was in no particular hurry to flash the check-ered flag. He took his sweet time thinking through each possible scenario. He had spotted the coast of Jamaica on the horizon, several hours before. He had originally flown to Puerto Rico, then sailed from there in a chartered boat. He wanted to be able to leave, either by air or sea.

Now he calmly waited for nightfall, drifting in his boat with the cooling trade winds. It was the famous 'blue hour' on the sea, just past sunset, extraordinarily serene and beautiful. Also magical and slightly unreal. He had finished five hundred more pushups on the deck of the boat, and he wasn't even winded. He could see half-a-dozen large cruise ships anchored near Ocho Rios. All around him were scores of smaller boats like his own.

He remembered reading somewhere that the island of Jamaica had once been the personal property of

Christopher Columbus. He remembered because he admired a time when a man could take whatever he wanted, and often did. His body was tight and hard, and he was bronze from three days of sun during his trip. His hair was bleached even blonder than usual. He'd had the drugs under control for almost a week now. It had been an act of will, and he'd risen to the challenge. He wanted to win.

Shafer felt like a god. No, he *was* a god. He controlled every move in his own life and the lives of several others. There were surprises left, he thought as he slowly sprayed his body with cooling streams of water. There were surprises for everybody who still chose to be in the game.

His game.

His plan.

His ending.

Because this wasn't just a game, it never had been. The other players had to know it by now. They understood what they had done, and why there had to be revenge. It was what The Four Horsemen had been all about from the beginning: *the endgame was revenge, and revenge was his . . . Or theirs? Who knew for sure?*

His father had taught him and his brothers to sail, probably the only useful thing he'd ever done for Shafer. He actually could find peace on the sea. It was probably the real reason he'd come to Jamaica by boat.

At eight o'clock he swam to shore, passing several of the smaller sailboats and a few motorboats. He found the physical exertion a neat antidote for anxiety and nerves.

He was a strong swimmer and diver, good at most sports.

The night air was peaceful and calm and fragrant. The sea was flat. Not a ripple disturbed the surface. Well, there would be plenty of ripples soon.

A car was waiting for him just off the coast road, a black Ford Mustang, glossy and shiny in the moonlight.

He smiled when he saw it. The game was progressing beautifully.

Famine was there to meet him.

No, Famine was there for another reason, wasn't he?

George Bayer was waiting on shore to kill him.

Chapter One Hundred and Twelve

George Bayer isn't in his room. He's not with Oliver Highsmith or James Whitehead either. Damn it to hell! He's loose.

The alarming message went out over the two-way radio. Sampson and I had been watching the south side of the hotel for close to eight hours, and we were sure George Bayer hadn't come our way.

We heard Andrew Jones's concerned voice on the radio. 'Remember that all of The Four Horsemen are agents like ourselves. They're capable and deadly. Let's find Bayer right away, and be extra alert for Geoffrey Shafer. Shafer is the most dangerous player. At least we *think* he is.'

Sampson and I hurried out of the rented sedan. We had our guns out, but they seemed inappropriate at the beautiful and serene resort. I remembered feeling the same way – nearly a year ago in Bermuda.

'Bayer didn't come this way,' Sampson said. I knew he

was concerned that Jones's people had lost Famine. We wouldn't have, but we were seen as backup, not the primary team.

The two of us quickly walked up a nearby hill that gave us a perspective on the manicured lawns rolling down toward the hotel's private beach. It was getting dark, but the grounds near the hotel were relatively well-lit. A couple in bathing suits and robes slowly walked toward us. They were holding hands, oblivious to the danger. No George Bayer, though. And no Shafer.

'How do they end this thing?' Sampson asked. 'How do you think the game ends?'

'I don't think any of them know for sure. They probably have game plans, but anything can happen now. It all depends on Shafer, if he follows the rules. I think he's beyond that, and the other players know it.'

We hurried along, running close to the hotel buildings. We were getting nervous and concerned looks from hotel guests we passed on the narrow, winding sidewalk.

'They're all killers. Even Jones finally admits that. They killed as agents and then they didn't want to stop. They liked it. Now – maybe they plan to kill one another. Winner takes all.'

'And Geoffrey Shafer hates to lose,' said Sampson.

'Shafer doesn't ever lose. We've seen that already. *That's* his pattern, John. It's what we missed from the start.'

'He doesn't get away this time, sugar. No matter what, Shafer doesn't walk.'

I didn't answer.

Chapter One Hundred and Thirteen

Shafer wasn't even breathing hard as he made it to the white-sand shoreline. George Bayer stepped out of the black Ford Mustang and Shafer watched for a weapon to appear. He continued to walk forward, playing the game of games for the highest stakes of all – his life.

'You bloody *swam*?' Bayer asked, his voice jovial, yet taunting.

'Well, actually, it's a fantastic night for it,' Shafer said, and casually shook water off his body. He waited for Bayer to move on him. He observed the way he tensed and untensed his right hand. Watched the slight forward slant of his shoulders.

Shafer took off a waterproof backpack and pulled out fresh dry clothes and shoes. Now he had access to his weapons. 'Let me guess. Oliver suggested that you all gang up on me,' he said. 'Three against one.'

Bayer smiled slyly. 'Of course. That had to be considered as an option. We rejected it because it wasn't consistent with our characters in the game.'

Shafer shook his hair, let the water drip off. As he dressed, he turned halfway away from Bayer. He smiled to himself. God, he loved this – the game of life and death against another Horseman, a master player. He admired Bayer's calmness, and his ability to be so smooth.

'Oliver's playing is so bloody predictable. He was the same way as an agent and analyst. They sent you, George, because they thought I'd never suspect you'd try to take me out by yourself. You're the first play. It's so obvious, though. A terrible waste of a player.'

Bayer frowned slightly, but still didn't lose his cool, didn't let on what he felt. He obviously thought that was the safest attitude, but it was how Shafer knew his suspicion was true. Famine was here to kill him. He was sure of it. George Bayer's cool attitude had given him away.

'No, nothing like that,' Bayer said. 'We're going to play according to the rules tonight. The rules are important to us. It's to be a board game, a contest of strategy and wits. I'm just here to pick you up, according to plan. We'll meet face to face at the hotel.'

'And we'll abide by the throw of the dice?' Shafer asked.

'Yes, of course, Geoff.' Bayer held out his hand and showed him three twenty-sided dice.

Shafer couldn't hold back a sharp laugh. This was so

good, so rich.'So what did the dice say, George? How do I lose? How do I die? A knife? A pistol? A drug overdose makes a great deal of sense to me.'

Bayer couldn't help himself. He laughed. Shafer was such a cocky bastard, such a good killer, a wonderful psychopathic personality. 'Well, yes, it might have occurred to us, but we played it completely straight. As I said, they're waiting at the hotel for us. Let's go.'

Shafer turned his back on Bayer for an instant. Then he pushed hard off his right foot. He sprung at Bayer.

Bayer was more than ready for him. He threw a short, hard punch. It struck Shafer's cheek, rattled, maybe even loosened a few teeth. The right side of his head went completely numb.

'Good one, George. Good stuff!'

Then Shafer head-butted Bayer with all of his strength. He heard the crunch of bone against bone, saw an explosion of dizzying white before his eyes. That got his adrenaline flowing.

The dice went flying from Bayer's hand as he reached for a gun, or some other weapon. It was in the back of his waistband.

Shafer clutched Bayer's right arm, twisted with all of his strength, and broke it at the elbow. Bayer shrieked in pain.

'You can't beat me! Nobody has, nobody can!' Shafer screamed at the top of his voice.

He grabbed George Bayer's throat and squeezed with superhuman strength. Bayer gagged, and turned the brightest red, as if all the blood in his body had rushed to his head. George was stronger than he appeared to be, but Shafer was speeding on adrenaline and years of pure hatred. He outweighed Bayer by twenty pounds, all of it muscle.

'*Noooo*. Listen to me.' George Bayer wheezed and gasped. 'Not like this. Not here.'

'*Yes*, George. *Yes, yes*. The game is on. The game that you bastards started. Tally-ho, old chap. *You* did this to me. You made me what I am. Death.'

He heard a loud, crisp snap and George Bayer went limp against him. He let the body fall to the sand.

'One down,' said Shafer, and finally allowed himself a deep, satisfying breath. He snatched up the fallen dice, shook them once, then hurled them into the sea. 'I don't use the dice anymore,' he said.

Chapter One Hundred
and Fourteen

He felt so damn good. So fine. God, how he had missed this. The mainline of adrenaline, the incomparable thrill. He knew it was likely that the Jamaica Inn was being watched by the police, so he parked the Mustang at the nearby Plantation Inn.

He walked at a quickening pace through the crowded Bougainvillea Terrace. Drinks were being served while the wretched song 'Yellowbird' played loudly. He had a nasty fantasy about shooting up the terrace, killing several dickhead tourists, so he got away from the crowded area immediately, for everybody's sake, but mostly his own.

He strolled the beach and it calmed him. It was quiet, restful, with strains of calypso music gently weaving through the night air. The stretch between the two hotels was eye-catching, plenty of spotlights, sand the color of champagne, thatched umbrellas at even intervals. A very nice playing field.

He knew where Oliver Highsmith was staying, the famous White Suite, where Winston Churchill and David Niven and Ian Fleming had all slept once upon a time. Highsmith loved his creature comforts almost as much as he loved the game itself. Shafer despised the other Horsemen, partly because he wasn't in their social class. Lucy's father had got him into MI6; the other players had been from the right backgrounds. Shafer's didn't quite match up. But there was another, more powerful reason for his hatred: they had dared to use him, to feel superior and throw it in his face.

He entered through a white picket-fence gate at the property line of the Jamaica Inn. He broke into a soft jog. He wanted to run, to sweat. He was feeling manic again. Playing the game had made him too excited.

Shafer held his head for a moment. He wanted to laugh and scream at the top of his lungs. He leaned against a wooden post leading up from the beach, and tried to catch his breath. He realized he was crashing and it couldn't have happened at a worse time.

'Everything all right, sir?' a hotel waiter stopped and asked him.

'Oh, couldn't be better,' Shafer said, waving the man away. 'I'm in heaven, can't you tell?'

He started walking toward the White Suite again. He realized that he was feeling the way he had the morning he'd nearly crashed his car in Washington. He was in serious trouble again. He could lose the game right now, lose everything. That required a change of strategy, didn't it? He had to be more daring, even more aggressive. He had to act, not think too much. The odds against him were still two to one.

At the far end of the courtyard, he spotted a man and a woman in evening clothes. They were loitering near a white stucco portico strewn with flowers. He decided they were Jones's people. They had staked out the hotel, after all. They were here for him and he was honored.

The male glanced his way, and Shafer abruptly lowered his head. There was nothing they could do to stop or detain him. He'd committed no crime they could prove. He wasn't wanted by the police. No, he was a free man.

So Shafer walked toward them at a leisurely pace, as if he hadn't seen them. He whistled 'Yellowbird'.

He looked up when he was a few yards away from the pair. 'I'm the one you're waiting for. I'm Geoffrey Shafer. Welcome to the game.'

He pulled a Smith & Wesson 9mm semiautomatic and fired twice.

The woman cried out and grabbed the left side of her chest. Bright-red blood was already staining her sea-green dress. Her eyes showed confusion, shock and then rolled back into her forehead.

The male agent had a dark hole where his left eye had been. Shafer knew the man was dead before his head struck the courtyard floor with a loud, satisfying smack.

He hadn't lost anything over the years. Shafer hurried toward the White Suite and Conqueror.

The gunshots certainly would have been heard. They

wouldn't expect him to run straight into the trap they'd set. But here he was.

Two maids were pushing a squeaking cleanup cart out of the White Suite. Had they just turned down Conqueror's bed? Left the fat man a box of chocolate mints to nibble?

'Get the hell out of here!' he yelled, and raised his gun. 'Go on now! Run for your lives.' The Jamaican maids took off as if they had just seen the devil himself. They would tell their children that they had.

Shafer burst in the front door of the suite, and there was Oliver Highsmith freewheeling his chair across the freshly scrubbed floor.

'Oliver, it's you,' Shafer said. 'I do believe I've caught the dreaded Covent Garden killer. You did those killings, didn't you? Fancy that. Game's over, Oliver.'

At the same time, Shafer thought, *Watch him closely. Be careful with Conqueror.*

Oliver Highsmith stopped moving, then slowly, rather nimbly, turned his wheelchair to face Shafer. A face-to-face meeting. This was good. The best. Highsmith had controlled Bayer and Whitehead from London, when they were all agents. The original game, The Four Horsemen, had been his idea, a diversion as he eased into retirement. 'Our silly little fantasy game,' he always called it.

He studied Shafer, cold-eyed and measuring. He was bright; an egghead, but a genius, or so Bayer and Whitehead claimed.

'My dear fellow, we're your friends. The only ones you

have now. We understand your problem. Let's talk things through, Geoffrey.'

Shafer laughed at the fat man's pathetic lies, his superior and condescending attitude, his nerve. 'That's not what George Bayer told me. Why, he said you were going to murder me. Hell of a way to treat a friend.'

Highsmith didn't blink, didn't falter. 'We're not alone here, Geoff. They're at the hotel. The Security Service team is in the grounds. They must have followed you.'

'And *you*, and *Bayer*, and *Whitehead*! I know all that, Oliver. I met a couple of crackerjack agents outside. Shot 'em dead. That's why I have to hurry up, can't tarry. The game's on a clock now. Lots of ways to lose.'

'We have to talk, Geoff.'

'Talk, talk, talk.' Shafer shook his head, frowned, then barked out a laugh. 'No, there's nothing for us to talk about. Talk is such an overrated bore. I learned to kill in the field, and I like it much more than talking. No, I actually love it to death.'

'You *are* mad,' Highsmith exclaimed, his grayish-blue eyes widening with fear. Finally he understood who Shafer was; he wasn't intellectualizing anymore. He felt it in his gut.

'No actually, I'm not insane. I know precisely what I'm doing, always have, always will. I know the difference between good and evil. Anyway, look who's talking, the Rider on the White Horse.'

Shafer moved quickly toward Highsmith. 'This isn't much of a fight – just the way I was taught to perform in

Asia. You're going to die, Oliver. Isn't that a stunning thought? Still think this is a bloody fantasy game?'

Suddenly Highsmith jumped to his feet. Shafer wasn't surprised. He knew he couldn't have committed the murders in London from a wheelchair. Highsmith was close to six feet and obese, but surprisingly quick for his size. His arms and hands were massive.

Shafer was simply faster. He struck Highsmith with the butt of his gun and Conqueror went crashing down on one knee. Shafer bludgeoned him a second time, then a third, and Highsmith dropped flat on the floor. He groaned loudly, and slobbered blood and spit. Shafer kicked the small of his back, kicked a knee, kicked Highsmith's face.

Shafer bent and put the gun barrel against Highsmith's broad forehead. He could hear the distant sound of running footsteps slapping down the hall. Too bad, they were coming for him. *Hurry, hurry.*

'They're too late,' he said to Conqueror. 'No one can save you. Except me, Conqueror. What's the play? Counsel me. Should I save the whale?'

'Please, Geoff, no. You can't just kill me. We can still help each other.'

'I'd love to stretch this out, but I really have to dash. I'm throwing the dice. In *my mind*. Oh, bad news, Oliver. The game is up. You just lost.'

He inserted the barrel of his gun into Highsmith's pulpy right ear and fired. The gunshot blew Conqueror's gray matter all over the room, and Shafer's only regret was that he couldn't have tortured Oliver Highsmith much, much longer than he had.

Then Shafer was running away, and he realized something that actually surprised him. He had something to live for. This was a wonderful, wonderful game.

He wanted to live.

Chapter One Hundred and Fifteen

Sampson and I sprinted toward the secluded wing of the hotel where Oliver Highsmith had his suite. There had been gunshots, but we couldn't be everywhere at once. We'd heard the pistol reports all the way on the other side of the Jamaica Inn.

I wasn't prepared for the bloody massacre scene we found. Two English agents were down in the courtyard. I'd worked with them both, just as I'd worked side by side with Patsy Hampton.

Jones and another agent, in addition to a team of local detectives, were already crowded into Highsmith's suite. The room was abuzz. Everything had turned to chaos and carnage in a burst of homicidal madness.

'Shafer went through two of my people to get here,' Jones said in an angry voice strained with tension and sadness. He was already smoking a cigarette. 'He came in shooting, took down Laura and Gwynn. Highsmith is dead, too. We haven't found George Bayer.'

I knelt and quickly checked the damage to Oliver Highsmith's skull. It wasn't subtle. He'd been shot at point-blank range and the wound was massive. I knew from Jones that Shafer had resented the senior man's intelligence, and now he'd blown out his brains. 'I told you he liked to kill. He has to do this, Andrew. He can't stop.

'Whitehead!' I said. 'The end of the game.'

Chapter One Hundred and Sixteen

We drove faster than the narrow, twisting road safely allowed, barreling toward James Whitehead's home. It wasn't far.

We passed a road sign that read: MALLARD'S BEACH – SAN ANTONIO.

Sampson and I were quiet, lost in our own thoughts. I kept thinking of Christine, couldn't stop the images from coming. *We have her.* Was that still true?

I didn't know, and only Shafer, or possibly Whitehead, could give me the answer. I wanted to keep both of them alive if I could. Everything about the island, the exotic smells and sights, reminded me of Christine. I tried, but I couldn't imagine a good conclusion to any of this.

We headed toward the beach and soon we were skimming past private houses and a few very large estates. Some of the estates had long, winding driveways that stretched a hundred yards or more to the main house.

In the distance I could see the glow of passing house lights, and I figured that we had to be close to James Whitehead's. Was he still alive? Or had Shafer already come and gone?

Jones's voice came in spits on the radio. 'This is his place, Alex. Glass-and-stone house up ahead. I don't see anybody.'

We pulled in near the crushed-seashell driveway to the house. It was dark, pitch black and satiny. There were no lights anywhere on the property.

We jumped out of our cars. There were eight of us, including one team of detectives from Kingston. The detectives were Kenyon and Anthony, and both were acting nervous.

I didn't blame them. I felt exactly the same. The Weasel was on a rampage and we already knew that he was suicidal. Geoffrey Shafer was a homicidal-suicidal maniac.

Sampson and I ran through a small garden that led to a pool and cabana area on one side, an expanse of lawn and the sea on the other.

We could see Jones's people beginning to fan out in the grounds. *Shafer had come into the hotel with guns blazing. He didn't seem to care whether he survived. But I did. I needed to question him. I had to know what he knew. I needed all the answers.*

'What about this prick Whitehead?' Sampson asked as we hurried toward the house.

It was dark near the water, a good place from which

Shafer could attack. Dark shadows stretched out from every tree and bush.

'I don't know, John. He was at the hotel briefly. He's a player, so he's after Shafer, too. This is it. Endgame. One of them wins the game now.

'He's here,' I whispered. 'I know it.'

I could definitely sense Geoffrey Shafer's presence. I was sure about it, and the fact that I *knew* scared me almost as much as he did.

Shots came from the darkened house.

My heart sank and I had the most disturbing and contradictory thought: *Don't let Geoffrey Shafer be dead.*

Chapter One Hundred
and Seventeen

One more target, one last opponent, and then it was over. Eight glorious years of play, eight years of revenge, eight years of hatred. He couldn't bear to lose the game. He'd shown Bayer and Highsmith a thing or two; now he'd demonstrate to James Whitehead who was truly 'superior'.

Shafer had noisily crashed through thick foliage, then waded waist deep into a foul-smelling swamp. The water was distressingly tepid and the oily green scum on the surface was an inch or two thick.

He tried not to think about the swamp, or the insects and snakes that might infest it. He'd waded into far worse waters during his days and nights in Asia. He kept his eyes set on James Whitehead's expensive beach house. One more to go, just one more Horseman.

He'd been to the villa before, knew it well. Beyond the swamp was another patch of thick foliage, and then a chain-link fence and Whitehead's manicured yard. He figured that Whitehead wouldn't expect him to come through the swamp. War was cleverer than the others though. He'd been committing murders in the Caribbean for years, and not even a blip had shown up to suggest a pattern to the police. War had also helped him in the matter of Christine Johnson, and that had gone perfectly. It was a mystery, inside a mystery, all inside a complex game.

Shafer lost track of everything real for a moment or two – where he was, who he was, what he had to do.

Now *that* was scary – a little mental breakdown at the worst possible time. Ironically, it had been Whitehead who had made him dependent on uppers and downers in Asia.

Shafer began to slosh across the fetid swamp, hoping the water wouldn't be over his head. It wasn't. He waded out and climbed over the chain-link fence on the far side. He started across the back lawn.

He had the most powerful obsession about destroying James Whitehead. He wanted to torture Whitehead – but where would he find the time? Whitehead had been his first handler in Thailand and then in the Philippines. More than anyone, Whitehead had made Shafer into a killer. Whitehead was the one he held responsible.

The house was still dark, but Shafer believed War was in there.

Suddenly a gun fired from the house. *War*, indeed.

Shafer began to zig and zag like an infantryman thoroughly trained in combat. His heart was thundering.

Reality came in odd stop-and-go movements. He wondered if Whitehead had a nightscope on his gun. And how good a shot he was.

Whether he'd ever been in combat.

Was he frightened? Or was he excited by the action?

He guessed the doors to the house were locked and that War would be crouched low, hiding inside, waiting to take a shot without too much exposure. He had never done his own dirty work though. None of them had; not Whitehead, not Bayer, not Highsmith. They had used Death, and now he'd come for them. If they hadn't agreed to meet in Jamaica he would have come after them one at a time.

Shafer broke into a full sprint toward the house. Gunshots exploded from inside. Bullets whizzed past. He hadn't been hit. Because he was so good? Or because War wasn't?

Shafer suddenly threw both arms up in front of his face. This was it. He dived through the large picture window in the loggia.

Glass exploded everywhere as the window blew into a thousand small pieces. He was inside!

War was here, close. Where was his enemy? How good was James Whitehead? His mind was filled with important questions. A dog was barking somewhere in the house.

Shafer tumbled across the tile floor, hit the leg of a heavy table, but came up firing anyway. *Nothing*. No one was in the room.

Suddenly he heard voices outside – at the front. The police were here! Always trying to spoil his fun.

Then he saw War trying to run. Tall, gangly, longish black hair. War had blinked first. He was heading toward the front door, looking for help from the police, of all people.

'You can't make it, Whitehead. Stop! I won't let you get out! Stay in the game.'

Whitehead apparently realized he couldn't get out the front door. He turned towards a stairway and Shafer followed, only a few steps behind. War turned sharply, and fired again.

Shafer flicked his hand at a wall switch and the hall lights flashed on.

'Death has come for you! It's your time. Look at me! Look at Death!' he screamed.

Whitehead kept moving and Shafer calmly shot him in the buttocks. The wound was large, gaping, and Whitehead screamed like a stuck pig. He whirled and fell halfway down the stairs. His face slammed against the metal railing as he fell.

He finally lay writhing at the foot of the stairs, where Shafer shot him again. This time between the legs, and War screamed again, loudly. He moaned, then began to sob.

Shafer stood over Whitehead, triumphant, his heart bursting. 'You think sanctions are a game? Is this still a game to you?' he asked in the softest voice. 'I believe it's great fun, but do you?'

Whitehead was sobbing loudly as he tried to speak. 'No, Geoffrey. It's not a game. Please, stop. That's enough.'

Shafer began to smile. He showed his enormous teeth. 'Oh, you're so wrong. It's lovely! It is the most amazing mind game you could imagine. You should feel what I feel right now, the power over life and death.'

He had a thought – and it changed everything, changed the game for him and for Whitehead. This switch was so much better than what he'd originally planned.

'I've decided to let you live, not very well, but you'll live.'

He fired the semiautomatic again, this time into the base of Whitehead's spine.

'You will never forget me, and the game will continue for the rest of your life. Play well. I know that I shall.'

Chapter One Hundred and Eighteen

The moment we heard the gunshots we ran toward the main house. I raced ahead of the others. I had to get to Shafer before they did. I had to take him myself. I had to talk to him, to know the truth once and for all.

I saw Shafer slip out a side door of the house. Whitehead must be dead. Shafer had won the game.

He was running toward the sea, moving fast and purposefully. He disappeared behind a small sand dune shaped like a turtle. Where was he going? What was next for him?

Then I saw him again. He was kicking off his shoes and getting out of his trousers. What was he doing?

I heard Sampson come running up behind me. 'Don't kill him, John! Not unless we have to,' I yelled.

'I know! I know!' he called.

I plunged ahead.

Shafer turned and fired off a shot at me. The distance

was too much for anyone to be accurate with a hand-gun. Still, he was a good shot and came close. He knew how to use a gun – and not just from a few feet away.

Sampson was kicking off his sneakers, pulling away his pants. I did the same with my sweats and T-shirt.

I pointed out to sea. 'He must have a boat out there. One of those.'

We saw Shafer striding into the low waves of the Caribbean, heading into a cone of light made by the moon.

He did a shallow dive and started to swim in a smooth-looking crawl stroke.

We were down to our underwear. Nothing very pretty. We both made shallow dives into the sea.

Shafer was a very strong swimmer and he was already pulling ahead of us. He swam with his face in the water, lifting it out sideways after several strokes to catch a breath.

His blond hair was slicked back and stood out in the moonlight. One of the boats bobbing out there had to be his. Which one?

I kept a single thought in my head, stretch and kick, stretch and kick. I felt as if I were gathering strength from somewhere inside. I had to catch Shafer – I had to know the truth about what he'd done to Christine.

Stretch and kick, stretch and kick.

Sampson was laboring behind me, and then he started to fall even farther back.

'Go,' I called to him. 'Go back for help. I'll be all right. Get somebody out there to check those boats.'

'He swims like a fish,' Sampson called.

'Go. I'll be fine. Hold my own.'

Up ahead I could still see Shafer's head and the tops of his shoulders glistening in the creamy white moonlight. He was stroking evenly, powerfully.

I kept going, never looking back to shore, not wanting to know how far I had come already. I refused to be tired, to give up, to lose.

I swam harder, trying to gain some sea on Shafer. The boats were still a good way away. He was still going strong, though. No sign of tiring.

I played a mind game of my own. I stopped looking to see where he was. I concentrated only on my stroke. There was nothing but the stroke; the stroke was the whole universe.

My body was feeling more in synch with the water and I was buoyed as it got deeper. My stroke was getting stronger and smoother.

I finally looked. He was starting to struggle. Or maybe it was just what I wanted to see. Anyway it gave me a second wind, added strength.

What if I actually caught him out here? Then what? We fought to the death?

I couldn't let him get to his boat before me. He'd have guns on board. I needed to beat him there. I had to win this time. Which boat was his?

I swam harder. I told myself that I was in good shape, too. I was. I'd been to the gym every day for almost a year – ever since Christine had disappeared.

I looked up again and I was shocked at what I saw.

Shafer was there! Only a few yards away. A few more strokes. Had he lost it? Or was he waiting for me, gathering strength?

The closest boat was no more than a hundred, a hundred fifty yards away.

'*Cramp!*' he called out. 'Bad one!' Then he went under.

Chapter One Hundred and Nineteen

I didn't know what to think, or exactly what to do next. The pain on Shafer's face looked real; he looked afraid. But he was also an actor.

I felt something underneath me! He grabbed hard between my legs. I yelled and managed to twist away, though he'd hurt me.

Then we were grabbing at each other, struggling like underwater wrestlers. Suddenly, he pulled me under with him. He was strong. His long arms were powerful vices, and he held me tightly.

We went down and I started to feel the coldest, most serious fear of my life. I didn't want to drown. Shafer was winning. He always found a way.

Shafer stared into my eyes. His blue eyes incredibly intense and manic and crazed. His mouth was closed, but it was twisted and evil-looking. He had me; he would win again.

I pushed forward with all of my strength. When I felt him straining against me, I reversed directions. I kicked out with my leg and caught Shafer under the jaw, maybe in the throat. I hit him as hard as I could and he began to sink.

His long blond hair floated up around his face. His arms and legs went limp.

He went down and I followed him. It was dark this far under the surface. I grabbed one of his arms.

I barely caught him. His weight was pulling me with him toward the bottom. I couldn't let him go. I had to know the truth about Christine. I couldn't go on with my life unless I did.

I had no idea about the water's depth. Shafer's eyes had been wide open and so had his mouth. His lungs must be filling with water.

I wondered if I'd broken his neck with the kick. Was he dead, or just unconscious? There was some satisfaction in the idea that I'd broken the Weasel's neck.

Then it really didn't matter. Nothing did. I had no more breath. My chest felt as if it would collapse. There was a fire spreading wildly inside me. Then a severe ringing started in both ears. I was dizzy and I was starting to lose consciousness.

I let Shafer go, let him sink to the bottom. I didn't have a choice. I couldn't think about him anymore. I had to get to the surface. I couldn't hold my breath any longer.

I swam frantically up, pulled at the water, kicked with all of my might. I didn't think I could make it; it was too far to the surface.

I had no more breath.

I saw Sampson – his face was looming above. Close, very close. It gave me strength.

His head was framed against a few stars and the blue-black of the sky. 'Sugar,' he whispered.

He held me up for a while, let me get my breath, my precious breath. My head continued to swim. We both trod water.

I let my eyes explore the surface for some sign of Shafer. My vision was blurred, but I didn't see him. I was certain he'd drowned.

Then Sampson and I slowly paddled back to shore.

I hadn't gotten what I needed out there. I hadn't been able to learn the truth from Shafer before he drowned.

Once or twice I glanced behind to make sure that Shafer wasn't following us, that he was gone. There was no sign of him. There was only the sound of our own, exhausted strokes cutting into the tide.

Chapter One Hundred
and Twenty

It took two more exhausting days and nights to finish with the local police investigation, but it was good to keep focused and busy. I no longer had any hope of finding Christine, or discovering what had happened to her.

I knew it was remotely possible that Shafer hadn't taken Christine; that it was some other madman from my past, but I didn't give that possibility more than a passing thought. I couldn't go there. It was too crazy an idea, even for me.

I'd been unable to grieve from the start, but now the monstrous finality of Christine's fate struck me with all of its brutal force. I felt as if my insides had been hollowed out. The constant, dull ache I had known for so long had become a sharp stab of pain that pierced my heart every waking moment. I couldn't stop, yet I felt as if I were never fully awake.

Sampson knew what was happening to me. There was nothing he could say, but he made comforting small talk.

Nana called me at the hotel, and I knew it was Sampson's doing, though both of them denied it. Jannie and Damon got on the phone, and they were both sweet and kind and full of life and hopefulness. They even put Rosie the cat on for a friendly long-distance meow. They didn't mention Christine, but I knew she was always in their thoughts.

On our final night on the island, Sampson and I had dinner with Jones. We had become friendly, and he finally told me some facts he had withheld for security reasons. He wanted me to have some closure; he felt I deserved that.

Back in 1989, after Shafer arrived in MI6, he was recruited by James Whitehead. He had reported in to Oliver Highsmith, and George Bayer had worked for him. Shafer had performed at least four sanctions in Asia during the next three years. It was suspected, but never proved, that he, Whitehead, and Bayer had murdered prostitutes in Manila and Bangkok. These murders were obviously the precursors to the Jane Does, and the game. All in all, it had been one of the worst scandals in the history of the Secret Service. And it had effectively been covered up. That was how Jones wanted to keep it, and I had no worthwhile objection. There were already more than enough unfortunate stories to keep people cynical about their governments.

Our dinner broke up at around eleven and Jones and

I promised to keep in touch. There was one bit of disturbing news, though no one wanted to overstate the significance of it: Geoffrey Shafer's body still hadn't been found. Somehow that seemed a fitting end.

Sampson and I were due to catch the first flight to Washington on Tuesday morning. It was scheduled to leave at ten past nine.

That morning, the skies were swirling with black clouds. Heavy rain teemed on our car's roof all the way from the hotel to the Donald Sangster Airport. School-kids ran along the side of the road, shielding themselves from the rain with flopping banana-tree leaves.

The downpour caught us good as we tried to dash out from under the cover of the tin overhang outside the rent-a-car depot.

The rain was cool, though, and it felt good on my face and head and on the shirt plastered to my back.

'It'll be real good to be home,' Sampson said as we finally made it under the cover of a metal roof painted a bright yellow.

'I'm ready to go,' I agreed. 'I miss Damon and Jannie, Nana. I miss being home.'

'They'll find the body,' Sampson said. 'Shafer's.'

'I knew who you meant.'

The rain hammered the airport's roof without mercy, and I was thinking how much I hated to fly on days like this, but it would be good to be home, to be able to end this nightmare. It had invaded my soul, taken over my life. In a way, I suppose it was as much a game as any that

Shafer had played. The murder case had obsessed me for over a year, and that was enough.

Christine had asked me to give it up, Nana had asked, too, and I hadn't listened. Maybe I hadn't been able to see my life and actions as clearly as I did now. I was the Dragonslayer, and all that it meant, the good and the bad. In the end, I held myself responsible for Christine's kidnapping and murder.

Sampson and I tramped past the colorful concession stands without any real interest, barely a passing nod. Street hawkers, called higglers, were selling wooden jewelry and other carvings, but also Jamaican coffee and cocoa.

Each of us carried a black duffel bag. We didn't exactly look like vacationers, I was thinking. We still looked like policemen.

I heard a voice calling loudly from behind, and I turned back to look at the commotion coming up from the rear.

It was the Jamaican detective, John Anthony, calling out my name in the noisy terminal, coming our way in a big hurry. He was walking rapidly, a few steps ahead of Andrew Jones, who looked powerfully dismayed.

Jones and Anthony at the airport? What in God's name was happening now? What could possibly have gone wrong?

'The *Weasel*?' I said, and it came out like a curse.

Sampson and I stopped, and they finally caught up with us. I almost didn't want to hear what they had to tell us.

'You have to go back with us, Alex. Come with me,' Jones said, slightly out of breath. 'It's about Christine Johnson. Something's turned up. Come.'

'What is it? What's happened?' I asked Jones, then Detective Anthony, when the Englishman was slow in answering.

Anthony hesitated, but then he said, 'We don't know for sure. It could be nothing at all. Someone claims to have seen her, though. She may be here in Jamaica, after all. Come with us.'

I couldn't believe what he had just told me. I felt Sampson's arm wrap tightly around me, but everything else seemed unreal, as in a dream.

It wasn't over yet.

Chapter One Hundred
and Twenty-One

On the road out of the airport, Andrew Jones and Detective Anthony filled us in on what they knew. I could tell that they were trying not to build up my hopes too much. I'd been in the same untenable situation many times, but not as a victim of a crime.

'Last night we caught a small-time local thief breaking into a house in Ocho Rios,' Anthony said as he drove, the four of us packed tightly in his Toyota. 'He said he had information to trade. We told him we would hear what he had to say, and then we would decide. He then revealed that an American woman had been kept in the hills east of Ocho Rios, near the town of Euarton. There's an outlaw group lives up there sometimes.

'I learned about it only this morning. I called Andrew and we hurried to the airport. The man says she was called Beatitude. No other name was used. I contacted your hotel, but you had already left for the airport. So we came out here to get you.'

'Thank you,' I finally said, realizing I had probably been told as much as they knew.

Sampson spoke up. 'So why does this helpful thief appear now, after all this time?'

'He said there was a shooting a few nights ago that changed everything. Once the white men died, the woman wasn't important anymore. Those were his words.'

'You know these men?' I asked Detective Anthony.

'Men, women, children. Yes, I've dealt with them before. They smoke a lot of ganja. Practice their hybrid religion, worship the Emperor Haile Selassie, y'know. A few of them are small-time thieves. Mostly, we let them be.'

Everyone in the car grew quiet as we hurried along the coast road toward Runaway Bay and Ocho Rios. The storm had passed quickly, and suddenly the island's hellified sun was blazing again. Sugarcane workers with machetes on their hips were tramping back into the fields.

Past the village of Runaway Bay, Detective Anthony turned off the main road and headed up into the hills on Route A1. The trees and bushes here were a thick jungle. The road eventually became a tunnel boring through vines and branches. Anthony had to turn on the headlights.

I felt as if I were drifting through a mist, watching everything as if in a dream. I understood that I was trying to protect myself, but also that it wasn't working.

Who was Beatitude? I couldn't make myself believe that Christine was alive, but at least there was a chance, and I clung to that. I had given up weeks before. Now I allowed myself to remember how much I loved her, how I missed her. Suddenly, I choked hard, and I turned my face toward the window. I went deep inside myself.

Bright light shone in my eyes. The car exited the brush after two or three miles that had seemed much longer on the twisting road. We were entering lush hills that looked something like the American South back in the fifties and sixties – maybe like Georgia or Alabama. Children in dated clothes played in front of small run-down houses. Their elders sat on uneven, slanted porches and watched the occasional car drive past.

Everything looked and felt so incredibly unreal to me. I couldn't focus.

We turned onto a skinny dirt road with a thick, high corridor of grass running between deep tire ruts. This had to be the place. My heart was pumping loudly, and it sounded like a tin drum being pounded in a tunnel. I felt every bump in the road like a hard punch.

Beatitude? Who was the woman they were holding? Could it possibly be Christine?

Sampson checked the load in his Glock. I heard the mechanism slide and *click*, and I glanced his way.

'They won't be happy to see us, but you won't need the gun,' Anthony said, turning to us. 'They probably know we're coming. They watch the local roads. Christine Johnson might not be here now, if she was even here at all. I knew you would want to check for yourself.'

I didn't say anything. I couldn't. My mouth felt incredibly dry and my mind was a blank. We were still involved with The Four Horsemen, weren't we? Was this Shafer's play? Had he known we'd eventually find this place in the hills? Had he set a final trap for us?

We arrived at an old green house with tattered white cloth over the windows and a burlap bag for a front door. Four men immediately came outside, all of them sporting dreadlocks.

They walked toward us, their mouths set hard, their eyes blazing with distrust. Sampson and I were used to the look from the streets of Washington.

Two of the men carried heavy field machetes. The other two wore floppy shirts, and I knew they were armed beneath the loose-fitting clothes.

'Just turn around, go back, mon,' one of them shouted loudly at us. 'Get out of here while you can.'

Chapter One Hundred and Twenty-Two

'**N**o!'

Detective Anthony got out of the car with both hands held high. So did Sampson, Jones and I.

There was the beat of traditional drums coming from the woods directly behind the main house. A pair of lounging dogs raised their lazy heads to look at us, and barked a few times. My heart was thundering faster now.

I didn't like the way this was going.

Another one of the men called to us, 'I and I would like you to leave.'

I recognized the phrase of speech. The double pronoun represented the speaker and God, who live together in each person.

'Patrick Moss is in jail. I'm Detective Anthony from Kingston. This is Detective Sampson and Detective Cross. You have a woman here. You call her Beatitude.'

Beatitude? Could it be Christine?

One of the men with a machete hanging from one hand glared and spoke to Anthony. 'Galang 'bout yuh business. Lef me nuh. Nah woman here. Nah woman.'

'This *is* my business and we won't leave you alone,' I said, surprising the man that I understood his dialect. But I know Rastaman from DC.

'Nah woman here. Nah American,' the man repeated angrily, looking directly at me.

Andrew Jones spoke up. 'We want the American woman, then we'll leave. Your friend Patrick Moss will be home by tonight. You can deal with him in your own way.'

'Nah American woman here.' The original speaker spat defiantly on the ground. 'Turn around, go back.'

'You know James Whitehead? You know Shafer?' Jones said.

They didn't deny it. I doubted we'd get anymore from them than that.

'I love her,' I told them. 'I can't leave. Her name is Christine.'

My mouth was still dry and I couldn't breathe very well. 'She was kidnapped a year ago. We know she was brought here.'

Sampson took out his Glock and held it loosely at his side. He stared at the four men, who continued to glare back at us. I touched the handle of my gun, still in its holster. I didn't want a gunfight.

'We can cause you a whole lot of trouble,' Sampson said, in a low, rumbling voice. 'You won't believe how much trouble is coming your way.'

Finally, I just walked forward on a worn path through the tall grass. I passed by the men, lightly brushing against one of them.

No one tried to stop me. I could smell ganja and sweat on their work clothes. Tension was building up inside me.

Sampson followed me, no more than a step or two behind. 'I'm watching them,' he said. 'Nobody's doing anything yet.'

'Doesn't matter,' I said. 'I have to see if she's here.'

Chapter One Hundred and Twenty-Three

An older woman with long and wildly frazzled gray-and-white hair stepped out of the front door as I reached the scarred, unpainted steps. Her eyes were ringed with redness.

'Come with me,' she sighed. 'Come along. You nah need no weapon.'

For the first time in many months I allowed myself to feel the tiniest flash of hope. I didn't have any reason to, just the rumor that a woman had been kept here against her will.

Beatitude? Something to do with blessedness and happiness? Could it be Christine?

The old woman walked unsteadily around the house and through light bushes, trees, and ferns out back. About sixty or seventy yards into thickening woods she came to half-a-dozen small shacks, and she stopped. The shacks were made of wood, bamboo, and corrugated metal.

She walked forward again and stopped at the next-to-last shack in the group.

She took out a key attached to a leather strap around her waist. She then inserted the key and jiggled it.

She pushed the door forward and it creaked loudly on a rusty hinge.

I looked inside and saw a plain, neat, and clean room. Someone had written *The Lord Is My Shepherd* in black paint on the wall.

No one was there.

No Beatitude.

No Christine.

I let my eyes fall shut. Desperation enveloped me.

My eyes slowly opened. I didn't understand why I had been led to this empty room, this old shack in the woods. My heart was ripped in two again. Was it some kind of trap?

The Weasel? Shafer? Was he here?

Someone stepped out from behind a small folding screen in one corner of the room. I felt as if I were in free fall, and a small gasp came out of my mouth.

I didn't know what I had been expecting, but not this. Sampson put out his hand to steady me. I was barely aware of his touch.

Christine gently stepped into the shafts of sunlight coming from the single window in the shack. I had never expected to see her again.

She was much thinner and her hair was braided and longer than I'd ever seen it. But she had the same wise, beautiful brown eyes. Neither of us was able to speak at first. It was the strangest moment of my life.

I had gone cold all over and everything was moving in slow motion. It seemed supernaturally quiet in the small room.

Christine was holding a light-yellow blanket, and I could see a baby's head just peeking above the crown of the covers. I walked forward even though my legs were trembling and threatening to buckle. I could hear the baby softly cooing in the nest of blankets.

'Oh, Christine, Christine,' I finally managed.

Tears welled in her eyes, and then in mine. We both stepped forward, and then I was awkwardly holding her. The little baby peacefully gazed up into both our faces.

'This is our baby, and he probably saved my life. He takes after you,' Christine said. Then we kissed gently, and it was so sweet and tender. We held on for dear, dear life. We melted into each other. Neither of us could believe this was actually happening.

'I call him Alex. You were always right here,' Christine told me. 'You were always with me.'

London Bridges, Falling

Chapter One Hundred and Twenty-Four

His name was Frederick Neuman, and he liked to think of himself as a citizen of the European Community rather than any single country, but if anyone asked he claimed to be German. His head was shaved close and it made him look severe, but also more impressive, he thought, which was an amazing accomplishment.

He would be remembered as 'quite tall, thin and bald', or as 'an interesting artist type', and several people *did* see him that week in the Chelsea area of London. *He wanted to be remembered. That was important.*

He shopped, or at least window-shopped, on the King's Road and Sloane Street.

He went to the cinema on Kensington High Street.

And Waterstone's bookshop.

Nights, he would have a pint or two at the King's Head. He mostly kept to himself at the pub.

He had a master plan. Another game was beginning.

He saw Lucy and the twins at Safeway one afternoon. He watched them from a safe distance across rows of baked beans and aisles of shoppers. No harm, no foul, no problem for anybody.

He couldn't resist the challenge though. The dice started to play in his head. They rattled the number he wanted to hear.

He kept walking closer and closer to the family, careful to keep his face slightly averted, just in case, but still watching Lucy out of the corner of his eye, watching the twins, who were perhaps more dangerous.

Lucy was examining some wild Scottish salmon. She finally noticed him, he was sure, but she didn't recognize who he was – obviously. Neither did the twins. Dumb, silly little girls – mirrors of their mother.

The game was on again – so delicious. He'd been away from it for a while. He had book money, his advance, which he kept in Switzerland. He had bummed around the Caribbean after his escape by boat from Jamaica. He'd gone to San Juan and been tempted to act up there. He'd finally traveled to Europe, to Rome, Milan, Paris, Frankfurt, Dublin – and at last home to London. He'd only strayed a couple of times on the whole trip. He was such a careful boy now.

It felt just like old times as he got oh so close to Lucy in the shopping aisle. Jesus, his physical tics were back. He was tapping his foot nervously and shaking out his hands.

He'd have thought she might have noticed that, but she

was such a vacuous blonde cow, such a cipher, a waste of time; even now, as he got closer and closer, only a foot or two away.

'Oh Loo-cy . . . it's Ricky,' he said, and grinned and grinned. 'It's me, *darling*.'

Swish. Swish. He swiped at her twice, back and forth, as they passed like strangers in the aisle at Safeway. The blows barely crisscrossed Lucy's throat, but they cut her inches deep.

She dropped to her bony knees, both hands clutching her neck as if she were strangling herself. And then she saw who it was, and her blue eyes filled with complete shock and pain and what seemed to be terrible disappointment.

'Geoffrey,' she managed in a gurgling voice, as blood bubbled from her open mouth.

Her last word on earth. His name.

Beautiful for Shafer to hear, recognition that he craved, revenge against all of them. He turned away, forced himself to, before he did the twins as well.

He was never seen again in Chelsea, but everyone would remember him for as long as they lived.

God, would they remember.

That tall, bald monster.

The one in all-black clothes, the inhuman freak.

The heartless killer who had committed so many awful murders that even he had lost count.

Geoffrey Shafer.

Death.

Turn the page for a preview of the next
compelling thriller featuring Alex Cross . . .

JAMES PATTERSON

ROSES ARE RED

Prologue

Ashes, Ashes

Chapter I

Brianne Parker didn't look like a bank robber or a murderer – her pleasantly plump baby face fooled everyone. But she knew that she was ready to kill if she had to this morning. She would find out for sure at ten minutes past eight.

The twenty-four-year-old woman wore khakis, a powder-blue University of Maryland windbreaker, and scuffed white Nike sneakers. None of the early-morning commuters noticed her as she walked from her dented white Acura to a thick stand of evergreen trees where she hid.

She was outside the Citibank in Silver Spring, Maryland, at a little before eight. The branch was scheduled to open in about ninety seconds. She knew from her talks with the Mastermind that it was a freestanding bank with two drive-through lanes. It was surrounded by what he called big-box stores: Target, PETsMART, Home Depot, Circuit City.

At eight o'clock on the dot, Brianne approached the bank from her hiding place in the evergreens under a colorful billboard obnoxiously offering McDonald's breakfast to the public. From that angle she couldn't be seen by the female teller who was just opening the glass front door and had momentarily stepped outside.

A few strides from the teller, she slipped on a rubbery President Clinton mask, one of the most popular masks in America and probably the one hardest to trace. She knew the bank teller's name, and she spoke it clearly as she pulled out her gun and pressed it against the small of the woman's back.

'*Inside*, Ms Jeanne Galetta. Then turn around and lock the front door again. We're going to see your boss, Mrs Buccieri.'

Her short speech at the entrance to the bank was scripted, word for word, even the pauses. The Mastermind said it was crucial that a bank robbery proceed in a specific order, almost by rote.

'I don't want to kill you, Jeanne. But I will if you don't do everything I say, when I say it. It's *your* turn to talk now, darling. Do you understand what I've just told you so far?'

Jeanne Galetta nodded her head of short brown hair so vigorously that her wire-rimmed glasses nearly fell off. 'Yes I do. Please don't hurt me,' she gasped. She was in her late twenties, attractive in a suburban sort of way; but her blue polyester pantsuit and sensible, stacked-heeled shoes made her look older.

'The manager's office. *Now*, Ms Jeanne. If I'm not out of here in eight minutes, *you will die*. I'm serious. If I'm not out of here in eight minutes, you and Mrs Buccieri die. Don't think I won't do it because I'm a woman. I will shoot you both like dogs.'

Violets are Blue

James Patterson

'Makes Kay Scarpetta's lot look positively fairytale' *Mirror*

This is James Patterson's sixth No. 1 bestseller in a row, and perhaps his best.

Around noon, I got a call on my cell phone. 'Just checking in,' the Mastermind said. 'How is San Francisco, Alex? Lovely city. Will you leave your heart there? Do you think it's a good place to die?'

The Mastermind of ROSES ARE RED is back – and he's hot on Alex Cross's trail. His cold, taunting threats leave Alex angry and deeply concerned for his family's safety.

Meanwhile, Alex is drawn into his most bizarre investigation yet. Two San Francisco joggers are found dead – bitten and hung by their feet to drain the blood. Further murders in California, and then on the East Coast as well, completely baffle Alex and the FBI. Is this the work of a cult, of role players, or even of modern-day vampires? Desperate to stop the deaths, Alex teams up with Jamilla Hughes, a savvy woman detective, and the FBI's Kyle Craig. But Alex has never been closer to defeat, or in greater danger. In a shocking conclusion, he must survive a deadly confrontation – only to learn at last the awful secret of the Mastermind.

Praise for James Patterson:

'A master of the suspense genre' *Sunday Telegraph*

'James Patterson's gift to thriller fans is D.C. homicide detective and psychiatrist Alex Cross' *Washington Times*

'Brilliantly terrifying . . . so exciting I had to stay up all night to finish it' *Daily Mail*

978 0 7553 4935 7

headline

Four Blind Mice

James Patterson

Alex Cross is preparing to resign from the Washington Police Force. He's enjoying the feeling; not least because the Mastermind is now in prison. Also, Alex has met a woman, Jamilla Hughes, and he is talking about the future.

Then John Sampson shows up at the house, desperate for Alex's help. Three young military wives have been savagely killed during a 'girls' night out' and Sampson's friend, a master sergeant at the army base, stands accused.

Uncovering evidence of a series of suspicious murder convictions, Alex and Sampson are determined to infiltrate the closed world of the military. But what is the army trying to hide? And do the mysterious symbols daubed on the homes of the accused mean that there are more sinister forces at work?

With his trademark razor-sharp plotting and adrenaline-filled action, James Patterson takes us on a sensational rollercoaster tale of suspense, politics, and intrigue that proves once again that he is, quite simply, in a class of his own.

'Makes Kay Scarpetta's lot look positively fairytale' *Mirror*

'James Patterson does everything but stick our finger in a light socket to give us a buzz' *New York Times*

'Brilliantly terrifying' *Daily Mail*

978 0 7553 4936 4

headline

Now you can buy any of these bestselling books by
James Patterson from your bookshop or *direct from his publisher*.

Miracle on the 17th Green *(and Peter de Jonge)*	£7.99
Suzanne's Diary for Nicholas	£7.99
The Beach House *(and Peter de Jonge)*	£7.99
The Jester *(and Andrew Gross)*	£7.99
The Lake House	£7.99
Sam's Letters to Jennifer	£7.99
Honeymoon *(and Howard Roughan)*	£7.99
Lifeguard *(and Andrew Gross)*	£7.99
Beach Road *(and Peter de Jonge)*	£7.99
Judge and Jury *(and Andrew Gross)*	£7.99
Step on a Crack *(and Michael Ledwidge)*	£7.99
The Quickie *(and Michael Ledwidge)*	£7.99
You've Been Warned *(and Howard Roughan)*	£7.99

Alex Cross series

Cat and Mouse	£7.99
Pop Goes the Weasel	£7.99
Roses are Red	£7.99
Violets are Blue	£7.99
Four Blind Mice	£7.99
The Big Bad Wolf	£7.99
London Bridges	£7.99
Mary, Mary	£7.99
Cross	£7.99
Double Cross	£7.99

Women's Murder Club series

1st to Die	£7.99
2nd Chance *(and Andrew Gross)*	£7.99
3rd Degree *(and Andrew Gross)*	£7.99
4th of July *(and Maxine Paetro)*	£7.99
The 5th Horseman *(and Maxine Paetro)*	£7.99
The 6th Target *(and Maxine Paetro)*	£7.99

Maximum Ride series

Maximum Ride: The Angel Experiment	£7.99
Maximum Ride: School's Out Forever	£6.99
Maximum Ride: Saving the World and Other Extreme Sports	£6.99